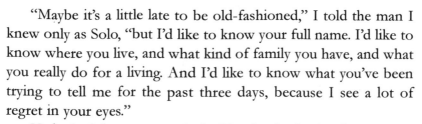
"Maybe it's a little late to be old-fashioned," I told the man I knew only as Solo, "but I'd like to know your full name. I'd like to know where you live, and what kind of family you have, and what you really do for a living. And I'd like to know what you've been trying to tell me for the past three days, because I see a lot of regret in your eyes."

He looked down at me grimly. "Don't mistake that for a change of heart. Whatever I've done here, I wanted it to happen. And I'll always want you. I don't have the words to tell you how much."

I held out my hands. "Then what you have to say can wait a little while longer." His face convulsed in a smile, a rebuke, surrender. We were lost. He pulled me to him then picked me up off the floor. We kissed like lovers after a long separation. I dug my fingers into his back and arched against him. Instantly we were on the bed again, him twisting sideways and jerking my robe open, his mouth on my breasts and stomach and lower, then holding my face and kissing me on the lips as I cried out along with him.

I loved him, whoever he was. I simply did.

The Novels of Deborah Smith

Miracle
Blue Willow
Silk and Stone
A Place To Call Home
When Venus Fell
The Beloved Woman
The Stone Flower Garden
Sweet Hush
Charming Grace
Alice at Heart
Diary of a Radical Mermaid
The Crossroads Café
A Gentle Rain

Anthologies:

The Mossy Creek Hometown Series
The Sweet Tea Series

# The Stone Flower Garden
## Deborah Smith

Smyrna, Georgia

◄B

Bell Bridge Books
PO BOX 67
Smyrna, GA 30081

ISBN: 978-0-9802453-7-0

Bell Bridge Books is an Imprint of BelleBooks, Inc.

Copyright 2002 by Deborah Smith

Printed and bound in the United States of America.

A hardcover edition of this book was published by Little, Brown & Co. in 2002
A mass market edition of this book was published by Warner Books in 2003

We at BelleBooks enjoy hearing from readers. You can contact us at the address above or at BelleBooks@BelleBooks.com

Visit our websites – www.BelleBooks.com and www.BellBridgeBooks.com.

10 9 8 7 6 5 4 3 2

Cover design: Debra Dixon

Cover photo: Nancy Tripp - Dreamstime.com

Interior design: Linda Kichline

# Prologue

On a dark spring night twenty-five years after I helped bury my Great Aunt Clara Hardigree, I found myself digging her up. I felt as if I was playing the lead in a scene from some grotesque southern soap opera. Scarlett O'Hara does the gravesite scene in Hamlet.

*Alas, poor Clara, I knew her well.*

A propane camp lantern hissed and flickered among the ferns by my feet. I dug for my great aunt's bones as quickly as I could in the moonlit woods. A huge marble urn loomed over me, its cascading marble flowers and marble vines poking my shoulders and head like hard fingers. The Stone Flower Garden was as much a part of the forest, as much a Hardigree symbol, as Clara's hidden grave. I shivered. Appalachian mountains as old as the earth looked down on my shame, and beyond the deep glen with the bones and the marble urn, the lights of Burnt Stand, North Carolina, my sleeping hometown, winked knowingly at me.

*We always suspected you weren't cut from the strongest Hardigree stone.* The Hardigree name stood for unbreakable women and unbreakable marble. But I, Darl Union, granddaughter of Swan Hardigree Samples, great-granddaughter of Esta Hardigree, had cracked.

And it was all because of a man. I looked up at Eli Wade, the man whose trust I'd betrayed, just as my silence had betrayed his wrongfully accused father, twenty-five years earlier. Eli watched me with no understanding of what I was about to show him.

I finally found Clara's skeleton no more than an arm's length down in the loamy forest sod. When I was a child, watching my Grandmother Swan dig the grave, it had seemed like a mile. Now Clara was just dirty bones waiting to be pulled up one at a time. Perhaps I should have brought one of Swan's finest linen tablecloths to wrap her in. A monogrammed one. We Hardigrees set a nice table.

The only thing that startled me was a necklace I plucked from the grave soil. When I wiped its small pendant and held it to the lantern light, I saw the twinkle of a diamond set in a tiny, polished chip of milk-white Hardigree marble. Grandmother had one just like it. So did it. It was a tradition in our family. Not a family crest, but the next best thing: Hard stone on hard stone, tinged with the soil of our ambitions.

I shivered again. *Done, then.* Every piece of infamous misery lay exposed. Nausea rose in my throat and I sat back on my heels with Clara's pendant clasped in my fist, my head bowed, my eyes shut. As a child I never meant to help Grandmother murder her and blame it on someone else. Like all the unforeseen fates — hate and true love and success and failure — it just happened.

"Your father didn't kill Clara," I told Eli. "Swan and I did."

Eli looked at the grave in shock, and then, slowly, back at me. Ineffable sadness and anger began to crowd the night air between us. I believed at that moment that he could never forgive me, and I could never forgive myself. "How could you do this to me?" he asked.

"Family," I whispered.

Children lose their innocence piece by piece. The layers are carved away until our hearts have been exposed and polished into an unnatural gloss. We spend the rest of our lives trying to remember why we ever loved so passionately and how we dreamed so simply, before life chiseled us down to the core.

# Part One
# 1972

## 1

When I grow up, I'll live somewhere as flat as spit on a marble table, Eli vowed. He was ten years old, homely, dirt-poor, smart, determined, and on an uphill course in his young life. Eli sweated and heaved as he helped his father, Jasper, push their overloaded pick-up truck up the frying-hot pavement of an unusually well-kept mountain road. The Wades had been moving uphill for two weeks, rising from their familiar Tennessee hill country into the Smoky Mountains, crossing the state line into western North Carolina then straight up the backbone of the tallest southern highlands. The damned old red-rusted truck had fainted on every steep grade.

Cooking pots, kerosene lanterns, and a rusty charcoal grill clanked on the sides of the truck's camper back like metal fish struggling on stringer lines. Low tree limbs tried to snag the dingy mattresses and lawn chairs bound atop. A dish cloth flapped from one of the camper's cranked-open side windows, as if waving at plain Annie Gwen Wade, Eli's mother, who plodded stoically along the mown roadside with sweat streaking her face and Eli's four-year-old sister, Bell, clinging to her neck.

Eli squinted ahead, watching sweat drip from Pa's grim face and thick arms. Pa maneuvered the steering wheel with one hand and threw his weight into the truck's open door frame. Eli winced. Sweat, poverty and pride clung to the Wade family like dust from Pa's quarry jobs. He was both ashamed of his father and fervently devoted to him. Suddenly Eli noticed a thin pine tree along the roadside. Five small handpainted signs were tacked in a row down its trunk.

God Bless President Nixon.
Jesus Won't Save Hippies.
Stop the war.

The first three were ordinary enough. He'd seen their kind all along the backroads. But the bottom two signs popped out at Eli like neon.

BURNT STAND, N.C. IS BUILT ON BLOOD, FIRE AND WHORES.
JEZEBEL'S DAUGHTER RULES HERE.

Good godawmighty. "Hey, look, Mama," Eli said loudly, directing attention to the signs with a jab of his hand.

Mama gasped. "You turn your eyes away."

"What do they mean?"

"I'm not sure how to tell you, so you don't look."

He bent his head and kept pushing. What kind of place were they headed to? When they rounded a curve Eli glanced up through wet, dark hair, scrubbed a dirty forefinger across the lenses of his cheap glasses, and saw the most amazing thing. There, white against the deep evergreen forest, stood two towering pillars of pinkish-white marble, one on each side of the road. Both sported handsome marble plaques filled with finely carved words. Eli gaped. More signs. Did Jezebel rule at the Pearly Gates?

"Now *these* here words are worth lookin' at," Mama said in soft awe. Eli read the plaques out loud, for Pa's sake. Pa, bare-eyed, could pick out the finest crack in a slab of marble, or find a shooting star across the Milky Way. He just couldn't read.

"'Welcome to Burnt Stand, North Carolina,'" Eli read in a heavy drawl. "'Marble Crown Of The Mountains.' And the other sign says, 'Home of the Hardigree Marble Company. Established with pride in 1925 by Esta Hardigree, who lit the fire of progress and never let a stone go unturned for commerce.'"

Beyond the strange marble monuments were huge fir trees and blue-green mountains. The rhododendron-hemmed two-lane led up an escalating hill between high mountain forest so deep it cast cool, blue-black shadows in the broiling August sun. Eli and Pa pushed the truck a few more yards, finally cresting that last, torturous hill.

"My god," Pa said suddenly. Eli, Mama, and Bell gathered next to him in the middle of the road, gazing in stunned silence at a pristine valley and a kind of a town they'd never imagined.

"It's pink," Eli said.

Burnt Stand blushed, deceptively innocent under the sun.

*

Pink. My whole life was pink. Pink town, pink marble fortune, pink marble mansion, pink frothy clothes, pink skin. My name was Darleen Swannoa Union, but it might as well have been *Pinky.* Swan Hardigree Samples, my grandmother and namesake, kept me scrubbed and shaded so much I was probably the only white seven-year-old girl in Hardigree County, North Carolina, who had no freckles. I was the heir to the Hardigree Marble Company, a princess of southern mountain marble. I was pink and miserable.

We were in the dog days of summer. The air felt like a warm wash cloth over my nose. At night the frogs and crickets and whippoorwills outside my ornate bedroom windows at Marble Hall sang sadly, as if waning summer moons were a call to mourn. Not many weeks earlier, terrorists had killed nearly a dozen Israeli athletes during the Munich Olympics. Our local Baptist minister said that proved the end of the world was near, which made sense to me, since Jerusalem was in Israel.

The ground seemed to bake on a stone griddle. Burnt Stand hunkered over the state's only major marble vein. Polished pink stone gave the courthouse, the city offices, the library, and other downtown buildings a sheen of old-world elegance, an almost Mediterranean lightness among the green mountain forest. Barnyard fences glistened with it. Cast-off chunks lined our flower gardens. Back-yard tomatoes draped themselves on rough marble walls. The chamber brochure claimed every house and public edifice contained at least a foundation or trim of our precious bedrock. For decades tourists had come just to view our fabulous town square and stroll our marble sidewalks.

I hated those sidewalks. On that miserable summer day in 1972 they burned my pink-toe-nailed feet even through my pink sandals. Yet I stood under the awning in front of the Hardigree Marble Showroom as Grandmother commanded that I do whenever I waited in public: Shoulders squared, head up, hands clasped around my pink straw purse in front of my spotless pink jumper with the embroidered pink rose on the front. Itchy sweat flattened the pink ribbons that streamed from my long French braid. I was a sturdy brunette child with dark blue eyes interested in seeing the world without a pink veneer.

Standing next to me, nearly identical in her own pink jumper and ribboned braids, was my best friend and only playmate, Karen Noland. Karen and I shared a tutor at Marble Hall, my grandmother's estate, and didn't attend public school. We were never allowed to play with other children in town, and could only run free in the woods behind the hall. We were lonely but adored each other. We were both orphans being raised by our grandmothers. Swan Hardigree Samples and Matilda Dove, my grandmother's assistant, had known each other all their lives, and so had their dead daughters—our mothers—and so had we. There was only one major difference between my family and Karen's.

We were white, and they weren't. Even in our cloistered town, defined and ruled by my grandmother, that made *all* the difference.

I couldn't say Karen and her grandmother, Matilda, were black, because they were more of a honey color, with pale hazel eyes and long coarse hair the color of chocolate ice cream. Neither Karen nor I had ever seen a picture of Karen's dead mother, Katherine, so we had no idea what color she had been. Karen kept a picture of her father on her nightstand, and he was a nice looking black man in a Marine uniform. I knew only that Karen and Matilda were not the same as us, but not the same as the black people on farms around town, not *black as the ace of spades*, as people said. And I knew only that I loved them dearly.

"Wish we could walk down the street to the Hall," Karen

whispered from the side of her mouth, as we stood at attention, sweltering. "We look like fools.".

"Only white trash and nobodies tread the side of the road like a gypsy," I intoned. It was a favorite saying of our grandmothers.

"Hot pink fools," Karen insisted.

I sighed. It was true. We stood like silly marble statues in front of the Hardigree Marble Showroom, where the south's well-to-do could order anything from a ton of marble flooring to a hand-carved cherub. Across from us, on the shady town park at the center of the square, an immodest replica of the Parthenon served as our park gazebo. *Given to a grateful citizenry by Esta Hardigree, 1931*, a plaque on the Parthenon confirmed. A group of ordinary children chased each other wildly across the park lawn. My heart ached with enforced dignity. Karen made a mewling sound. We could not violate our grandmothers' edicts.

As we stood there sweltering under our peculiar status—one little pink white girl and one little pink honey girl—an odd site appeared beyond the dip in West Main. An old pickup truck entered the square between giant magnolias along the marble sidewalk, creeping along without any apparent human guidance. Pots and pans swung from ropes on the camper back. The truck rattled like a cow bell. Mounds of boxes and burlap bags were strapped to the top with ropes, and a rusty pink tricycle had been chained to the truck's front bumper.

From our sidewalks, our park, and our shop fronts, people stared. I craned my head and finally made out a tall, handsome but rough-looking man pushing the truck from the driver's side. A thin, brown-haired woman walked behind, the skirt of her limp polyester dress swaying above her thin tennis shoes. She carried a little girl who burrowed her head into her mother's neck.

And then, I saw the boy.

He was tough looking, with skinned black-brown hair except for a shaggy lock that fell across his high forehead and his thick, black-rimmed glasses, the kind old men wore. His body looked long and thin inside faded jeans and a t-shirt. He bent his slender shoulders to the truck's back corner like an ant pushing a boulder. Lean muscles strained in his arms. He looked like a boy Jesus, pushing a pick-up truck instead of pulling a cross.

*No, a Gypsy boy,* I thought for redemption's sake, though there'd never been evidence of Gypsies traveling through Burnt Stand, before. At least the boy was in charge of his world, moving it. My world was as rooted as the marble cherubs in the Hardigree showroom window, and I had no control over any of it. I watched with fascination as the rattling truck inched around the oval circuit of the town square, then headed toward me. Slowly, the boy and his world eased into a small, empty parking space directly in front of the Hardigree Marble Showroom's elaborate white doors and soaring arched windows. Twenty feet from Karen and me. We had a front row seat.

"Strangers and white trash," Karen whispered fearfully, and backed up until she was pressed against the marble façade of the showroom offices. She gave me a comical Lucille Ball look of horror. "You better come over here with me!"

I shook my head. The exciting, frightening outside world had suddenly parked right before me. The boy's chest heaved. He dragged a hand over his glasses, smearing dirt and moisture on them as he raised his head. When he spotted me, he did a double take. I knew I looked like a big, pink-dyed Easter chick, and my face burned with humiliation. As if he couldn't be certain I was real, he pulled his glasses off and cleaned them on the tail of his white t-shirt. I stared at him openly, and he stared back. His eyes were large, brown, and soulful, with long lashes. The most beautiful eyes I'd ever seen. He tilted his head as he tried to see me without aid. "Yep," he said. "You're still pink."

"Eli, you wait right here with Bell," the woman said, setting the little girl down next to him. "Your pa and me'll be right out, you hear?"

"Yes, ma'am." He took his baby sister's hand. She slammed herself against him and hid her face in his stomach. His mouth flattened in resignation, but he patted her on the head. His mother looked my way and smiled shyly. "Hello," she said. "You're the prettiest sight."

"Hello, ma'am," I replied primly. "And thank you." Grandmother had trained me in graciousness via innumerable teas, dinners, and picnics. I had been presented to the governor, the vice president, and more than a few marble barons, including an Italian man friend of hers who barely noticed me except to call me *il mio piccolo e aumentato*. My little rose. Italian for pink. "How do you do, ma'am?"

"Why, pretty good, thanks."

"Annie, let's go." The hard-looking man scraped a comb through his dark hair and rubbed his face with a towel he pulled from the truck's cracked vinyl dash. He ignored me and went instead to Carl McCarl, my grandmother's handyman. Carl McCarl shuffled like an old, bald bear as he mopped marble sidewalks and washed down buildings. He was in a bad mood. Grandmother had ordered him to go up on the main road when he finished there, and tear Preacher Al's signs down off the pine tree again.

Preacher Al had been a stonecutter in the old days, but he went crazy at some point, forcing Great-Grandmother Esta to throw him out of town. He only preached through his pine tree pulpit, and everybody ignored him. Swan said he was a sad old man, and her mercy toward him always amazed me. Carl McCarl went up on the road regularly and took down his lurid signs. Swan would never explain their meaning to me.

"Excuse me," the boy's father said to Carl McCarl in a deep, working-man's drawl, the voice of cornfields and textile mills, long-haul truck routes and late-night roadhouses. "My name's Jasper Wade. I'm here to see Tom Alberts. Said to look for him at the Hardigree showroom here in town. Is this it?"

My ears pricked up. Tom Alberts was my grandmother's business manager, handling the grubby details of firing and hiring workers at the quarry and the showroom. Hardigree Marble employed over 300 people. A good third of Burnt Stand's workforce.

Carl McCarl turned slowly and stared at Jasper Wade for a long time. Jasper Wade scowled and flexed his massive forearms. "You got a problem with me, Mister?"

"Go round back. Around that corner, yonder. Down the alley. Ring the doorbell at the office sign. And don't worry about that there truck. I'll get you a mechanic to look at it."

Jasper Wade's face loosened with surprise. His expression said his whole life had been hard work and back doors, and any kindness was unexpected. "Thank you kindly." He motioned for his wife to come along. I watched them walk down the burning sidewalks and disappear down a marble alley at the end of the block. Carl McCarl watched him until he disappeared. I had never seen the old man so interested in just another stonecutter, or in anyone, for that matter. He wiped his forehead with a hand that trembled, then shuffled inside the showroom.

I shrugged off his strange behavior as I returned my attention to the boy, pondering how to test him. *Greetings*, I said to people, instead of *Hello*. I had read the salutation in a Victorian book of manners, and it clung to me like the scent of a comforting nosegay, a test to find the other lonely souls in the world. This happened because Swan kept me so isolated and spoke to me as if I were a small, pink adult. And so I had become a caricature, like a bad reproduction of a classic marble vase. A faux child. No one ever responded in like to my salutations. My whimsies were far too ponderous. My heart pounded. "Greetings," I said loudly. I waited for him to say something stupid.

After a moment spent chewing a thought, the boy nodded. "Greetings," he answered seriously, the first boy who ever had.

I smiled in disbelief. "My name's Darl Union. What's yours?"

"Eli Wade."

"Is that your sister?"

"Yeah." His little sister burrowed deeper into his stomach, clutching his t-shirt in her small fists and hiding her face.

I looked closer at her. "Can she breathe like that?"

He shrugged. "Aw, she's a trout. She's grown herself some gills."

This was the funniest thing I'd ever heard, and now I fully admired Eli Wade's way with words. I opened my mouth to say so, but from the corner of my eye I saw trouble coming. The children in the park included several older boys, all white except for Leon Forrest, the son of a tobacco farmer. Leon lounged nearby, skinny and dark as night, scowling and grimy in old jeans and a t-shirt. He was waiting for his daddy to come out of the feed and seed store.

He sneaked peeks at Karen every time he saw her in public. He had a crush on her. She ignored him..

My stomach clenched as a gang of boys left the park and bounded our way. "Darl, Darl, you come over here with me!" Karen hissed. I didn't budge. Eli's shoulders tightened and his head came up. He pressed his glasses high against the bridge of his nose and scoured the other boys with a look. In return, they offered some creative spitting and sneering. Stonecutters' sons. Tough as rock.

"What the heck kind of truck is this?" one said. The others joined in.

"I ain't never seen nothing so sorry."

"You all live in that thing?"

Eli said nothing. As if expecting the worst, he pried his little sister from his shirt front, picked her up, then opened the truck's passenger door and set her on the faded vinyl seat. She whimpered, gave the scene outside one quick, terrified look, then scooted down, out of sight. I heard her sobs. When Eli faced the gang again they closed in a little. One of the more swaggering types hooted and shot out a hand. He prodded Eli's shoulder. "Hey. Hey. What's wrong with that girl—is she some kind of retard?"

Eli punched the boy as quickly as a black snake snatching a mouse. The boy tumbled backwards into the others. Suddenly everyone was yelling. Eli stood there with his feet apart in dirty tennis shoes, his fists drawn up like a boxer's, his whole attitude quiet and deadly. Heat fogged his glasses. *"Get him,"* a boy yelled, and they all stepped forward. Fists began swinging. One of them slammed Eli in the mouth, and he went down. The others piled atop him.

My life as a statue was over.

I leapt in a pink heap atop the downed boys, clawing and slapping as I pushed my way to Eli. I heard Karen squealing and looked up just enough to catch her bounding forward in my defense. One of the boys shoved her, but suddenly Leon Forrest had that boy by the collar of his shirt, shaking him. When the rest of the boys realized two girls and tough, black Leon Forrest were in the fight—and not just any two girls—they backed off as if poisoned. Eli Wade got to his feet and wavered in place, blood streaming down his chin. I was sprawled on the pavement.

The whole gang stared at me, the color draining from their faces. The pink rose appliqué had been half-torn from my skirt, my pink hair ribbons were akimbo, and I was in a furious pink froth, with my skirt halfway up my waist, revealing pink panties. I glared from them to the row of fingernail scrapes on my arm, oozing blood. "S-s-sorry," one boy said.

"Aw, shit," another intoned.

"He's *mine*," I said. "You leave him alone or I'll tell my grandmother to *fire* your daddies from the quarry." I was devoid of mercy or nobility in the heat of the moment. I felt a hand under my armpit. Eli pulled me to my feet then stepped in front of me gallantly while I jerked my skirt down. He squinted behind his fogged glasses, but his fists were steady. "Git, assholes," he said to the boys. They turned and ran.

My breath backed up into my skull, and I felt dizzy. When my eyes cleared, Eli was looking at me with a frown. I shook my head. "Don't be afraid. I didn't mean it about their daddies. All the stonecutters belong to us Hardigrees. Now those boys know you're one of them."

Blood dripped from his nose, and he wiped it furiously. "I don't belong to *nobody*. Leave me be." He climbed into the truck, hauled his wailing sister out, and shut the door. "Shussh, Bell," he soothed, as he sat down on the running board with her in his lap. "Nothing ain't hurt but our pride."

Karen snatched my arm and swung me around. "Look at you! Oh, Darl! We're going to be in trouble." One of her braids was mangled. Crisp, wiry brown hair tufted from the ruined plait like stuffing from a pillow. "You okay, Karen?" Leon Forrest asked, as he hovered nearby. "Your do's comin' undone."

She whirled toward the tall dark farm boy as if he intended to stain her much paler brown skin. "You go on. Shoo. Go away."

"As long as you ain't hurt."

"I'm f-fine," she sputtered. "Go on, boy. Thank you. Bye."

He sighed as if he could live on that small gratitude, then headed down the sidewalk, his shoulders hunched. I gazed unhappily at Eli and his sister. She burrowed her head in his stomach and sobbed. He sat there stoically, ignoring me.

At that moment Karen's grandmother, Matilda, drove up in her gold sedan and slid out of the big car in a quiet whoosh of fine fabric. Matilda was an imposing woman, tall, slender, and impeccably neat in a tailored blue dress, her thick chocolate hair molded into a short, fashionable hairdo, her skin light enough for freckles. Only degrees of skin tone separated her from Swan, in terms of their majestic effect on people. "What in the world?" she asked, and her hazel eyes flashed angrily at Eli. "Who are you, young man?"

He stood, prying his little sister away for a moment. He bobbed his head to her, a polite gesture few white children made to colored women. "Eli Wade, ma'am."

She went very still, her hand rising, slowly, to her throat. "Wade," she said softly. Like Carl McCarl, she seemed stunned..

"He didn't do anything wrong," I said quickly. "I'll take the blame for him. He's *mine*, Matilda. Please?" I smoothed my hand across my arm, swiping blood from my scratch. I had seen this in a movie. Blood rituals. Before Eli Wade could pull away I drew my finger through the blood beneath his nose, then dabbed it on my own cheek. Unaware of any other forces swirling around us, I met the slow, amazed heat of Eli's stare. "My stonecutter." I told him.

I had decided we were cut from the same rock.

*

*The past is carved in stone. Never leave the pieces for someone to find.* Swan Hardigree Samples had written that rule on a slip of paper when she was a girl, and had never forgotten it. The warning ran through her mind now as she held a yellowed photograph at her desk in the dark luxury of her library at Marble Hall. Matilda pulled an armchair beside Swan's desk and they bent their beautiful heads together over the photograph.

It had been taken on a rolling back street in Burnt Stand on a spring day in the mid-1930's. Swan's aging mother, Esta, posed with jaunty elegance before the scaffolding and the piled stone block of yet another fine marble home she was building. *Esta Houses*, she called them. She was building her own town, building her own version of the past, and grinding the rest to dust. A tight bow of dark material banded her ample hips in a long-waisted dress. Her bodice sagged a few inches too low, revealing a crevice of fine bosom below a neck with skin going as soft as pale crepe.

Around her, workmen posed awkwardly, their hats in their hands, obedience in their eyes. Behind her on a rough pedestal of tumbled stone, gazing out steadily at the camera, Swan herself stood in the glory of a 19-year-old's future, lovely and reserved in a long slender skirt and high-buttoned white blouse, her eyes stern but still capable of warmth and humor. Her younger sister Clara lay on her side atop a low stone wall, dressed in schoolgirl cotton but lounging like a southern Cleopatra, even to the sly expression on her face. Off to one side, away from the whites, Matilda stood much as Swan did, with steady decorum and quiet command, a heavy cameo closing her blouse at the throat. Strangers assumed she was a live-in colored companion, or a personal maid of some kind.

Behind and above them all, framed by the unfinished marble walls of the house, a tall, dark-haired white man stood with his long legs braced apart on scaffolding. He was dressed in worker's clothes and had the muscular build of a stonecutter, but there was more pride than humility in his face. He'd hooked his thumbs in loose pockets over long thighs. He seemed to be standing easily atop the world. Their world.

His name had been Anthony Wade.

"What a handsome sight Anthony made that day," Matilda said. "We could barely keep our eyes off him."

"But he only had eyes for you." Swan put the photograph back in a small marble-and-wood box with a lock on the lid. She flicked the dial and handed the box to Matilda. "I wish you hadn't kept that."

"It's the only picture I have of him." She paused, her throat working. "Thank you for helping me find his family." They touched hands for a moment. Swan nodded to her, but grimly. "This family of Anthony's came long after he left Burnt Stand," Swan reminded her. "You owe them nothing."

"I owe Anthony," she said.

"If Clara hears about us bringing them here, you know there'll be trouble."

"She won't hear. No one remembers Anthony but us—and old Carl. No one else will associate the Wade name with him." She rose, and took the box. "I have to help Anthony's son and his family, Swan. I have to try."

Swan nodded wearily. She indulged Matilda, though she herself had long since given up on sentiment and kindness of the overt variety. She and Matilda had survived hard childhoods, small-minded dictates, men who came and went, and daughters who never understood and died young. She feared that bringing the Wades to Burnt Stand was a mistake she'd regret for the rest of her life.

"Send Darl in," she told Matilda.

Matilda frowned. "She's claimed Eli Wade as her personal project. She'll defend him. I don't know what to make of it. You should have seen them together. Like two little warriors."

*An amazing child*, Swan thought. She steepled her chin on one hand, and shut her eyes. Darl was bright, smart, beautiful, loving. Her future could be ruined so easily. Like fine hard stone, she had to be chiseled just right. Swan would not make the same mistakes she'd made with Julia, Darl's mother.

"I'll let her have the boy for now." Swan opened her eyes and looked at Matilda. "She'll understand her place and his, soon enough."

"Don't we all?" Matilda said sadly, and left the room..

*

"Why, Darl, you favor your grandmother more every day," an elderly woman had cooed to me one day as I stood in the Burnt Stand Soda Shop, waiting for Swan.

"No, I think she looks more like her Great Aunt Clara," an elderly companion insisted.

"Oh, don't say that. Don't put that curse on the child."

"But Clara was beautiful!"

*"She was as ugly as sin."*

I stood there listening in horrified confusion as they heatedly debated my mysterious great aunt's morals—and then I watched them snap shut like turtles when Swan arrived. And so I knew: Clara was so evil she could embarrass our family name in public, something a Hardigree must never do.

But now, I had done it, too.

I waited for Swan's judgment on a teak bench in the hall outside her library. My feet tapped an uneven rhythm on the marble floor, and I shivered. Swan had recently outfitted the old mansion with air conditioning, and I missed the hum of ceiling fans and warm breezes. "Help," I whispered to a fireplace portrait of my dead mother, Julia Samples Union. She smiled down at me in useless debutante beauty.

Everyone said she'd been a very sweet person, and very soft. I dreamed of her at night, and of my father, who had been nothing but a young Hardigree company stonecutter. I had never known either of them. I was just a baby when he killed himself and my mother by driving too fast on a mountain road just outside town. He didn't mean to. Men never did, Swan said.

My great-grandmother, Esta, stared down at me from another wall. Her portrait was nearly life-sized, and had been painted in the late 1930's, not long before she died. Esta was only in her fifties then, and still conveyed curvaceous beauty and power. She gazed out at the world with just the slightest taunting lift to one brow. An ice-blue ball gown hugged her breasts and spread from her waist like a flower, and around her throat a tiny Hardigree pendant—marble with a diamond in the center—hung from a snarl of pearls and sapphires. Swan wore one just like it.

Beside her, a massive portrait of her husband, my great-grandfather A.A. Hardigree, portrayed him as a darkly handsome man with burning eyes. He had started the quarry and built the original town of Burnt Stand, then died when a fire destroyed most of the town in the 1920's. I was afraid of him, and could only think of him being roasted. Nearby, my grandfather, Dr.

Paltrow Samples, smiled blandly from a portrait encased in marble trim. He had come from a prominent Asheville family, and had died of a heart condition before I was born. Swan rarely spoke of him, just as she rarely spoke of my dead mother, or of Great Aunt Clara, who lived in Chicago.

There was no portrait of Clara anywhere in our house. She was the unspoken monster who might get me if I didn't learn to be a lady. Not that Swan told me that in so many words, but even as a child I knew it was a bad sign when someone's name was never mentioned.

If I weren't careful, I'd end up just as invisible.

The library's massive oak doors clicked softly. I jumped up, clutching my hands behind my back as if shackled. Matilda stepped out. "You may go in," she said gently. "It's all right." She patted me on the back. Matilda had a core of warmth that Swan lacked. I nodded and swallowed hard.

When I stepped into the library soft shards of light glimmered on a crystal chandelier. Swan rose from her desk. I shivered again, although my grandmother would never lay a hand on me, and rarely even raised her voice. She was fiercely protective of me, firmly instructive, extremely proud. I wanted to please her.

"You disobeyed my strictest rule about our behavior in public," Swan said in her cultured drawl. I could only nod shamefully.

She moved across the room with the hipless grace of a *Vogue* model, dressed in a pale linen skirt, a white blouse, and low-heeled white shoes. A single strand of pearls graced her throat, matching small pierced earrings. She wore a gold wristwatch, a diamond encrusted wedding ring, and her Hardigree pendant. Swan was only in her early fifties, still stunning, with shoulder-length brunette hair she had just begun to touch up with color. Her eyes were even bluer than mine, with arching brows.

"You've never disobeyed me, before."

"I'm sorry."

"Sorry you got caught?"

"Yes, ma'am. I mean, No, ma'am."

To my astonishment, the thinnest little smile cut her mouth. "Tell me exactly what happened." She settled behind a heavily carved desk and tapped a gold fountain pen on the dark marble surface. Imported. A gift from the Italian marble baron.

"You always say we have a duty to our employees, so I thought I needed to do my duty, and they were hitting him, and I just couldn't stand there."

"This boy, Eli, strikes me as troublemaker. He was barely provoked, it seems, before he started swinging at the other boys. What do you think?"

"I think he's used to being made fun of and having to fight back. But he didn't hit anybody until they picked on his little sister."

"I see. So he's a noble person, in your estimation?"

"He helped me up. He stood in front of me so I wouldn't get knocked down, again."

"I see. Be that as it may, I don't want any more trouble between you and Eli Wade."

My heart sank. "Yes, ma'am." Swan never issued casual orders.

"Don't ever lower yourself to the level of your inferiors."

"Yes, ma'am."

"But do fight for what is yours."

I stared at her, bewildered. "Ma'am? So it's all right?"

"This time." She waved me away. "Go."

I leapt for the doors, a huge weight lifting from me, though I realized my grandmother's complex rules had become more tangled than ever. When I was older I'd understand that I'd impressed her. The meek might inherit the earth, but not Hardigree Marble. I halted at the huge doors, and looked back. "Where are the Wades going to live, ma'am?" I always called her *ma'am*.

Swan had already opened a drawer and removed a stack of ledgers to consider. She looked at me over them, a little impatient. "At the Stone Cottage. I needed a caretaker for it."

I bit back a gasp. The Stone Cottage belonged to us; in fact it sat not ten minutes' walk away in the vast wooded property behind Marble Hall. This meant the Wades were special. This meant Karen and I would no longer be all by ourselves in the woodlands where we played our solitary games. Unbelievable good luck had come to me.

I had been born between a rock and a hard place. A pink rock.

But now my small, lonely, protected world had just increased in membership by one fascinating soul.

Eli Wade.

# 2

*She's lookin' at us like we're up for sale.* The thought burned Eli's brain as he, Mama, Pa, and Bell lined up on the tiled floor of Swan Hardigree Sample's fine, antique-filled office at the Hardigree Marble quarry. She sat at her desk, studying them. She was the most beautiful woman Eli had ever seen, not how he'd pictured anybody's grandma. Behind her, standing like a guard, was the beautiful colored lady, Miz Dove. Miz Dove kept looking at Pa as if the sight was a stinging balm to her eyes. Eli couldn't figure her out.

"Have you done any work as a maid?" Swan Samples asked Mama. And Mama nodded eagerly. "Yes, ma'am."

"Mrs. Dove—" Swan gestured at her—"may contact you. She runs my estate."

Mama bobbed her head at her, then at Miz Dove. "Thank you, ma'am." Miz Dove inclined her head in return.

"What is your girl's name?" Swan asked Pa. Bell shivered in Pa's arms, her thin legs sticking out of a homemade dress. She burrowed her head in the crook of his neck. He protectively cupped one big hand around the back of her head. "Annette Bell, ma'am. She's mighty shy. We can't get her to talk much. Just born that way, a doctor said."

"Weaknesses of birth can be overcome by willpower and discipline, Mr. Wade."

Pa's shoulders hunched. He couldn't read, no matter how hard he tried. People like Swan were the reason he guarded his shameful secret so fiercely, and why it tormented him so much. The weakness of it. Eli burned with grief and embarrassment, watching him. "Yes, ma'am, we're working on her," he said finally.

Her gaze turned to Eli. He tried to give her a poker face, but she saw through it. "Why are you frowning at me, young man?"

He felt Mama and Pa's worried eyes on him. *Think quick, stop giving yourself away!* His struggle to produce a bland expression made a muscle twitch beneath his right eye. The weaker of the two. He pushed his glasses up. Guess she'd tell him that eyeball just needed more willpower. "I . . . was frowning at that paintin' behind you and Miz Dove, ma'am," he lied quickly.

She arched a brow. On the wall behind her, a huge painting depicted a half-naked Lady Liberty leading Washington and his troops across a storm-tossed sky. "What disturbs you about it?"

"Well, if Liberty really wanted General Washington to take her serious, wouldn't she've done better to cover her bra with some armor?"

Mama darted one hand out and pinched the back of his plaid shirt. One more word, that clutch said, and I'll pinch skin. Eli darted an apologetic glance up at his father, and saw anger. But when he forced his gaze back to Swan, she was looking at him differently. "The best armor is often invisible." He said nothing to that. Every word risked more trouble. "You're a thinker and a student," she said.

"Yes, ma'am."

"Good. Keep it up." She paused. "But don't ever frown at me, again."

He nearly strangled. He looked at Pa, and Pa nodded. This was a dogfight, and they had to roll over in defeat. Let this woman bite them on the balls, if she had a mind to.

Eli shivered with fury. "Yes, ma'am."

He would never forget.

\*

When I heard Eli had poked fun at Swan's Liberty painting, I was stunned. What kind of brave soul was he? Didn't he understand my grandmother's power? She never tolerated disrespect.

Just the year before she had broken off her friendship entirely with a lady of great social esteem, who lived in the mountain city of Asheville. Asheville was a hair-raising 90-minute drive from Burnt Stand, across two steep ranges with twisting roads. Swan and I stayed at the woman's Asheville estate whenever Swan hosted balls or gave parties at the Grove Park Inn, which with its towering lobby and massive stone verandah was the most elegant hotel in all of North Carolina, to me. I loved it because it wasn't pink, and it wasn't made of marble, and it held no dark mysteries, unlike Burnt Stand.

*Burnt Stand—the town so full of vice the Devil burned it down.*

I read that inscription on an old photograph in a North Carolina history book I found in the Asheville lady's living room bookshelves. The photograph showed Burnt Stand in the early 1920's, not long before the fire that killed my great-grandfather. My great-grandmother, Esta, escaped with Swan, baby Clara, and Matilda, the daughter of a black servant.

It was easy to see why Esta decided to rebuild the town in unburnable marble. The original burg was just a collection of awful log and tarpaper buildings crowding the valley. Every tree had been cut down, a mule and wagon were mired in the mud of what was now Main Street, surly groups of men and unkempt-looking women lounged on warped wooden boardwalks, and even our glorious blue-green mountains appeared dull. In one corner, the anonymous diarist had drawn an arrow to a cloud of dust. "Only a half-mile to the quarry and no trees, so on a windy day all of A.A. Hardigree's gals turn pink. Hah hah."

I showed the inscribed picture to Swan. "What's vice, Grandmother? Why does this man say 'hah hah' about the girls? Wasn't Great-Grandfather a nice man? What kind of girls did he have? What's this picture mean, ma'am?"

"It means my friend is no longer my friend," Swan answered coolly. "She has very poor taste in history books, and very little respect for my good name." Swan took the book from me and said no more. But we never visited that woman's home, again.

\*

The Stone Cottage was another of the mysteries associated with my family's past. Great-Grandmother Esta had built it in the late 1930's, at the same time she built Marble Hall and all the fabulous Esta Houses in town. It included three bedrooms, a parlor, a dining room, a kitchen, and even a detached one-car garage—all in pink marble, of course. An azalea-rimmed dirt lane led to it from a back road on the opposite side of Marble Hall's property.

When I was a child Swan told me only that the place had been Esta's guest house, which seemed peculiar to me, since it was hidden from Marble Hall by several hills and the Marble Creek hollow, and reaching it from the Hall required a long hike through our back woods, past the Stone Flower Garden, another peculiar but magical place.

Swan sent Carl McCarl to do regular maintenance but never visited the cottage herself. Occasionally some friend or business acquaintance in need of solitude would move in for a month or two, but before the Wades arrived the cottage had been empty for several years.

Now, it glowed with light.

"They're living in a haunted house for sure," Karen whispered as we lay on our stomachs at the edge of a laurel thicket on the hill above the Stone Cottage. Karen had a fixation on death and ghosts, since her father had died in Vietnam when she was a baby and her mother, Katherine, had died of some unknown disease not long after. I tried not to wonder if my own parents remained in the ether.

Karen slapped one golden hand at a mosquito that buzzed past her precisely braided brown hair. "This boy better be worth it," she said. We lay flat in the woods. I worked up a bulb of liquid on my tongue and bombed a mosquito in mid-flight. "Got one."

"You're gross."

"At least I'm not scared of ghosts."

"You just don't know better." She craned her head. "The Stone Cottage is *full* of spirits."

"Nah, this is just a lonely place, not haunted."

"I bet our mothers' ghosts are around here."

"Why?"

"They used to play in these woods. My grandmother said so."

"Huh. They didn't stay," I said flatly. "So they must not have been very happy here. And they don't care about us anyway, so

they're not hanging around." I brushed gnats from my face and
hoped no green snake or centipede would crawl out of the leaf
mold into my cut-off overalls. Suddenly, I saw movement at the
cottage. "There he is!"

We flattened ourselves more and watched Eli emerge from the
cottage's handsome back door. It was early September by then,
just past Labor Day, a feasting time of late summer when every
road intersection in the county hosted a barbecue stand selling
pork sandwiches, Brunswick Stew, and pork ribs sopping in rich
sauce. We had already spotted Eli's mama and daddy's arrival in
the now-working truck. They'd carried shoeboxes packed with food
into the house. Jasper Wade had been on the payroll of Hardigree
Marble for nearly a month.

Eli carried a dripping section of ribs in his bare hands. As he
stood on the cottage's back patio alone he savored that cheap
country meal as if it were the finest gourmet food, catching the
sauce on his tongue, licking the bones. He got sauce on his
eyeglasses and had to stop to clean them. He licked the sauce
from the lens before he polished them.

"He's not much to look at," Karen whispered. "Ol' bug-eyed,
four-eyed, kind of skinny—"

I elbowed her. "He's poor. He just needs to fatten up. I think
he's really handsome. And noble. He's been places, and he doesn't
just have to stand around waiting on something. He's like Galahad,
or . . . Chad Everett on *Medical Center*."

"Noble? Huh."

My heart twisted as I watched him go over the cleaned bones
a second time, sucking them for even the last remnant of flavor.
The new school year would start the next week, and since Karen
and I were schooled at Marble Hall I wouldn't get to see him,
much. "Noble," I repeated. "And handsome."

Karen groaned with exasperation. "What do you think you're
going to do? Turn him into your boyfriend? Your grandmother's
never going to let you have a boyfriend, until she picks one out
when you're grown up and she wants you to get married."

"I can have a boyfriend whenever I want one!"

"Hah. Are you crazy? You and me are important people. We

have to marry rich men."

I reared up on my elbows. "I'll marry anybody I want!"

Karen gasped. "Sssh, you fool! Get down!"

I flattened myself again, but it was too late. Eli stared right up at our hiding spot. His jaw tightened. He threw the bones into the bushes and charged up the hill. The hair stood up on the back of my neck. Beside me, Karen shrieked, "Run!"

And we did.

I tore through the woods, scrambling up hills and sliding down gulleys, stumbling over the exposed gray roots of a big beech, hearing Eli's furious footsteps gaining on me. Karen sprinted down a narrow deer path and deserted me entirely. Soon I heard only my own soft shrieks, my panting breath, and Eli's feet. I headed for the only place I felt safe.

I crested a steep knoll, started down it, then tripped on muscadine vine and sprawled into a narrow, shadowy glen. I realized where I was the instant before my forehead struck a smooth, hard, moss-speckled base of marble. The thud shook my brain, and I went very still, flat on my back, watching golden stars swim in the air. Above me, intricately carved marble flowers and vines curled down from a huge pink-marble vase, taller than a man. Around me, weathered marble benches hunkered among ferns and honeysuckle vines, and pink marble urns stood empty, waiting for fresh plantings that never came. I had run to the Stone Flower Garden, and it had trapped me in its marble arms.

Eli crashed down on his knees beside me and cupped my face between his hands. "Jesus. Don't pass out or nothing." His own face was pale, and any anger he'd felt seemed to have vanished. "I'll get creek water." He disappeared for a minute, and when he returned he held out the bottom of his sopping white t-shirt in his hands. I sat up woozily, leaning against the massive vase behind me, as he patted the cool, dripping shirt to my forehead and cheeks. "What'd you think?" he almost yelled. "That I was gonna chase you down and kill you?"

The stars faded and my head cleared. "Well, you were running like it! You sounded mad!"

"I was. But I wasn't gonna hit you or nothing. I don't hit girls."

"You just chase them like a wolf." I touched a finger to the egg-sized knot rising on my scalp. He pushed his black-rimmed glasses up his nose and studied my head, then looked into my eyes. His hands, lean and already strong, plucked at leaves on my overalls. "You gonna cry?"

"No. I'm a Hardigree. I cry marble tears and spit marble spit."

He whistled under his breath and sat back on his heels. "You're a sneak, that's what."

"I only wanted to see if you were doing okay in your new home."

"Look, I just want to be left alone and not screw up nothing. My pa needs this job here. He hadn't had no good job in six months. The quarry in Tennessee closed on him. Quarry work is all he can do."

"Why? He looks big and smart."

For a full five minutes I waited, but he said nothing. "He's not smart," Eli said finally. "Not in any way that counts." Silence. His head drooped.

Pangs of sympathy shot through me. "Is he a good daddy, anyway?"

"Yeah."

"Okay. Then be glad. I don't have a daddy. *Or* a mama."

He stood up, frowning. "How come?"

"They ran off the road when I was a baby. You can still see the scrapes on the big rocks down below Hightower Ridge."

"I'm sorry."

"My daddy was a stonecutter at Hardigree Marble. Like yours."

He stared at me. "Jesus."

*Jesus.* He was going to hell. All right, I'd go with him. "*Damn*," I said bravely.

He suddenly became aware of the hidden glen surrounded by deep forest, and his eyes widened as he studied the giant marble flower vase. "What kind of place is this?"

"A good place to hide, except when *you* are chasing me. My great-grandmother built it. Nobody knows why."

"I bet there's magic, here."

Excitement shot through me. *He understood.* "Lots of it."

"Who comes here?"

"Just me. My friend Karen's scared of it." I hesitated. "But you can come here. I won't mind."

His eyes hardened. "Why are you bein' nice to me? What do you want? I'm not your kind."

"I say you *are*." When he went quiet again I sighed with disappointment. I got up, brushed leaves off my overalls, and began to make my way, weak-kneed, up the opposite slope.

"Hey," he called. I stopped and turned. He looked up at me in a way that made my heart patter softly. "I ain't ever gonna be *pink* like you," he declared. "But I think you're a fine shade of friend."

I fell in love with him that day, at only seven years old.

*

*Why is she nice to me?* Eli wondered constantly. Back in Tennessee he'd grown used to being ignored or teased, called white trash, poor, four-eyes, ugly, and worse, the son of a dummy who couldn't read, the brother of a sister who barely spoke. He'd fought all those fights alone, until the pink girl took up his cause.

*Greetings,* Darl Union had said like a princess.

*Greetings,* he had answered, like a prince.

And now she had shown him the fantastic hidden garden. Magic and good luck began to come to him. The garden, with its stone flowers, was changing his family's lives.

Eli discovered his mother crying with joy every morning when she cooked up grits and fried eggs in their nice new home, even if the strange little house didn't belong to them and was only free board from the Hardigree Marble Company. For years they'd lived in rented rooms, old trailers, even the truck for the last few weeks. They'd never had a house, before, especially not a marble one. The air was cool and sweet. Ivy curled up the cottage's walls and draped the cornices of the roof. The walls, inside and out, where a cool, clean, pink. The whole place made him think of Darl Union.

"Not enough sun for a garden," Pa complained, but even he couldn't find fault with anything else. The kitchen appliances were clean and decent and all worked, there were two handsome bathrooms with big marble tubs, and at night the little cottage glowed with light from wrought-iron wall sconces and ceiling fixtures. There was even a washing machine.

When Eli lay next to Bell on their shared bed at night, clean from a tub bath, he cradled an old paperback copy of Gulliver's Travels to his chest and swore he'd do whatever anybody asked, if his family could only, please Jesus, stay there until the hard times faded behind them like a bad taste. He went to the Stone Flower Garden every day, and prayed some more.

Pa hung a wallet-sized picture of Grandpa Wade on the living room wall near the fireplace. It was the only picture they had of him, and was tattered. Grandpa had cut it from a bigger picture, Pa said, but didn't know what the bigger picture was or where it was taken. Grandpa had been the best stonecutter in five states then, before a quarry accident left him nearly crippled. Pa had not been born yet. The picture was taken before Grandpa, already a ruined man, had met Grandma Wade. She'd married him regardless and made their living working as a cook and a nurse. He'd killed himself drinking when Pa was just a boy.

But in the picture he stood, young and handsome, in the open wall of some grand marble house he was building, his legs braced apart, his thumbs hitched on his pants, his smile turned just a little downward, as if somebody below had earned it more than the rest of the world.

Eli always wondered who that someone was, and where his Grandpa had been so happy.

*

Over the fall and winter I spied on the Stone Cottage innumerable times, catching a glimpse of Eli as he helped his mother hang clothes outside to dry. His father came to the quarry office one day when Swan was there, and hat in hand, asked permission to clear a half-acre near the cottage for a spring vegetable garden. "You do good work, Mr. Wade," Swan answered from behind her big mahogany desk with the marble inlay, "and so I grant my permission." This was a stunning show of praise from a woman who rarely found anything or anyone worthy of reward.

During the bitter cold months of winter I hunkered on the knoll above the Stone Cottage in my soft woolen coats and cashmere sweaters, watching Eli and his father cut down large hemlocks, firs and white pines in the family's new garden spot. I could see Eli shiver in a thin army jacket and ratty yarn cap. I watched Jasper Wade shiver, too, but neither of them ever gave up and went indoors. Jasper patiently taught Eli to use a dangerous chainsaw so heavy it sagged Eli down when he held it. I'm sure Jasper could have saved time cutting the trees himself, but he didn't.

Each time a mighty tree fell through the combined efforts of father and son, gruff, unemotional Jasper Wade put an arm around Eli in a quick, rough hug, and I saw Eli's upturned grin of pleasure. I knew, then, without being able to put it in words, that Eli adored his father the way I loved Swan. I yearned to earn one smile, one hug, one ounce of expressed love, just one..

Annie Gwen regularly came outside, bringing hot drinks and stoking a fire they built from chopped branches. Bell, bundled in blankets and cheap polyester scarves, prodded the edges of the fire with a stick. Annie Gwen got marshmallows and hotdogs, and often the family sat around the fire at the end of a long day, roasting such simple food in the flames. Bell curled up in her mother's lap and Eli sat cross-legged on the ground between her and his father. Sometimes, Annie Gwen would sing old country songs, and Jasper smoked a cigarette, listening. The pungent, sweet pine scent of their fire rose to me and I inhaled it with a loneliness that nearly tore my skin.

This was the scent of a loving family.

*

Eli crept through the deep mountain woods the next March, scuffing his jeans and camouflage hunting shirt – a disguise, because he was very methodical. He had waited for the trees to sprout enough leaves to hide him. He glimpsed the pink Hardigree mansion through the woods and inhaled sharply at its size. He crawled under a thicket of laurel on the ridge facing the mansion's back gardens until finally he had a clear view. His breath caught in his throat. The first spring gnats swarmed him. He stared in worried awe at the splendor before him.

The mansion crowned the opposite ridge like a pink palace in a painting of Shangri-La in one of his books. Marble balconies and soaring windows glistened in the sun. Big, draping willows and dogwoods surrounded the house, and the lawn of the back yard looked as green and smooth as the felt on a pool table. There were amazing flower gardens, and a marble gazebo, and a pool! A personal, private swimming pool! All held together by an incredible stone terrace across the back—a wall of pink marble blocks at least thirty-feet tall. A marble staircase zigzagged down that wall and ended at a kind of patio at the edge of the forest.

Dappled in sunlight, that secluded patio curled around a large pond with a slender marble fountain, shaped like a pagoda. Water trickled delicately from the pagoda's marble roof. Flowering white water lilies floated on the pond's surface, and as Eli watched, a gold-and-white fish the size of a large trout crested for a second. The sight was amazing, even for an avid reader such as Eli. His mind filled with stories of exotic locales and fabulous ways. Darl had a private fish pond, with monster-sized goldfish and a miniature pagoda. She lived like the child of a Japanese samurai.

He had barely caught his breath when his eyes returned to the top of the terrace, and an eerie current prickled his skin. Spaced between towering snowball bushes were a dozen large, marble swans. They sat in fixed glory atop the terrace in the space between each big shrub. They stared straight at Eli fiercely, a flock of angry-looking marble birds, as if daring him to breach the pink wall of their namesake's fortress. They were guards. The Devil had incubi and succubae.

Darl's grandmother had marble birds.

He made himself stare back at them, angry and scared, wanting to throw a few rocks at them then run like hell. Suddenly a door opened in a gleaming glass sunroom across the back of the mansion. His heart stopped as Darl's grandmother walked out. She appeared from the giant pink mansion as if she knew he'd trespassed to the very edge of her castle moat. He flattened himself beneath the big green leaves of the rhododendron.

"Goodgodawmighty," he whispered. She looked like a movie star in a black bathing suit, black sunglasses, and a long, see-through black robe. She walked past the pool and went to the edge of the terrace, stroking her dark brown hair back from her face, gazing into the woods. Eli's skin drew up a size smaller. He couldn't move. But she was coming his way.

She went down the long marble steps and halted on the patio. He watched in amazement as she knelt by the fish pond and dabbled her fingers in the dark water. A second later she lifted one of those foot-long goldfish from the pond and stood, holding the poor thing up in front of her like she meant to eat it alive or watch it drown in the air, just for fun. The fish struggled wildly. She didn't let go.

Finally, just as the fish began to give up, she knelt and slid him back into the water. With a relieved flip of his tail he disappeared. She rinsed her hands and flung water from them, then rose and climbed the stairs. She tossed her robe aside and dived into the blue pool. She was in charge. She could play God. Nobody could drown *her* in air or water.

Eli released a long, fearful breath. He had seen her in her full armor, now.

## 3

"Stand up, Mister Wade." The fifth grade teacher, Mrs. Dane, glared at Eli through her square, amber-rimmed glasses. She held his test papers in one hand as if she meant to flail him with them. She looked capable of ax murder—small, lethal, strong, with a roll around her middle and a face like a pug dog. She wore a blonde wig that let strands of her own brown hair escape around the edges. She always seemed on the verge of coming unstuffed.

The hair rose on Eli's neck. He slid from his desk as slowly as syrup draining from a bottle. He hated being called on in class, hated standing up in his Salvation Army flannel shirt and his floppy jeans, which were already too short for his growing legs. The faintest trace of snickers rose around him like a bad stink. He adjusted his black-rimmed glasses, fingering a scuffed place on one temple. Mrs. Dane squinted at him through her fancy amber windows. He gazed back, resolute.

"Mister Wade," she said evenly. "You finished this math test in five minutes. The rest of the class needed a whole hour." She slapped the papers down. "You cheated."

"No, ma'am," he said simply. "I sure didn't cheat. Ma'am."

She shook his papers. "Then explain how you did this."

"I just . . . don't have to think much. The numbers just come right out."

"Like pus," some boy whispered. "He's a Pus Head."

The class's chorus of muffled giggles was silenced by one slap of Mrs. Dane's hand on her desk. Eli's face flamed. "Come to the board," she ordered Eli. His knees quivered. He walked slowly to the front of the room then stood like a soldier at attention. Mrs. Dane scribbled on a notepad. "Multiply these figures on the board. Two-hundred-and-seventy." Eli picked up a piece of chalk and wrote the number. "Times Two-hundred-and-fifty." Eli wrote the second number. "The answer is sixty-seven thousand and five hundred," he said.

"Don't be funny with me, mister!"

"I don't feel funny at all, ma'am. That's the answer, ma'am."

Mrs. Dane worked the figures on her notepad. A blush rose in her cheeks. She frowned. "All right. Right." Eli's chest filled with a rush of relief. But her mouth thinned in challenge. "Six thousand and seven, divided by twelve."

He didn't even bother to write the figures on the board. "Five hundred-point-fifty-eight. That gets you within point zero four of an even number."

She scribbled. She gasped. Her head snapped up and she peered at him incredulously. "Two million and twenty one times sixty-seven!"

"One hundred and thirty-four million, one thousand, four hundred and seven." He paused. "Even." Mrs. Dane sat down, worked the figures on her pad, then threw her pencil down. She raised her head again, gaping at him. She tugged distractedly at her blonde wig, and a whole swath of mousy brown hair cascaded from behind one ear. *I made her brain blow a hairball*, Eli thought. She pointed at him. "You're a genius."

A wave of pride washed over him. He'd kept his temper, believed in himself, and won this humiliating contest. When he looked at the rest of the class, they were as wide-eyed as rats staring at cheese.

The Big Cheese. Him.

"Greetings," he said.

*

Swan took me to the quarry offices on most Saturdays to observe, to do small bits of paperwork, to learn the hard business of hard stone. I sat at my own small desk in the corner of her office, glancing wishfully out a large picture window at the open sky, the wide deep box of the marble pit, and the men at work with cranes and cutting tools. I preferred the carving factory next door, where I was allowed to stand in certain areas with safety goggles covering my eyes, watching the master craftsmen grind, cut, and polish the stone. On Saturdays the men could bring their sons for an hour to teach them the trade. No girls were allowed. Except me.

On that crisp Saturday in March there stood Eli, his boyish hands sunk into oversized leather gloves, his face and clothes covered in dust, a bandana tied over his nose and mouth. He worked alongside his father, and he never looked up at me when I was looking at him, though I did catch him watching me. I looked away then slyly whipped my gaze back. Caught him.

Swan suddenly, astonishingly, exited her office and strode onto the factory floor, something she rarely did when the dust flew. She cut quite a figure in the new career-woman fashions of the seventies. That day she wore a pantsuit—tailored blue slacks with a matching jacket. A colorful silk scarf made a belt at the jacket's waist and trailed from her right hip like a referee's flag. The heels of her imported blue pumps clicked on shards of marble. A choker of pearls graced her throat. Every muscle in her tall, svelte frame moved in the perfect synchronicity of confidence; every man in the plant looked up at her as she passed. She was still so beautiful; she could have been Scarlett O'Hara's older sister, or Jacklyn Smith's lookalike mother on *Charlie's Angels*.

I, of course, was dressed in a pink wool jumper and pink, knee-high ski boots.

She stopped at Jasper Wade's work area and beckoned him with a crook of a finger. When he threw off his face mask and set down his grinder, she said, "Come along to my office, Mr. Wade. And bring your son."

I couldn't imagine what she wanted with Jasper and Eli, but I beamed at Eli because I was to be included. As he tugged his bandana down and wiped his glasses his big, chocolate eyes did not evade me, and I saw the worry in them. My heart twisted. "She never fires anyone herself," I whispered as we trailed her and his father. "She makes Mr. Albert, her manager, do it. So don't worry about your daddy."

He glared at me. I frowned at him. We entered the office. Swan sat down and pointed me to my own little desk. His father appeared worried, too, even standing there so tall and strong, a dark-haired and handsome man covered in marble dust and sweat and submission, even on a cold spring day. He and Eli stood in a marble-tiled area just inside the office door, not daring to set even one grimy foot on the fine Turkish rug beneath our own feet. I sat down morosely at my handsome marble-topped desk and crossed my hands on the cold stone.

"Mr. Wade," Swan said, "I understand from his schoolteacher that Eli is a math genius."

In the stunned silence that followed, I gaped at Eli, and his father's eyes widened, as well. "He's good with his brain, ma'am," Jasper finally said. "And I reckon yes, the boy's real good with figures. He's been doing the checkbook for my wife and me, and he's never made a mistake. Not once."

"How old was he when you allowed him to begin keeping your family accounts?"

Jasper looked at Eli. "Do you know, son? I'm not sure."

Eli's guarded expression said he wasn't certain he should admit anything. He swallowed hard. "Six years old, Pa."

Jasper's eyes gleamed. He looked back at Swan. "Yeah, I reckon he was in the first grade then, ma'am."

Swan sat back in her tall, upholstered office chair. She steepled both hands to her mouth, studying Eli with her intense blue eyes, as if calculating his value in fine stone. Suddenly she leaned forward and tapped numbers into an adding machine on her desk. The machine whirred and clanked and slid a paper receipt from its top. She tore the slip of paper from its berth and hid it in one hand. "Eli, quick, in your head. Do this arithmetic. What's one hundred and twenty three times forty two?"

Eli gazed at her and didn't blink. "Five thousand, one hundred, and sixty six."

Her brows arched. "Correct." I nearly fell out of my miniature office chair. He was brilliant! She calculated another figure on the machine. "Eight hundred and ninety five divided by eighty two."

"Ten point ninety one," he said without missing a beat.

Swan grilled him with ten more exercises. He never hesitated, and he never missed an answer. She tossed the slips of paper on her desk and leaned back in her chair again, propping her chin on the back of one graceful hand. Her gaze rose to Jasper's. "Mr. Wade, I want Eli to work part-time after school in the office, here. I want him to learn accounting from Mr. Albert. Of course he's just a child, but he's no ordinary child. I provide one college scholarship every year for a deserving student from this town. If he proves himself to be a scholar and a gentleman, I expect he'll receive that scholarship when he graduates from Hardigree High School. He'll study business and accounting over at Duke University in Chapel Hill, and then he'll return here to work for me."

This was amazing. She had singled the Wades out to live in our own Stone Cottage, and given Jasper Wade permission to cut down hundred-year-old trees in our forest, and now she was vowing to send Eli to the state's finest university someday. She recognized his nobility!

Jasper Wade looked too surprised for words. Eli's mouth opened and shut. He stared into space until finally his gaze came to me. *You're special and she knows it, so act happy!* He must have seen the excitement in my face. But in return, I only saw anger and misery in his. He was going to be owned by Hardigree Marble, whether he liked it or not.

"Nobody in my family ever went to college," his father said slowly.

Swan nodded. "Then it's about time. You have a rare opportunity to change the entire course of your family's future. Any sacrifice is worth that."

"Yes, ma'am. His mama'll be beside herself. This is her dream."

"Good. Then make it come true."

"Thank you, ma'am. Thank you. He will." Jasper looked down at Eli. Pride and command glowed in Jasper's harsh face. His eldest child, his only son, had just been handed a chance to work with his mind instead of his hands. A chance to be somebody. "What do you say, son?"

Eli stared up at him, searching his unyielding expression. Slowly, Eli turned toward my grandmother. A weight heavier than every slab in the quarry seemed to settle on him. "I'll do it. Thank you, ma'am."

It was the sound of defeat. I would own him, someday, but against his will. Tears rose in my eyes. A hollow victory.

*

This, then, was the dark side of wealth and power: In order to have that power, you had to take something away from other people, you had to control them for your own best interests, and you had to be responsible for them. I spent that whole dark spring brooding over my power-wielding future and the beaten look that settled in Eli's eyes when Swan clamped the manacles of Hardigree Marble around his young life. All right, so here was my solution: When I inherited him, I'd set him free. And then I'd marry him.

I didn't really want to marry anyone, but I'd do it for his own good. I had no role models for married bliss, but I'd try to learn. My mother had been killed by marriage, and as for Swan, of course, she was a self-contained entity, a cool puzzlement outside the realms of marital convention. My grandfather, the doctor, was just a mild-mannered bald man in a photograph. For all I knew my mother had been an immaculate conception. I watched Swan gracefully entertain men among her guests at parties, but I never saw her kiss one. The Italian marble baron occasionally happened to show up when we traveled to New York, and at those times Swan would leave me in the care of some New York socialite or other, some friend of hers from her youth, and she and the marble baron would spend late nights on the town. But that was all.

Matilda's husband, Mr. Dove, was a faceless mystery. She lived alone with Karen in one of the smaller Esta Houses, a fine 1930's bungalow of river stone trimmed with marble, on a shady town street not far from Marble Hall. It was no secret that Swan had given the house and five acres of woodland around it to her as a young woman. Whatever this generosity smacked of—a remnant of the retainer system born in slavery, or white Hardigree noblesse oblige—Matilda had no doubt earned the marble-supported roof over her head. Pride and independence seemed to drive her as hard as they drove my grandmother.

And then there was Great Aunt Clara, she of the sinister silences and shrouded history. So much for studying Great Aunt Clara's example.

Men, it seemed, were only window dressing in the Hardigree female universe. Just the pediment that held up the vase for admiration, not to be confused with a solid foundation or a permanent decoration. I couldn't imagine Swan doing the thing a woman had to do to get a baby. Karen had told me all about the process, from the laying down naked and the kissing to the poking and the gooey result. I had to believe Karen was telling me the truth, since she'd gotten the information from a copy of *The Joy Of Sex* she found in a box at the Hardigree County Library, where Matilda sent books Swan had donated. But I couldn't fathom it.

Swan would never undress for a man—she didn't even show herself to me. I'd never caught her in anything less revealing than a fabulous nightgown and a long, white-silk robe. She had a whole collection of those. Besides, Swan would never allow anyone—man, woman, God, or Satan—to get on top of her.

I knew that for sure.

*

Every May Swan held a weekend party at Marble Hall for her alumni class at the Larson School For Girls, in Asheville. Even a cousin of one of the Vanderbilt descendents had attended while Swan was there as a teenager, since at that time various Vanderbilt heirs still lived at their castle-like mansion, Biltmore, secluded on a vast estate along Asheville's borders.

Marble Hall was full of elegant matrons of southern society. Swan brought in extra help for the meals, the afternoon tea, the evening cocktails by our large marble pool and marble gazebo in the back gardens. It was Annie Gwen's first big event as our maid, and Eli was pressed in service hauling trash and washing dishes. In his spare time, he was supposed to baby sit Bell. It didn't work.

Bell Wade peered at me with terrified eyes from inside one of the big, whitewashed floor cabinets in the mansion's vast kitchen, where she'd burrowed into the pots and pans. She had a colander on her head. Wisps of her fluffy, dark hair poked through the sieve holes. She was dressed in tiny cut-off jeans and a tiny Sesame Street t-shirt. "Here she is, Eli. She's hidden like a rabbit."

He grimly knelt beside the open cabinet door, hiking the knees of his overalls. I was dressed in a pink organdy shift with pink patent-leather slippers. "Baby Sister," he crooned softly, holding out his hand. "Come on here. You look like something from outer space."

She stared at us with huge dark eyes and didn't move.

"We have to get her out of there before Matilda catches her." I darted looks at a butler door to the dining room. Matilda and Annie Gwen were just on the other side, serving luncheon platters of tomato bisque and almond chicken salad to Swan and her twenty-five classmates. "Matilda has your mother polish these pots like they're fine silver!"

"Well, now they're a crown for Bell." Eli carefully laid a hand on the tiny girl's hand. She clutched a stew pot in her lap, and held on hard. "Comeon, Baby Sis, come on out for me." Eli never lost patience with Bell, though she tried him all the time. I hiked my slender pink dress up a little and got down on my knees. "Come out this instant," I ordered in a cool, dry tone. "Time is money, and you are two nickels short of ruining my schedule."

Eli gritted his teeth and gave me a narrow look. "I don't need your help." He jabbed a hand inside the cabinet and latched onto his sister's wrist. "Outta there, Bell." She uttered a soft squeal but he dragged her out anyway. I caught pots and pans hurriedly, trying to keep them from clanking. Bell braced a tiny, tennis-shoed foot against the cabinet's door frame. Eli grunted, wrapped both hands around her leg, and jerked.

She slid onto the marble-tiled floor as if birthed from a stew-pot womb. In the bright sunshine streaming through the kitchen's high windows I saw how pale she was, how utterly terrified of this place and its strange people. She shook with fear. Eli winced and pulled her to him for a deep hug. "It's okay, Baby Sister."

But it wasn't. Slowly, a yellow stream of urine slid from beneath her bottom. I leapt up. The clatter of footsteps on the hall floor outside the butler's door made us jump. I shut the cabinet door. "Just hide her," I told Eli. "Go up the backstairs. There's a linen closet right near the top. Get inside and close the door. I'll come in a minute."

Eli frowned as he stood and hoisted Bell into his arms. "What are you going to—"

The steps were almost at the door. "Go!"

He bounded out an arched doorway in the kitchen's back corner. I heard his feet on the narrow servant's stairway, then blessed silence. I faced the butler's door, my breath short. It swung open, and Annie Gwen pushed her way through. She carried a large, empty silver tray. Her brown hair was pulled back in a crisp bun, and she wore a pink maid's uniform with pink tennis shoes. Her kind, plain face lit up in a smile when she saw me. "Miss Darl, honey, what you need, sweetie?"

I sagged with relief and put a finger to my lips. "Bell tinkled." I pointed to the floor.

Annie Gwen gave a soft yip of dismay. "Where is she?"

"Eli took her upstairs. I'll go help him dry her off. It's all right."

Annie Gwen leapt to a utility closet and pulled out a mop. I bounded up the backstairs. The house closed in on me, dark and cool and as quiet as a big marble mausoleum. At the top of the landing I carefully inched open the wide, louvered door of the linen closet. Eli sat in the floor of the dark closet with Bell huddled in his lap. He'd wrapped her in one of Swan's finest monogrammed bath towels. Her soggy shorts and her flower-print panties lay on the floor. "It's okay," I said, and explained. He exhaled. "Now I just got to get her some dry clothes."

"I'll get her some. I've got a whole trunk full of my old clothes. Just wait." I shut the door and hurried up another flight of back stairs. My personal bedroom was a small, pink suite on the mansion's backside. It overlooked the pool, the gazebo and the back gardens. I could even see beyond the pink stone terrace to the shallow koi pond far below. Along that terrace, interspersed with shrubbery, the line of tall marble swans guarded Hardigree secrets, including my small one about Bell.

I dug in a white cedar chest until I found a frilly pair of shorts and ruffled panties. These looked the right size. All was well. I hurried back down the stairs and had just opened the linen closet door an inch when I heard steps on the long marble staircase at the hallway's other end. I tossed the clothes to Eli. "It's just one of the guests," I whispered. "I'll talk to her."

He wrapped his arm tighter around poor Bell. "Just don't let nobody open this door."

"I won't." I shut it, then planted myself in a tall, upholstered wing chair nearby, as if I was just part of the décor, a small part. The hall was wide and long, the marble floor covered in a full-length carpet of delicate scrolls and fleur de lis. Along its length were more sitting areas. Paintings of English landscapes and good reproductions of the old European masters hung on the walls. I swung my legs as if perfectly relaxed, hoping the guest wouldn't even notice me in the rich shadows. The hall was lit only by the sun filtering through a tall window at the far end.

A doughy blonde woman in a pale silk midi-dress huffed her way to the top of the marble staircase. Her face was flushed. She swayed a little on her feet. "Why, little Darlene, wha'you doin'?" Her genteel, magnolia-soft voice was kindly but slurred. She'd had one too many Bloody Marys for lunch.

"Just sitting, Mrs. Colson." She lumbered my way and sat down near me on an antique, velveteen loveseat. Her bleary eyes filled with tears. "You look just like Julia, sitting there. That was one of her favorite spots. She used to play with her dolls in that linen closet. She called it her special doll house."

I stopped swinging my feet. Goosebumps rose on my skin. Swan's friends never spoke of my mother to me ordinarily. "Was she as pretty as her pictures?"

"Beautiful. A beautiful brunette with big blue eyes, just like you."

"Was she smart?"

"No, honey, she was foolish and reckless. But she was certainly sweet."

We sat there gazing at each other for a moment, while I absorbed such honesty. Mrs. Colson began to talk about Swan and my mother, how close they'd been, how both had been full of smiles and laughter around each other, how Swan had adored her and indulged her. A small pain twisted my heart. My mother had

had a real mother. Why couldn't Swan love me that way?

Mrs. Colson rambled on, shaking her head sadly. "It was just too bad about her and Katherine. Poor Katherine. Just wild blood. But what else could you expect from that mix?"

Katherine Dove. She was talking about Matilda's daughter, Karen's mother, the unknown girl we'd never seen in a picture, never heard discussed. I slid out of the chair, as stiff as a soldier. Mrs. Colson clamped a moist, doughy hand on my arm and peered at me tearfully. "If it hadn't been for that girl's bad influence, I expect your mother would have been fine. You poor child. Don't you ever feel bad about her. You might not have had a good mother, but you have a wonderful grandmother."

My breath cut my windpipe. "Didn't my mother want me?"

Mrs. Colson smoothed her hands up and down my arms, uttering soft sounds of comfort. "Well, no, but your grandmother wants you. And when Swan Hardigree Samples wants somebody, they don't get away." She released me, stroked one hand across my hair, then rose the hall and disappeared into a bedroom, pulling the door shut behind her.

I turned blindly, weeping without tears, numb. I opened the door to the linen closet. Eli still sat in the floor, holding Bell in his lap, wrapped in the towel. She had hidden her small face in the towel. SHS, Swan's monogram, was all I saw of her face. Eli looked up at me with his large, dark eyes, somber with sympathy, and I knew to my horror he'd heard every word Mrs. Colson spoke. "Darl," he said gruffly. The first time he'd ever spoken to me by my name.

I gasped for air. "I'm going to the stone flower garden." I left him there and hurried down the back stairs, then out a door to a sunroom, then out the sunroom door into the bright spring afternoon. I skirted the back gardens behind tall snowball hedges then went down a set of stone steps along the back terrace. In a moment I was racing past the Japanese goldfish pond and into the deep woods, sliding and falling on the forest floor of matted leaves, briars tearing at me. When I reached the sunken glen I threw myself down next to a bench and pillowed my face in my arms, sobbing.

Eli followed me, carrying Bell. They sat down in the leaves beside me. Of all wonders, he put his arm around my shoulders. "This is a good place, a safe place," he said. "When we come here we don't have to be who we are. We'll just be who we want to be. All right?"

I raised my head and nodded. Suddenly a small, soft hand touched me on the arm. Eli and I both looked down at Bell in amazement. She pointed at the shorts I'd given her. Pink ones, of course. "I'm pink, now," she whispered. Her eyes were sorrowful, her voice sweet and melodic. She patted my arm. "Like you."

"Glory be, she's talking," Eli said softly. She had a talent for compassion, and I'd unleashed it by crying in our magic garden. I scrubbed my eyes and sat up. Eli and I traded amazed looks. The strength of Eli's arm around my shoulders felt good. He nodded to me. "We'll be ourselves, no matter what," he said.

From then on, he and Bell and I met often in that hidden, peculiar garden, hoping and dreaming together in the only safe world we knew.

## 4

Three years passed. Eli still kept to himself, counting his family's new life every quiet, safe day like a miser afraid to turn his back on pennies, but poured out his dreams to Darl in the garden. He never said he hated working in the office at Hardigree Marble, but he thought she suspected. Just as he suspected she was lonelier than any other human being on the face of the earth, except when they were together. The world turned in small, quiet circles, with them at the center..

*Godawmighty, it's Leon Forrest hisownself, and if looks could kill, everybody in this town would be stone-cold dead.*

That was Eli's first thought on the winter afternoon when the older boy slunk into the offices at Hardigree Marble to fill out paperwork for a quarry job. Eli looked up from a corner table where Mr. Albert had him adding payroll invoices as fast as his fingers could fly with a pencil. Leon stood there like a thundercloud. He was fourteen, now, over six feet tall and thinner than Eli, who was nearing the six-foot mark, himself. Leon's skin was black as tar, and his hair jutted in nappy tufts no matter how much he tried to pick it into a preened Afro. His folks had gone bust at farming, and now he was dropping out of school to work at the quarry. He hunched his shoulders inside an old army coat. His bitter gaze fell on Eli. "What you watchin' me for?"

Eli clenched his pencil and refused to look away. "I dunno. Guess we're in the same boat. I gotta work here, too."

"Huh. What you're doin' ain't work."

"Beats rasslin' marble in the cold." Eli tapped a ledger. "This is *smart* work."

"You sayin' I ain't smart enough to do what you do?"

"I got no idea. But I'd teach you how to keep these books if they'd let me. I hate doin' it."

"I could keep books. I like books. I'm sure not gonna rassle marble all my life."

"You sure will if you don't learn to do something else. I've seen how that just naturally happens around here."

Leon fumed. Mr. Albert saw him from his office window and, scowling, hustled into the front room. "Don't you loiter in here, boy. Your daddy'll come by and fill out your forms for you." He pointed to the picture window that overlooked the quarry. "Get on out there and tell that tall man in the blue coat I said to put you to work."

"Yessir," Leon mumbled.

Mr. Albert grimaced at Leon's overalls and mud-covered farm boots on the office's carpeted floor. "And don't you ever walk in here with dirty feet, again." He turned on his heel and left the room. Eli looked at Leon Forrest sympathetically and saw the humiliation in his face. "That man in the blue coat is my pa. Just do what he says and he'll be fair to you. You'll be okay."

Leon stared at him. "Day'll come when nobody around here tells me where or how to walk." He stomped out.

At six Mr. Albert closed the office for the night. The cold afternoon was settling into an icy dusk. "We're done, Mr. Genius," he ordered. Eli gratefully donned a heavy scarf and his padded canvas jacket then loped to the secluded parking lot to wait for Pa. There were only a few pick-up trucks left in the graveled area, and steep hills covered in fir and hemlock surrounded it, making a natural arena. The air turned his breath to frost. Eli shivered and stared in dismay as three rough-looking young black men dragged Leon out of the woods, swinging at him with their fists. Eli recognized none of them. Leon plowed into the trio, and all four tumbled in a mauling heap among the trucks.

*I could go get Pa*, Eli thought first, but there wasn't time. He crept over, ducking behind truck beds, until he was close enough to hear the wild grunts and curses. Leon was getting the shit beaten out of him. As Eli watched, one of the young men flashed a switchblade knife. Eli stood up and yelled like a banshee as the man swung the knife at Leon. Everybody jumped. The tip of the blade only caught Leon across the cheek but left a nasty gash. Red blood poured down Leon's dark jaw and neck.

His breath like the white puff of a steam engine, Eli lunged at the young men with his fists up. The sight of a tall, skinny white boy yelling maniacally and landing punches on them must have raised prospects of white Burnt Stand policemen and white trouble in general. "Fuck you, dude," the knife-wielding fighter said. He slashed at Eli, then he and the others sprinted for a low silver sedan and left in a hail of gravel and dust.

Eli stood there defiantly for a few seconds, then wavered and looked down at himself. His jacket's spongy filler protruded from a foot-long cut in the canvas directly over his stomach. He shakily opened the jacket and made sure his guts were still in place. Leon moaned and sat up. Eli hurried over and knelt beside him, grimacing at his bruised and bleeding face. The skin of his cheek had been opened like a zipper, the line showing red meat in the black skin. "Reckon you're gonna need some stitches," Eli said.

"Hell, no. My family got no money for stitches." Leon jerked Eli's coat open. "Did they cut you, too?"

"Nah. I'm too skinny and the coat's a size too big."

"You're crazy. Stay out of my trouble."

"What's your trouble?"

"Aw, those shits are from over at Ludawissee Gap. One of 'em said some bad things to my sister Prig. She owns a grocery store over there. They always comin' in, stealin' from her. I took me some kin and we went over and kicked some ass. They just returnin' the favor."

So Leon had a sister to protect. Eli recognized the nobility and honor in that instantly. He would tell Darl about Leon's heroics. Then he could slip in news of his own close escape from gutting. Darl would be impressed. "You did good," he told Leon. "But fist fightin' won't you get you very far. I've given it up as best I can."

"Huh. So you think you're cured of the itch? You punched at them bad mothers like a idiot. Who you think you are? Joe Frazier?" Leon smiled painfully then slapped him on the back. They got up, and Eli pulled a wad of filler from his sliced jacket. "Here. You can put this to your face 'til you get home."

Pa walked into the lot about then, casting looks in the dusk for Eli. "Comeon, you need a ride?" Eli said to Leon, but figured

Leon wouldn't take help from white folks. He was right. The older boy shook his head. He clamped the stuffing to his bloody cheek and started off through the woods. Then he turned and looked back. "Some day," he said, "I'll help you out, too."

Eli took all vows seriously. "I'll thank you kindly, when you do."

He told Darl about Leon, and she whispered the incident to Matilda, and Matilda made certain Leon Forrest got his face sewed up by a doctor. Leon's troubles sparked a chord in her, and she discreetly took him underwing, after that. She'd kept herself and Karen aloof from the few black families around Burnt Stand, and those families rejected her in kind. Eli always wondered if helping Leon was her only way of telling them she was sorry.

This, he decided, was the magic he and Darl made together.

*

On my tenth birthday, a Sunday in late September, Swan and I sat across from each other in the formal dining room at Marble Hall, eating off fine china filled with roasted chicken, sweet corn muffins, and cold black-eyed-pea salad. I was so pleased to have a rare meal alone with her, to have earned her full attention. As usual, we'd attended the morning sermon at Burnt Stand Methodist, a historic marble sanctuary adorned with a plaque warning God that Great-Grandmother Esta had built it.

Annie Gwen pushed through the butler door, carrying a silver tray where something bulky lay shrouded in a white napkin. She smiled at my surprised look, set the tray on the room's stalwart antique buffet, then reached under the napkin and pulled out the plug end of a brown extension cord. My fork froze over my salad as I watched her plug the cord into a wall socket.

She looked at Swan, who nodded her dismissal. "Happy Birthday, Miss Darl," Annie Gwen said, then left the room. I gazed from the plugged-in mystery to my grandmother. She rose from the table, as elegant as always in a calf-length skirt and matching jacket, favoring a soft amber shade for the season. I was still stuck in pink.

"You're ten years old," Swan said. "That's a milestone." She pulled a bottle of champagne from a silver bucket on the buffet, then filled two tall crystal flutes with the golden liquid. She topped the champagne with orange juice from a silver pitcher. "Your first mimosa. Come here."

I stood and moved warily to the buffet, still eyeing the electric whatever hidden under the crisp white napkin. For all I knew she intended to brand me. Swan handed me a champagne glass and I held it high, mimicking every adult I'd ever seen at a party. She clicked hers to it, the sound like a fine chime. I waited for her to say something, even Happy Birthday, but she didn't. I sighed and put the glass to my lips. So this was how it tasted to be halfway to adulthood. Sweet, tangy, with a rush of effervescent warmth all the way to my toes.

I drank the entire glass in one gulp. I wanted to be grown so badly. To make her even more proud of me. "Don't ever do that, again," Swan ordered. Blinking, already a little giddy, I gave her a bewildered look. Her eyes flashed. "Don't inhale an alcoholic beverage as if you're a barroom drunk downing a beer. Sip it. And always leave at least an inch in the bottom of the glass. Never be a glutton, particularly where alcohol is concerned. And never have more than two drinks at a time—and no drinks at all if you're alone in the company of a male."

"Yes, ma'am."

She took my glass and set aside with her demurely unemptied one. "I have a present for you."

I stared at the covered platter. My tongue felt thick. "Will it hurt?"

"What?"

"Nothing. I'm sorry, ma'am."

She pulled back the edge of the napkin, revealing a beautiful gold jeweler's box. She held it out, and opened the lid. I made a soft sound of pleasure as I gazed at the delicate pendant on a fine gold chain. A flat dewdrop of pink marble had been encased in a gold filigreed rim. The twisted gold held a one-carat diamond in the center of the stone. "It's just like yours!"

"Yes. That's the point." She lifted the necklace out and laid the box on the buffet. Swan pulled an identical pendant from beneath the soft collar of her jacket. "I received mine from my mother when I was ten. If you'll look at her portrait, you'll see she's wearing one." Swan paused. Her mouth curled just slightly. "My sister Clara has one, as well. And—" Another pause, then she said quietly —"I gave your mother one when she was your age. All of us, we Hardigree women. We all wear one."

"You loved my mother. Do you love me?" I blurted.

Her expression became instantly implacable. "You are my granddaughter," she said, "and my only heir. That's very important to me."

All my joy, my excitement and pride, vanished. She couldn't even say the words. *Why* was I so undeserving? She slid the opened necklace around my neck and latched it. The short chain held the pendant high on my chest. Swan pulled the napkin off the silver tray.

I stared at what appeared to be some kind of needle gun. My head reeled. "This is a soldering iron," Swan said. Swan slid her fingers under my necklace. She folded the napkin and tucked it beneath the chain's latch. I froze. She made a shushing sound. "I'm only going to solder the lock."

"Why?"

Her unwavering blue eyes bored into me. "Because it's our tradition, and I want you to honor it. Because mine is soldered shut, and so was your mother's. And Clara's. And your great-grandmother's. All soldered."

"You mean I can never take it off?"

"That's right."

I stood there like a prize calf while she maneuvered the soldering gun and a bit of silver soldering wire over the latch. I smelled a smoky, acrid scent, and my stomach rolled. *She doesn't love me, and that's why she's putting a chain around my neck. Like I'm a dog. I'm wearing a dog tag.* "There," Swan said, and stepped back. "Done."

"Thank you, ma'am," I managed to say.

At the first diplomatic chance I left the dining room and rushed outside, down the terrace steps, past the koi pond, and into the woods, where I threw up.

*

"No way, Baby Sister, not that one." Eli snagged the balloon just as Bell was about to tie it to the low branch of a young sassafras seedling. The tree had sprouted from the earth a year ago on the slope of the stone flower garden. Though he, Bell, and Darl had raked and pruned and tidied the wild glen, they'd decided to leave the sassafras, with its funny, mitten-shaped leaves.

Bell frowned as Eli took the balloon by its string. "What's wrong with it?"

"It's pink. No pink."

She made a tenderly aghast face. "Oh! Darl would hate that!" Eli let the air out and stuffed the limp balloon in a pocket of his jeans. He checked the wristwatch his folks had given him for his thirteenth birthday, three months earlier. "All right. It's time. I reckon I'll go over the hill and wait for her now. You be ready."

Bell smiled. "I will." At seven she was still quiet and easily spooked, but there was no comparison to the huddled toddler who had shivered at any stranger's glance. Dressed in cut-offs and a t-shirt, she bounded behind the stone flower vase and hunkered down. Eli nodded his approval then walked up the hill, adjusting his glasses as he went.

Mama and Pa had bought him metal aviator frames, which he didn't mind so much. He got his hair trimmed neatly once every six weeks at the Burnt Stand Barber Shop, where his and Pa's coarse black locks fell on the pink marble floor just as nicely as any man's hair in town. Gone was the side-skinned, chopped-top look of his first year.

Everything was looking up. There was talk at the quarry that Pa might be promoted to foreman soon. Mama had saved enough money from her job as a maid at Marble Hall to purchase an oak-veneer living room suite at a discount furniture store in Asheville, and Pa had proudly added twenty dollars to buy two fancy lamps at the flea market.

*This is how the world runs*, he thought somberly as he sat down to wait for Darl on the wind-ravaged trunk of an old oak. *You have to give a lot just to get ahead a little.* God and Swan Hardigree Samples had been good to his family, but his family had worked hard for that favor, and Eli would never do anything to damage their streak of good luck. He heard footsteps in the leaves and stood quickly. His mood brightened as it always did when Darl appeared at the top of the next hill. She waved and he raised a hand in return.

She never wore pink when she escaped to the woods. Her mink-brown hair curled in long waves down her shoulders and the front of a blue blouse. She'd grown at least four inches over the past few years, and was going to be a tall, slender girl, like her grandmother. Her arms and legs were long and strong, her skin as soft as silk, her eyes, even from a distance, the deepest blue. He watched her approach with a new feeling that tormented him inside more every day. He loved her, but he shouldn't stare at her this way. She didn't even have bosoms, yet.

For every noble moment they spent in the hidden garden reading books to each other and to Bell, talking about life, and listening or dancing to songs on a portable radio, he now spent an equal—but far less dignified—amount of time fantasizing about girls in ninth grade who had large breasts, about lingerie models in the Sears catalog, and even about perversely shaped pears and bell peppers at the Burnt Stand Supermarket, a fact that embarrassed him helplessly.

Yet here she was, his dearest friend, his faithful supporter, his lonely love, Darl Union. Her face was a little sad, but so many times she looked that way, just burdened, until he spoke to her. He liked the way her eyes lit up when she saw him.

"Stop right there." He strode to her, whipping a blue bandana from his jeans' pocket. "I got to blindfold you. Bell and me got a surprise."

"Huh. I'll fall over a cliff, and that'll be a surprise."

"Aw, hush. I'll lead you." He inhaled the sweet scent of her clothes and skin as he carefully tied the scarf behind her head. Before he covered her eyes she looked up at him with sad-eyed trust, disrupting all his noble thoughts, merging gallantry with hormones. Once the mask was in place he pushed a strand of her hair back from her face, then took her by one arm. "Just walk along with me."

"I can do that."

He guided her carefully up the hill. When they overlooked the Stone Flower Garden he gently tugged the bandana off her head. "Happy Birthday." She laughed and clamped her hands to her face as if caught in a prayer. Brightly colored balloons filled the deep glen. Anchored to the flower vase, the benches, the sassafras seedling, and the rhododendron shrubs, they bobbed and danced in the warm, early-autumn air.

"Happy Birthday, Darl!" Bell called softly. She popped from behind the flower vase's wide pediment, balancing a lopsided little cake with white icing on her upturned palms. Ten candles flickered atop it.

"Oh, it's wonderful," Darl said softly. She grabbed Eli by one hand and they rushed down the slope. "How pretty," she said of the cake.

Bell blushed and preened, ducking her fluffy, dark-haired head, overcome. "I made it," she whispered.

"You did? Even better."

Eli squeezed her hand. "Make a wish and blow out the candles."

Darl's expression quieted, and she gazed somberly at the funny little cake with its fragile lights. "I wish you and Bell were my family."

Bell beamed at her, and Eli succumbed to a warm tide of pleasure mixed with foreboding anxiety. "You're not supposed to wish it out loud."

Bell gasped and nodded fervently. She believed wholeheartedly in magic. "It won't come true!"

Darl's gaze hardened. "I'll make it come true. Somehow." She blew out the candles fiercely then looked up at Eli.

His heart twisted. He took a small packet from his pants pocket, and held it out. The gift was wrapped in neatly folded white tissue paper. She pulled the paper open as if it was the finest silk. Inside lay a small piece of marble, honed to a perfect oval shape and highly polished. "I made it for you," Eli said. Carved in its center was an elongated figure eight. "That's a math symbol," he explained gruffly. "It stands for infinity. Forever."

She kissed him. Just rose on her toes before he realized what she meant to do, took him by the shirt front, pulled him forward, and kissed him quickly on the lips. His face burned and hers turned red as well. She met his eyes then looked away quickly in a rare bout of shyness. "Forever," she whispered.

Nobody knew quite what to say after that. Eli and Darl sat down on the ground around a bench, pushing at balloons that rubbed against them tenderly, dipping their fingers into white icing and soft cake, not looking at each other as they ate, or at Bell, who began to giggle at them.

Eli savored every second and thought his heart would break. The sweetest taste would always be Darl. Forever.

*

It was a warm, bright October Saturday, in the middle of the month. I remember the stark silhouettes of the long row of oaks that lined the drive to Marble Hall, the quietness of the earth, the hushed quality inside the mansion that day. A hard autumn rain had stripped the last of the fall leaves the night before. My thoughts were stripped bare and lean, too, for the winter ahead.

I sat in a window seat of the library, curled up in its upholstered pillows, warming myself in the sun as I avidly read a new book called *Watership Down*. Somewhere in the mansion Swan was on the phone with her caterer and decorator, planning the holiday season parties she would give both in Burnt Stand and Asheville. Matilda was away for the weekend, and Karen was napping in my bedroom. Annie Gwen, who often quietly managed the kitchen and house on her own now, was dusting in the living room.

In an hour I planned to don my coat and meet Eli, Karen, and Bell at the garden. I had endured painfully formal dance lessons in cotillion classes at an Asheville dance school, and I was teaching Eli to waltz. But usually he wouldn't dance at all. Bell, Karen and I would sway and gyrate while he stretched out on the ground in his own patch of sunshine, grinning at our silliness.

A mantel clock ticked and shushed. I turned a page in my

book. A trickle of foreign sound reached my ears, but I ignored it as if it were a buzzing fly. It grew louder, and I raised my head, listening. A car coming up the drive. Nothing odd about that. Swan must have invited some of the town ladies to drop by. They knew better than to refuse Swan's invitations.

"I'll get the door," I called to Annie Gwen. I wandered into the high, chandeliered foyer and peeked out one of the sidelights around the Hall's ornate double doors. A bright red Trans Am sports car purred up the oak-lined driveway. I did a double take. Swan didn't associate with the kind of people who drove Trans Am's. The car's top was up, and I couldn't make out the driver. I opened the massive doors and stepped onto the portico's wide marble apron, framed by a pair of tall, lean cedars in marble planters. I sunned myself in the autumn heat and squinted.

A woman. A dark-haired woman, her eyes covered by sunglasses, drove the blister-red car. She swung it into the courtyard, nearly clipping an island of planters and manicured shrubs. The tires squealed as she braked inches from the polished stone steps to the portico. Such a dramatic entrance left me breathless and amazed. She flung her door open and curled herself out. High-heeled red boots hit the pink bricks. Skin-tight designer jeans enclosed long, lean legs. She threw back her shoulders in a fringed leather vest. Her voluptuous breasts bulged against the buttons of a white blouse so sheer I could see her little black bra through it. Her lipstick was cherry red, her hair an upswept tangle of curls.

I gaped at her. A wild woman, on our very doorstep.

She stared straight at me with a cocky smirk beginning to slither across her mouth, pulling several creases on the upside, accenting the softening skin of her jaw. She wasn't as young as she wanted to look, but she was exactly as sarcastic as she meant to be. "Why, if you aren't a perfect little copy of your goddamned grandmother," she drawled.

Anger prickled my skin. I snapped my mouth shut and lifted my head regally. "Ma'am, only trashy people speak that way to me."

She laughed. "Oh, God. Just like Swan!"

Behind me, the mansion's doors opened with a deep, elegant

swoosh. I turned quickly. Swan stood there looking at our visitor. They could not have been more different in dress and manner. Swan was a fashion plate in her typical weekend casual wear, meaning tailored slacks and a soft gray sweater with pearls. The visitor was a blue-plate special from a roadside diner.

Neither said a word. Swan's eyes, as cold as arctic blue ice, never left the woman, who stared back, frozen and sullen. The silence stretched out. My lungs ached with held breath. They were like gunfighters in an old western movie, one daring the other.

"Draw," I said urgently.

The visitor whipped her glasses off. I gasped. Her blue Hardigree eyes gazed at Swan the way a mongoose stares down a cobra. "Hello, Sister," the woman said.

The sound Swan made was almost a hiss. "Hello, Clara."

*

"And then she got out four or five huge suitcases and dragged them indoors," I went on quickly, my words tumbling over each other. "My grandmother just stood there. Grandmother didn't say *Stop*, or *No*, or *You're not welcome here*. Grandmother just let her go in. And so my . . . my Great Aunt Clara took all her suitcases upstairs and went into the biggest guest bedroom in the house and slammed the door. And Grandmother went in her office and shut *that* door. And I just stood there with my eyeballs up on poles like a snail, trying to see what was going to happen next."

Eli, Karen and Bell sat before me in the stone flower garden. Eli's angular face was tight with concentration. Bell's mouth made a permanent *Oh*! of intrigue. Karen whistled under her breath. Eli finally squinted in thought and shook his head. "Well, it doesn't have nothing to do with you, and that's all that really matters to me."

I leaned closer to him. "Do y'all ever hear your mother say anything about my grandmother and Clara? I mean, I'm sure Matilda knows things about us that she won't tell, but maybe she talks to your mother."

"Mama's quiet as a mouse," Bell whispered. "That's where I

get it from."

"I've got to figure this out. Grandmother and Clara hate each other. But nobody will tell me why."

Eli frowned and pushed his aviator glasses higher up his nose. "You just stay outta their way. If they get to whacking each other or pullin' guns or firing atomic missiles, give a yell and I'll come get you."

My heart melted. "I'll hide beside the koi pond and yell Duck! when the bombs fire."

"Not Duck," Karen corrected drily. "Swan."

Everyone burst into chortles—that was the effect we all had on each other, even in dark moments. In the midst of it we heard a distant clanging sound. Karen and I and jumped up worriedly. A brass bell hung from a handsome oak post in the back gardens. Grandmother and Matilda used it to call us from our forest rambles. "We have to go."

Eli and Bell scrambled to their feet. "Watch out for ducks and Clara!" Bell cried. I hugged her. "I'm not afraid of Clara. She's so red I'd see her coming a mile away. She can't sneak up on me."

Eli frowned. I loved to look into his protective gaze, his eyes so dark they sweetened him like syrup. "You yell if you need me," he said quietly. "Promise."

I wanted to kiss him. I got the urge under control and merely nodded.

*

A thick knot of anxiety filled my stomach as soon as Karen and I came within view of the back terrace. Matilda stood at the top, watching for us. Her graying brown hair did not move in the afternoon breeze; her golden face was set in a frown, her body looked rigid in a tailored dress of umber wool. We hurried up the stone steps. "Darl, go pack your weekend bag," she ordered crisply. "Your grandmothers's sending you to my house with Karen for a few days."

"Allright!" Karen said happily.

"Are Grandmother and Clara going to fight?" I asked.

"Clara has come for money, and when she gets as much as she wants, she'll leave. It's only a question of how much your grandmother will give her, and when, and how long Clara will wait." I couldn't believe Matilda told us that. It was more than anyone had ever confessed before.

I grabbed Karen's hand and we hurried inside to pack my things. I listened to the tension in the house, to the stealthy, bewildering silence of Grandmother and her sister, waiting for their blue-eyed bombs to explode in my world.

\*

"I don't mind staying here," I whispered to Karen, as we huddled under a downy quilt in her four-poster canopy bed that night. The room was done in fluffy cream colors and bright yellows. Even a photograph of Karen's Vietnam-hero father in his marine uniform sat on her dresser in a cream-and-yellow frame. "It's not pink."

She snuggled closer to me in a flannel nightgown. The mountain days could be hot in autumn, but the nights turned cold. "If you weren't a white girl, you could come to visit all the time. People wouldn't talk."

"I wish you could visit overnight at Marble Hall with me. Nobody dares talk ugly about my grandmother's guests."

She snorted her disgust over my simplistic views, then sighed. "I wish we were sisters."

"Me, too." We linked hands. "We wouldn't be like my grandmother and Clara. We'd like each other."

"Except people wouldn't let us. I'm a nigger, Darl."

That word hung in the air like a shadow demon. She'd said it so plainly it had little power. Yet even our cloistered lives had not been able to escape it. I looked across the darkness at the yellow trimmed walls, the yellow lace on the room's creamy curtains, even the yellow picture frame with Karen's black father gazing out proudly in the glow of a yellow nightlight. "It doesn't matter what people say."

"You don't know what they call me and Grandmother when we go someplace by ourselves."

"They'd never dare! Swan wouldn't let them."

"Not around here. I mean when Grandmother and me go to Asheville. Ladies stare at us in the shops. Once, I heard one say, Well, I swear, look at those fancy niggers. And when we stopped at a gas station once the man who pumped the gas said to Grandmother, You must work for a rich white lady. She sure lets her nigger drive a nice car. It's always like that, Darl. It's why Grandma and me *never* go far alone.".

"I'll always protect you. I promise."

She snorted. "I don't want you to protect me, fool. Besides, you can't even do it. The rest of the world isn't like Burnt Stand."

My heart ached. What good was power and money if I was still helpless to defend my most-loved people? "Dammit. Dammit." I pounded the pillows. I felt as if every muscle in my body had clenched.

The rest of the world was like Clara.

## 5

Matilda left to run errands the next afternoon, and Karen fell asleep on the living room couch with her schoolbooks spread around her and a forbidden episode of *Days Of Our Lives* playing on Matilda's only concession to tawdry entertainments—an old black-and-white television. I put a pink sweater over my pink wool skirt and pink blouse, slipped from Matilda's handsome bungalow on pink tennis shoes, and headed one mile due west through hilly woods and across the narrow dirt roads of secluded mountain farms.

The October afternoon was hot; I wound the sweater around my waist. The sun made deep slanted shadows through the golden autumn trees when I finally walked up the marble-stoned driveway at Marble Hall. It wasn't five o'clock, yet, so I knew Swan might still be at the quarry offices or at the marble showroom in town. I skirted the front of the house and sneaked through the clipped boxwood garden on one side. I had a kitchen door key, and I planned to use it. I'd quietly seek out Clara inside the mansion and see if her lethal aura sizzled like ice in the warm fall air..

I didn't have to go that far. I stepped out of the boxwoods garden through an open wrought-iron gate in the tall marble wall that enclosed that side of the back yard. There in the bright sun beside the swimming pool, sunning herself on a plushly pillowed, white wicker lounge chair, sat Clara.

Completely naked.

I stopped like a fawn before a wild dog, hoping the mere act of standing still would hide me against the pink garden wall. Perhaps this was why Swan always clothed me in pink—camouflaged for my own safety. But it was too late. Clara's lounge chair faced me. She tilted her head forward, and a smirk crossed her mouth. I couldn't see her eyes behind large, white-rimmed, octagonal sunglasses, which gave her the alien appearance of a mutant insect in a horror movie. Maybe she was thinking of eating me alive, just for fun. Her tinted brunette hair fell in wide curls from a jaunty topknot. Her long, lean legs jiggled provocatively as she crossed them at the ankles.

She was 48 years old but still had the lithe body that made Hardigree women so alluring and quick on the attack. I'd never seen a naked person in the flesh before, much less a relative. I stared helplessly at her bare breasts, which rode high on her chest with manufactured roundness, and I tried desperately not to notice anything about her crotch.

"Come here, Darling Darl," she drawled softly. I was surprised at the friendliness in her tone. "I won't bite."

"I just stopped by for a, hmmm, visit, Ma'am. Just to pick up some more clothes."

"Right. Sure." She slid further down on a long blue pool towel, its ends trailing onto the pink marble surface of the pool patio. As if humoring my modesty she flipped one trailing end of the towel over her groin, though she made no effort to cover her breasts. "Come here and visit." She gestured at a wicker chair nearby. When I didn't budge her eyebrows arched over the white rims of her glasses. "Not afraid of your own great aunt, are you, Hon? I can't believe Swan raised a sissy."

I marched toward her with grim dignity. A pungent aroma hit my nostrils, and I saw the ashtray half hidden beneath her lounge. A strange, homemade cigarette wafted its smoke into the air. Next to it sat one of Swan's finest Baccarat martini glasses, empty. I knew plenty about liquor but I'd never smelled marijuana before. I sat down on the edge of the chair with my knees pressed tightly together, as if the exotic, burnt-rope scent might creep up my skirt and make me want to throw off all my clothes, too.

And then, gathering my wits, I saw it. The necklace. The marble and diamond pendant hung from a gold chain around Clara's neck just like mine and Swan's. My heart eased with familial relief. How bad could she be if she still honored our Hardigree traditions? "I have one of those pendants, too, ma'am." I slid my necklace from the pink collar of my blouse.

She uttered a throaty laugh. "Branded for life. I ought to rip mine off and throw it in the nearest toilet, but it's about the only thing of my mother's I got to keep when Swan kicked me out of town. I was only sixteen at the time. Do you know that story?"

I stiffened, once again uncertain. "No, ma'am." I stood. "I better go. I have clothes to find."

Clara held up a reassuring hand decked with long, white-nipped nails. "I'm only bitching at you because I'm bored. I can't leave the premises." She laughed. "Swan has me under house arrest."

"What—what did you do wrong, ma'am?"

"I was born with all our family's worst traits, Darling Darl, if you believe Swan."

I slid my hand in my skirt pocket and clenched a small marble stone Eli had given me. Clara scared me, and I needed the comforting feel of Eli's talisman. "She's never told me much about you."

"Of course not. I live on the dark side of the Hardigree planet. Where all the fun is." She leaned forward. Her breasts swayed. I felt hypnotized. Clara grinned. "I can tell you stories about our family . . . but I won't."

I gripped the stone harder. My palm was slick with nerves, and the stone scooted backwards as if oiled. It shot from my skirt pocket and clattered on the patio stones. A jumping bean couldn't have been more agile. It skittered and bounced toward Clara. She dropped her long-clawed hand to the patio surface and scooped it up. "Aw, you've got a little marble keepsake. Isn't that sweet? What's this figure eight mean?"

"Nothing, ma'am." I held out a hand. "May I have it back, please?".

"No." She closed her fist around it. "Tell me what it means, or I'll throw it in the pool."

I shivered. "The eight means nothing. Really. Nothing. And everything. It's not an eight. You're supposed to look at it sideways. It's a math symbol. It stands for infinity. Forever."

"Hmmm. God, you're a queer little thinker, aren't you?"

"May I have it back, now?"

"Not yet." She opened her hand, flipped the stone over and perused the other side. She cackled. "Now, we're talking. A heart.

And initials. D.U. That's for you. And E.W. Hmmm. Darl's got a boyfriend. Who's E.W.?"

"He's just a friend."

"No, he's a boyfriend. And he cuts stone."

"No, Ma'am. No."

She laughed. "A stonecutter's kid, that's who he is! Oh, shit, that's perfect!" She held her breasts, leaned back in the chair, and laughed like a truckdriver. In the meantime she tossed the stone at me. I grabbed it in mid air and hid it in my skirt pocket again. Clara pulled her sunglasses down the tip of her nose and gazed at me with amused disgust. "Don't you understand? Swan's trying so hard to suck the life out of you, but you're struck with the family curse. See, we can't keep our hands off men who work with stone—and the dirtier, the better. Give him up, Hon. He'll ruin you or kill you or break your heart. And if he doesn't, Swan will."

She was so smug, so evil. My pride overcame common sense. "My boyfriend's the smartest person in town, he's a genius, and he'd never do anything to hurt me. Grandmother even hired him to work with the ledgers at the office. He's going to the university in a few years. He's not just going to cut stone all his life. And he's not dirty!"

"Oh, yes, he is, and he'll cut stone, one way or another. Is he handsome?" Her sly expression returned. "Handsome and rough around the edges? That's how we like our men. Unpolished but hard. Poor and proud but not too proud to do what we tell them to do. Treat him like a pet puppy right now, Hon. But when he's old enough to piss on you, get rid of him. Or Swan'll do it for you."

Fury stoked my blood. I advanced on her with my fists clenched. "You've got a nasty mind and a nasty mouth. I see why Grandmother never invited you to visit us. Well, let me tell you something. Eli Wade is the best boy in the world. And—"

"What did you say his name is?" Her mouth popped open.

"Eli Wade. His parents and his sister and him came here three years ago, and they work hard and they live in the Stone Cottage. His mother works as a maid for Matilda so you know that means she's a good person. Plus Grandmother has given the Wades special favors— and you know she doesn't do that for trashy people. And—"

"Wade. Wade? Oh, my God." Clara whipped her sunglasses off and stared at me as if she couldn't say the name often enough to make her believe it. For once there was no hint of humor or sarcasm in her eyes. She looked stunned. "Wade. You're sure that's their family name?"

I took two steps back. Her intensity unnerved me. "Yes."

"Where did they come from?"

"Somewhere in Tennessee."

"What do they look like—the men. What does this Eli's daddy look like?"

"I don't know what you mean. He's a big tall man, with muscled arms, and he's kind of quiet—"

"Does he have dark hair and dark eyes?"

"Yes, but—"

"I'll be goddamned." She stared into space, her blue eyes shifting as if she were comparing notes on a mental blackboard. I stared in anxious confusion. She leapt to her feet, throwing the towel around her naked body like a toga. She trembled. Her eyes were almost feverish. "Get out of here," she spat at me, "and don't tell anybody we talked about the Wades. And don't you goddamn dare tell anyone I'm going into town." Gone was any pretense of affection or even tolerant cynicism.

"I thought you weren't supposed to leave the house."

"All bets are off. The whole damn game is different now—if what I think is true." She threw back her head and made a furious, groaning sound. "Swan and Matilda," she sang softly. "You lying bitches.".

Clara strode to the house, slung open one of the French doors that faced the pool patio, and disappeared inside. I stood there in shock. Dread filled me.

Clara had been held at bay by magic, like some demon or evil spirit.

And somehow, I'd just set her free.

\*

Eli's head swam with dreams of the future. Good luck didn't

come in single bursts—he was convinced of that, just seeing how nothing but good seemed to happen to Darl's grandmother. Good luck was a sum that multiplied itself in ratios as pure as life itself. Once you set the calculation going in your head and believed in the numbers, that luck grew.

And now it had paid off for the Wade family.

"Let's celebrate, Son." Pa proclaimed the occasion with a rare smile, his eyes alight as the bartender at Neddler's Place set a tall mug of beer before him and a small glass filled with beer before Eli. Neddler's was a joint in the woods off a backroad outside Burnt Stand. It had a jukebox, a bar, pool tables and a smell like a bathroom floor. The floor was made of scrap marble, and the bar was topped with a slab of the stone, too. Photographs of the quarry hung among stuffed deer heads and neon beer signs on the shabby plywood walls.

"To Jasper Wade, the new foreman," a man called out, and several dozen stonecutters stood with their mugs or bottles in hand. "Boss Wade, Boss Wade," they chanted. Eli leapt to his feet and clasped his own glass of precious beer. "To my Pa," he said proudly. "Boss Wade."

Everyone drank. The beer slid down Eli's throat like bitter tonic. He fought not to gag, set the glass down on the bar, and smiled at his father, who gave a deep laugh. Pa had never looked so happy in his entire life. "We'll get on home in a minute and tell your mama and Bell the good news," Pa said. "And you know what? When I get the first paycheck with the raise on it, we're all goin' out to eat. Somewhere all the way to Asheville. With tablecloths. And candles."

"That'll be great, Pa." Eli hiked himself back onto the bar stool carefully. His knees felt drunk, but it suddenly dawned on him that he was tall enough for his feet to reach the bar's marble footrest almost as easily as Pa's did. Almost six feet tall. Almost a man. He adjusted his aviator glasses and could swear the world looked different—better every day. If Pa could be this happy and earn a promotion to foreman despite not being able to read, then what other endless possibilities existed?

Eli thought of Darl, who made him feel capable of moving

mountains. *I'll get into college on my own*, he thought excitedly. *I don't need a Hardigree scholarship. That way I won't have to come back here and work for the marble company to pay Swan back.* He'd come back for Darl when she was old enough, because he'd have money by then, he'd be a college graduate—and rich, no doubt. He'd take his family away from here, and he'd take Darl. They'd see the world, and the world would see them.

Neddler's old wooden door swung inward, clattering a chain on its latch. Heads swiveled as a newcomer entered the windowless bar. A shaft of cooling autumn sunshine pierced the room's dim and smoky interior. Eli squinted at a startling female silhouette against the open doorway. Long legs in tight jeans, feet in high-heeled boots with thick soles, a bulge of tightly-bloused breast against the sunshine, a pile of hair tangled on her shoulders. The silhouette stepped inside, and a man near that end of the bar rushed to shut the door.

The jukebox was between songs, and silence ruled as all conversation stopped dead. Men halted with their cues posed over the pool tables, their mouths open and their eyes riveted to her. Everything about her said *sex* in letters as bright as the neon bar signs. In their low light she almost passed for a woman under thirty, but her blue eyes were as predatory as an old hawk. She brushed a dark brunette curl away from her face and searched the bar as if she could pierce any man there with a killing look. Eli felt a tingle of alarm and intrigue down his spine and through his groin. His face warmed. Who was this strangely familiar lady?

Creighton Neddler, the aged, white-haired owner and bartender, jerked to life. "Miss Hardigree," he said loudly, looking around as if to make certain he broadcast the name to every stonecutter in the room. "We're, uh, we're glad to have you. Can I pour you a beer?"

She didn't bother to answer, but instead kept studying the men. Eli's breath stuck in his throat. *Hardigree. This was Darl's Great Aunt Clara?* That made her somewhere near Swan's age, old enough to be somebody's grandmother. He darted a glance at Pa, whose face said anything to do with a Hardigree female of any age in this bar couldn't be good for men who depended on Swan's paycheck.

Pa set his mug of beer aside and stood. He had to look after his crew. His drawling voice, deep, uneducated, but firm, echoed through the small bar. "Ma'am, I'm the new foreman at Hardigree Marble. My name's Jasper Wade. What can we do for you?" Are you lookin' for somebody?"

Her gaze settled on him like a pulse of electricity. A quick flick of her eyes encompassed Eli but then returned to Pa, narrowing and widening. She tilted her head and looked at him from other angles, and to Eli's amazement, her expression shifted between anger and a kind of pain. With a snap of her head she walked to Eli and his father, stopping close enough to touch Pa.

Which she suddenly did.

Eli almost choked as she lifted her hand and stroked her fingertips along his father's jaw. Pa's shoulders went rigid, and he jerked his head away. She thrust her hand higher and caressed his cheek. Eli struggled not to shout, *Get away from him!*

Pa couldn't shove her away—couldn't lay violent hands on any woman, because Pa didn't manhandle females, not for any reason. Yet Pa couldn't take a step back, because how would that look to the men? Everyone was staring. "Ma'am," Pa said in a strained tone, "I'd appreciate if you'd take your hand off me. I'm a married man, and I'll have to move your hand away for you if you keep on."

She lowered her hand but studied him, her head thrown back and her chest rising hard on each breath. Bitterness entered her eyes, and she smiled. "You do look just like him. It has to be true. Your daddy was Anthony Wade, wasn't he?"

After a stunned moment, Pa said warily, "Yes, ma'am."

A low sound exploded from her lips. "From Wichitaw, Tennessee."

"Yes, ma'am."

"The Payson Marble Quarry. That's where he worked in Wichitaw, before he came here."

Eli was speechless. What was going on? When he sidled around Pa and looked at his face, he saw grim bewilderment that matched his own. "Ma'am, my daddy died when I was a boy. A good thirty years ago. I don't know what you're gettin' at. Are you sayin' you knew him?"

She laughed. "Knew him? Oh, I knew him— before you were born. I knew him when he was the talk of the town around here. No man could cut stone the way Anthony Wade did." She emphasized that with her head tilted. The words sounded nasty.

The color rose in Pa's face. "Ma'am, my daddy never lived in North Carolina, and he never worked for Hardigree Marble."

"How would you know? It was before you were born, I said. Hell, yes, he lived here." She paused. Her voice rose. "My mother brought him here. He built Marble Hall for her. He built all the Esta Houses in town. He built the Stone Cottage and the Stone Flower Garden." She smiled like a cold, tight cat. "He did whatever she told him to do—and he built this town."

Eli could barely breathe. His Grandpa Wade, the cripple and alcoholic, had done all that? They were living in a cottage of stone he'd cut and set with his own hands? He'd carved the fabulous statuary in the Stone Flower Garden, and designed the marble that made up every fine house in the whole town? Why had he kept all that glory a secret? Pa looked stunned. Around him, the men gawked in electric silence. "Ma'am," Pa said finally, "I believe I'd know if my own daddy had ever done something that grand. I believe he'd have told my mother all about it. I think you got the wrong man."

She stepped closer. She smelled of perfume and cool night air. Her eyes gleamed. She touched Pa's face, again, pressing a fingernail into the flesh of his cheek. He stepped back from her. Her eyes flashed. "He didn't want anyone to know," she said in a low voice, "Because he was a kept man. *He was my mother's whore.*"

Pa looked as if she'd slapped him. He turned slowly and gripped Eli by the shoulder. "We're leavin', son. Right now." Then, to Clara Hardigree, "I don't believe a word you say, but if you were a man I'd kill you."

*I'd kill you.* The violent threat didn't even phase her, but it made Eli gag. Pa gave him a firm push and they moved past her toward the door. The hair stood up on Eli's nape. All of Pa's fellow stonecutters, men who called him Boss Wade now, as an honor— were watching this godawful humiliation.

"I'll tell you another thing," Clara Hardigree called out as they reached the door, loud enough for all to hear. "I know how your daddy came to be crippled. A dozen of his own men— stonecutters—threw him out of town and nearly beat him to death. You want to know why?"

The whole world was exploding. Eli braced his feet apart as he watched the blood drain from Pa's face. Clara Hardigree smiled. "Because he wasn't just a whore. He was a nigger lover, too. You might want to be nice to Matilda Dove's little girl." Clara paused, savoring the coup de grace. "She's his granddaughter."

*

I slipped back to Matilda's house around dusk, and Karen shrieked with disgust over my adventure without her. When she saw my despair she quickly backed down, and we locked ourselves in her bedroom. We spent the rest of the afternoon endlessly discussing my encounter with Clara, and what Clara's strange behavior might mean.

Matilda returned at dinnertime, looking tired and distracted after doing errands for Swan. We ate a silent meal of tuna sandwiches and vegetable soup. I wanted to confess about Clara, but the words stuck in my throat. Matilda put on a long blue house robe then sat in the living room with a delicate glass of undiluted bourbon in her hand. I had never seen her drink, before.

"All right, here's the news," she said to us finally. "Clara has gone out on the town, and no one knows where. She promised Swan she wouldn't leave Marble Hall, but she did. If for any reason she should stop by this house, I expect the two of you to scat upstairs and not to so much as poke your nose out of the bedroom door while I talk to her."

"Because she's a bad person?" Karen asked quaintly, and shot a knowing look at me.

"Yes." Matilda gave us a flat look. "She's cruel and irresponsible, and her reputation in this town is very poor. Now, that's all I can say. Swan does the best she can with the situation, and we have to help her as best we can."

"Maybe she won't come back; maybe she's gone home to Chicago," I said.

Matilda looked at me. "No, Darl. Evil never retreats that easily."

She was out there, doing something terrible, because of me.

## 6

Even in the worst of their hard times Eli had never seen Pa
the way he saw him after they came home from Neddler's. "It'll be
all right, Jasper," Mama begged. She sat in the floor at Pa's feet,
looking up at him with tearful supplication, hugging him around
his knees.

Pa hunched over in the big easy chair Mama had ordered from
Sears as his birthday present that summer. He held his head in his
hands. An oak fire crackled inside the ornate marble hearth, sending
shadows above the lamps and onto a shelf filled with Mama's
dimestore ceramic collection. The living room of the Stone Cottage
was warm and friendly, the way Mama always made it, but nothing
helped.

Eli's eyes kept going to Grandpa Wade's tiny photograph. Bell
clung to him with her arms around his waist and her tear-streaked
face pressed against his stomach. Pa wasn't crying, but Eli heard
pure agony in his voice. "I'm done for. If what that woman said's
true, the Wade name is gonna be nothing but a bad joke around
here from now on."

Mama held him. "It's a lie, Jasper. Clara Hardigree's just crazy
and mean. People whisper she's never been anything but trouble.
Even Miss Swan can't bear her and can't bear to have other people
see what she's like. That's why Miss Matilda told me not to come
to work while Clara was here."

Pa looked at her with patient despair in his rugged face. "Annie
Gwen, don't you understand? Miss Swan and Miss Matilda were
just tryin' to keep her from findin' out your name. *Wade*. They
were tryin' to hide us."

Mama gasped. They sat in silence, their heads bowed together.
Neither of them were eloquent people, and both depended on
actions, not words, to express their hearts. Eli watched in misery
as Pa stroked a hand over her pale brown hair and down her thin

back. "I've never been a smart man, not able to read and all, but I've tried so hard to make you proud of me. I'm sorry."

Mama clutched his hand. "I *am* proud of you. What your daddy did forty years ago's got nothing to do with you. And if having colored kin oughta make you ashamed, then just about every white person in the world's got something to hide, too."

Pa cupped her chin in his hand and looked down at her fiercely. "You know my mama raised me to treat colored folks fair, and hell, Matilda and Karen are just one shade shy of white, but Annie Gwen—there are men at the quarry who hate coloreds and hate anything to do with 'em. I'm the foreman of those men, now. All they're gonna see when they look at me from now on is a man who's got colored kin in this town."

She shook her head wildly. "You listen to me. This is as fair a place as we've ever lived. Miss Swan don't tolerate petty nonsense. Even a few hateful knotheads at the quarry can't change her mind on you being the new foreman."

Pa wrapped his arms around her and hunched over her. "Everything we got in this place is our right by work and sweat and tears. We earned it. I swear to you and I swear to God—I'm not leavin' here without a fight."

*

Eli lay in the dark in his twin bed across the room from Bell, listening to the low murmur of his parents still talking late that night. Everything felt restless and miserable—Eli hadn't taken off his jeans and sweatshirt, just as Bell, sleeping fitfully, still wore all her clothes. He heard Mama and Pa step into the hall, and the sound of the truck keys jingling. "I'm just gonna go back and ask Creighton Neddler what the men said amongst themselves after I left," Pa told her in a low voice.

Eli sat up, straining to hear his mother's soft, anxious reply. "Please let this wait 'til mornin'."

"I can't. It's killin' me. I'll be back home soon. Don't worry."

Killing. For the second time that day Pa had talked of the word. Eli slid from bed, opened a nearby window, and climbed out. By the time Pa cranked the truck's engine Eli was already hidden quietly in the truck's bed with one hand on the inside latch of the camper top.

He wouldn't let Pa fight alone. The odds were moving against him.

\*

Eli shivered in the truck's cold bed, peering furtively out the cracked window of the camper top. Neddler's Place was a scrap-marble bunker with a tin roof and boarded-up windows with beer signs on them, not a pretty place in the daytime and even rougher after midnight. It sat by itself off a narrow back road halfway up Doe Ridge, one of the wild mountains that ringed Burnt Stand. The parking lot was only dimly lit by a streetlamp nailed high up the side of an electrical pole. Cold mountain air curled over the ridge and raked the empty tree limps.

Beside a couple of other pick-up trucks and Neddler's sedan, only one car waited on the shadowed lot—Clara's blood-red Trans Am. She'd stayed at the backwoods bar all this time? *Godawmighty,* Eli thought. *What kind of lady does that?*

He unlatched the camper top's door, pushed it upwards, then climbed out over the truck's tailgate and stepped quickly into the shadows outside the streetlamp. With a thick wooden slap, the bar's front door popped open. Eli jumped.

Pa strode angrily from the building with his fists shoved into the pockets of his green hunting jacket as if he wanted to keep himself from punching somebody. Old Mr. Neddler followed him, scrubbing both hands on a bartender's apron. "I'm not throwin' you out, Jasper, I'm just tellin' you to leave the situation alone for now. I got enough trouble tonight with her inside my place. I've had to chase off most of my customers tonight just to make sure she don't get half the quarry crew fired for trying to get in her panties. I guarantee you, Swan Samples would sure fire the ass of any man who touched her sister, even though it'd damned sure be Clara's own fault."

Pa pivoted and faced the elderly barkeep. "It's not right—

somebody like her havin' the power to hurt people with talk about the past. Hell—she can't even prove it's true." He hesitated. "*Did my daddy fuck Esta Hardigree?*"

The old man sagged. "The gossip was that he spent more time at the Stone Cottage laying the old lady than laying the stone."

Pa groaned. Listening in the darkness, Eli burned with embarrassment for Pa, for their family, and suddenly, as the thought struck him, for Darl. Her Great Aunt Clara was rich white trash and her great-grandmother had been—what? He knew how much he loved Darl then, to think of her misery as much as his own.

"Go on home," Neddler urged Pa. "The men who want to think bad of your family name will do it anyhow, and the rest will know better. And maybe word won't get to Miz Swan about any of this."

Pa nodded wearily then turned toward the truck. Suddenly Clara Hardigree stepped out of the bar's doorway. One look could tell she'd been drinking the past few hours. Her walk was a looser sashay, almost a taunt as she crossed the parking lot. A cigarette trickled smoke from her right hand. She flicked the butt away with the skill of a truckstop waitress. "If you're leaving, I'm disappointed. You're not living up to your daddy's reputation."

Pa looked down at her with a muscle jumping in his cheek. "Keep away from me."

Neddler tried to block her path but she sidestepped him like a cat. In a flash she careened up to Pa and put both arms around his neck. She pressed her thighs against his and tilted her head back. Pa dragged her arms down so roughly she staggered back, stumbled over her own high-heeled clogs, and fell. Mr. Neddler reached for her but missed. She sprawled on her side and slapped at Mr. Neddler's hand. Eli was petrified. Pa stood over her. "I told you I'd kill you if you were a man," he said. "If you hurt my family I'll kill you, regardless."

He turned and went to the truck, slung the driver's door open and got inside. Eli leapt forward but couldn't move fast enough. He watched from the shadows as his father unknowingly left him behind. Clara Hardigree climbed to her feet furiously. "Nobody talks to me that way." She walked to the Trans Am, snatched the keys from her jeans' pocket, slid inside the low, sleek car, and within seconds skinned rubber onto the road down Doe Mountain. Her taillights disappeared behind the truck's.

"Goddamn her," Mr. Neddler muttered aloud, his voice carrying on the wind. "Maybe she'll run off a mountainside and spare us all more trouble."

Eli backed into the darkness, quivering with worry and anger. He'd have a long walk home that night, but the walk didn't scare him.

Clara Hardigree following Pa down a dark road did.

*

It was nearly dawn. I lay in bed beside Karen in an agony of indecision. I should call Grandmother and tell her about my conversation with Clara. I had provoked Clara to run off, to run wild. But I'd have to tell Swan about our Wade discussion, too, and I couldn't risk that. The morality of the dilemma made me bundle myself in a tight, fetal ball next to the soundly sleeping Karen, pulled up so tight I could kiss my own kneecaps.

I heard a rock hit a window pane and crept out of bed. When I looked down into Matilda's side yard I saw Eli looking up at me in the moonlight. I waved to him, then pulled a robe around my shoulders, tiptoed downstairs and out the back door. I ran to him in the moonlight. "What's wrong? What are you doing?"

"I been walking home from Neddler's."

"What were you doing at *that* awful place? What's wrong?"

He clenched my hands in his. His shoulders hunched under a denim jacket. His breath puffed ragged and white in the frosty air. "I don't know how to tell you . . . how to say what happened, about your . . . I just hate to say any of it—"

"Clara!" My voice broke. "Something's happened because of her, hasn't it?" He looked shocked but nodded. I poured out my conversation with her by the swimming pool at Marble Hall. He pulled me out of the light and we huddled on a marble bench in the deep shadows of a golden-leaved oak. He told me what Clara had said about his family at Neddler's Place.

The tale filled my brain like an overblown balloon. Eli's grandfather had lived here in Burnt Stand when he was a young man? He'd worked for my great-grandmother Esta? And built the very Stone Cottage and the Stone Flower Garden that Eli and I loved so much? And he'd . . . he'd had sex with Matilda? He'd made a baby with her? Katherine had been their daughter? *Karen was his granddaughter?* I thought my skull would explode. I pressed my palms to my temples and held my head.

Eli hung his head. "You know what people'll say about my family, when this gets around."

"No, I don't know. What do you mean?"

"That we're related to Matilda. We've got black kin."

"But you're not black."

"Doesn't matter. Pa says there are men in his crew who'll never look at him the same way. They'll say his pa was a . . . that Grandpa Wade liked black women."

"But your father didn't do anything wrong. None of you did. Only your grandpa. And Matilda, I guess, but I just can't imagine—"

"Hey!" Karen called softly. "What's going on?" Eli and I jumped. She scurried across the backyard, her breath puffing. She hugged a yellow-and-white afghan around her nightgown, and in the moonlight she looked like a pretty butterfly with a golden face. *If it's all true*, I thought in amazement, *then she's Eli's cousin.*

Eli stood. "Aw, we're just up to nonsense. I just had to see Darl."

"Eli Wade, you're a crazy fool boyfriend, and you're gonna get us all in trouble." She bounded up to him and playfully punched him on one shoulder. He stared down at her for a moment, then held out one hand. "Shake on it," he said.

"What?"

"Trouble. So we're all in trouble together, I guess."

"All right." She slid her hand into his and pumped it vigorously. I stood up and put my hand atop hers and his. "Me, too," I said. "All for one and one for all."

I met Eli's somber, honorable eyes. We couldn't tell Karen what we'd heard, not yet. It might be a lie. It might blow over. That night we couldn't yet fathom all the consequences  Clara's mean-spirited declaration might have on Matilda and Karen and Eli's family, or mine.

So we held hands and hoped nothing else mattered.

*

Eli lay in bed, pretending to sleep in the pale light of morning, when he heard his father come home. He sat up rigidly. Across the room, Bell turned once, frowning and mewling in her sleep, then was quiet. Eli listened with his heart in his throat as Mama's footsteps rushed down the cottage hall's marble floor. "Jasper? Where have you been? I was scared to death."

"I was just drivin' and thinkin'. I'm sorry. I sat up on Cheetawk Point just lookin' at the stars for a long time."

"What happened?"

"Nothing. Creighton Neddler told me Clara's always caused trouble, and yeah, that my daddy was a lady's man. I don't know. I can't think anymore. I've got to get an hour or two of sleep 'fore I go to work. I won't lose my job. I promise you. I promise you."

"Stop worryin' and rest. I love you so," Mama crooned. "Get these sweaty clothes off and get in bed."

Eli felt as if his nerves were on fire. After they shut their bedroom door he clenched his hands to his head. Thoughts whirled and jumped. Where had Pa been? What had become of Clara Hardigree? And why hadn't Pa told Mama about seein' her again?

*

Clara seemed to have disappeared. I felt as if I'd been wrapped in a cloak of needles. Somehow no word of her bald-faced visit to Neddler's had gotten to Swan yet; and the gossip about the Wades and Matilda was still circling among the stonecutters, whispering itself to their wives, their children, their friends. Certainly no one wanted to be accused of handing it to the next inner ring of the Burnt Stand solar system. Swan was our sun, and the closer one carried news to the sun, the more likely that one would get roasted alive.

That afternoon I worked at the quarry offices filing invoices, and Eli finished totaling a long ledger of monthly accounts for Mr. Alberts. Swan barely spoke to anyone and looked infinitely combustible. I saw blue fire in her eyes and a straight-backed dignity that said Clara was in deep trouble just for disobeying Swan's edict about roaming the countryside. My skin itched when I thought of Swan learning what Clara had said at Neddler's.

Eli looked hollow-eyed. He kept finding excuses to go to the picture window over the quarry pit. Down there, his father guided a massive saw blade into a wall of coarse stone. Water flew and sizzled off the blade's cooling system; Jasper Wade did not look up and did not speak to anyone. He simply cut the stone with a quiet ferocity that chilled me.

The weather had turned cold. No one would catch Clara sunning naked by the pool that day. It was almost five, and I was sick at my stomach, wondering what had become of her, and what would happen, next. We heard a shout outside. Eli and I rushed to the picture window along with Mr. Albert, a thin, balding man who could not fit the stereotype of a bean-counting manager more than he did.

What we saw made my heart stop.

Preacher Al, he of the roadside signs condemning sin and Hardigrees, stood on a narrow wooden footbridge that had been built across one end of the quarry's square chasm. He was ancient, grizzled and bearded, a wild-eyed Old Testament preacher whose frayed jeans and black sports coat might as well have been holy raiment. He held up a piece of cardboard at least four-feet square. He'd painted it white, with the words in blood red:

JEZEBEL'S OTHER DAUGHTER
HAS RETURNED TO SPEAK THE TRUTH

"He's talking about Clara," I whispered to Eli.

Several men raced up a metal staircase to the narrow walkways at the top of the quarry, easily fifty feet above its stone floor. Jasper Wade led the way. Eli clenched his hands on the window sill. The catwalk had rails, but they were only hip high, and

Preacher Al's balance was bad—combined with rheumatism and high blood pressure that made him dizzy even when he wasn't seeing Biblical apparitions. He swayed, holding the sign overhead with both hands. "You brought your whore sister and the son of the sinner here to test this town's godly spirit, again," he yelled toward us.

"He's talking about my pa," Eli said in soft horror. "The son of the sinner."

Preacher Al obviously thought Swan was in the office watching him, but she'd left minutes earlier to look at a new grinder in the carving factory. "Flaunt not the sanctity of the Word," Preacher Al bellowed towards us. "The sin of the father is ripe in the son! The sister and the mother of shame begat more shame! Swan Hardigree! Come out of your den of iniquity, woman, and swear off your family's ways!".

I groaned. I leaned onto the window sill and watched Jasper Wade and several other men pose at the entrance to the catwalk. It was too narrow for a posse to cross. Eli's father gestured to Preacher Al to walk toward him. When that didn't have any effect, Jasper took a step onto the catwalk.

"Stay back, Demon Wade," Preacher Al screamed at him. "Your father was a pawn of Hardigree lust and he slept with the dark races!"

Jasper halted, scowling. Eli shivered visibly. At that moment, my grandmother appeared at one end of the adjacent bridge. "Oh, dear God," Mr. Albert said beside us. "Miss Swan is onto him now."

She looked lethal. She went down the high, narrow catwalk with the cool stride of a woman on a Sunday stroll. The men saw her coming and pressed themselves to one side as she eased past them. She put a hand on Jasper's arm and shook her head. He frowned but stepped back.

She quickly strode onto the catwalk that held Preacher Al. She looked straight at him and didn't hesitate. She didn't say a word. He began backing away along the catwalk, waving his sign and yelling garbled Biblical phrases at her. She kept walking towards him. Suddenly, his face convulsed in fear and he climbed over the rail, clinging to the outside of it with one hand, flapping his cardboard sign with the other, and still yelling at her. "I knew the truth then and I know now," he bellowed.

She halted calmly and began to speak in a low voice to him. Eli and I couldn't hear her, but later we learned what she said. *Anthony Wade was kind to you. He saved your life one day in these pits. It's your own fault you let my sister talk you into betraying his secrets. That's what you have to live with. Or die with. It's your choice.*

Eli's father and the other men at the intersection of the catwalks behind her called out to Preacher Al. *Drop the sign, Preacher! Climb back over!* But they were no balm for the hellfire the old man saw in Swan's eyes. He raised his right arm as if attempting to shield himself with his pathetic sign. A corner of the stiff cardboard caught him in one eye, and he jerked his head. In doing that, he fumbled his grip on the railing. And he fell. His mouth open in silent oration, screaming, he fell fifty feet and landed flat on his back on the quarry's marble floor.

You didn't have to look at him twice to decide he was dead.

I leaned against Eli. He gripped my arm. His breath rasped. "She killed him with a look."

I could only nod.

*

Swan took me back to the mansion with her, along with Matilda and Karen. We were barricaded behind marble walls. The weight of doom pressed in on me. Karen—who still did not know the Wades were her relatives—cooed her sympathy over the terrible thing I'd witnessed. She held my hand while I slept. Even so, I had terrible dreams about Preacher Al all that night after he died, seeing him land with a sound like a split watermelon on the quarry floor.

The next morning there was still no sign of Clara. I left Karen asleep and wandered downstairs in my nightgown, clutching my stomach. Matilda met me at the foot of the stairs. "Go back up there," she said. "Your grandmother and I are discussing what Clara told people about your Great-Grandmother and Anthony Wade." Matilda paused. "And about me." What she said was very serious, and not for your ears, or Karen's."

"But I know already."

"And we're very sorry about that."

"Are you going to tell Karen? I don't think she'll mind knowing she has white kin."

Matilda laid a cool, golden-brown hand along my face. Her hazel eyes softened. "What do you think of me, after what you've heard? Be honest."

"I don't know what to think." I paused. "But I still love you."

Swan walked out of a side hallway, her face so cool and perfect, her svelte body clothed in soft gray slacks and a matching cashmere sweater. When she saw me she said. "It's time we talked."

I shuddered. "I'd appreciate a little information, ma'am."

She led me into the living room and sat down facing each other on brocaded divans with marble feet. She cleared her throat. "Certain types of gossip can harm everything you'll inherit someday. I want you to remember that we have built something very fine in this community. The town itself, the good people who come here to live because of its unique beauty, the good jobs we provide for two hundred men, the charities we support, the decency of this entire town—all of that is a factor of Hardigree money and determination. We built this town, and we take care of it. We have responsibilities. Do you understand?"

"Yes, ma'am. We're very lucky."

"No. Luck doesn't come to everyone. You make good luck for yourself. If your Great-Grandmother Esta hadn't been willing to take charge of her own fortunes, this town wouldn't exist. Nothing fine would have grown here. Self-worth isn't carved in stone, Darl. It's carved here." She placed her fingertips over her heart. I put my hand over my own heart, and nodded.

"Now. The terrible things your Great Aunt Clara said are the truth. At least part of the truth."

"You mean, Eli's grandpa really did work for us way back when?"

"That's right. Almost forty years ago."

"And he liked . . . Great Grandmother?"

"Yes, he did."

"He liked Matilda, too?"

"Yes."

The miserable truth sank in. "But now everything's ruined."

"Yes. When people don't know the facts, they can only gossip and wonder. But when proof is available, they can be very ugly. Unfortunately, the proof is living in our own Stone Cottage."

I clawed my hands together. "Please, ma'am, don't say you've got to fire Eli's daddy and send his family away. Please, don't."

"I have no choice. I don't want people to compare them to Matilda and Karen and cause trouble. Do you want Karen to be treated badly?"

"No, but—"

"Matilda is one of our own. My reputation protects her. But I can't protect everyone. The Wades have to go."

*I'll die, I'll turn into stone without Eli here*, I thought. I wanted to beg Swan, but I knew better than to give her an even greater reason to send the Wades away. "But if Matilda wants them here—if they're kin to Karen—"

"I've told Matilda I'll make certain Jasper Wade finds a good job elsewhere. Matilda understands. She has to think of what's best for Karen's reputation in town. And honestly, it's best for the Wades, too. Ugly gossip does no one any good."

"It shouldn't matter that they're kin to the Doves. What difference does that make? Matilda and Karen are just like us!"

"You'll have to be older before you comprehend the stupidity of mankind."

"No, I understand right now. You just can't send Eli away."

A new current raked the air. She leveled a searing look at me. "I think you'd better know that Eli's fate is of no concern to you, and even if he stayed I wouldn't let you keep him."

"If everybody else in our family gets to love who they want, then I will, too. And I won't have to pay Eli to love me, the way Great-Grandmother paid Anthony Wade."

Swan stood, bent over and slapped me so hard I heard my neck pop. She'd never hit me before in my life. It made ice bloom inside me, but strangely enough, I was suddenly stronger. I blinked once then stared up at her without a shred of regret or humility, just daring her to hit me, again, but then I saw her eyes glisten with tears.

We heard the sound of a car. Swan left the room at a fast walk, and I hurried after her. Matilda met us in the foyer. "It's Clara," she said.

## 7

Clara pulled up in front of the mansion in her fire-red Trans Am. She climbed out wearing what must be a new outfit, since she'd left with none of her luggage in tow. "*Neiman Marcus*," she said, waving a hand at the creamy wool pantsuit she wore. "I've been shopping. I drove down to Atlanta. Crossed the state line into Georgia and just kept driving south, making my shopping list as I went. God, Atlanta makes Asheville look like a countrified dump, when it comes to shopping." She held up her right hand. Morning sunshine glinted off a diamond ring. "How do you like it, Sister? You paid for it. You're paying for everything." Clara smiled. "I've got the key to your heart, now, don't I? And the key says 'Wade' on it. Hello, Matilda. How does it feel to be the one they gossip about in town? You always wanted Anthony Wade back, but all you could find was his son. Forty years too late, too."

Matilda looked down at her and only said, "You're as sad a soul as you've always been."

Clara laughed and started up the steps to the portico. Swan blocked her way. "You're never setting foot in this house again."

"The hell I'm not." But even Clara wouldn't dare push Swan aside. Clara grimaced. "Look, I'm going inside and pack my things, and then we're going to talk about my future income."

"You've very wrong about that."

Clara looked a little flustered. "All right, so I'll go through the back door at the kitchen. I have a key to that." She pivoted and went down the steps, then strode along a marble walkway toward the gardens and the pool. Swan and Matilda walked after her. I followed without hesitation, my nightgown fluttering around me.

"The back door is bolted from the inside," Matilda said as they reached the pool patio.

Clara swung around. "Why?"

"I bolted it," Swan explained. "Because I know how your mind works."

"All I want is more money, Sister. As much as I'd like to see you squirm, I just want more of my share of the family fortune."

"I've taken care of you all your life. You don't need more."

"Taken care of me?" Her voice rose. "*Taken care of me?*" Suddenly, she noticed I stood nearby, listening. I had sidled around the pool and found myself a vantage point near the low marble wall of the back terrace. Clara whirled toward me and came around the pool's edge at a half-run. "Let's talk, Darling Darl. Don't stand there trying to look  discreet, girl. Be a big mouth like your old Auntie Clara. I've got some family history for you."

I drew back but she snatched me by one arm. Her bitter blue eyes seethed as she looked from me to Swan and back to me. "Your Great-Grandmother Esta owned the biggest whorehouse in town. Swan and I were born in that whorehouse. And so was Matilda. A.A. Hardigree fathered all three of us. Of course, Matilda's mother was a colored whore. That makes Matilda our half-sister. Isn't that interesting?"

My head snapped back as if she'd hit me. By then Swan was beside me, and she twisted Clara's hand off my arm, then pushed me toward Matilda, who took me by the shoulders. Swan and Clara faced each other. I felt dizzy with the words Clara had just hurled at me. "Stop, right now," Swan said to Clara between gritted teeth.

But Clara peered gleefully around her. "Darl, your great-grandmother never married A.A. Hardigree. But she decided she wanted to be a lady and raise her daughters as if they had a name, so she burned the whole damned town down and made sure A.A. fried in the process. Then she produced a marriage certificate and a will, so she got the quarry. And *that's* when she and her daughters became southern ladies. We dragged little Matilda, our darkie half-sister, along for charity's sake."

"If you stop now," Swan repeated, "I'll give you the money you want, and you can leave."

"You know what your grandmother did to me, Darl? She sent me off to a goddamned reformatory when I was sixteen years old. A prison for girls. Run by goddamned nuns. That's where I spent two years. She got rid of me—because I talked about our family. I told the truth. I caused trouble. Matilda got to stay and have Anthony Wade's baby, but I got sent away." She leered at Swan and Matilda. "But I always come back, don't I? I'll always talk. And you'll always have to live with it."

"Not anymore," Swan said. Swan slapped her hard enough to click Clara's teeth together. Clara put a hand to her jaw and stared at her sister with slitted eyes, tinged with fear. The look on Swan's face was the same as the killing look she'd given poor Preacher Al.

Swan hit Clara again. Not a slap, this time, but a full broadside with the flat of both hands to Clara's chest. Clara stumbled backwards. Swan stepped lithely after her, shoved her, then drew back a hand and slapped her once more. Matilda screamed. I yelled, "*Watch out!*" Clara stumbled against the terrace wall and grabbed wildly at one of the marble swans. Her hand latched around one of their elegant marble necks.

But my grandmother's minions were not about to save the one person who could destroy everything Swan had built. Clara's fingers clutched frantically but slipped off. She fell over the terrace wall, twisting as she went, disappearing down the sheer drop.

I didn't see her hit the marbled lip of the koi pond below, but I heard the godawful thud, just like Preacher Al's. I leapt to the terrace wall. Swan threw out an arm and blocked me. I was so upset, so blind with horror, I might have easily plummeted over out of careless hysteria. Matilda joined us. We three stared at the scene below.

Clara floated, face-down, in the pond. Bubbles rose around her head. "She's still breathing," I yelled. I writhed from Swan's grasp and ran to the steps. By the time I reached the bottom Swan and Matilda were quick on my heels. I was about to climb into the shallow pond when Swan locked both hands around my waist. "We'll pull her out," Swan said calmly. "You run up to the house and get the first-aid kit. Hurry. Don't take time to phone for help or tell Karen. Don't say a word. Just go inside."

That made sense. "Yes, ma'am!" I bolted back up the steps. When I turned at the top I saw that Swan had not gotten into the pond, but instead had Matilda by the shoulders and was talking to her in a voice so low I couldn't hear the words. Matilda gestured toward Clara and tried to pull away, but Swan shook her lightly. Then Swan climbed down into the pond. She waded to Clara and stood over her, but made no move to turn Clara over. Bubbles still flooded the surface around Clara's head, but Swan simply prodded Clara's shoulder with a finger. Matilda, frozen on the pond patio, turned her back on the scene and covered her face.

I didn't know what to think—what were they doing, what did it mean? I raced inside the mansion and dragged our first-aid kit from the kitchen pantry. I was sobbing for air when I galloped back down the terrace steps with the kit clutched in my arms. Swan and Matilda sat on the pond's marble border. Matilda pillowed Clara's head on her lap and bent over her, crying silently. Clara's mouth and eyes hung open. There was no color in her face. I dropped to my knees and held out the kit as if it contained a full team of doctors. "I have ointment, and gauze, and . . . " My voice trailed off. "I should have run faster . . . "

Swan's flat blue stare silenced me. "No. There's nothing we can do."

I uttered a long cry of despair and hunched over my useless first aid kit. Swan sat there as I gagged and cried, calmly waiting. She looked over at her sister's corpse and stroked a strand of wet hair from Clara's forehead. There was the slightest tremor in her fingers, but she gave Matilda a steady look. "This is my doing, not yours."

"No. I let you do it." Matilda clasped a hand along Clara's lifeless cheek. "I always prayed we could change her. I never understood why she had to hurt herself and everyone else, too." Matilda bent her head over Clara's again. She smoothed Clara's hair back from the dark red splotch on one temple, where her head had struck the patio edge. "I'll stay with her while you call the police."

Swan didn't move. Matilda raised her head. They traded a charged look, Swan's gaze flat and decisive, Matilda's going from bewilderment to shock. "*Swan*," she said.

"I confronted Preacher Al yesterday and he fell off the catwalk. Today I argued with Clara and she fell off the terrace."

"This was an accident. No one's going to accuse you of

deliberately—"

"Clara left town two days ago. In my mind, she simply never came back."

"Swan, we can't, we can't just—"

"You know gossip doesn't go away, and you know how it can come back to haunt us. Clara has hurt us enough. I won't have her blood smeared on my reputation — or yours — for the rest of our lives."

"But on top of everything, you're suggesting—"

"After what she's done to us over the years, does she deserve to hurt us even more?"

Silence. Matilda's face took on an expression I had never expected. Pure loathing filled her eyes. "No. You're right."

Swan nodded. I sat there staring at Clara's dead face, nausea surging in my stomach and up my throat, my fingernails scraping bits of bright paint off the first-aid kit. "What—what's going on?" I finally managed to whisper.

My grandmother looked at me without blinking. "We're going to bury Clara in the woods. And never tell a soul."

*

I have very little memory of the rest of that day, or the night that followed it. I know that old Carl McCarl lumbered from the driver's cab of a huge furniture truck that evening, drove Clara's red Trans Am up a ramp into the truck's vast interior, then carried it away. I know that late that night when Karen and I were in bed Matilda and Swan dragged Clara's body, wrapped in a sheet, to the stone flower garden.

I followed them in the darkness and hid on the knoll above the garden. I watched them dig the grave by lantern light near the base of the flower statue, and put Clara's body in it. I watched Matilda say a prayer over the shallow, open hole. Swan put a hand on her shoulder, but showed no other sign of compassion. And then, they covered Clara with dirt.

I staggered back to the mansion and waited on the patio by the pool, sitting cross-legged under the light of a lamppost. When they climbed the terrace stairs they took one look at me and halted. I asked, "Are we murderers?"

Matilda knelt down, held me tightly and told me *No, don't ever think that way.* But my grandmother, less willing to spin the truth, looked me straight in the eyes. "We did what had to be done," was all she said.

*

I didn't leave the mansion for a week. I dreamed at night of the ground erupting in the stone flower garden, of Clara crawling out and walking, mildewed and ashen, through the woods and up the terrace steps, into the mansion, up the stairs, into my room. Preacher Al floated along behind her. Blood dripped from his ears and his gaping mouth. Clara and Preacher Al wouldn't confront Swan. Swan would stare down even the dead. But me, they could get to.

*Why did you let me die?* Clara asked. She loomed over me, ghastly and evil, dripping dirt and worms. *Why didn't you hurry faster with that first-aid kit? Why didn't you at least bury me in the vault with our family? Why didn't you speak up? I'll haunt you the rest of your life.* Preacher Al moaned at me. *The sins of Jezebel are on you, too, now.*

One night their faces dissolved and Swan's replaced them. I jerked upright and there she was, in the flesh and the darkness, leaning over me. She looked angelic in her creamy white robe and nightgown. The smallest hints of gray had recently escaped from her brunette hair at the temples, but even so her hair cascaded around her face with vital life.

She stroked my hair away from my sweaty brow and laid the backs of her cool fingers on my cheek. "Don't dream," she ordered softly. "It will all be better in time. You'll forget what happened but remember why we did it. And you'll be stronger for that wisdom."

*She killed Clara. If I don't do what she wants she might kill me, too.* That grotesque thought entered my mind like a snake and curled around me. "I'm fine," I lied, shivering under the covers. "I'll never tell anybody." For a moment she was silent, and something in her deep blue eyes said she might admit her own pain. But she got the better of herself. "Good," she answered.

The next day I forced myself to go to the garden and make certain Clara hadn't left. I couldn't make myself go all the way into the glen I'd once loved so much, so I halted a few yards up the slope. Swan had carefully pulled the loam, filled with tiny roots, back into place. It hid the disrupted ground like a mat. My grandmother's talent for covering up Hardigree sins was remarkable.

Suddenly I heard a rustling sound. Bile rose in my mouth. Clara must be clawing her way up. I swayed weakly. "Darl!" It was Eli, cresting the opposite ridge, so tall and gawky and bespectacled yet so dear and gentle. He hurried around the edge of the glen and halted before me, his dark eyes filled with concern. "Where have you been?" he demanded urgently. "I've been here every day, waitin' for you."

"I've been sick, that's all. With the . . . the flu."

He touched my cheek. "You got no fever. You're cold, not hot."

"I'm almost well." I turned my face helplessly into the palm of his hand. It was an adult gesture, romantic and sensual, and yet as innocent as my desperate loneliness. He didn't look much better than me, his eyes tired, his skin pale. "I'm going to hug you," he said, and then he did it, just holding me deep in his long, boyish arms, and me holding him. He caught his glasses in my hair. After awhile we both stirred awkwardly and stepped apart.

"My pa doesn't know what to expect. Have you heard anything?" Eli asked. I shook my head. I think Swan had promised Matilda to leave the Wades alone for now. Too much happening too fast would only draw more attention. Eli studied me urgently. "Has Clara come back yet?"

Swan had told me exactly what I must say if anyone asked me that question. I looked up at my best friend and true love, and I lied. "She went home to Chicago."

The breath soughed out of him. He shut his eyes, then opened them.

"When?"

"Right after that night at Neddler's. Swan made her leave town.

I didn't know about it 'til later."

"So you didn't really see her go, yourself?"

"No, but she . . . went."

"*Thankyougod*," burst out of him in one word. He grabbed me by the hand and pulled me down the hill. He sat down on the bench not more than a foot from Clara's burial spot. Although he tugged for me to sit beside him, I braced my knees and stared at her hidden grave. A wave of sickness overcame me. "I have to . . . go." I ripped my hand from his then stumbled up the slope of the glen, where I fell to my knees and vomited milky water. He hurried after me, knelt and put an arm around my shoulders. "You *are* still sick. Comeon. I'll walk you home."

With his help I got to my feet. Leaning against him, holding one of his hands in a knot against the pit of my stomach, I made it all the way to the base of the terrace, where I looked at the koi pond and vomited again. Then I pushed him away and ran up the stone steps without looking back.

*

Eli took the first punches and gave them back twice with a force that made his attackers grunt. But the older boys were thick-shouldered football players for the Hardigree County High Warriors, and he was outnumbered. In less than sixty seconds they left Eli sprawled among the metal trash cans outside the loading dock of the school cafeteria. Blood speckled him from a cut over one eye, and his ribs hurt. He gasped for breath. "Next time get you some niggers to help you fight," one boy said. And the other added, grinning, "Hey, he can just call his kin, can't he?"

After they walked off, Eli found his glasses under a trash can lid. The aviator frames were twisted and broken. He climbed to his feet. The world without glasses was a blur, a prison. He made his way slowly around the school's perimeter to the road in front of the school, then into the woods for a two-mile hike to the quarry. It took him over an hour because he kept blundering and getting lost. When he reached the quarry he waited in the woods by the back lot where the employees parked. Late that afternoon Pa finished for the day and walked out to the truck.

Eli stepped forward, half-blind, bruised, his head throbbing. Pa strode up to him, clasped his face beneath the chin, and studied him painfully. "Can you take it, son?"

"Yeah. Can you?"

Pa nodded. The knuckles of his right hand were swollen. One of the rednecks on his crew had said, "Maybe I don't have to listen to no orders from the son of a nigger-lover." And Pa had showed him why that idea wouldn't work.

"Get in the truck," Pa said. "I'm takin' you over to the eye doctor to order you some new glasses."

Eli nodded. He climbed gingerly into the truck. As they drove they said nothing. Eli couldn't bring himself to ask about that night at Neddler's. Clara was gone. That was all that mattered.

*

Eli went to the stone flower garden every day, but Darl never returned. He stopped going to the garden and instead chopped wood outside the cottage until his shoulders ached and blistered wet his hands. One cold afternoon Bell watched him worriedly. She darted forward like a bundled snowman in her quilted jacket and sweatpants, snatched up the frayed kindling as it spewed from his ax, then stacked it on the cottage's marble stoop as if he might split the stone next.

Eli levered the ax into the top of a log with a furious downswing. *Darl doesn't want anything to do with me now. She won't say so flat out, but me being Anthony Wade's grandson is what makes her sick. Wades are nothing but trouble to her family now.*

Maybe Wades were nothing but trouble to themselves, either. Maybe the good luck was subtracting from itself, not multiplying. Matilda Dove had told Mama not to come back to work at the mansion, at least not for now. And though Swan hadn't fired Pa at the quarry, Mr. Albert suddenly didn't have any accounting work for Eli to do after school each day..

Eli swung the ax again. He still looked at Pa with gut-level misery because Pa had lied to Mama about seeing Clara at Neddler's late that night. Maybe Pa just didn't want her to know Clara had come onto him, that she'd followed him—how that looked. But it wasn't right, it was a fracture in the solid stone of Pa and Mama's trust for each other, and Eli's trust in Pa.

Eli sent a shard of wood flying with the next cut of the ax. Bell cried out as the slender stick of rough wood hit her in the mouth. She clasped her hands to her face and began to cry. God, seven years old but sometimes she was still like a baby. He ran to her and pried her hands away. Blood oozed from a split in her lower lip. "Oh, Baby Sister, I'm sorry." Unbidden and surprising tears formed in his own eyes. He scrubbed them away but they returned.

Bell stared at his tears in shock, and her own tears halted. "Eli," she moaned, and patted him on the cheek. "Nothing used to make you cry. What's the matter?"

Eli shook his head. He was her big brother, a man in his family, and it was two weeks before Christmas, a good time trying desperately not to turn bad. Yet he had never been lonelier in his life, because Darl had deserted him.

*Our luck's running out*, he thought, but didn't say it.

8

Christmas finery draped Marble Hall inside and out. All the main rooms downstairs hosted trees covered in ornaments and lights. Every table held a glittering holiday centerpiece. Pots of red poinsettias filled every corner. I saw red blood and Clara's red Trans Am everytime I looked at them.

Matilda brought Karen over one afternoon, and she ran upstairs to my bedroom. I sat in a pink-pillowed window seat, just staring out toward the terrace, the woods, the stone flower garden. Karen sat down opposite me. "What are you doing?" she asked brightly.

I could only look at her and think of all the things she didn't know. That not only was her grandmother Swan's half-white sister, but her grandfather was Anthony Wade. That our grandmothers had started their lives as the daughters of prostitutes—an image barely formed in my mind but vivid with horror. That she and Eli were cousins. That she and I were, too. Only I was privy to such secrets. The Hardigree curse.

"What are you doing?" Karen demanded a second time. "Fool. Are you listening?"

"I'm trying to think straight," I said. "I don't feel good."

"You've had the flu longer than anybody I've ever known."

"I'm a slow healer."

She frowned at the stack of heavy, leather-bound books in the floor by my feet. I'd brought them up from Swan's library. Hoisting one volume into her lap, she hooted at the pink slips of stationary I used as bookmarks. "What are you reading?"

"They're law books."

"Law books?" She flipped open the book to a marked page. "*Accessory*," she pronounced slowly and dramatically. Karen rolled her eyes. "What's that?"

"It means you didn't do it but you can go to jail, anyway."

She once again rolled her eyes at my strange interests, shut the book, then yawned and kicked off her loafers. Karen curled up on the window seat with her feet in my lap. I rested both hands on my pale-brown cousin's yellow-trimmed socks, my fingertips touching the warm golden skin of her ankles, thinking how much I loved her. I stared out the window once more. I missed Eli desperately but could not bear to set foot in our garden again. I couldn't confess to him, couldn't confess about Clara and Great-Grandmother Esta, whorehouses and Swan and Matilda and what lay beneath the loam of the stone flower garden, to anybody.

At that point I wouldn't have minded being put in the electric chair as an accessory to murder, but I didn't want to incriminate Swan and Matilda, too. What would Karen do without her own grandmother in a world as cruel as ours? So I couldn't tell anyone, or ask anyone's advice.

No one. Not ever.

I was set in stone.

*

One week before Christmas Eve, a fisherman spotted Clara's Trans Am sunk in twenty feet of water in Briscoe Lake. The big mountain lake was an hour's drive west of Burnt Stand, inside the vast Nantahala National Forest. *Land of the Noonday Sun*, the Cherokee Indians called that forest, set in mountains so steep their shadows hid everything except a sports car.

"We've got the car out and the state crime lab boys are lookin' it over," Chief Lowden, the head of our police force, reported to Swan. "So far, they haven't found anything." I sat on the living room divan nearby, listening as calmly as a judge. Chief Lowden, a big, burly, red-headed man known for benevolence mixed with practical brutality, kept frowning and looking my way. "Miss Swan, do you think Darl ought to hear all this?"

"My granddaughter isn't an ordinary child," Swan answered. "Go on."

"Well, ma'am, we're bringing in divers to search the lake. For hmmm, well, for a body."

Swan nodded calmly, as if he were talking about a stranger,

not Clara. "You may find one."

"You said your sister left here the evening she was seen at Neddler's Place."

"Yes. She told me she was driving back to Chicago. That's the last I saw of her. I didn't know she was going to the bar on her way out of town. But I wasn't surprised."

"Ma'am, I realize you and Clara aren't close, but wouldn't she have called you when she reached Chicago, just to let you know she got home safe?"

"No. We often went years without speaking."

He sighed and nodded. Everyone in town knew Clara was our family outcast. Her damaging influence and our family's sordid past swirled around us; even marble walls couldn't keep that out. "I'm thinking she got a wild hair and tried to go cross-country to the interstate," Chief Lowden went on. "Somehow she made a detour to the lake. The forestry service says the gravel road was open to visitors around that time. Looks like she drove off a little wooden bridge over a cove nobody visits much."

Swan didn't blink. "My sister was reckless. It's possible she was drunk when she left Neddler's."

"I do remember her totaling two or three vehicles when she was drinkin' as a teenager." He winced. "Sorry."

"It's all right. I've never pretended to understand her motives. What she might have been doing at Briscoe Lake alone is beyond my imagination. In fact, I don't want to imagine it."

"No, Miss Swan, you sure don't." Chief Lowden, who owed his new patrol car and the five-man police department's recently renovated offices to a donation from Hardigree Marble, spent a minute or two apologizing for the bad news. Swan inclined her head in a regal acceptance of the sympathy. He left with his hat in his hands.

I began to shake. Swan walked over to me, cupped my chin in her hand, and looked down at me almost sadly. "Forget everything except the truth you want to live with," she said. Then she went to a massive, marble-topped bureau and poured herself a glass of wine from a cut-glass decanter with an elaborate H etched into its silver stopper. Swan took a deep swallow of wine and shut her eyes. When she opened them any lingering concern had vanished. "Remember that, Darl. Your life is your reputation, and your reputation is your fate."

I sat there on the divan, scraping my fingernails against my raw palms.

When he heard the news that Clara hadn't gone back to Chicago after all, Eli bent his head on his arms, and cried.

*

Everyone in town was abuzz with the news from Briscoe Lake, where divers found no trace of Clara's body. The unfolding drama fueled even more talk about her lurid revelations concerning our family, the Wades, and Matilda. Still, Swan's pride wouldn't allow her to cancel the annual Hardigree Marble Christmas party, a soiree so entrenched in our town's traditions that we were celebrating its fiftieth year.

"Is she going to send Jasper Wade away from here?" I asked Matilda.

Matilda nodded and looked away. "After the holidays."

So the week before Christmas I stood beside Swan, her in a soft gold midi-dress and me in pink with red holiday trim, inside the door of a cavernous, heated revival tent set up in a clearing beside the quarry. Several hundred people—company employees, their families, the town's mayor and other notables, pretty much anyone and everyone of consequence in our immediate universe—milled among tables of food and eggnog. A hired Santa and his hired elves entertained the children with small gifts of toys and candy. A raised dance floor occupied the tent's center, under basketball-sized clusters of mistletoe and red ribbon. Multi-colored Christmas lights dangled from the tent's steel rafters. A small dance band played holiday music.

"Welcome," Swan said formally to each entering guest, most of whom were modest country people who blushed and stammered.

"Greetings," I said.

I ached with tension and disappointment. Eli and his family

hadn't arrived and must not be coming. "There they are," Karen whispered. She stood behind me, near Matilda, who kept her on such a short leash those days I rarely got to see her, either. Looking like a sweet, pale-mocha elf in a green-and-gold dress, she still had no clue the social controversy involved anything but Clara's disappearance.

My heart raced as Eli, Bell, Annie Gwen and Jasper finally showed up at the tent's garland-draped entrance. The family was dressed in their Sunday best. Bell brightened at the sight of my smile but tugged nervously at the hem of a floppy jumper. Her brown hair was held back by a plastic bando bearing a sprig of plastic holly and red berries. Annie Gwen looked pale but stoic in a simple brown dress with a plaid jacket. Jasper stared straight ahead, his rugged face set like a statue's, yet women craned their heads at the handsome sight of him in a suit and tie. The suit may have come from the Sears catalog and the tie from the sale bin of the Burnt Stand Thrift Shop, but he had become the stuff of notorious fantasy.

I had eyes only for Eli. He wore a blue suit like his father's, with a plain red tie askew and tightly knotted. The hems of the pant legs were already too short for his ankles, and his thick, bony wrists showed at the end of the jacket sleeves. He burned me with a look that searched me for a thousand answers, his eyes going dark with concentration behind his glasses. I quivered inside from the need to talk to him. Suddenly I knew how it felt to be grown at ten years old, my childhood chiseled away. And I saw that his boyhood was gone, too, that he really was a tall and somber young man at 13. "Greetings," I said brokenly.

He didn't answer.

"Welcome," Swan said to Jasper and Annie Gwen.

"Thank you, ma'am," they said in unison, but their eyes were worried and scanned the crowd. People stared back, whispered, darted looks their way and not. For one frozen second Jasper looked past Swan and traded a searching gaze with Matilda. She held the scrutiny of her lover's son with a grim dignity that matched his own. One golden hand clasped the perplexed Karen by a shoulder. Her other hand remained clenched against her deep burgundy dress..

Swan turned away, her mouth set, her face neutral. "Darl, come along. We have other guests." She had upheld a Hardigree tradition of hospitality, but now her turned back said she was done with Jasper Wade. She made a very obvious gesture of rejection by gliding away into the mass of Hardigree employees. People pulled back on either side of her path like courtiers in a royal court, then closed behind her and looked at the Wades, deserted in her wake.

Swan was so accustomed to me following every command of hers that she didn't look behind to see if I obeyed. I hadn't. My heart was breaking. I could see the spectre of total ostracism dawning on Jasper Wade's face. His future in Burnt Stand was gone. The men he worked with knew he'd fallen from Swan's grace, and like animals in a pack they were only waiting to see how long he'd fight not to be driven away.

"What's going on?" Karen asked. "Why is everyone acting so strange?" A black boy, one of the sons of the sturdy black farmers who kept to themselves outside town, ran up to her and spit on the floor in front of her gold slippers. "Why don'tcha go play with your white kin?"

"What are you talking about, fool?"

"The Wades," he spat. "They're your kin. Whitey."

It happened so fast even the horrified Matilda was not been able to prevent it. An instant later Leon Forrest strode out of the crowd and the boy ran in fear. Leon halted before Karen like a hapless courtier in a cheap polyester Sunday suit. "It don't matter what you are," he said to her. "Don't matter to me. It's okay."

Karen, her mouth open in astonishment, looked from him to me and then at her grandmother. "Come with me," Matilda ordered, then clamped an arm around her shoulders and drew her out a side exit. Karen struggled and stared back at me desperately, then at Eli, who winced. Her expression crumbled. I knotted my hands and swayed. I was falling through the earth, my heart beating inside the marble bedrock below my feet. Matilda and Karen disappeared outside the side exit. Now Karen would learn everything I knew about our family. Except that we had murdered Clara..

I walked numbly to Eli. I watched his face. Anger became sadness became uncertainty became sacrifice. I knew it was too late for him and his family, and so did he. The little band across the way began to play some quiet Christmas song. I held out my hands. "Would you like to dance?"

He was a bad dancer—and always had been. He said nothing for a second, looking down at me with as much misery and reserve as my own. "The only place we belong together is in the Stone Flower Garden."

That nearly killed me. I struggled with my voice. "No, I belong with you anywhere.".

A deep breath lifted his chest. He took me by one elbow and we stepped up on the dance floor. We stood there by ourselves, surrounded by the collective stare of the whole town. Eli and I faced each other, formed our hands and arms into some semblance of a formal embrace, then stepped slowly in rhythm with the music. When the song ended not one person in the audience moved or spoke. Surprise, disapproval, and fearful wonder filled the huge tent.

"Son," Jasper Wade said grimly, from behind us. "That's enough. We're leavin'."

Eli held my gaze for another full five seconds. His mouth moved in a whisper so low I felt it rather than heard it. "Greetings," he said as a goodbye.

My eyes filled with tears. "Greetings."

He and his family left the tent. Stranded in the middle of the dance floor, I turned and looked straight into my grandmother's merciless blue eyes.

*

The next day, Mr. Neddler walked into Chief Lowden's marble-walled office at the Burnt Stand police station. "Chief, I don't know if this means anything, but it's been worrying me since Clara Hardigree's car turned up." Creighton Neddler described Jasper Wade's late-night confrontation with Clara outside the bar, how angry Jasper had been, how he'd shoved her hard enough to make her fall, how he'd threatened to kill her, and how determined she'd been to catch up with Jasper when she sped down the dark mountain road.

Chief Lowden repeated every word of that conversation as Swan escorted him into our elegant living room at Marble Hall. "Miss Swan," he finished, "the last person to see your sister alive was Jasper Wade that night, and he had a reason to do her harm. I hate to think the worst, but I do."

"Grandmother," I said, as a warning. "*Grandmother.*"

Swan's face said the Clara situation had grown serious beyond her patience. A coldness even more startling than her usual seeped from her perfect skin. "Leave the room, Darl."

I shook my head. I wouldn't let her do this to Eli's father. But then, what could I say? *We did it, Chief Lowden. Grandmother and Matilda and me. Let Clara drown in the koi pond and dragged her body through the woods in the night and buried her in the shade of the stone flowers. Take us all to prison.* Oh, Matilda, Karen. I couldn't drag them down with me. "Grandmother," I repeated between clenched teeth. "Mr. Wade is not a murderer. I just know it."

Her eyes seared me. The battle between us had become a silent, full-scale war. "I'm sure you're right. But Chief Lowden is only going to ask Mr. Wade some questions."

The chief nodded. "Little Darl, you're a sweet girl who likes to think the best of folks, and I agree with you. I promise you this is just part of my job. I'm just goin' to drop by the Stone Cottage after I leave here and talk to Jasper Wade and ask him to explain some things, and it'll all be settled. Nobody's going to get hurt, Honey."

*People are already hurt,* I wanted to scream, but I was frozen inside my skin. I was learning what to give away and what to keep close. "All right," I said. I manufactured a large sigh as if satisfied, then turned and walked slowly out of the living room under Swan's intense scrutiny. When I was free to run, I raced to the back of the house, out the French doors, past the pool now covered with its winter tarp, and down the terrace steps into the woods.

\*

A wooden trailer to haul their belongings. Some furniture and

knicknacks. A new engine for the old truck. A bundle of cash—
their savings account from the Bank of Burnt Stand—tucked safely
in a cardboard box under the truck's front seat. Those were the
only obvious signs that three years of life in Burnt Stand had
changed their lives for so much better and so much worse. Eli
tried not to think how shabby they'd still look as they drove through
town on their way out. He jerked the rope tight on a kitchen chair
he placed atop the furniture stacked on the trailer. Tears stung the
backs of his eyes. Misery and anger as deep as the cut of an ax
separated him from the boy he'd been.

"That's the last of it," Pa said, slinging a coat into the truck's
front seat.

"Here," Mama said, carrying a bulging cardboard box from the
cottage. Eli leapt to take it from her. "Yes, Mama?" Her eyes were
swollen from crying. "Can you find a place for this? Careful now.
It's turkey sandwiches and all the fixin's. Put it in the camper where
it won't get mashed.

"Yes, ma'am."

This would have been their Christmas Eve dinner, to be enjoyed
at their nicely set table while they watched a Christmas concert on
television. Now it was traveling food pressed into cheap plastic
containers and sandwiches in waxed-paper wrapping. Eli wanted
to yell. He wanted to fight somebody. When he carried the box to
the back of the truck, Pa was bent under the camper's half-door
rearranging trash bags filled with clothes and other possessions.
Pa straightened, saw the family's entire Christmas dinner crammed
inside a box, and his face went white. "Goddamn," he said slowly
under his breath. He turned and slammed a fist against the side of
the truck. "Goddamn my daddy, goddamn this town, and goddamn
Clara Hardigree."

Bell sobbed out loud at the violent words as she emerged from
the cottage. She burrowed her face into a grocery bag overflowing
with Christmas decorations in her arms. "I don't want to leave
here. It's our home!" Mama ran to her and pulled her close.

This was the tableau the family presented when Eli turned
wearily and saw Darl burst from the rhododendron thicket on the
hill above the cottage. "Eli!" she yelled. He ran to meet her. Her

long hair was tangled with twigs and bits of dried leaves, her face
with flushed. She gasped for air. "I ran . . . as fast as I could. Eli,
Chief Lowden is—"

"Get your breath. Shush." He put an arm around her and helped
into the yard. She moaned when she saw the packed truck and
trailer. "No!"

Eli straightened with his last ounce of dignity. "Listen, you go
away. You go back up that hill and don't turn around. I won't say
goodbye. I won't. I'll write to you when we get somewhere."

She clutched his shirtfront and shook him. "Eli, the police are
coming for your daddy."

Pa strode forward. "*What?*"

*Godawmighty, Pa*, Eli thought. *Did you do it?* Darl's arrival was
too late to give much warning. They already heard the sound of
cars on the cottage's narrow dirt road. Two tan-and-blue Burnt
Stand police cruisers rumbled around a curve in the forest and
pulled into the yard. Chief Lowden hoisted himself from the lead
vehicle and waved at everyone with strained geniality. His brawniest
officer, a thick-necked church deacon and ex-marine named
Canton, climbed from the second one.

Eli watched the officer unsnap the holster of his service
revolver and lay one thick hand on the gun's butt. Officer Canton
had spoken to an assembly at the highschool one day. He prided
himself on taking the worst calls. In a town where one murder a
year set a record, this was the worst call.

"Annie, keep everybody back," Pa ordered. He met Eli's eyes.
"Son, you take care of your mother and sister."

Guilt soured Eli's throat. "Yessir." He stepped in front of his
mother and sister, but couldn't stop Darl from joining him. He
was secretly grateful, but pushed her behind him, too. She, Mama,
and Bell pressed against his back, holding onto each other, and to
him.

Pa faced the chief. "We're leavin'. I'm not waitin' for Miz
Samples to fire me."

Chief Lowden sighed heavily. Behind him, Officer Canton
stood with his feet apart and his hand still on the butt of his gun.
"Not so quick, Jasper," the chief said. "I got to talk to you. Just be

straight with me."

"I'm an honest man."

"Good. 'Cause I hear you had a second run-in with Clara Hardigree that night at the bar up on Doe Mountain." Eli felt his mother's fingers convulse in shock against his shoulder. His heart sank as the chief described every detail of the ugly scene Eli had witnessed along with Mr. Neddler. Mama made a soft sound of horror. Pa, who had his back to them, seemed to hunch his big shoulders more with every word. The chief studied his face. "Where'd you go after you drove off with Miss Hardigree following you?"

"He came straight home," Mama called hoarsely. "He was here the rest of the night."

Pa pivoted and looked at her with tears of love and regret in his eyes. "*Annie, don't,*" he said gruffly. Then he turned back to face the chief. "My wife's tryin' to help, but I don't need to cover up nothing. I'm tellin' you the truth. I let Clara Hardigree go by me, then I drove up to Cheetawk Point and sat lookin' at the stars and thinking things through. I come home just before dawn."

Chief Lowden shook his head sadly. "I'm sorry, Jasper, but that means you've got no alibi. I'm sorry to put it this way, but you had time that night to kill Clara Hardigree and drive an hour to Briscoe Lake and dump her body with her car. You had time to commit murder that night, Jasper, and you had reason."

Pa clenched his fists. "I didn't kill Clara Hardigree and dump her in that lake. That's crazy."

"I hope so. But you're gonna have to come into town with me and answer some more questions."

"*Are you arrestin' me?*"

"Now, let's not call it that. I just want you to tell your story for the record. Just go over it a few times with some fellows from outside the county, and you give me your fingerprints, and things like that. Comeon, now. Get in my car and let's go onto town and get this over with. I'm not even sayin' you'll spend a night in jail, man. Just cooperate and come talk to some folks."

Pa didn't move a muscle. Eli's legs went weak. He knew what Pa must be thinking. Raised with nothing, his own father killed in a quarry accident when he was a boy, hampered by something in his brain that scrambled every word he tried to read, ignored in every way except for his skill with marble, brought here as a charity case, built up, and now torn down—Pa couldn't take anymore. To be accused of murder in front of his wife, his son, his fragile daughter, to be told that he would be taken into town in the back of a police car, where everyone could see his final shame. It was one day before Christmas Eve, and Pa's whole lifetime of bad luck had caught up with him.

"Just go talk to the police," Eli called. "Pa, I'll go with you."

His father shook his head imperceptibly. "Chief, I'll pack up my family and be out by tonight, but I'm not going to your jail. Not even for questionin'."

"I can't let you go, Jasper. Get in my car, man."

Pa turned instead and walked to the truck. Chief Lowden gaped at him. "Hold on, Jasper. You're making me nervous, and Officer Canton doesn't *like* it when I get nervous." Canton lifted his revolver from its holster. Pa opened the truck's driver door and reached beneath the front seat. Eli suddenly realized what Pa had put there beside the box with their money in it. *No, no, don't, Pa, don't.* Eli opened his mouth to yell the words, and Mama, knowing also, screamed.

Pa lifted a pistol from beneath the seat.

"Jasper Wade, drop that gun," Chief Lowden called. Canton lifted his own revolver. Pa only held the gun in his palm, not pointing it, but he brought it up in the air and his hand began to shift into place around the handle and the trigger. "Get out of my yard," Pa said. "I'm taking my family and leavin' this town. That's all I want."

"Put the gun down!"

"I can't do it." Pa curled his finger over the trigger. Maybe he only meant to fire a shot toward heaven, just one bitter bullet in God's direction before he laid the gun on the hood of the truck and went with the police as he'd been told to do, but he never got the chance.

Officer Canton shot him through the heart.

## 9

I lay in my bed in the dark, drugged on some kind of tranquilizers and just aware enough to hear the drifting words spoken between Swan, Chief Lowden, and our family doctor. "Doc, I swear to you I got her away from the scene as soon as I noticed her standing there," the chief said. "She was wild. I had to drag her. You saw how she was when you got here. Just crazy hysterical." My room was in shambles, things broken, clothes strewn. I'd smashed out panes of glass in the big window looking toward the woods. My hands were bandaged.

"I want this child kept under sedation for at least the next week," the doctor whispered. "Possibly much longer than that."

"I don't think that's necessary," Swan said. Her voice sounded tired.

"Miss Swan, in the past month she's seen Preacher Al fall into the quarry, she's lost her great aunt, and now she's watched a man shot to death. She'll end up with a nervous breakdown, Miss Swan."

"No, she'll be the strongest soul you've ever met in your life. She's already stronger than either of you can imagine."

"She'll be *hard*, Miss Swan. Not just strong. Peculiar and hard."

"Both those traits can be an asset. The world is not particularly kind to weak women."

The men gave her an astonished look. The doctor cleared his throat. "Be that as it may—the only way you're going to keep her in this house right now, and keep her from hurtin' herself – is to keep her drugged."

After a long silence, Swan said, "Write a prescription and I'll have it filled."

The men left. I dimly felt Swan's hand on my face, and opened my eyes. She sat down beside me on the bed. The rush of her fine perfume filled my mind. The scent of her perfume would make me ill, after that night. "When I was a little girl," she said in a low voice, as if beginning a bedtime story, "I learned to cry quietly, so the men in my mother's house couldn't find me."

I blinked slowly, burning inside. Cry? My grandmother had *ever* cried? "They were not *friendly* in a way a little girl would like," Swan went on. "I taught Matilda to cry silently, as well. We had the same father, but he didn't protect either of us. As for our mothers—Matilda's mother worked for mine, and she was colored, of course, so she meant less than nothing to our father. She died of a disease certain working women suffered from in those times, and my mother—your great-grandmother Esta—was left with Matilda to raise.

"Mother debated sending her to a colored orphanage in Asheville, but I begged her not to do it, and finally, she relented. *As long as you're a good girl, I'll let you keep her*, she said, as if we were still in slave times and could own a person. In Mother's mind, none of us were better off than slaves of some kind or other. She made her living selling women to men, after all..

"From then on, Mother told everyone Matilda was my own little colored maid, and that made her a novelty. Mother's customers found it charming. But Matilda and I  knew we were half-sisters. We knew we could only depend on each other. Together we discovered all the best hiding places in my mother's large house. The other women could never find us." She paused. "And neither could the men."

Swan took one of my bandaged fists between her hands. I think she assumed I was too drugged to remember anything she was telling me, but every word branded itself on my brain. "We were about five years old when Clara was born. Our father, A.A. Hardigree, was drunk at the time, and he spent that evening downstairs in the company of one of the women who worked for Mother. Matilda and I hid in a hallway armoire and peeked out at him as he staggered from the woman's room. His clothes were half-buttoned and he stank of liquor and sweat. He was a big, handsome man, with hands like a stonecutter but so finely dressed you knew he'd never cut marble again. He owned the quarry. He'd built the town for his men to use. He ruled like a king. We watched him in terrible awe and fear. Then we heard a sound on the stair landing above us.

"My mother had managed, somehow, to make her way out of her rooms and came to the landing. She clutched the railing and looked down at him, cursing him, crying. A bloody white nightgown clung to her body. She had long brunette hair like yours and mine, and the fiercest blue eyes. She was amazing, terrifying, beautiful. "I just gave you a second *white* daughter," she said. "Doesn't that mean anything to you?"

"He threw his head back and smiled up at her as if Clara's birth were a joke. *Sons and marble stone have value*, he said. *But what's a whore's daughter worth? Not a damn thing.*" Swan traced the bandages on my hand with her fingertips. "I think that must have been the night Mother decided to save us all from the fate he intended. She decided to make something of herself, and her two daughters, and their little colored half-sister. The next summer—right in the middle of the worst drought in years—she woke us late one night and sent us out of the house—Matilda and me, carrying Baby Clara—with one of her women to watch over us. The woman hurried us up the hill out of town and through the woods, but then she broke down crying—she was afraid of the dark mountain woods, and afraid of my mother, too, and so she simply left us there.

"Matilda and I huddled in the dark, holding Clara. We had no idea what was happening. The hills were mostly cleared of trees then—just acres of stumps left, ugly and barren. It was easy to see the town in that languid summer heat, watching the lightning from a dry storm play over the shacks and shanties and wooden houses that made up Burnt Stand then. I'll never forget how suddenly the buildings went up in flames, as if a dozen fires had been set at once. The heat and smoke rose up the hills toward us, and we ran.

"There was a spring—it's long since dried up—but it existed, then, up on Bald Stone Trace, among the rock outcroppings in the woods there. It made a wonderful little pond. Matilda and I loved it. We thought fairies lived in the water. We went to that spring and sat down in the edge, finally able to breathe. Clara was gasping. We bathed her and she was all right. I've never forgotten how safe and free we felt there—how *important* it felt to save ourselves and

Clara, how proud we were. I've loved water ever since.

"My mother's house was a huge wooden Victorian with a tarpaper roof, and it burned like dried cornstalks. People ran screaming, some of them on fire. We never saw our father come out. He died in Mother's bed, people said. People said the heat lightning set the town on fire. And Mother said nothing.

"But suddenly she produced our father's will, and she hired a lawyer from Asheville to defend it. She swore he'd left the quarry to her. She swore the will named her as a wife. And she won. So, from then on, she was Mrs. Hardigree. Everything belonged to her—the horrible ruins of the town, the quarry, his name, his money. She never looked back. And we tried not to, as well."

Swan sighed deeply and bowed her head. "But Clara never understood what we came from. She grew up very differently from Matilda and me. She never felt real fear. She never suffered humiliation. She never understood what made us so careful, so determined to raise ourselves from our past. Mother became very busy with the business of making money off the quarry and building her marble town. She ignored Clara—let her run wild. Perhaps Mother hated her for those words our father had spoken the night she was born. I don't know. My mother never explained very much about her thoughts. She and I were never *close*."

Swan smiled thinly. "Matilda and I tried to teach Clara to be a lady, but it was hopeless. She couldn't comprehend why we were so intent on being respected. We understood that money and power and reputation are as easily lost as won. Clara understood only that she had been born rich, beautiful, and free to do as she pleased.

"By the time we were teenagers Mother was rich enough to begin her grandest building schemes here in town. She wanted a master stonecutter to build a mansion for her—and to build fine houses in her new town, all out of marble. She put out word at all the quarries in the south until she found a man named Anthony Wade, in Tennessee. He was an incredible-looking young man, big and dark-haired and handsome, poor and not well educated, but gentlemanly. He was brilliant when it came to construction and stonework. He had natural instincts for calculations and logic." She paused. "Like Eli, he was, perhaps, a kind of genius."

I made a low, angry mewling sound and tried to pull my hand away. She wouldn't let me. *"Listen to me, and understand,"* she ordered. "Given a chance in any other place and time, he might have become a famous architect. Coming here was his chance, good or bad, to make a name for himself. *There are no opportunities without sacrifices.* You have to learn that."

She shut her eyes for a moment, then went on. "Mother brought him here and quickly took a fancy to more than his work. She was growing older then—losing her fine looks but still a beautiful woman. I believe she was truly taken with him, and he was—" Swan hesitated, searching the air for words—"he was not *unhappy* to be favored by her charms. At least not at first. The Depression was just ending, jobs were still short, people were desperate. She *owned* her stonecutters. She controlled the entire town.

"She set Anthony Wade to work building this mansion, and the Stone Cottage, and the Stone Flower Garden. She filled the cottage with fine furniture and insisted he live there like a country prince. He became something of a celebrity around here. Then she set him to work building fine marble houses and public buildings in town. People were awed by his talent. They didn't know he had other talents where my Mother was concerned. All the time, he was just a walk away, at her beck and call."

Swan paused. "I hated Mother for the whispers that began to rise about her and Anthony Wade. And I hated Clara, who was barely past childhood but already had a bad reputation with every young man in town—except Anthony Wade, who never gave her more than a passing glance." Swan was silent, shutting her eyes, then opening them hard and bright. "You see, he dallied with Mother out of practical necessity, but he had fallen in love with *Matilda.*

"I should have seen that coming. Matilda was so confused, so hurt by her place in the world. She and I were tall, sophisticated lookalikes in so many ways, yet we were treated so differently by society. She was darker than a white person, and her hair was coarse, Negro hair. She was stunning but she couldn't pretend to be white, and the kind of treatment she received from white men was despicable. She became very aloof and distrustful. I tried to help her, but there was little I could do to change the world in which we lived.

"I attended private college in Asheville and took her with me, regardless of the talk it caused—me bringing my *maid* along everywhere. We boarded with relatives of the Samples family— that's how I met your grandfather. Matilda wasn't allowed to attend college or go to any of college functions with me, which was very painful for us both. She found a job as a clerk in an insurance company owned by a very prominent colored man. He sold insurance policies to colored people all over the state. Matilda didn't love him, but she was lonely, and he was persistent. She began to see him. They were soon the crème of colored society. Everyone believed she'd marry him.

"We came home during summer vacation on the eve of my engagement to Dr. Samples. One day Mother sent us to the Stone Cottage to deliver sketches she'd drawn for yet another house she wanted Anthony to build in town. I never risked my reputation alone with him, so I took Matilda with me. We drove Mother's big, flashy Cord down to that secluded place, both of us a little nervous and high-handed. Anthony Wade was Mother's hired man. We knew all that that implied.

"The most startling sight met our eyes when we arrived. He'd built a small pen beside the cottage, and in it were two tiny fawn deer. Twins. He was feeding them cow's milk from a teat bucket, just as if they were orphaned calves. Their mother had been killed by dogs, he told us. He'd found them in the woods and was having a time trying to keep them fed and alive. He looked exhausted but wouldn't stop tending them. We'd never seen anything as gentle as his attention to those babies. *May I help you feed them?* Matilda asked. She was enthralled. She rarely spoke to white men, preferring to keep her distance. But she couldn't resist, this time.

"And as for Anthony Wade—I will never forget this—he looked at her as if she were a princess who had deigned to speak to him. *Once a lady like you touches them,* he said, *they'll want to live for sure.* Matilda put her hand to her heart as if to mark the spot where he'd just taken it. From then on she went there every day to help him feed the fawns. *I saw her fall in love with him that day, and him with her.*"

Swan sighed deeply. "Of course it was such a problem—a white man and a colored woman. I begged her to stay away from him, but it was useless. He was just as desperate to be with her as she with him. They even talked of marriage—of running away together, somewhere, where such a thing might be legal." Swan hesitated, and a gritted tone came into her voice. "I knew the outcome would be disaster. I should have known Clara would provoke it.

"Clara discovered them together at the cottage. She was sixteen years old, childish and viciously jealous. She told Mother about Anthony and Matilda—and then she told *everyone.* The whole town soon knew that Anthony Wade had been caught with Esta Hardigree's colored *maid.* Mother became murderous. She went to Preacher Al—who was no preacher then, but a big thug of a stonecutter—and paid him to take some men down the cottage and beat Anthony to death. Matilda heard what she intended and sent Carl McCarl to stop them in the midst of the terrible brutality.

"Carl had worked as a stonecutter since the old days in town. He had known Matilda's mother—he was a favorite customer of hers before my father commandeered her services exclusively. I believe Carl truly loved her, and he was devoted to Matilda, as if she were his own daughter.

"Carl saved Anthony's life, but not before the men had beaten him so badly he was ruined for life. Carl carried Anthony to a hospital over the state line in Tennessee and left him there. I paid the medical bills. No one expected Anthony to live. He did live, but he was scarred and damaged. As soon as he could walk, he disappeared.

"Mother threw Matilda out of our home and told her never to come back. I hid Matilda with friends in Asheville. I thought she'd die over losing Anthony. *And worse—she was pregnant with his child.* That news reached her colored beau—the insurance man—and he cut off all contact with her. Mother threatened to disinherit me if I continued to help her. It was a terrible time—and Clara gloated over it all. Wonder of wonders, I managed to keep all of this turmoil so quiet that your grandfather's family didn't suspect at first, but then the rumblings about my family began to reach them. I was engaged to him, by then. I knew I had to do something to save my future and Matilda's."

Swan was silent for a moment. I drifted in and out, the lurid, tragic story wafting through my mind, mingling with death and grief and shame and the pain I had seen in Eli as he and Annie Gwen held Jasper in their arms, covered in blood. A tapestry of unspeakable images began to wrap me in stone chains. Swan said finally, "Then Mother died unexpectedly, and that changed everything." There was another long silence, while drugged horror crept over my brain. I couldn't put a name to what she was hinting, just as I could only steep in a nameless understanding that Clara's death had been no accident. "I sent Clara away to a kind of school in Illinois," Swan went on. "Run by Catholic nuns."

*A kind of school.* My head whirled. A prison.

"I made certain I inherited everything from Mother—the quarry, this house, all the money. Suddenly, any qualms the Samples family may have had—any whispers or rumors they'd heard about my family—paled in comparison to my fortune. I married your grandfather and we came back here to live. When Matilda's daughter was born in Asheville she was as white as you or I. Katherine. She was a beauty. Dark-haired and dark-eyed—like Anthony Wade— but as pale as pink stone. Hardly a colored child.

"I brought her here and told your grandfather she was the orphan of a distant cousin of mine. We kept her to raise. Then I brought Matilda home, and I gave her a house in town and a job managing this household for me, so she was able to be with her daughter. A year later, your mother was born. Julia and Katherine—what a lovely pair they made. Matilda and I raised our daughters together, keeping our secrets from them, indulging them but training them to be ladies, to have pride. They were fine girls, smart and beautiful and strong. Katherine had no idea she was anything other than a white Hardigree. She enjoyed all the privileges that that entailed. Matilda protected her with painful pride."

Swan hesitated. Her words were coming slower, harder. "Clara returned suddenly when Julia and Katherine were about to graduate from the Larson School in Asheville. They were both so excited about the prospects of college the next fall—they talked constantly of joining sororities, of all the wonderful young men they'd meet. Their lives were golden.

"Clara had not fared so well. She'd worked her way through a series of notorious men with money, and she'd acquired the trashy attitudes of lowlifes and gangsters. She was in her late thirties then—and she knew her appeal to that kind of man was beginning to fade. She wanted an income from me. I said No. I underestimated her vindictiveness. In revenge—" Swan's voice slowed to a lethargic drone—"she went to Katherine and Julia and told them our family history including the fact that Katherine was Matilda's daughter."

Swan stopped. I stared at her haunted expression in a hypnotic daze, my mind an open wound into which she poured one scalding secret after another. "Clara threatened to spread the word to all their school friends, to the society who had accepted them, to everyone who revered the exquisite Hardigree cousins. I was devastated, and Matilda, too. I gave Clara the money she wanted, and promised her more in the future. I bought her silence and she left, but the damage was done.

"Your mother and Katherine never recovered. They were so young, so cloistered in this pink, innocent world Matilda and I had created for them. Now they had to deal with the fact that they were the granddaughters of outcast women—and that Katherine was a mixed-race girl on top of that. Katherine was so upset, looking at Matilda, whom she'd adored as if she were family but still just a dear employee. Now she knew this was her *mother*—a colored woman who couldn't stay at the finest hotels when we traveled unless I listed her as my maid—a woman who couldn't use a public bathroom or a fountain marked for whites only. This was Katherine's mother. This was Katherine, now.

"Both she and Julia were inconsolable. They accused us of hypocrisy, of lies, as if somehow we were to blame for the heritage from which we'd tried so hard to shield them. They were heartbroken and ashamed and thoughtlessly cruel. Both saw only one solution—to rebel bitterly against their life, here—just flailing out in anger and pain at any likely target. Katherine rejected us all and ran away. I was so afraid Julia would do the same thing—I made her a prisoner here, threatened her, had her watched, wouldn't let her go anywhere alone. And of course, that only made her more determined to hurt me."

Swan looked down at me with something almost like apology on her face. "She was a princess trapped in a castle, and your father must have seen it as his duty to rescue her. And she *wanted* to be rescued—particularly if her hero was the lowest and last man I'd pick for her. A stonecutter. She was pregnant by him— and secretly married to him—before I realized she'd outsmarted me.

"And so I, in my desperate, mistaken wisdom, tried to control her new husband with a show of generosity—the gift of the stone cottage, and a foreman's job at the quarry. He was easy to persuade. But your mother hated me for manipulating him, and began to hate *him* for accepting it all. They were never meant to be together—he was rough and uneducated, and she quickly realized they had no future together. They fought, but she refused to leave him—just to spite me, I think. When you were born, I took you away from them. The day your mother and father died they were rushing to a court hearing in Asheville, trying to regain custody of you." She paused. "In fighting me, they realized they were a family. But it was too late."

Whether she was telling all this to me—a tranquilized, traumatized ten-year-old girl—as an apology, an explanation, a bizarre attempt at comfort, or all three—I now knew that my mother had not deserted me. It was the only bright thought I clung to. Swan watched me quietly. "You've absorbed every word," she said. "Amazing."

She cupped my bandaged hand a little tighter. "Now hear the rest. We found Katherine finally, in New York. She'd spent some time working for one of the civil rights organizations, and she'd met a young man doing that same work, a young colored man, and she'd told him her mother was colored, and she married him. I suppose she loved him. I don't know. He was drafted and went to Vietnam, and he was killed there, in combat. A week later Katherine left her little girl, Karen, with a friend. And then she killed herself.

"Matilda and I went to New York, and we took Karen, and we brought Katherine's body back here, and we buried her beside Julia, in an unmarked crypt. People don't know it, but she's there—in the Hardigree mausoleum. We brought Karen to be raised with you. We knew that some day we'd have to tell you and her as much of the truth as we could—when you were old enough to hear it." Swan hesitated. "It seems that time has come."

I moved my mouth, but no words came out. Swan put her fingers to my lips. "We made a well-intentioned mistake three years ago by seeking out Anthony's family and bringing them here. Matilda wanted to help them, but we failed. I'm very sorry. I promise you that. But I've told you all this because I want you to understand: I have only one true regret." She paused. "I should have drowned Clara when she was a baby, that night at Bald Stone Trace."

Everything she'd told me—every warped and yet desperately sad fact about her life and Matilda's, our mothers, ourselves, Anthony Wade, Clara—all paled next to the remorseless destruction she'd forced others to endure along with her. She forced me to accept our heritage as a rite of passage, and I made peace with it the only way I could. "I hate you," I whispered.

She looked away, then back. Her gaze went hard and dry. "If it were that easy to stop loving someone, I'd believe you."

She left me there in the darkness, and I shut my eyes.

*

Eli, Mama, and Bell buried Pa in the cemetery of the same run-down Tennessee church where Anthony had been buried decades before him. It was just south of Nashville, and for the next two days after the funeral Eli drove the truck up the interstate toward anywhere—he didn't care, and neither did Mama or Bell. At a truckstop motel one night he said to them, "I'm goin' to take care of us." Bell, who had shrunk into silence for a week by then, suddenly sobbed, "Did Pa do it?" And Mama broke down crying again. "No, no, he never did, he never could."

"I'm goin' to take care of us," Eli repeated in a daze. Deep in his heart he believed his father had killed Darl's great aunt, and he would remember the look in Darl's eyes as Chief Lowden dragged her away, a look he interpreted as not just shame for him but shame for loving him and shock over his father's obvious guilt. Eli's anger and grief and vows to make something of his family would never change the rejection he believed he'd seen in her eyes.

He had lost Darl forever.

\*

I had lost Eli. I could never go after him, never tell him the truth, never expect forgiveness. I had no right. No matter where I went or what I did with my life from that time on, no matter how I dealt with Swan and how I escaped her plans for me—which I would do—I would remain trapped in memories, my secret guilt as unchanging as our stone flowers. Some mystic instinct, memories merging with experience, began to whisper to me. My mother hadn't deserted me. Swan had driven her away. I couldn't get away from Swan myself yet, but I would some day.

Between a rock and a hard place, only love and defiance could survive.

When I was taken off medication, sometime in February or March I believe, I went into a small plain room upstairs at the mansion, filled with storage boxes. I dug in them until I found clothes my mother had worn as a teenager. She'd been smaller than me, so the slender tan skirt and white blouse fit even though I was younger than she'd been when she wore them. I even found a pair of her penny loafers. Swan had kept everything, trying to seal my mother's memory away from us both. As I grew older I would understand my grandmother's pain because I had pain of my own, but I'd never forgive her.

Even my mother's shoes fit me. I wouldn't follow her path, but now I knew, at least, why she'd walked it. I dressed in the tan skirt and white blouse then went downstairs. Swan stood beside a central table in the chandeliered foyer, her eyes distant, her hands idle on a thin marble vase she held. In my brief glimpse of her before she saw me, she appeared unspeakably lonely. I hesitated on the bottom stairs, but marble gives away even the sound of a heartbeat. She heard my footsteps and looked up.

For one second I must have been my mother to her. Swan's hands fumbled. The marble vase fell and cracked in two on the marble floor.

I didn't even flinch.

"No more pink," I said.

# PART TWO
## Twenty-five years later

## 10

On a late autumn afternoon when the heat rose like a vapor, Eli flew his twin-engine Cessna along the Mississippi River outside Memphis, Tennessee. Pine forest and marsh aproned the ancient waterway, warning him to stay above them. *Ace it, the odds are easy*, he thought grimly. He'd landed the Cessna in South American jungles, in Canadian mountains, in western desserts and coastal fishing burgs where alligators groaned in the swampy ditches near the plane's wheels. He was 38 years old, with a weathered, homely-handsome face, the rich, dark eyes of his boyhood, his father's broad-shouldered build, no wife, no children, and over fifty million dollars in the bank. Gambler, investor, inventor—he'd seen the world wherever a smart play took him.

But there was nothing smart about this day's mission.

Now the grand old mother-river of his native south spread like a long silver lake beneath him. He found a landmark on its banks and swung low over the trees, angry and a little reckless. Construction swaths appeared in the forest, the land gaping in torn sections of dirt and heavy machinery. The top of a billboard-sized sign flashed beneath him. Rivercross Landing, he recalled that it said. Estate homes from $300,000.

He found the long, straight stretch of paved boulevard that was the development's main entrance road, then guided the plane down into the alley between the trees in a harrowing exercise of skill and determination. *Han Solo*, a flight instructor and more than a few passengers had dubbed him. *Solo*. The nickname had stuck. Eli craned his head, calculating distance and speed expertly as the wooden construction skeletons of behemoth homes flashed by. Touch down. Flat land. He taxied the plane slowly, dust whirling from the deforested homesites on either side, until he reached a white construction-office trailer bearing a Canetree Development sign next to the door.

A worker ran up to him as he stepped down. "What do you think you're doin', you crazy SOB—" the man halted. Eli was well over six feet tall, with thick arms and large, big-knuckled hands. The grime of hard labor covered his thick-soled workboots, old khaki's, and sweat-stained blue shirt. He'd given up glasses for contact lenses, then laser surgery in the past year. He knew how rough he looked at that moment, and so did the worker. The man stepped back. Eli nodded to him. "I'm Alton Canetree's brother-in-law." Eli jerked his head toward the trailer. "Is he in there?"

"Sure. But he's, uh, he's havin' a bad day. Nobody's seen him much."

"I bet." Eli flicked an ace of hearts into the air, caught it with his fingertips, then palmed it like a magic coin. Patience. Temper. He counted to ten. The numbers never let a man down. As he strode to the trailer he slipped the old card into his shirt pocket and flexed his fists.

He snatched open the metal door so roughly it slapped the side of the trailer. As soon as he stepped inside he frowned at Alton, who lay stretched out on a vinyl sofa asleep with one arm thrown over his eyes, his golf shirt wrinkled, his pants flecked with cigar ashes, and his sandy hair matted with sweat. A half-empty bottle of bourbon and an ashtray filled with half-smoked cigars teetered at the edges of a short metal file cabinet Alton had pulled close to the couch.

Eli hesitated, feeling a pang of surprise and concern. Alton wasn't much of a smoker or a drinker ordinarily. In the five years he'd been married to Bell he'd never been less than dependable. He'd become Eli's surrogate brother and a second son to Mama. He clearly doted on Bell, and she loved him dearly in return. Their first child, Jessie, a daughter, was six months old. Alton adored her. All of which made what he'd done impossible to understand.

"Alton, goddammit, wake up." Eli skirted the file cabinet, bent over him, and took him by the shirt. One hard shake and Alton sat up, staring at Eli with bleary, bloodshot eyes. Eli winced. Alton hadn't just been drinking. He'd been crying. Eli clasped him by the shoulders. "What happened? Why did you walk out on my sister?"

"I didn't know what else to do. I love her too much to go on the way we are."

"Look, I know she has some strange ideas. But you don't pack up and desert your wife and baby. You don't leave your family."

"Eli, one of her crazy psychics has finally gotten to her this time. All she talks about is what happened when y'all were kids in North Carolina."

Eli groaned silently. Bell's obsession with the past was nothing new. Just like Mama, she had never given up, even when there were no answers. But Mama had channeled the torment into prayers and church work, while Bell had turned to tarot-card gurus and psychics. "Look, it's her way of dealing with what happened to us. You know how unpredictable she is. This is just a phase. If she's spending too much on her soothsayers, send me the bill."

"It's not just the damned psychics, anymore. It's gone way beyond that. And I don't want your money. If it was just money I know you'd bail us out. I won't let you."

"Whatever it is, you're coming to Nashville with me right now. We'll talk on the way. I'll help you and Bell work things out. As bad as you look, she looks worse. Comeon. She and the baby are with Mama."

Alton shoved himself off the couch and staggered to his feet. "It's not that easy." His voice rose. "One of her swamis told her you all have to go back where your father died. Go back to that town—that place you lived. Bell's psychic says the truth's in the dirt, *buried*, some kind of bullshit, I don't know—I gave up trying to reason with Bell over this one. She's on fire since little Jessie was born! She says she owes it to our daughter to prove her grandpa wasn't a murderer."

"I don't care what some half-assed fortune teller told Bell to—"

"Eli, your sister went behind my back and made a deal that wipes out our savings." Alton shoved his hands through his hair. "She bought a half-million dollars worth of land without telling me."

Eli froze. "What land?"

Alton bowed his head into his hands, then uttered a sound between a sob and a bleak chuckle. "The land where you-all lived in North Carolina. With that marble cottage on it and that garden—whatever the hell you called it."

Eli stared at him. "The stone flower garden."

Alton nodded. "She says she's going back and dig it all up."

*

Eli made the quick flight back to Nashville that afternoon in one of the bleakest moods of his life. He'd kept his boyhood promise to himself to find flat land. In a way, staying on the level had become the defining drive of his life. And yet he kept moving over the face of the world, a natural loner, always gaining altitude. When he looked back he saw Burnt Stand, that one pink town in North Carolina, the one place he never landed, where nothing had ever been even, or level, and unanswered questions could never be settled. Even after so many years he still thought of Darl every day.

He landed the plane on a neat, paved air strip amidst rolling pastures and wooded hills with Nashville's famed skyline on the distant horizon. The acreage he had bought a few years before lay only a few miles from the old cemetery where Pa had been buried. Mama went every week to visit the grave, and had donated thousands of dollars to the tiny country church that owned the cemetery. She was happy being near Pa.

Eli climbed into a mud-spattered SUV he'd left at the private runway and drove down a dirt road between fenced pastures dotted with cattle and horses. When he wasn't traveling Eli worked the farm, trying to sink himself into the land, to put down roots. But he, Mama, and Bell had moved around so much for so many years that for him, at least, staying in one place felt unnatural.

*Keep moving and don't look back*, he often caught himself thinking.

He passed barns, outbuildings, and the small brick house where the farm's manager and his family lived. The irony of that arrangement—the comparisons with his own childhood—always made him a little uneasy. Now he was the landlord, commanding a tenant family, though he prided himself on fairness and good pay. When he crested a knoll the yards of the main house spread out before him, verdant and pretty, the last of the summer flowers still blooming. Deep, cool shadows hovered under massive shade trees. The house he'd built for his mother stood among them with the quiet grace Annie Gwen had wanted in a home—roomy but simple, copied from a picture of a white-clapboard farmhouse she'd found in Southern Living magazine.

His mother met him at the front door with a look of soft worry on her face. Annie Gwen Wade was now almost sixty years old, straight-backed but a little plump, favoring an arthritic right hip, her light brown hair going gray and cut in a short, fluffy style by a high-priced Nashville salon. She was dressed in one of her favorite plain blue jumpers and a t-shirt, with a baby blanket and a burping towel draped over one shoulder. "You couldn't get Alton to come back?" she moaned. Eli shook his head and swept his mother into a deep hug. "But he loves her. And I'll take care of the problem."

"How?" His mother pushed herself back. Her eyes were haunted. "Did he tell you what Bell did?" Eli nodded. "She says Miss Swan put the land up for sale, and—"

"I know, Mama, I know. Alton told me the details."

"She's lost her mind! She wants to dig up the very soil where we lived in Burnt Stand, but she doesn't even know why."

"We're not going back there. And nobody's going to dig."

Mama raised one hand and closed her fist around the diamond crucifix Eli and Bell had given her one Christmas. Bell chased whimsies. Mama prayed for signs. "If I thought there was any way to show that your pa didn't kill Clara Hardigree you know I'd do it. But this is foolishness."

"No, it's not, Mama," Bell said from above them. "It's destiny."

Eli stepped inside the foyer and looked up a whitewashed staircase. Bell stood at the top, barefoot, dressed in jeans and a tear-splotched white silk blouse. At 32, she was still delicately sweet and a little odd, with her mother's caramel-brown hair and the same dark Wade eyes as Eli. Annie Jessamine Canetree—Jessie—was cradled, asleep, in her arms.

"We're never meant to go back there," Eli told her.

"We'll be haunted the rest of our lives if we don't! Haunted," Bell emphasized, crying and rocking the baby. "I don't want my daughter to grow up haunted, too."

Eli scrubbed a hand over his hair while he fought an urge to yell at her. "Your psychic doesn't know what she's talking about. There's nothing buried there but bad memories."

"No, things don't happen by coincidence. After my psychic told me the truth is buried where we lived I hired a lawyer to see—just to see what he could find out about Swan Samples and her property—she's in her late seventies, now, and I thought maybe she'd turned everything over to Darl, who might—"

Eli slammed a hand on the stair banister. "You didn't contact Darl, did you?"

"No, no, I just had the lawyer talk to real estate agents in Burnt Stand." Bell clasped the stair railing and came down slowly, clutching Jessie to one shoulder. Mama limped up the first few stairs and anxiously took the sleeping baby into her own arms. Bell held out both freed hands to her brother in supplication. Her eyes gleamed. "And the lawyer found out that Swan Samples put the back acreage behind Marble Hall up for a sale a year ago! The Stone Cottage, the Stone Flower Garden, everything! She meant to sell it! That's not coincidence, Eli! We were meant to buy that property!"

"You made the deal with Swan Samples? She knows it's you?"

Bell shook her head. "I hid because I didn't want my lawyer to upset her with the truth. She's an old lady now."

"You didn't think she'd get a clue she'd been lied to when you sent men with pickaxes and bulldozers to pry up the forest?"

"Maybe she'll be pleased—surely she wants to know the truth about her sister. They never found Clara's body in that lake."

"It's a big, deep lake. No surprise."

"Someone killed Clara Hardigree, but it wasn't Pa. I'm going to dig on the land until I find something that tells us what really happened."

"You're not going to find anything," Eli said, his voice lower and more controlled than before. "Or prove anything except that we're a bunch of fools with money, now."

Bell turned to him raggedly, trembling, her eyes filling with anger. "Why don't you want to believe in Pa? How can you act as if he did it? Don't you want to clear his name? He was our daddy. He loved us. He doesn't deserve to be called a murderer. I don't want my daughter to grow up hearing that her Great-Grandpa Anthony couldn't keep his pants zipped and her Grandpa Jasper killed a woman. Do you want to tell your children that someday?"

Eli hesitated. He felt Mama's eyes boring into him. "I don't have any children and I don't expect to have any." Mama moaned and rocked Jessie when he said that.

Bell threw up her hands. "Eli, don't you see what's wrong with you? Why you live the way you do—like an old gypsy hermit, flying all over the country and dabbling in computers and making money and sleeping with women here and there who just happen to look like Darl Union—"

"*Bell*," Mama said.

Bell took a long look at the warning expression on Eli's face and blanched a little. "Big Brother, I'm sorry, but you know your life's not right. It's all because of Pa, isn't it? You're haunted, just like me and Mama. Going back to Burnt Stand is the only way to get over it."

Eli gripped the stair banister. "There's nothing buried on that property that can change what Pa may or may not have done. I say leave it alone and get on with our lives."

"Get on with our lives? The way you have? I know what you've been doing the past few years. Mama knows, too. We're not stupid."

"I'm just trying to do something good with my life and my ill-gotten money." A sharp smile cut his mouth.

"We know about Darl and the Phoenix Group."

Silence. The poignant accusation colored the air and set Eli in grim silence. Bell gripped his clenched hands. "You can't go on trying to be part of her life without her knowing. Eli, it's not right—not fair. Not to her, and not to you."

"She has no reason to ever want to see me again. To see any of us."

"You don't even know if she hates us. You don't know if she believes Pa did it."

"She believes it," he said between gritted teeth. "There're a few things I won't ever forget in my life. One is the sight of Pa on the ground with blood pouring out of his heart—" he halted as their mother's face began to compress into misery. He took a deep breath. "And one is the look in Darl's eyes."

Bell began to cry in earnest. "That's why we have to go back." She touched his clenched hand gently. "Eli, don't you ever wonder if Darl suffers the way we do? That maybe she needs to know what really happened, too?"

"We might only end up proving that Pa killed her great aunt."

Mama, who had been listening to Eli's betraying doubts in silent agony, spoke up quietly. "Is that what you're afraid of, son?"

After a stark moment, he nodded. Her faced went white and she sat down on the stairs, cradling the baby protectively. Eli grabbed her by one elbow, and Bell rushed down the steps. "Mama!" Bell slid Jessie from her grasp then sat down beside her, clutching one of her hands. Eli stroked her hair.

Mama straightened and wiped her eyes. "Your pa was a good man, and in my heart I know he didn't kill Clara Hardigree. Maybe we'll look like fools for diggin' in the old dirt, but I don't mind. Bell's right. We do have to go back to that land, and we have to look for something, and just pray we find a truth we can bear." She held her children and her grandchild closer, studying her cynical son and damaged daughter with a mother's heartache.

Eli felt as if a weight had settled on him.
*Darl.*

\*

When he was at the farm outside Nashville Eli spent most of his time in a small, windowless building he'd constructed in the woods within walking distance of his mother's house. A small sign on one door said Solo, Inc., the name of an all-purpose corporation he'd created for himself. The building included a spartan bedroom and kitchen, but they were almost afterthought. Some rooms were filled with books and CDs on mathematics, science, and technology. Others were a jumble of tables and shelves crowded with electronic tools and testing equipment, computers, and the various systems related to them. A web of cables draped the plaster-board ceilings and snaked along the tile floors. Eli's passion for such things had led him to invest wisely in the start-ups of several small high-tech companies, each now worth a fortune. He could afford to surround himself with soulless accessories.

And yet that night, sitting in an old leather recliner amidst all of those implacable and ulitmately logical, passionless silicon brains, he typed a command and a large computer screen filled with the opening credits of the Larry King show. King explained the night's topic and guest, then turned to that guest as the camera switched to a wider shot.

"Welcome back to the show," he said to Darl. Eli exhaled slowly. She took the breath from him so many times, but never knew. He'd tried to put her out of his mind for years after he left Burnt Stand, because wondering about her was too painful.

Now he sat back in his chair and watched her on national television. "I wish I didn't need to be here again," she told King. "No offense, but still."

"I understand. For viewers who don't know what the Phoenix Group is, tell us."

"It's a non-profit legal defense foundation. There are five attorneys and a small support staff. We're based in Washington, D.C. The foundation is headed by Irene Branshaw, a retired federal court judge."

"You take on death penalty cases. To date the foundation has freed twenty men from death row. The public tends to hate defense lawyers who do that."

"DNA evidence proved those men were innocent. The purpose of the foundation is not to manipulate the system and set guilty men free. It's to provide justice for the wrongly convicted."

"But Frog Marvin's case is different. There's no doubt he killed two police officers. Are you trying to get him off?"

"No. I'm only asking that his death sentence be commuted to life in prison."

"He's scheduled for execution in Florida next Wednesday. Any luck with the most recent appeals?"

"No, but there's still a week. I'm not going to let the state of Florida kill a child."

"You always make a point of referring to 'Frog' Marvin, who's 39 years old, as a child. Why?"

"He has the IQ of a second grader," she answered in a dulcet voice. "Think of putting a seven-year-old boy to death. That's Frog." She riveted King with the politely decorous but knife-sharp gaze that had made one commentator say drolly she had gunslinger eyes at high noon. Waves of brunette hair softened her intense face but did nothing to mitigate her searing blue eyes. Her features were beautiful, her skin—there was no better description— porcelain. Yet she was spartan in dress and attitude, favoring strictly tailored business suits, and the Marvin case had worn on her like no other. Eli had watched over recent months as she'd grown thinner and more drawn looking. Sharper. Sadder. More dangerous.

King turned to the camera. "For viewers just joining us, twelve years ago Frog Marvin and his older brother Tom were convicted of killing two Florida police officers during a convenience store robbery. Tom's serving a life sentence but Frog got the death penalty because he did the shooting."

Darl shook her head and raised her right hand in a now-wait-a-minute rebuke. Eli always noticed that she wore no rings, and very little other jewelry. The Hardigree pendant hung from a fine gold chain around her neck, catching the studio light against the blue lapel of her suit. *She's loyal to her Grandma*, Eli thought.

He steepled his chin on one fist. She would always be Swan's granddaughter, always a Hardigree, and he would always be the son of the man who had probably killed her kin. "Tom ordered Frog to shoot the officers," she went on. "Nobody disputes that or the fact that Tom was an abusive bully who'd terrorized Frog since they were boys. Every eyewitness to the robbery testified that Frog said, "I don't want to hurt them," and Tom screamed at him to fire the gun or he, Tom, would hurt Frog. Frog shot the officers, then dropped the gun and began to cry."

"The officers' families were on this program last week. They say those circumstances shouldn't matter."

"I have total sympathy for them—but the man who killed their loved ones was *Tom* Marvin, not Frog Marvin. Frog was only doing what he was told. He clearly didn't have the capacity to defy his brother.".

"You've taken this case very personally."

"I take every case personally."

"You've gotten to know Frog Marvin pretty well?"

"I've been working on his case for five years. He was one of my first assignments after I joined the Phoenix Group."

"Before that you were a public defender in Atlanta."

"For a number of years, yes. I was hired by the Phoenix group not long after it was formed, in 1996."

"You're not going to get rich working for the government and charity foundations. Ever think of hanging up your shingle in the big-dollar world of private law practice?"

"The rich can buy their own brand of justice in the world. They don't need me."

"Cynical?"

"Realistic." She went on explaining the foundation's work. Her voice was low, genteely southern, well-modulated, a little husky and drawling, extremely sensual. She was a natural on television, just as in court. *I could listen to her forever*, Eli always thought. She'd become something of a celebrity for her television interviews. Eli had stored all of them on CD. He never missed one.

"You've gotten death threats over the Marvin case?"

She nodded and shrugged. Her attitude said she was capable of eviscerating anyone who stalked her. She had her grandmother's alluring, blood-curdling, unfathomable blue eyes. But to Eli she was still the pink girl who lay behind those eyes. "That comes with the territory."

Eli lurched out of the chair and snatched a cell phone from among a table cluttered with electronic test equipment. He punched the speed-dial function. A few seconds later he said, "William? Tell me about the death threats."

When he got off the phone he paced. Darl continued to talk calmly to Larry King as Eli ground his fingertips into his palms. "What would you like to see happen to Frog Marvin?" King asked her.

"I simply want his sentence commuted to life. I'm not arguing that he should be freed."

"If everything fails, he'll be executed by lethal injection next Wednesday. Will you be there as a witness?"

"On the front row, if I have to. I've been with him all along. I won't desert him at the last minute."

"A Florida newspaper editorial called you a shark with blue killer eyes. Are you that tough?"

"Absolutely."

"Can you watch Frog Marvin die, if you have to?"

She didn't blink. "Death isn't that difficult to watch," she answered finally. "The hard part is living with it."

King turned to the cameras. "When we come back we'll take your questions for Darl Union, attorney for Frog Marvin, the mentally handicapped convicted murderer scheduled to die in Florida next week."

Eli sat down slowly, watching her face until the scene cut to a commercial. She looked pale, tired. *The hard part is living with it.* What did she live with? How bad were her memories of Clara and his father? Of him? His thoughts whirled. He understood her fixation with death in a way few people could. He understood why a helpless, childlike man like Frog Marvin would make her fight with all her energy and devotion. This 35-year-old woman had once been a little girl in pink who dived into a cluster of fighting boys to save a stranger.

An outrageous plan began to form in Eli's mind. "Godawmighty, goddamit, you can't go to her that way," he said at the idea, and put his head in his hands.

But he knew that he had to find out what might be between him and her, to meet her on neutral ground before he had to tell her about Bell's addled plan to dig up the land behind Marble Hall, but most of all he knew he owed it to her to be where she needed him, where death stalked the helpless. He knew he had to try.

After twenty-five years, he and Darl would meet again.

## 11

I'd lost. No more chances. No more appeals. Frog Marvin was going to die. And it was my fault.

Wednesday morning, dawn. A hot September day seeped onto the horizon of central Florida, far from the fantasies of Disney World or the friendly beaches of the Atlantic and the Gulf. A few hours earlier the governor had refused to intervene in Frog's case. I stared bleakly at the cusp of the pink and maroon sunrise as I stood in a fenced yard outside the prison. The light was very dim; the smell of mown grass, pine thickets, and swampy culverts clung to the heavy air; the frogs had just stopped singing.

*Frog.* I winced. I hadn't slept more than five hours in the past two days, and when I did I dreamed about Eli and Jasper and Clara and even Preacher Al, all as raw as a new quarry pit. Eli was always thirteen years old to me, calling out *Pa, no!* as his father fell from the gunshot. My silence, my fear, my loyalty to my own kin—had condemned him. Now I'd failed Frog Marvin, too.

"Time to go back inside," I said to the young man and woman who chainsmoked a pack of filter-tips. They were law-student interns for the Phoenix Group. Their moral support had been limited to following me around and—when they thought I couldn't overhear—whispering to each other that I was about to crack. They might be right. My feet were leaden. My body felt like a cold wire inside a rumpled blue jacket and matching skirt. I stopped at the door held open by a guard, and spent a moment wiping bits of grass and dew off my black pumps. Anything to distract my own thoughts.

"I'm ready," I lied. I followed the guards into a secluded cell. Frog lumbered gallantly to his feet. An elderly prison minister stood beside him, looking shriveled. Frog was huge, with a round, florid face and bulging green eyes, thus the nickname. At first sight he looked like a monster. "Miss Darl," he said urgently, his voice a thick, backwoods drawl. "I was fearin' you might feel too bad to come see me one more time."

"Frog, I've never broken a promise to be here for you, have I?"

He looked at me tenderly. "No, Miss Darl."

"I was just upset when I had to tell you what the governor said. I needed some time to myself, time to think about anything else I could do. But there isn't anything else, Frog. I'm so sorry. I wish I could start over. I'd do everything different. I wouldn't make the same mistakes."

"Oh, no, Miss Darl, don't blame yourself. Everybody says you're the best lady lawyer they've ever seen." He twisted his big hands together and shifted from one foot to the other. "I did something bad and I guess I . . . I guess I oughta just go on and die."

"Frog, you only did what your brother made you do. I don't want you to die for that."

"I . . . I have to, though. They say so."

I nodded. My eyes burned, my throat was a knot. Frog looked at me and his lower lip quivered. "Don't be sad," he whispered.

"I'm sad because I let you down."

"Miss Darl, don't you say that. I was scared of you at first when you come to be my lawyer. You got mean eyes. But then you smiled at me and I saw you were sweet. And you been sweet to me ever since. You couldn't let me down. You built me up."

The minister cleared his throat. He produced a small prayer card from the Bible he carried. He held it out to Frog. "Mr. Marvin, let's read this out loud together."

Frog fumbled the card in his thick fingers, and his face turned red. My stomach twisted. Frog couldn't read. I took the card. "I'll read it for you, Frog."

"Does it say what heaven's like?"

The minister drew back his head and inhaled as if filling his lungs with rhetoric. "Heaven is beyond our comprehension, Mr. Marvin. It's brimming with the light of goodness and . . . "

"You'll have a nice girlfriend and a home with a place to play basketball," I interjected, drawing on favorite themes Frog had discussed with me. "Hambone will be waiting for you as soon as you die, and your grandfather Bo, too. Both of them. As soon as

you fall asleep, they'll come to you." A pet mutt named Hambone
and a kindly grandfather were Frog's only gentle memories. His
whole life had been handicapped by mental retardation, poverty,
and terrifying abuse.

Frog stared at me with urgent hope. "They'll be right there
when I die?"

"Yes. All you have to do is fall asleep, and they'll come to
meet you."

"How do you know?"

I hesitated. "Because dead people visit me in my dreams."
*Nightmares*, but I didn't say that.

"And you really know when they're there?"

"They're always there," I confirmed. "Just waiting for me to
shut my eyes."

Frog exhaled raggedly. "I can do that, then."

"Time to go, Ms. Union," an official said at the door.

"Miss Darl," Frog whispered. "I'm scared."

My body clenched. I wanted to do something, anything, break
down the walls, rush this grown child outside and away to a world
less cruel. "Let me hug you," I whispered. He engulfed me in his
arms. When I finally stepped back he looked at the minister
frantically. "Give her the present!"

The minister sighed and pulled a small, bulky item from the
pocket of his jacket. "Mr. Marvin asked me to purchase this for
you."

I gently pulled white tissue paper apart. Inside was a white
plastic heart with tiny flowers painted on it. "My heart is yours
forever," Frog said.

I nearly lost my mind. Frog was Jasper Wade, he was me, he
was Eli, he was every vulnerable memory I'd sunk deep inside me
all those years. Once again I would watch someone die. "I'll keep
it safe, Frog." I kissed him on the cheek. "I love you." It was
probably the first time in his adult life that anyone, woman or
man, had told him that. He began to cry. "Now, I can go to heaven,"
he said.

A few minutes later, dazed, I walked into the small room where
Frog would be killed. A young male reporter from a Florida TV

station said queasily, "I don't know how you can do this."

I said nothing. I didn't know, myself.

A woman from one of the cable news services leaned toward me as we sat down in rows of chairs. "I heard the Phoenix Group is paying for Frog Marvin's cremation. I heard a rumor you're having his ashes sent to your hometown in North Carolina. True?"

I ignored the question, and she called me a cold bitch under her breath. Every nerve in my body thrummed. When the officials led Frog into the other side of the room and strapped him to a gurney with his massive arms anchored to armrests, he began to tremble and looked my way. "Miss Darl, I'm going to close my eyes now, and I'm gonna keep 'em shut until Hambone and my grandpa come to get me." He paused. His mouth quivered. "I'm not scared, because you're here waitin' with me until they come, Miss Darl."

I nodded, unable to speak. The antiseptic stink of the room, the hum of the air conditioner, the buzz of an overhead light fixture roared inside me. I saw Clara and Jasper, air bubbles in the koi pond, blood on the ground before the Stone Cottage. I saw Eli lurching to his dying father's side, and I saw the hollow stare in his eyes when Chief Lowden dragged me away. Now I saw Frog Marvin stretched out on a gurney as if crucified, and I saw the technician start the IV drip that would make him sleep without waking, all because I had somehow not done or said the right thing, once again. I began to scream silently. Clenching the tiny plastic white heart, I held it against my cheek, where Frog could see that I wouldn't let go.

Frog smiled and shut his eyes..

He never opened them again.

\*

Chaos. Dozens of protesters rallied behind picket lines outside the prison entrance, waving their placards and chanting for the television cameras. About half were for killing Frog. About half were against. The scalding white light of video cameras recorded the crowd for various networks and local television stations. A line of police officers kept everyone behind barricades. A hot semi-tropical sunrise slanted across the placards. I only noticed the hateful ones.

KILL THE COP KILLER.
JUMP INTO HELL, FROG.
ONE LESS PIECE OF CRAP IN THE WORLD.

The police officers sweated and looked uncomfortable. "Darl, I cannot let you do this," William Leyland said, as I started walking toward the throng and the cameras. Phoenix's security coordinator sounded fierce, which was hard for William to do with his musical Caribbean accent. He laid a burly, mocha-colored hand on my arm. "Come, now, Darl. You *cannot* do this. It's irresponsible. I have cars waiting and the others are already in them. We have to go. Speaking to these protesters will do no good."

"It will do *me* good." I pushed his hand away and strode forward. The cameramen turned their lights on me about the same moment the crowd realized I was Frog's lawyer. The anti-death penalty group applauded. The rest surged forward with glittering eyes.

"I hope you got to see your murderin' retard  die, bitch," a woman yelled. One of the anti-death penalty protestors shoved her, and the police broke them up. William rushed after me and tried to block more contact. "This could cause a riot," he said under his breath. "Please stop."

"I can't." I stepped to the edge of the barricade. I still clenched Frog's plastic heart in one hand. With my other hand I pulled a folded slip of paper from the side pocket of my wrinkled jacket. "I want to read you-all something. It's from a social worker's report about Frog Marvin and his brother. It was written in 1979, when Frog was about twelve and Tom was fifteen." I cleared my throat then read loudly, and slowly, "Frog shows severe fear and is covered in bruises. Often goes to neighbors' house in hysterics, begging them to hide him from 'monsters.' Boys' alcoholic uncle is only adult in the home. Neighbors report beatings of both boys and beatings of Frog by Tom. Tom broke Frog's jaw and arm last year. Tom has killed or tortured animals in front of Frog. Doctor's exam shows signs of sexual abuse in Frog." I stopped. "Frog Marvin grew up in a chamber of horrors. Nobody cared enough then to stop it, and nobody cares enough now. *We're* the monsters in Frog Marvin's world."

I saw a few chagrinned and queasy looks around me, but many belligerant ones. A small, fleshy man bulled his way to the front of the crowd. "Lady, it's whiny liberals like you that let scumbags like him run free. I don't care how the stupid bastard grew up. I don't care if he was too scared of his brother to get away. I don't care if he only had half the sense of a goddamned rock, all right? He killed two cops and he deserved to die." He snatched the paper and the toy heart from my hands and held both high. "What kind of shit is this? Liberal excuses," he yelled.

"Shutup, you ignorant redneck asshole," someone from the anti-death penalty group called out. That crowd began shoving forward. There were shouts and screams. People began grappling with each other. The camera crews turned their white-hot lights and lenses on the brawl. I leaned over the barricade, snagged the front of the man's shirt, and reached up for Frog's gift and the paperwork. The man tore the paper into pieces then dropped the plastic heart on the ground and stomped it beneath his shoe. "Take that to court," he said with a smirk.

An unknown fist flashed by me and slammed into his mouth. The fist didn't belong to William, who was urgently trying to push me aside. The punched man staggered back and was engulfed by the shouting, shoving crowd. By then the melee had begun to push the barricade over, guards and police were invading the pack and prying people apart, and I was almost knocked down. "Get her out of here," William yelled to the person who had punched my tormentor. A strong arm curved around my waist. My feet left the ground.

I struggled and gasped as the unseen rescuer pulled me out of the crowd. When he set me down I turned to shove him away. "Let me go, goddammit. I have to get my heart out of there—" My voice halted. I stared up into large, burnt-brown eyes and an angular face topped with dark hair. Something, deep inside me, said *Look at him and remember.* Remember what? I shook my head.

"I'll take care of it," the stranger said in a deep southern accent that went into my bones. "Your heart. I'll take care of it."

William ran up to us. "Go. Go with this fellow. Please."

"Go where?"

"Irene has made plans for you. Please go. This man is an old friend of mine. I'd trust him with my life and you can, too. You can count on him. His name is Solo. No worries, now. Please, go."

"William, I can't—"

"I'm takin' her," the stranger named Solo said abruptly. A rental sedan sat on the opposite side of the two-lane prison entrance. Solo pulled me to the passenger side and jerked open the door.

I clutched the door frame and held on, staring at the fighting, yelling mob I'd provoked, heartsick. Solo put a hand on my shoulder, and the contact made me swivel to look up at him with desperate shame. I had only added to the circus atmosphere around Frog's death. "What have I done?" I asked in a choked voice.

There was a fiercely proud expression in his eyes. "You made 'em look at themselves too hard, and what they saw was ugly. Now get in the car. When it's all over but the shoutin', it's time to back up and breathe."

"I haven't taken a deep breath in years."

"Then let's go get some air."

He gently pushed me into the car. I nearly suffocated on my own shame, and put my face in my hands.

\*

Solo had a small plane waiting near the prison. Judging by its weathered paint job and scuffed interior, it was used to hard action. My luggage was already stacked in the passenger seats when he opened the hatch. I climbed in next to him in the cockpit, then stared blindly out as the world slipped by below us. Within an hour the vast Gulf of Mexico begin to glimmer to our west.

St. George Island curls like a sandy eyebrow along Appalachicola Bay, on the waters of the Gulf, looking toward the Caribbean and Mexico. People call that part of Florida the Forgotten Coast. Since it's in the curve below the state's panhandle, less kindly souls call it the armpit. Far from the interstates, it sports only quaint old fishing towns, oyster bars, and wide, uncrowded beaches fronting dunes and vacation houses perched on concrete pilings.

Irene Branshaw, the retired federal courts judge who headed the Phoenix Group, had decreed that I go to a house she owned there. I was being gently kidnapped, and this new security consultant of William's—Solo—had been assigned the unenviable job. I didn't want to know more about him, not even his full name. I wanted to exist in a vacuum where my responsibilities began and ended with myself.

Fat thunderheads piled up on the horizon. Wind gusts buffeted the plane. Solo manuevered the controls calmly, but his expression was intense. The day grew from dawn into a burning sun, behind us. I was running from the heat of Hell, and taking this stranger with me.

Neither of us spoke. I sat with my hands unfurled and laying palm up on the coffee-stained skirt of my suit, my head back on the seatrest, my mind blank. He said something under his breath as he watched the control panel.

I lifted my head. "Is something wrong?"

"No. I was just calculating my fuel weight in relation to airspeed."

"Are we running out of gas?"

"No. It's just a hobby of mine. Counting, calculating." He hesitated. "Breathe," he ordered gently.

I nodded, put my head back again, and shut my eyes. I could count on him, William had said. So maybe he was good with numbers.

*Good with numbers.* Somehow, reassuring.

I slept despite myself.

Frog died again, in my dreams.

*

Solo and I landed at a tiny airstrip among pine forest on the island's western end. Irene kept an old Jeep there. Solo piled my luggage in the back along with a battered leather tote of his own. I stared at his tote and tried to form an opinion, which was difficult. I hadn't eaten much in two days, and the heat plus an empty stomach made me see firefly stars. "Thank you, but I intend to go on alone from this point," I said, leaning against the Jeep, sweating in my business suit.

He studied me carefully, turning a dog-earred ace of hearts in his fingers as he did. "The odds are against your plan." As if proving his prediction right, my knees buckled and I clutched the Jeep's side. Solo picked me up and set me in the Jeep's passenger seat. "Relax," he ordered. "I won't get in your way."

I sat there in dizzy, nauseated silence as he drove the main road that ran the length of the island. We passed through a sandy community of restaurants and tourist shops then entered more pine forest. He turned in at a lane that disappeared through the pines. When the lane left the woods we drove among sandy hummocks covered in sea oats. The vast expanse of the Gulf waters spread before us. He stopped the Jeep in a yard behind a multi-level, pearl gray house with a tiled roof the color of coral. The house sat on a dozen pilings, at least fifteen feet above the parking area underneath. Beyond the house, low dunes and blue sky filled with dramatic white clouds framed the ocean.

I made sure I got inside without his help—climbing the long flight of stairs from the parking area methodically, as my head whirled. "Thank you but I'll get my own luggage, later," I said, but he brought it up anyway. The house was decorated in handsome pale furniture and deep coral couches. On the front of the main level, a long deck stairstepped down to the dunes. Irene had made certain the kitchen was stocked. I took a bottle of water from the refrigerator, shrugged my business jacket onto a chair, pulled a notepad and a pen from the suitcases Solo propped inside the door of the master bedroom, then walked outside unsteadily.

A pair of cushioned lounge chairs waited under a long, coral-roofed gazebo facing the ocean. It took all my willpower to make the short trek to one of the chairs. I sat down in the gazebo's breezy shade, slid my stockinged feet out of my pumps, and quickly drank a gulp of the water, enough to revive me. Then I bent my head over the pad and began doggedly scrawling notes about Frog's case. I had phone calls to make, statements to be written, no time for rest or grieving.

"I'm not here to judge," Solo said behind me, "but whatever you're doing can wait until you feel better. I'll fix you some food."

"No, thanks. You can leave, now. I'll call William and tell him I don't need you. I appreciate everything you've done but I'm fine. I have work to do. I have to think."

Silence. It lengthened into the slow rush of waves on the beach and the cries of gulls. Finally he said, "I guess you didn't notice the house."

"It's a fine house. No problem."

He came around in front of me, a tall, lean man with big shoulders, moving gracefully. He was dressed in soft khakis and a light shirt with the sleeves rolled up. He seemed to be the kind of man who dressed as an afterthought, and wore his clothes as practical coverings, not a fashion statement. On a better day I would have noticed much more about him. "Yes?" I said.

"Well, let me fill you in," he said patiently. "There must have been a helluva storm last night. There were tree limbs all over the runway and the main road, and the house is missing some shingles and a couple of pieces of siding. The electricity's off—that water you're drinking is probably tepid—and there are two good-sized pine trees laying against the far side of the roof." He paused, scowling. "But what worries me the most is that the alarm system is out. And the battery back-up didn't even kick in."

I raised my head slowly. Everything was a dull, vaguely curious blur. I hadn't noticed anything he'd described. "Can you fix any of it?"

He dropped to his heels at the end of my lawn chair. His eyes were all I could keep in focus. Large, dark, so familiar. I pushed the strange thought away. "I can fix everything," he said. "Except you." When I stared at him he frowned and rose to his feet. "All right, I'm not real good with words. I'll get to work. But I'm not leaving you here alone. I'll take an upstairs bedroom."

"We'll talk about this arrangement later." I went back to my notepad with dogged concentration, forcing my fingers to write. I intended to list every legal move I'd made on Frog's behalf, starting with the day I'd taken over his case five years earlier. Every move, and every mistake. I'd analyze it all endlessly, until I knew exactly where I'd failed him.

Mr. Solo, whoever he was, left me alone, or at least let me think I was.

*

I woke sometime that night, still wearing my business clothes, still on the lounge chair. The muggy ocean breeze made my skin feel salty. Dozens of crumpled sheets of paper lay around me. My day's attempt at logical thought had scattered in the night wind at the edge of the continent, looking like strange little dust balls on the weathered deck. A half-moon sent pale light beneath the gazebo. My head throbbed. I felt weak and disoriented. When I sat up my glance fell on a low table that had appeared beside my chair. A tray of fruit, cheese, and bottled water sat there. Solo's work, while I slept.

I put a shaking hand on an apple, brought it to my mouth, and bit in. Suddenly I was starving and I ate everything on the tray, stuffing food into my mouth, then gulping down the water. When I finished I abruptly bowed my head on one arm atop the table edge. Everything from the past day rushed over me again. Everything from the past twenty-five years, too.

My life made no sense, and there was no resolution for the ghosts and the guilt that haunted me. I'd left Burnt Stand the day I turned eighteen. I put everything I could fit into a small car I'd bought with my savings, and drove a few hours' south, into Georgia. When I reached the sprawling skyscrapers and green suburbs of Atlanta I stayed in a cheap motel room and took a job waitressing at a midtown diner called The Peanut Room, where photographs of former President Carter lined the walls. I applied at Emory University for the pre-law program.

Swan ordered me to come back, then reasoned with me, then offered a few dignified bribes, but when nothing else worked, she cut me off without a penny. I know my decision to escape from her broke her heart—I had come to understand that the rules she enforced were as painful for her as for me. She only understood one way to preserve the tenuous Hardigree reputation she'd fought so hard to build. By sheer, stubborn domination. So I fought back in like kind.

I got into law school with a student loan, working two jobs to support myself. I lived on friends' couches or in their spare bedrooms for the next five years, but by god, when I finished no one owned me and my guilt-riddled memories but myself. I turned down a bevy of prestige job offers from law firms and went to work as a public defender in the Atlanta courts. The money I made for the next few years was just enough to rent a cheap apartment and cover basic necessities, but I didn't mind. I was an obsessive worker, a martyr to a cause, a loner. The occasional man who crossed my bedroom door couldn't compete with my entrenched and often maniacal devotion to my calling. I intended to save every innocent person on the face of the earth. No other Jasper Wade would die on my watch. As for my guiltier clients—and most of my clients *were* guilty—they were all Great Aunt Clara to me, deserving due process and a fair trial, at least. A few years later, when Irene Branshaw contacted me about working for the Phoenix group, I knew I'd found the perfect channel for my constant, torturing need to redeem myself.

Until I failed Frog Marvin.

"I can't go on this way," I whispered to the island's night wind. I got up, staggering, and looked through the moonlight at the beach and the ocean. Some dark urge said, *Just walk in and don't look back.* I didn't know what to do with that godawful thought, and it made me frantic. I didn't want to die, but I didn't know how to live, either. I turned blindly, raising my hands to my tangled hair, holding the sides of my head as if my brain might explode. My gaze fell on the other lounge chair, a dozen feet or so from mine.

I halted, staring. In a bright ray of moonlight I saw my temporary housemate stretched out, sound asleep, on the long, low chair. *Solo.* I went over to him and stood, frowning down at his pleasant, rugged face and athletic body. Now dressed in a t-shirt and faded jeans, his face at rest, he looked vulnerable. He slept on his back with his thick forearms looped over his chest and his large, knobby bare feet crossed at the ankles—a very guarded way to rest. He'd burrowed his head against a matted throw pillow that matched the lounge's paisley cushions. His dark hair was tossled in stark contrast against the feminine background.

I stared dully at the closed laptop computer that sat on the deck below his chair, along with an empty mug and an insulated coffee pot. He'd obviously tried to keep himself awake as long as possible. A few feet away a bizarre, anonymous thing glinted on the deck like a metal spider in the moonlight. The gadget was no more than a foot tall. Some kind of intricate robotic toy.

Bewildered, I turned and walked back to my chair. The ocean gleamed and rumbled ahead of me. A night filled with pinpoint white stars spread over it. The dunes stood out as white tops and deep shadows. As I watched, small, pale crabs scurried across the sand. I squared my shoulders. I'd walk in the surf. I'd confront the ocean. I'd confront every burden in my lopsided life, and try to make some sense of them. *And maybe you'll decide to take that long walk into the water*, an inner voice whispered.

My hands shook. I spent a moment lifting my wrinkled blue skirt and pulling my pantyhose down, then shoved the hosiery aside. Barefoot, I headed to the end of the deck and started down a short set of wooden stairs. Suddenly, the robotic 'toy' emitted a pulsing, high-pitched shriek. I whirled around. The thing clattered toward me like a metal crab.

Solo was out of the chair and standing within two seconds. The robot kept scurrying my way and shrieking. Solo swept the moonlit deck with a quick, predatory arc of his head. When he spotted me he relaxed visibly and pulled some kind of remote control from his jeans' pocket. With a press of his thumb, the robot quieted. "Sorry," he said. "It's a gizmo I built. A gimmick with motion sensors. But it works." He walked toward me. "Are you all right? What do you need? Takin' a moonlit stroll? Good. I'll come along behind you. Don't pay me any attention. I'll just follow."

I stared at the robot. "Goddamn that thing." I was shaking.

"I figured you might wake up and take a walk or a swim. I

thought I ought to know. It's a mighty big ocean."

Did he suspect I needed protection from myself? I managed, on weak knees, to climb back up the steps and walk toward him. I suddenly felt foolish, exposed—and terribly depressed. I halted an arm's length from him. "I'm tired, but I don't need an escort. I'm only going for a walk."

He studied me closely. "Let me tell you something. I know all about your work for Phoenix. I know how hard you tried to save Frog Marvin. I've seen what kind of person you are, and I've got a pretty good idea what you must be thinking right now." He paused. "And I'm not gonna leave you alone with those thoughts."

My skin became a tourniquet. I could feel the blood draining from my face and a spring of relieved grief gushing inside me. *How do you know me that well?* His homey language, his deep drawl, his face. His face. Those dark eyes. "You're right about some of it," I whispered. "But what happened was my fault, and I can't forget that."

Solo gave me a long searching look, myriad emotions passing through his shadowed face, the intensity burning me. I could have sworn I saw tears in his eyes. No. Another trick of the moon. He reached out a hand as if to touch my arm, then stopped himself. He dropped his hand to his side. "He'd want you to be happy. He'd want you to believe you did all you could for him. I guarantee it."

The timbre of his deep, sincere voice vibrated through me, unhinging my common sense. "You may know me, but I don't know much about you."

"I know this much: I'm not letting you take any walks alone." He paused. "If you try, I'm not above wrestling you inside and locking you in your bedroom."

My skin turned cold. I stared at him in disbelief, then realized he was completely serious. He'd threatened me. "Tomorrow, I'm leaving," I said. "And you won't stop me." I walked angrily inside the house. After I entered the master bedroom I heard him follow me indoors. He moved around the spacious, peach-and-coral Florida kitchen, opening and closing the whitewashed cabinets, then I heard him walk carefully across the white-carpeted living-room floor, as if trying to be quiet. Then, silence. No sound of him climbing the stairs to the other bedrooms.

I opened my door a sliver and looked out. He'd lain down on a couch. The electronic tracking device sat in the middle of the room. I shut the door, paced unsteadily for a few minutes, then sat down on the master bed's pearl-gray coverlet, shivering, furious. I lay back, knotting the cloth in my hands, suffocating on my own dilemmas.

Within five seconds I fell asleep.

*

*Tell her. Tell her who you are.* The thought drummed like an accusing chant in Eli's mind as he swam in the warm Gulf waters early the next morning. Each powerful stroke of his arms plowed the order deeper into his conscience. Tell her. Tell her the truth today.

*It's me. Eli. Whatever questions haunt you, they haunt me too. I have to go back to Burnt Stand and find the answers for us both.*

He prayed when he told who he was and what he wanted she'd remember some spark of the quick bond they'd formed as children. He prayed she wouldn't look at him and think only of what Pa probably had done to her great aunt. He prayed she wouldn't look at him and see a murderer's grown son.

Eli butterflied himself across a shallow wave then headed for shore. *I'll tell her as soon as I get back to the house. When she wakes up, I'll be waiting to talk to her.* He levered himself upright in the surf, found his footing, and scrubbed stinging saltwater from his face and hair, as tides of white foam and blue-green water played around his hips. He loved the ocean, loved the feel of something so endless and challenging it could only be an abstract joy, never summed up in manmade terms. It made him feel clean. Eli inhaled the rich air deeply—his eyes shut, his head back—then slung rivulets of water from his fingertips. He rimmed his thumbs beneath the loosely tied waistband of his black swim trunks, which had settled several inches below his navel. As he pulled the errant trunks higher on his lean hips, he opened his eyes.

Darl stood on a knoll of white sand not a dozen yards away, watching him.

She had gotten out of the house and gone to the ocean without him or his robotic gadget knowing. God, what a piece of work she was. The soft wind caused drying strands of her mink-brown hair to dance around her amazing face, curtaining her intense blue eyes, then revealing them. She never flinched from a somber study of him, even as he looked back the same way. A damp white nightshirt clung to her body and thighs, but her modesty saved little. Through the wet cotton he glimpsed a low-cut black bra and bikini panties. The silhouette of her high-breasted body and her strong stance on the dune, with the wind carrying her hair in front of her face, was a picture that would last in his mind forever. Aroused and helplessly miserable, he knew then that she was still his beloved Darl, grown and beautiful, dignified but damaged, dragging the weight of her childhood behind her just as he dragged his.

"I escaped," she called grimly. Then she stepped down the small dune and walked towards him, halting at the edge of the surf. She tugged her nightshirt away from her body, but the wind pressed the material to her, again. A slight flush in her face said she might feel uncomfortable, but her eyes, underscored by dark crescents of fatigue, bored into him. "I climbed over my balcony," she explained in a matter-of-fact way. "I just had to go out by myself this morning."..

Eli looked at her in speechless wonder. *Tell her who you are. Tell her now.* He stayed in the cool, hip-deep water, waiting for his physical reaction to ease. "When you were a little girl," he began carefully, "you always found ways to buck the system."

She went very still. "That's an odd thing to assume."

"But true."

Slowly, she nodded. "You're good at analyzing people. Or you've made it your business to research me as much as possible."

"You're not business to me. And you're not a stranger. I don't know any way to say this except to just—"

She held up a hand. "It's all right. I know what you mean. Yesterday you became a good friend to me." Her troubled eyes warmed with a sorrow and regret that left Eli speechless. "I want to thank you for everything. I want to thank you for not letting me walk out here alone last night. I was. . . exhausted, and confused. I scared myself last night. I don't know what I want to do next— I can't say I'm at peace with Frog Marvin's death, or happy with my work on his behalf. I have to study every angle of the situation. I have to think. I only know this much: I do need to be here, away from everything and everyone who wants to tell me how to feel right now. I just need to *exist* for a day or two. No past, no future. Just be." She smiled thinly. "And that, Mr. Solo, is my metaphysical thought for the day. Do you mind just 'being' with me?"

The weight of the situation settled on Eli. "Not at all," he said finally. "I'll make sure nothing and nobody bothers you while you're here. I swear."

The fervor of that remark raised a deeper blush in her cheeks and brought back the reserved look in her eyes. Eli silently cursed his choices. He'd learned so much from women—restraint and timing, the protective virtues of mating games. All cynical instincts, lost here on this beach, this morning. Darl smoothed the hair back from her face and gave him a polite nod. "I can see why William sent you with me. You're very comfortable with your sense of honor." She paused. "I envy you."

With that she turned and walked up a path between the dunes, touching her fingertips to tall sea oats that bent their grassy heads to her. Eli could only stand there, troubled and guilty on the edge of the only world they could share easily.

He couldn't tell her yet.

*

I never made the mistake of believing Eli would show up in my life someday. He no longer lived in the United States, and he'd probably never come back. I knew why. Ten years earlier, I'd tracked him down.

It was a bright spring morning in Atlanta, just a few weeks after I started work as a public defender for the district attorney's office. I was 25 years old, a bright-faced obsessive workaholic, fiercely proud of myself. I'd finally gotten my law degree and being able to afford my own small apartment, even though the one-bedroom efficiency crowned a creaky, gothic apartment building off Ponce de Leon, a schizophrenic boulevard where fine old homes shared their address with tattoo parlors, and where some of the city's sleaziest hookers occupied all-night diner stools alongside yuppie engineering students from Georgia Tech.

I looked at the amount in my checkbook that morning as I sipped hot tea at an oak breakfast table I'd scrounged from the vast selections of the Lakewood Flea Market, the city's largest monthly swap meet. Swan had sent me five thousand dollars as a graduation gift—she couldn't resist being proud of me, though she never said so. *You've proved your point*, her accompanying note said. *When you're ready to come home, Hardigree Marble can use your expertise in law.*

I intended to donate all of my grandmother's gift to charity, but then decided at least a portion of it had an equally appropriate use. I would give myself a graduation gift Swan certainly wouldn't like. I'd settle a question that had tormented me for years.

I picked up the phone and called a private investigator I'd met while interning with one of Atlanta's more notorious criminal defense attorneys. If you wanted someone found, even someone who didn't want to be found, this guy was the private dick of choice. "I want to find a young man named Eli Wade," I told him. I explained how little I knew about Eli's vital statistics: His age—he would be 28 years old then. His birthday—I remembered the date distinctly, because I'd marked it on my calendar as a child and always gave him presents. I knew his parents' names, and Bell's, of course. "He might be living in Tennessee," I told the investigator. "That's a long shot, but it's where he was born. I don't know where he and his family went after they left Burnt Stand, North Carolina, but I heard they buried Eli's father near Nashville."

That was very little to go on, the investigator told me. But he also said Eli's birthdate was a good detail for searching government records, and he'd see what he could do. I hung up the phone and stared out the tiny window over my sink. The grime of the city clung to a stately, blossom-covered dogwood tree begging for space against a cracked sidewalk. Across my shady residential street a battered yellow van sported a Confederate flag and a marijuana leaf emblem. God save Dixie, and pass the doobie. I felt like the dogwood, very alone in a world without much charm.

Three weeks later, my hired hunter called me over my breakfast tea with the news. "Eli Wade wasn't that hard to find," he said. "He's wanted by the Feds."

I clutched the phone. "Why?"

"He's a partner in an off-shore gambling business down in the Caribbean. He's been living there the past five years." I went very quiet. The investigator clucked his tongue. "Hey, it's not so bad. He's a young guy makin' a fortune off sports junkies. You get it? He's a high-priced bookie for Americans posting sports bets."

My heart sank. "He's a professional gambler?"

"Yeah. And a great one. High tech. Computerized. It's just too bad he'll be in deep trouble if he ever sets foot in the States again. Eli Wade is a man without a country."

"What about his mother and sister?"

"Living the life of luxury, looks like. He takes care of 'em real good."

"They live with him in the islands?"

"Yep. Mom's doing a lot of volunteer work with some church missionaries down there. Little Sister piddles around public relations for one of the big hotels. Your Eli keeps 'em way away from his line of work. They got a nice house, nice things." He paused. "You know, I wouldn't worry about this guy if I were you. Nobody can touch him down there. He's makin' big money, he lives a quiet life, he's doin' okay. He's a criminal, but only if he comes back here." He waited patiently as my choked silence filled the phone. Finally he said, "Look, Darl, you're a classy kid. I need to know what kind of info you're after, and what you don't want to hear."

"Tell me the rest." I felt sick.

"Well, if you're checking him out because he's an old boyfriend and you still got a thing for him, you oughta forget him. I mean, he's definitely got women down there. A girlfriend who runs a scuba business. Another one who's his bookkeeper. He's not lonely, and he's not mopin' around waitin' for you to show up, kid."

Of course I shouldn't have felt surprised, disappointed, or

betrayed. I was only ten years old when Eli left Burnt Stand. I was no dewy virgin now myself, and I'd attempted a couple of serious relationships during college. Still, the news about Eli added up to a strange mixture of victory and defeat. He'd survived and prospered, if not with honor. He was happy—happy to forget me and the three years his family had lived in Burnt Stand . . .

I'd always harbored the idea that I'd find him some day, go to him, and tell him the truth about Clara's murder. He deserved justice for his father. Hell, he deserved revenge. If it had just been about me I'd have let him do whatever he wanted to punish me, but I had Swan to think about, and Matilda—and Karen, because her grandmother's involvement in Clara's death was the one shock Karen had been spared when we were children. Karen had withdrawn from Matilda and from me after that year. When she was old enough she'd deserted Burnt Stand, just as I had. We hadn't spoken in years.

I put my head in my hands that morning and debated what to do. My family was in shambles. Eli had become a rich criminal. I suppose as an honorable lawyer I had a duty to save the world from unregulated betting on Knicks games, but I didn't.

I just cried in my tea, and tried to forget him.

## 12

I opened a pair of efficient gray suitcases and stared at only business clothes. When I'd packed for Florida the week before I'd been convinced I'd win Frog a last-minute reprieve and return to Washington quickly. My choice of casual wear came down to a wrinkled sleeveless white-linen shift, a pair of cargo shorts, and another white nightshirt. I showered, then donned the loose shift, wound my hair back in a damp braid, and put on narrow black sunglasses.

A hard tapping sound suddenly sounded above me. I shaded my eyes from hot sunshine pouring through the bedroom's sliding doors, which went to a private balcony. I tugged the doors open. The rumbling song of the surf poured in, along with a gust of briny air. I padded barefoot onto my balcony, and gazed upwards. Solo sat atop a folding ladder on the deck above me. He was nailing a section of windblown siding back into place.

The deepest blue sky I'd ever seen silhouetted him. He wore baggy, knee-length shorts, his bare feet were smeared with sand, and he'd slung his shirt over the ladder's utility shelf. As I had seen at the beach, his bare back was muscled, his chest was broad, and his skin was deeply tanned. A fine vee of dark hair trailed down his stomach. He clamped a row of small nails between his lips with intense concentration. Yet he sat with his long legs and knobby, handsomely ugly feet curled around the ladder's metal stanchions in an almost boyish posture that was very appealing. As I watched, he raised a hammer. Sinews flexed in his forearm, and he drove a nail into the siding with a single, expert stroke.

*We like our men rough and hard,* Clara had hissed at me that day by the pool. There was a part of me that always worried—irrationally, but still—that some genetic weakness really did doom Hardigree women to be either promiscuous or emasculating, or both. I held myself back from men, and intimacy, for me, required a long, thoughtful, restrained path. Yet there I stood, gazing up at

Solo. My skin began to tingle against the fabric of the linen shift. I drew back from the sensations with a rush of discipline as sharp as a steel trap.

"Could you use some help?" I asked.

He pivoted and looked down so quickly I was afraid he'd lose his balance. As it was, he smiled and lost all the nails. They clattered to the floor of the upper deck and several fell between the cracks, landing at my bare feet like hard raindrops. I knelt and began picking them up. "Let 'em go. I've got more," he called.

"Waste not, want not." I gathered the nails as he climbed down from the ladder.

"I bet you keep a little jar in your kitchen, full of leftover nails and paper clips and safety pins."

"Spoken like a man who keeps his own little jar."

"Hmmm. You nailed me on that one." He sat down on the deck, then stretched out near the edge, looking down at me. "Good to see you feelin' better."

I hesitated. "I slept last night."

"Good. Gimme my nails back, you thief."

He reached over the side. I raised the nails in my cupped palm. Solo carefully scooped them up with his blunt fingertips, brushing my palm as he did. We traded a charged look. "You're welcome," I said. Looking troubled, he nodded. I turned and walked back into my bedroom without offering another word.

I sat down on the bed and hugged myself.

*

A courier drove out to the beach house that afternoon, delivering a small box that Solo brought it to me at my bedroom door. Still working on the siding, he was drenched in sweat and smelled of fresh ocean air. He pulled his t-shirt on as he approached me. "It's safe," he said, pointing to the parcel's Washington address. "William told me he'd be sendin' it. I don't want you to open anything yourself."

"I get ordinary hate mail, Mr. Solo. Not letter bombs. And I know what this is. I asked William to overnight it."

He frowned as I attempted to pry open the heavily taped box with my short, plain fingernails. Solo pulled a steel folding knife from his trouser pocket and flicked open a serrated blade wicked enough to make me look at him in startled warning. He clamped a protective hand over mine, drew a fine line across the box lid with the knife's point, and the tape parted. As casually as that, he put the knife away and lifted his hand.

I opened the lid and sank my fingers through bubble wrap. When I lifted out the plastic heart Frog had given me my heart twisted. The toy was cracked and scuffed. A small white bow that had been glued to the top now hung from a frazzled string. I uttered a soft sound. Solo gallantly turned away. "I'll be outside," he said.

"Frog couldn't read." The words burst from me, not making much sense and apropos of nothing. Solo slowly pivoted back. I shook my head. He waited with a stillness that said this meant something to him. "I know," he said.

"Even in prison the other inmates taunted him. Called him stupid and retarded. He wanted to write apologies to the families of the policemen he shot, and I wrote the letters for him. I told him he shouldn't expect any answer, and he understood. Then he asked me to write to his goddamned brother in prison. 'I love you Tommy. I know you didn't mean to tell me to hurt anybody.' But Tommy Marvin never sent a word in return. Nothing. The bastard." I laid the heart back into the box. "Frog was convinced that Tommy didn't write back because he knew Frog couldn't read. 'He doesn't like people to know how dumb I am,' Frog told me. The humiliation hurt him more than anyone can imagine."

"I can imagine," Solo said quietly. "I know exactly what that does to a man." When I looked at him for explanation, he turned and walked outside. I heard him around the house, but I kept to my room, and we didn't see each other the rest of the day.

\*

The next morning Solo swam again, then threw a towel around his shoulders and stood on the beach writing something on a palm-sized computer. I watched him from my balcony, where I'd spread my papers on a small patio table. My head ached. I'd tossed in bed all night, filled with bad dreams, and looking out my door once to confirm that Solo slept on the living room couch again. I felt raw inside. This was the best I do for recuperation. The sun crept under the table umbrella, and I kept adjusting the umbrella for shade. The earth continued to turn. A revelation. I rested my chin on my fists and studied Solo. He glanced at the ocean, then at his handheld device, and wrote with the device's stylus, then looked at the ocean, again. I picked up a phone I'd pulled outside. My cell phone didn't work on the island. I called the Phoenix Group's offices in Washington.

"Where did you find this man?" I asked William. William Leyland was a mystery, himself. His soft Caribbean accent and calm demeanor undoubtedly masked some interesting history. If he had any political or racial issues as a black man, he kept them to himself. He applied the same mask to other people's privacy. All of us at Phoenix considered his opinions on security—and any assistants he hired—unimpeachable.

"Here and there," William said finally.

"I see. Is Solo his real name?"

"I believe it's a nickname. He chooses to go by it at times."

"You can't reveal even a few details from his personnel file? Is he ex-military, a former cop, a retired samurai?"

"Please. Such imagination. He's an absolute gentleman. I can tell you he's never been married, has no children, and owns the plane in which you flew two days ago. I can tell you he's quite the computer expert, and that he designed the software that protects the foundation's office files."

"You mean he wrote our encryption programs?"

"Yes, he created all of Phoenix's security programs and hardware systems. Including the security system at Irene's house there, at St. George."

"And he just moonlights as a personal bodyguard?"

"Not really. He simply wanted to participate firsthand in this instance."

"Why?" Silence. "William," I prodded.

"Because for a long time he has watched your work for the

foundation, and he respects you very much. And the Frog Marvin case was particularly personal to him."

"Why?"

"He comes from poverty. He understands the weak and helpless. I have spoken enough. Please, don't try to analyze him. Just accept him for the purpose he wishes to serve. He wants to make you comfortable, so you can rest."

"I've rested enough. I should catch a flight out of Tallahassee and go back to Washington tomorrow."

"I suggest not. Irene sends word you're not to set foot in the office or return to your apartment. Circumstances are not good, here."

The hair rose on the back of my neck. "What's happened?"

"The media is besieging the office for an interview with you about the melee outside the prison, and the police caught a gentleman spray-painting ignorant slurs on your apartment door." I shut my eyes. I could imagine the words, like those on the placards. He went on in a kind tone, "Another few days and the public interest in Frog Marvin's case will begin to fade. But please stay at the beach, for now."

"I seem to have no choice."

William paused. Then, with a certain grim pleasure, he said, "Sometimes God intends it that way, for one's own benefit."

"God isn't that concerned with any of us." I told him goodbye and laid the phone down, sick at heart.

On the beach, Solo turned and looked at me. He raised his hand. The ocean and sky framed him without making him seem small. He stood on the edge of the land as if he were my only lighthouse.

He suddenly made me glad to see him, and I raised my hand in return.

*

I'd become more of a drinker than I liked to admit, and that afternoon I went to a wet bar that occupied one corner of the house's large living room and poured myself a tall bourbon with a little water and ice. I sank down stiffly on a plush rattan couch, pushed aside a collection of coral that decorated a huge glass coffee table, and set out my laptop computer. But after two deep swallows of bourbon I slumped with my head in my hands and began to mourn for the spartan confines of my aging intown apartment, where comfort was an old recliner and books filled every available space. I kept picturing someone writing words on my door, the spray can hissing out *You Bitch* or *Go Fuck Frog in Hell*.

"Getting' good and plastered?" Solo asked. I straightened quickly. He stood in the open door to the deck, sweaty and bare-chested, a tool belt dangling from one hand. He dropped the belt, swiped at his torso with a white t-shirt, then raised his arms and pulled the shirt on. The erotic arch of his chest and belly seemed casual and unselfconscious, which made it even more appealing. I looked away as his head emerged from the shirt's neck. "Is the house back in order?"

"It'll do. Electricity's back on."

I rattled my glass. "I know. I have ice."

"Eaten anything today?"

I rattled the glass again. "Ice."

"All right. I'll fry up some whale blubber, and we'll play Eskimo. Be right back." He pointed at the stairs then disappeared up them two at a time. A few minutes later he descended. He was freshly washed, his dark hair wisping in damp waves as it dried. He'd donned light trousers and a blue dress shirt with the tail out, and was barefooted. Frowning, he walked over without invitation and sat on the couch beside me. His heat and clean-soap scent invaded my lightly cologned air. He glanced at a utilitarian steel wristwatch he wore, then reached for a remote control. "Time for your daily soap opera." He punched a button. Across the room a large television clicked on. He changed the channels until the opening credits of a show called *Attractions* filled the screen. "I hear you got a hometown friend on the show."

I stared at him. "I suppose that's something William told you about me."

"Hush. There she is."

A lithe and beautiful young woman in a jeweled evening gown appeared on the screen. Her slender, honey-colored hands gestured gracefully as she spoke to a black, heartthrob-handsome actor in a tuxedo. Her honey-skinned face—very much like mine in its features—was elegantly composed yet dramatically angry. Her hazel eyes gleamed sharply beneath exquisite black lashes. She wore her thick black hair in a combination of cornrows and silky extensions that trailed to her breasts.

This aloof, exotic, stunning creature was Karen. The world knew her now as   Kare Noland.

"Kare Noland does a helluva job playin' a cool cat like Cassandra," Solo said.

I looked at him a long strange time, sorting my options. "You watch this show regularly?" He nodded. I faced the television, took another swallow of bourbon, and decided to talk. "I call her Karen. She's my cousin."

News of my mixed-race family didn't seem to phase him. "You see her much now?"

"No. She left home about the same time I did—seventeen, eighteen— went into acting, didn't want any of the old ties. She told me we had nothing in common." I paused. "She said she'd decided to be black." I exhaled a long breath of bourbon-scented air and got up from the couch, then cast a frowning look down at Solo, who was studying me quietly. "And that, Mr. Solo, is the longest conversation I've ever had on the subject, with anyone. You have amazing powers."

"I'm a good listener. What you say to me, stays with me. I think you know that."

"I know you like to collect information. Numbers, facts, details."

"I like order. Trying to make sense out of things the only way I know how."

"I'm betting you already know that someone vandalized the door of my apartment in Washington."

He nodded. "Look, give it a couple more days and people won't remember Frog Marvin or why you fought for his life. The bastards'll move on to a new fight to pick. You'll be left alone."

He was right, unfortunately. No one really cared in a world where death, destruction and injustice could be reduced to an entertaining melee with the help of the media. But when you had been there first hand, outside the lights, inside the misery and suffering of another human being, the caring punched you in the stomach every day. I put a hand over mine and fought nausea. Solo took one look at my stricken face and said quickly, "That doesn't mean none of what you did was important."

"Was it? Did Frog's life or death mean anything, solve anything, change anything? Did I help in any way to make things better in his world or the world in general? No. He's dead, and I can't change that." I bent and snatched the remote control, then jabbed it at Karen's image on the television. "And there's someone I love, but I can't help her, either. And that's just the tip of my personal iceberg, Mr. Solo. I fail the people who depend on me and I can't seem to make a difference to the people I love." I snapped the television off and threw the remote on the couch.

Solo got up, stepped around the coffee table and took me by the shoulders. I froze at the personal contact. His angular face and dark eyes were serious, almost angry. "If I knew how to forget the dead and hold onto the living, I'd tell you the secret to it. I saw you on TV last week, too. I heard what you said—that watching death isn't the hard part. That living with it is. You were right."

"You've lost people you loved?"

"Oh, yeah."

"How did you get over it?"

"I'm not sure I ever have or ever will."

He let go of me, then walked to the big glass doors that filled the back of the house and stood looking out at the ocean with his hands on his hips and his shoulders slumped. I followed him. "Tell me what happened. Please." We stood together, looking out at the endless water.

"I saw my father die."

The floor seemed to tilt beneath my feet. No wonder this man made me think of Eli. "How?" I asked gently.

"In a . . . fight." It was clear he measured every word, and didn't like to let go of any. He turned and studied my reaction as he spoke. "Maybe he deserved it, but it wasn't fair."

"You blame him for his own death?"

"I guess I do. Not much of a son, am I?"

"I expect you were a very good son. These things get complicated. It's easy to spend the rest of your life trying to understand."

"I don't know that I ever will, like you said. I'm always looking for answers I'll never get. The rest of my family never really recovered from it. I've made it my business to take care of 'em and let 'em believe what they need to believe."

"That he didn't deserve it?"

"Yeah."

"But you really think he brought the trouble on himself?"

"I don't know. Probably. Either way, there's always a part of him—and me—I can't find. Out there." He gestured toward the ocean, the world. "He took it, and he didn't leave the answers."

"You hate him but you love him."

"Yeah. And that's hard."

I nodded, my brain on fire as I searched for discreet ways to describe my relationship with Swan, and Clara's death, and its effect. Solo was the first person I'd ever found who might understand. "Someone was . . . murdered in my family."

He went very still, searching my face. "Who?"

"A close relative. I can't . . . it's hard for me to talk about, even now. I was a child when it happened. I felt I was responsible for the chain of events that led to it. If I'd only done or said one thing differently." I lowered my gaze, defeated. "The same thing I've been thinking since Frog was executed."

"But you were just a kid."

I lifted my head and stared at him. "Even children know right from wrong. And I was a very odd, very old-minded child. I knew what was right, and what was wrong, and what I should have done.".

"Did they find the killer?" He spoke in a low voice, as I did. As if we were holding the lid shut on a seething Pandora's Box of memories still capable of destruction.

"The man who was accused of the murder," I said carefully, "didn't get much of a trial."

He stepped closer to me, scouring my face. "But you were sure he did it?"

I clamped down on my tongue, then felt the cool numbness of control come over me. It frightened me sometimes, how I could go stone-cold, giving away no shred of emotion, just like Swan. I stepped back from him. "Let's just say the system didn't work very well—for either side—and I learned early on that it's easier to accuse someone than to prove his innocence. That's why I became a defense attorney, instead of a prosecutor. I need the challenge of proving my innocence."

He tilted his head. "*Your* innocence?"

"I mean the accused's innocence." I turned, deeply agitated, and faced the window. His gaze continued to bore into me. *Redemption.* I was looking to this irresistible stranger for redemption. He was becoming a stand-in for the one person whose forgiveness I needed desperately. *Eli.* I abruptly turned away, glancing over the tiled floor until I found the leather sandals I'd left near one of the room's couches. I shoved my feet into them. "We need a change of scenery."

Solo calmly slid his feet into old loafers he'd left near the doors to the lower deck. "I noticed a beach bar on the drive here. I'll buy you dinner. We'll watch the sunset."

"Good. Let's not talk, anymore."

Either unoffended or unapologetic, he merely shook his head.

\*

We sat on the sand beyond the deck of a beachside tavern, watching a purple-and-gold sunset over the ocean's western horizon. Dusk sifted into the air. Oldies poured from speakers mounted on driftwood posts. Solo had polished off two imported beers. I drank only a bottled water, fearing I'd lose control all together. I sat defensively, with my arms wrapped around my knees. The ocean breeze ruffled my hair and swept moisture from my skin. Beside me, Solo leaned back on his elbows, with his long legs stretched in front of him. A tiny ghost crab skittered over his bare ankle and perched for a moment on the tongue of his loafer before darting away. Solo watched it with his eyes half-shut, and I watched Solo. "Nothing rattles you," I said.

"Plenty rattles me," he corrected.

"I watched you from my balcony this morning, when you walked to the beach. What were you making notes about?"

He turned his half-shuttered gaze on me. "I was calculating wave volume and velocity. Guessin' at the ratio of waves per minute, per hour, per millenium. It was just a game. I solve math puzzles to relax." He gave me a droll look. "Go ahead and laugh. Go ahead and say it. *I was countin' water.*"

I unfurled my arms and swiveled to look at him closely, shaken by every surprising charm of him and the poignant familiarity welling anew inside me. I remembered his fuel calculations during the flight to the island. I thought of the robot, the computer expertise, the encryption skills—all based on an intricate aptitude for electronics, engineering, and most of all, advanced mathematics. "I used to know someone who loved numbers and calculations the way you do."

Solo uttered a dry laugh. "Kind of an idiot savant, like me? A man of few talents?"

"He was the sweetest person I've ever known. He happened to be a math prodigy, as well."

"Hmmm. What did he do with that kind of brain? Become a professor? Engineer? Doctor? What?"

I scooped a bit of sand onto my palm, then watched it drain through my fingers. "No, unfortunately he became a professional gambler and bookie."

Solo sat up. When I looked at him, he hooked his arms around an updrawn knee and faced the ocean. His profile was clean and strong, his expression, troubled. "What's wrong?" I asked.

"Gettin' old and creaky." He hunched his shoulders, then stretched and nodded toward the uneven little hummocks of sand beneath us. "I made my bed and I have to lie in it. But just now I realized how hard it was, all along."

I regarded his odd words with a frown. He clasped his knee again and continued looking away from me, at the ocean. "So this good, sweet man, this genius, he didn't turn out so well?"

"I wouldn't say that. I only know he ended up in the Caribbean running a very lucrative off-shore betting business. I hired an investigator to find him ten years ago, and that's where he was."

"He must have been important, if you looked for him that hard. Old boyfriend?"

I hesitated. "You could say that, yes."

"You never looked him up, again?"

"No. It was an illegal business. He targeted Americans and used domestic phone systems. The same laws are applied to Internet gaming now."

"You couldn't love a man who broke the rules a little?"

"It's not that. It's none of my business. I'm not sure gambling should be against the law. If people want to waste their money, let them."

"But you were disappointed that he didn't turn out respectable."

"I think he did what he had to do to take care of his family. He had a hard childhood. I won't judge him." I looked at Solo quietly. "You said you lost your father and had to take care of your family. Would you tell me more about that?"

The look on his face was both restrained and wishful. He shook his head. "But if I was goin' to tell anybody, it'd be you."

I sat back and considered that for a moment. "You and I seem to sink into dark conversations and stop just short of admitting anything. I'm as bad as you."

We were quiet, after that. The night sky filled with stars. He asked me if I minded whether he smoked a cigar. I told him to go ahead. "I'm compulsive and rigid, but I'm not politically correct," I said.

"Good girl." He pulled a small cigar with an expensive label from a scuffed silver tube in his back pocket. I inhaled the fine aroma of the cigar and watched the smoke curl from his lips. It was such a masculine icon, so simple to ridicule but so appealing. "Do you hunt and fish?" I asked.

He squinted at me. "Do a little fishin'. Don't own a gun."

"Pacifist?"

"No. I've just seen enough killin'." The darkness in that simple statement broke the breath in my throat. I looked at him hard in the faint mist of the salt air. "I do understand," I said.

After a quiet moment, Solo spoke gently. "Don't sit around

thinkin' about how Frog Marvin died. It won't do him any good, and you got a life to live. You got work to do for others like him. They need you. Look, I'm not telling you anything you can't read in the Bible or anywhere else people hunt for reasons on faith. But it is just so."

"Tell me how you do that. How do you live in the valley of the shadow of death without fearing any evil? How to keep from losing everything good about yourself?"

"You keep hoping. You keep trying to make things right."

I smiled wearily. "It's all about the journey, not the destination. I see."

"It's all about the hope," he repeated. "And the love."

I met his eyes. This man had loved, and was loved. I was sure of that. Whether the loving including cadres of adoring women, or a close family, or dear friends, or all of those, he had a mantel of experience I apparently lacked. I thought of Swan and Matilda and Karen. Together we made broken pieces of what a loving family might be. "Stop that," Solo ordered. I looked at him. "Stop that hard thinkin'. You gotta feel, not think." He lifted his hand with the cigar pinched between his thumb and forefinger, and passed the gently drifting smoke over my head in a ceremonial circle. "Smoke carries bad thoughts away. That's an old Cherokee Indian idea."

Now I at least pegged his origins. With that tribal reference and his high-ridge drawl, he had grown up somewhere in the Appalachians. "You're a mountain man," I said.

He nodded. "Hillbilly."

"I wish your ceremonies really worked."

"You don't get it, do you? You gave Frog Marvin hope. And you gave him love. And he died happy. You did what you were put in his life to do."

He carefully placed the remnant of his burned-down cigar back in the silver tube, as methodical as a minister, the calm of his small ritual seeping inside me. I stared at him in desperate wonder. "That's the easy answer."

He shook his head. "Answers are usually easier than we want to think. It's the questions that'll tear a person apart."

I propped my elbows on my updrawn knees and my chin on my hands, and looked up at the stars above the ocean. "Thank you," I managed finally.

A heart-wrenching ballad by The Righteous Brothers began to play over the bar's outside sound system. Solo pivoted to cast a doubtful gaze on several couples who were wound around one another on the deck's small dance floor. "You want to know what rattles me? Dancing."

I sat perfectly still for a few seconds, watching him and watching the couples barely sway to the languid, romantic music. *Don't do it. Don't encourage this.* "I was raised by my very-southern grandmother. She sent me to ballroom dance classes in Asheville, North Carolina, the land of the genteel southern two-step. I'm an expert." I held out a hand. "Would you like to try?"

"I'll trample you."

"I'll take off my shoes if you'll take off yours. Bare feet can't hurt."

"Well, damn. If you insist." With feigned defeat, he took my hand and helped me up.

We slid out of our shoes then faced each other. My heart pounded. He still held my hand, his grip both snug and careful. I put my left hand on his shoulder. "Now, your right hand goes on my waist." He slowly clasped my left side just above the hip, pressing his fingers gently into the sheer white shift. I tucked his left hand, still holding my right one, against his chest, making certain to keep a buffer zone between our bodies. "We needn't be as clingy as the deck crowd."

"You're takin' the fun out of it."

"Humor me."

"Look, I'm just glad to be here."

We stepped slowly to the seductive, throbbing ballad. He did know how to move, regardless of his protest. My hand softened inside his. The slightest flex of his fingers registered on my flesh. I fixed my gaze on the collar of his blue shirt. In the middle of the song a small misstep on the uneven ground brought my bare foot atop one of his. "Hey," he said drily. "I'm not rough trade, lady, so watch your feet."

I couldn't help a quick laugh. He urged me to move closer with a subtle tug of his hand against my side, and I did. His breath brushed my face, and the clean, masculine scent of him filled my senses. He was comfort and sex and danger and faith. I raised my eyes to his as if he were a cathedral. We lost ourselves in looking at each other, hardly moving to the music at all.

\*

As we drove up to the beach house the outside lights automatically activated, filling the parking area beneath the stilted home with glaring light. When we reached a back staircase I hurried up the dimly-lit stairs, quickly reaching a narrow landing, where my feet plowed into a small cardboard box. Solo heard the soft sound of the collision and leapt up the stairs.

"Don't touch it," he ordered, and pulled me behind him. My gaze fell on the  embossed, gold-and-white packaging label of Hardigree Marble Company. My name and the Florida address were written in elegant cursive script. Above the typeset return address for the marble company the same hand had written the initials SHS. Swan Hardigree Samples.

"It's from my grandmother in North Carolina," I said wearily. "I doubt she's sent me a bomb."

Solo picked up the package. A muscle flexed in his jaw as he examined it. "Your grandmother must be worried about you. I guess you've called her by now. Haven't you?"

"We don't talk much. I don't go home very often."

"But you're close."

"We're . . . inseparable, but not close." A shiver went down my spine. As if she'd known I was feeling weak-willed, Swan had intervened. "My grandmother wouldn't have sent me something here if it weren't important. I need to go upstairs and open it."

After another moment spent scrutinizing the package, his expression went completely, carefully neutral. He insisted on carrying the package as we climbed. As if it really might explode.

\*

*My dear Darl,* the enclosed note on Swan's embossed stationary began. *I realize you have no intention of asking for my sympathy or support, but I have been gathering the news about you and do have concerns about your well-being. Having contacted the Phoenix offices in Washington, D.C., I was told by Irene Branshaw that you hope to bring Mr. Marvin's ashes to Burnt Stand for burial. I've taken the liberty of arranging for a place in our own church lot, and I've enclosed a sample of marble for Mr. Marvin's urn and grave plaque. It comes from one of the finest slabs I've ever seen. With your approval, I'll have the carvers begin work right away. You see, I am proud of you, and I do care.*

It had taken twenty-five years of estrangement and another man's execution to wring those words from my grandmother's heart. I sat down on a couch as I pulled bubble wrap away from the heavy square of marble she'd sent. Its glossy, striated surface was the delicate color of a pink tearose.

"Your grandmother sent you a chunk of marble," Solo said flatly, as if the irony in such a gift meant to something to him as well. He leaned against a wall in the shadows near an open sliding door, his hands sunk in his trouser pockets, his shoulders hunched, his expression dark.

"My grandmother is seventy-seven years old but still definitely unbreakable, and she's never given up on the idea that some day I'll come back and take over the family business." I flattened a hand on the cool marble. A strange reaction prickled my skin. Swan had sent a piece of us—who we were—to remind me that stone cracked at its weakest fissure. I stood, hugging the piece of marble in my arms. "I'm going to bed. Good night."

I walked past him without faltering, using all my willpower to glide bonelessly, head up, back straight, face smooth. Swan had built me on her own foundation and all the desperate pride hidden beneath it. I'd learned how to armor myself in thin air, just as she did. I didn't need anyone, including Solo. It was safer that way. As I reached the bedroom door Solo spoke in a gruff voice that stopped me in my tracks. "Sounds like to me your grandmother wants you to think you're made of stone. It's up to you to prove her wrong."

"I can't," I said, and closed my door.

## 13

*Throw that goddamned piece of Hardigree marble out a window before it poisons her. And goddammit, tell her who you are.* Eli swam the next morning with angry fervor, feeling the web of complications closing around him. He'd go back to the beach house right now, dry off, get dressed, brew some coffee, then plan every word before Darl woke up. He'd keep it clean and quick. He knew now that she didn't hate the memory of him, despite Pa's murderous legacy in her family. She'd told him things about himself as he'd never imagined she remembered him. He'd learned what he needed to know. That was all that mattered.

Eli dug his head deeper into the briny ocean water, sweeping his arms in high arcs that cut through the swells out beyond the surf. He couldn't change the accusation against Pa or the possibility that Pa deserved it. No matter what solace Bell craved, they weren't going to answer that question by digging for ghosts in Burnt Stand. But now he knew how Darl might react to the idea of searching, at least. She believed in fair judgements. She would give Pa's innocence a chance.

*She'll give mine a chance, too*, Eli decided.

He swam for the shore. Just as he took his footing on the island's sandy tidal shelf a wave rocked him and something thumped his left arm below the elbow. Even as years of experience swimming in the Caribbean jelled into a single warning thought, he jerked his arm up violently.

He'd been bitten by a small shark, probably a black tip chasing bait fish. The shark had clamped down on him by mistake. Blood gushed from a deep, crescent-shaped gash that circled half the muscle of his upper forearm. Eli lunged to dry land, holding his arm out from his body, dripping blood on the white sand. He stared at the wound, cursing softly when he realized how bad it was, then overcome by a surge of nausea and dizziness.

*Bad luck*, he couldn't help thinking. *Bad timing.*
Truth and opportunities were washed away in bad blood.

*

"You saved my ass, boy," someone bellowed in his ear. It was
a hefty, bald, tobacco-spitting redneck named Jernigan, at the
trucking company job where Eli had just been knocked five feet
by a sliding fork lip as he pushed Jernigan out of the way. Eli
looked down at the broken forefinger on his right hand. The bone
protruded and blood slithered everywhere. It was January, freezing
cold, and steam rose off his blood. His stomach roiled. He was
only fourteen and had lied about his age to get the job. They'd find
out now, someway, and he'd lose the paycheck. Mama's job clerking
groceries didn't pay much. They needed every penny.

Blood, Pa's blood. Failure and shame. He saw it on his hand.
His legs buckled. Jernigan caught him by the collar of his sweat-
stained thermal shirt and blew a gust of fetid silver breath on Eli's
face, as if dusting him off. "Don't pass out on me, boy, you're my
new favorite employee of the fuckin' month." And Jernigan, a big
tough middle-Tennessee bastard of a dock foreman, dragged him
to the company nurse.

Two days later, when Eli came back to work with his finger
splinted and his hand swollen like a fat glove, Jernigan's new liking
for him continued. "Com'here, you tall skinny shit," he ordered
affectionately, and shoved Eli into a dingy storage room near the
main docks. Eli stared at a dirty wooden table and the men around
it. Piles of cards, poker chips, and dollar bills covered the table's
center. "This young gentleman—" Jernigan guffawed—"has a way
with numbers. I don't want him to be a dumb-ass truck loader all
his life. Let's teach the boy a skill."

He slung out a chair, and Eli joined the men at the poker table.
"You got any problem playin' with a colored man?" Jernigan grunted,
pointing a stained finger at a beefy black trucker at the table. Eli
met the trucker's cool, dark eyes. "No sir, I got no problem at all,"
he said to the trucker, not Jernigan. The trucker nodded. "Then
take a drink, white boy." The trucker slid a pint bottle of gin Eli's

way.

Eli sipped the gin and nearly vomited, but managed to keep a blank face. He stared at the cards as another man gathered them, shuffled and reshuffled them, tracked them with grimy thumbs, then tossed them Eli's way. "Learn to shuffle," the man ordered.

Eli manuevered the deck awkwardly with his splinted finger, spilling cards, his face burning with embarrassment, his wounded hand throbbing, but a strange confidence grew in him each time he raked the deck. Fifty two cards, set in precise and logical arrangements, easy to remember. He looked down at them and saw his primitive shuffling efforts had scraped a soft scab on the palm of his hand, and a few dots of blood speckled his chapped winter skin. His head reeled, and he nearly passed out. But he held onto the cards, the future, the soothing count. Pa couldn't ruin this for him.

He was already feeling the numbers in his skin.

*

*Just count the cards. Count them in your head*, Eli told himself to keep from fainting. He stood over the beach house's white kitchen sink, pressing mounds of ice wrapped in paper towels to his arm and trying not to watch his own blood dribbling down the drain. He heard the door of the master bedroom open. Eli leaned heavily on the sink, light-headed and sweating. Blood had spattered on the tail of the striped dress shirt he'd managed to pull on over his wet swim trunks. He pressed his thighs to the sink cabinet. He hated his body's over-reaction to the smell and sight of blood, to the old trauma, but he couldn't control it. He saw Pa dying, every time. He tried to focus on Darl's footsteps crossing the living room. They sounded heavy, but then his senses were distorted.

He hid his bleeding forearm below the rim of the sink as Darl walked up to the kitchen's breakfast bar. She looked severe and elegant in tailored beige trousers and a crisply matching jacket. The Hardigree pendant hung in the center of a soft white top beneath the jacket. She'd wound her luxurious brunette hair up in a twist. Sunglasses covered her eyes. She was in her uniform, her armor.

And she was carrying her suitcases. Eli gripped the sink's edge tightly. Dammit, he'd played these odds all wrong. She was leaving.

She halted, frowning. "Are you sick? Your color is—you have no color."

"Can you get the first aid kit out of the cabinet over the microwave?" Her gaze went to the white tiled floor. She froze. Large splotches of blood trailed all the way across from the sliding glass doors to the deck. "What in the—" She walked around the end of the breakfast bar, saw his arm, and halted.

"I'm fine," he said. "A little shark snapped at me while I was—"

She tossed her sunglasses aside, snatched a clean dishcloth from a hanger and whipped it around his forearm, wrapping it tightly, then grabbed another one from a rack beneath the sink. As she bound the second towel his blood dabbled her hands and smeared the edges of her suit sleeves. The gore had no visible effect on her. He swayed a little, and she steadied him with an arm around his waist. Eli gritted his teeth. "Goddammit. I can't dance, and I nearly pass out at the sight of my own blood."

She glanced up at him, and for just a moment he saw fierce, undeniable affection in the cool landscape of her face. "Two left feet and a weak stomach," she accused. "And you're going to make me miss my plane in Tallahassee."

He calculated his odds and called her bluff.

"Good," he said.

*

"Wife? Girlfriend?" a nurse asked her at the small hospital on the mainland.

"His lawyer," Darl replied without a trace a humor.

Eli's head cleared enough to appreciate that. He'd managed to fill out the emergency room paperwork without Darl discovering his real name. He was glad when she insisted on following him into the cubicle where a doctor put several dozen stitches in his arm. She sat beside him on a metal stool, saying nothing, her eyes trained with hawkish intensity on the doctor's meticulous stitchery.

The chatty young physician told them he was the son of a shrimper and had gone to medical school rather than face a lifetime out in Appalachicola bay, working the nets. He kept glancing at Darl shyly—not an odd thing for any man to do—but her gaze remained riveted to Eli's arm. Abruptly she said to Eli, her voice hollow, "You could have bled to death."

"Not hardly," the young doctor interjected.

She lifted her gaze and lasered the physician. "I disagree. And don't patronize me with vague assurances."

The doctor gaped at her and blushed. Eli suddenly realized her face was pinched and ashen; a fine sheen of sweat covered her forehead. He grabbed her wrist with his free hand and fingered a racing pulse in the soft underside. "The Doc knows what he's sayin'. He's right." Eli craned his head to study her. "You look like a vampire got all your color. First I try to pass out, and now you. If we were wrestlers we could be a tag team."

"You should have called out for me the instant you walked in the house bleeding."

"Look, I may be a sissy, but at least I try not to keel over in front of women. Besides, it's not that bad."

"Yes it is," she said loudly. She leaned away from him, swaying a little. Pink splotches stained her cheeks. A rush of emotion broadsided Eli. *She doesn't deal with blood any better than I do.* Several people craned their heads in the adjacent cubicles. The young doctor stared at Darl and blushed harder. A heavyset nurse in pink scrubs lumbered up. "Got a problem here, lady?" she demanded.

Darl stood. "Yes, we have a problem. And don't stand there like a pink drill sergeant speaking to me in that tone of voice." She jerked her head toward Eli. "This man had to wait twenty minutes before his injury was treated. God knows how much more blood he lost in that time. *So don't stand there in your pink marble outfit and speak to me as if I'm the problem.*"

The nurse gave her a lethal, placid stare. "*Marble?* What're you talkin' about?"

Darl swayed on the last word, clearly realizing how little sense she made. Eli was on his feet by then, the doctor yelping as he leaned after him with the needle held at the end of a long surgical suture attached to Eli's skin. Eli snagged Darl around the shoulders with his good arm. "She apologizes," he told the nurse. "Now leave her alone, please-ma'am."

The nurse stalked away. Eli sat down and pulled Darl back onto the stool next to his. She steepled her hand over her closed eyes and shivered. He was trembling a little, himself. "I'm sorry," she whispered. He tightened his arm around her so fiercely she took a deep breath in self-defense, then gave up and turned her face into his shoulder. The young doctor gaped at them with a look that said a woman so high-strung had better be worth the trouble in bed.

"Let's get this done," Eli said. His tone made the doctor hurry back to his stitching. Eli cupped a hand to the back of Darl's head.

*I understand,* he wanted to tell her. *I know what you remember.*

*

My face tight with humiliation, I stared at the small fishing boats and cabin cruisers of a weathered marina on the bay in Appalachicola. The old fishing town was shabby and scenic, historic and laid-back. There were none of the ubiquitous miniature golf courses or water-ride parks, chain seafood restaurants, behemoth condo developments or souvenir shops that had overtaken most of the Florida coast. Eli nursed a cold beer and watched me like a hawk. We sat side by side at a scarred picnic table on the weathered screened deck of The Wild Oyster, a local restaurant. Around us, tourists and fishermen downed huge luncheon platters of fried seafood or slurped raw oysters doused in cocktail sauce. People cast curious glances our way. We made an odd couple, me in my beige-silk, blood-speckled business suit, him in a blood-spattered dress shirt, swim trunks, and loafers.

"I don't know what came over me at the hospital," I said, still facing forward and refusing to meet his eyes. "I made a fool of myself. I seem to be doing a lot of that, lately. I do apologize."

"Hey." The word was a gentle command. I hesitated, then swiveled reluctantly and met his scrutiny. "I say you've got nothin' to be ashamed of."

I nodded at the wide white bandage that encircled his left forearm. "How do you feel?"

He finished the beer in one long swallow. "Fine. My painkiller just kicked in."

"Good." I looked at the small fishing boats in the marina. "Then let's rent a boat and go out in the bay. Let's race over the water and inhale the wind. I'll pay."

"You just want to harass the sharks on my account."

"Oh, yes, I'm a good lawyer." My tone was sarcastic. I got to my feet with a flurry of motion. "I want to go where I can breathe."

"All right." He rose and tossed some money on the table. "I'll walk over to the marina office and see if somebody can take us. And I'll pay. Don't argue."

I stared at him. He had a stubborn look I'd begun to recognize. "That will be totally out of character for me."

"Good."

"I'll change clothes."

"Where? How?"

I pointed to a corner bar where a bartender sold blue cotton t-shirts and short cotton shorts with the restaurant's logo. *Come Out Of Your Shell At The Wild Oyster*, a slogan beamed in neon orange lettering.

"You're takin' a big leap off a short fashion dock," Eli said, looking as if he'd like to picture me in thin, soft cotton. "How fast can you do it?"

I gave him a cynical smile. "I'm ready to jump right now."

*

The bay was miles wide, shallow, and as smooth as glass. In the distance, modern bridges and causeways girdled its horizon like white stone islands in the sun. A small flotilla of shrimpers and oyster boats crisscrossed the waterways as easily as gulls. But close to the mainland shore, where Eli geared a large speedboat at a lazy pace, the bay belonged only to him and Darl. She sat on the bow with her bare feet curled under her and both hands draped over the deck rail. Her face was turned in profile to Eli, her eyes drinking in a world of pine woods, marshes, and sand bars. She'd taken her hair out of its braid. The wind tossed the mink-brown waves around her shoulders and plastered the thin blue t-shirt and shorts to her body. The shorts clung to tops of her thighs, freeing long, sculpted legs. Her hips flared voluptuously from a small waist, and her breasts showed in beautiful outline. He recalled her mentioning that she was an avid walker, sometimes covering five miles a day on a track near her Washington D.C. apartment. But she was no athlete, she said. She just had to keep moving.

Now, in a rare mood because of him, she had become still. She watched the scenery, and Eli watched her.

The bay's dark water slapped rhythmically against the speedboat's hull. Cool, damp air rushed over their faces. She tilted her head back, shut her eyes and inhaled, then looked at him. "The bay smells like fresh watermelon," she called. He nodded, mesmerized by the sight she made. Blue sky, blue eyes, ripe blue body. She pointed at the bow. "Do you want to sit up here and let me drive awhile?"

"Steer," he corrected mildly. "Not drive."

"I grew up in the mountains, not around water. You know boats, obviously."

"I've owned a few."

"On lakes?"

"On the ocean."

She regarded this new bit of information with her head tilted and her eyes thoughtful, as if adjusting his place in her files. "How much did you pay to rent this boat without the owner coming along to drive—steer—it?"

"Enough to make him dance when he ran off to count my money."

"Thank you. Thank you for doing that."

"No problem. I'm enjoyin' the view." He looked at her without skimming the meaning, and she didn't turn away. When she finally pulled her gaze to the water again, it seemed a guilty gesture. She stood, looking forward, she reached into a pocket of her shorts. Eli frowned at the unknown talisman she plucked out. She rubbed her fingers over it.

The water suddenly shimmered and came alive. She frowned at the sight and looked back at him in question. Eli quickly brought the boat to an idling stop and made his way to her side. She pointed. A huge school of tiny fish flashed silver and white as they swirled in perfect unison. "Bait fish," Eli explained. "Around here they call 'em Poggies."

Darl held the mysterious pocket item close to her side but reached out over the water with her other hand. "Hello, Poggies. I bring you greetings from the world of air."

*Greetings.* Eli looked at her with his heart aching. Her childhood catch phrase tore into him like a fine wire, cutting the connection between conscience and clear thought, leaving only nostalgia and desire. "Greetings, they say back," he returned gruffly. "Greetings, Darl."

She straightened slowly, staring at him. Eli stepped so close to her he could see the swift pulse of her heart where the t-shirt clung to her left breast. His own heart was pounding, too. He looked at the Hardigree pendant hanging against her chest. "You wear one totem and carry another." He gestured toward her clenched hand. "Would you tell me about 'em?"

For a moment he feared she'd shake her head. The look in her eyes was fragile. But then she slowly raised her fist to the necklace. "This is for family." She paused. "It reminds me that I'm capable of . . . *anything.*" She curled the last word on her tongue as if it were acid. Slowly, she held out her fist and unfurled it, palm up. "And this is for inspiration." She paused again. Her throat worked. Then, softly, "For the love and hope you talked about the other night."

Eli looked down at her hand. In it lay the smooth chip of marble he'd made for her twenty-five years earlier. She'd burnished the infinity symbol to a smooth trace in the stone. He couldn't speak. She searched his face worriedly. "Don't try to understand me, Mr. Solo."

"Too late." Eli raised his hand slowly, then slid his fingers into her hair at the spot where it cascaded behind one ear. She didn't move away. Her troubled gaze flickered from his eyes to his mouth, and back. "Greetings," he said again. The breath soughed from her. "Greetings." He bent a little and fitted his mouth to her lips. A sweet, easy kiss. The sensation made him sigh, and she answered it. On his next breath he slid his arm around her back and kissed her more deeply. Darl opened her mouth, but didn't put her arms around him. He touched the tip of his tongue to hers and she reciprocated, then shivered. "Stop," she whispered.

Trembling himself, Eli stepped back. "Are you all right?"

She nodded, her eyes never leaving him. She seemed to vibrate with restraint and a certain ferocious melancholy. Eli returned to the cockpit and slid the boat into gear. She watched him the whole time, her eyes troubled as she clenched the gift he'd given her when they were children, her knotted hand held low over her body. Eli's heart hammered and he prayed silently.

*Please, let her know it's me.*

*

I had kissed a man I barely knew and fitted Eli's soul to him. Solo owned me from that second on. All he wanted from me was myself, and I could give him that. I'd had his blood on my hands. His affection was the only pretense of redemption I had won fairly.

That evening we returned to the beach house, built a small driftwood fire between the sand dunes, and shared a blanket, watching the sunset. We traded sips from a bottle of pinot grigio and ate cold boiled shrimp from a bowl laced with lemon juice and cocktail sauce. The pale sand crabs skittered around us. Solo tossed them tiny bits of food and made bets on which crab would be bold enough to snatch the offerings first. "A dollar on that little guy by the sea oats," he said. "He'll go the distance."

"No, that pony will fade in the stretch. He'll never make it past the pile of clam shells. I'm putting my dollar on the big one crouched near the gull feather."

"Nope. Too slow for the field. He's a plow-crab, not a race-crab."

I smiled, and he returned it. By the time we finished the wine and the shrimp, it was dark and I owed Solo seventeen dollars. "I'll give you my marker," I said, and drew my name in the sand behind us.

He squinted at the signature, then at me. "I better call it in right now, before the tide rises."

We'd been waiting for any excuse, the air electric between us, the humor soft-spoken and tender, the night completely arrived. In the shadows and flickering firelight I took his hand. *Eli.* I saw what I wanted to see. I kissed him. Just as on the boat, that first contact was sweet, a polite greeting. But the second kiss sent us down on the blanket, arms curling around each other, our soft sounds mingling with the rush of the surf.

He was everything I wanted him to be, and more. Once we were standing naked in my moonlit bedroom, with the balcony doors open and the ocean's night sounds cascading over us, he put his hands under my thighs and lifted me off the floor. I gasped and angled my legs around his hips as he pressed my back against a cool, pale wall. He levered his body against mine, with the hard tip of his erection couched against my stomach. I had never felt so molded to another human being, so intricately open to sensation. We tore at each other's mouths and arched together, holding on for dear life. *Darl,* he whispered, but I couldn't call him by name— I was afraid I'd call him Eli and break the spell. I kissed him roughly, Eli's unspoken ghost hidden in my throat. "Lay me down, now. I'm not really made of stone."

"You never were," he said, and burying his face in my hair as if I were a soft blanket enfolding him, he carried me to bed.

*

I woke on my side in soft morning sunshine, facing him just an arm's length away. I inhaled his breath, warm and musky but pleasant, the essence of this good, strong stranger who covered my skin, inside and out. We'd fallen asleep finally, just before dawn, and this was the furthest apart we'd been all night. My right hand lay cradled inside his on the pillow between our heads. His thick fingers arched over my hand protectively, just as I continued to welcome him with one outstretched foot tucked between his ankles.

We couldn't stop touching each other, even when we slept. I slowly turned his broad hand in mine, looking at its weathered skin and broad calluses. What had this techno wizard done to earn a working-man's palms?

I studied his plain, rugged face, the deep sweep of his dark lashes on his angular cheekbones, his beard shadow, the boyish fan of coarse, dark hair over his high forehead. During the night I had seen him in unguarded moments, glimpses in moonlight, pain and hunger and devotion. He had given me what I'd given him—desperate mysteries. Just looking at him made me bite back a moan. I was damp and tender and disheveled, the night like hot, sweet wax inside me, coating old fears, clouding old shames. I'd always held back from loving any man. Honest love demanded full trust, and I would never share my childhood secret with anyone.

Not even this one.

I slipped away from him by slow degrees, holding my breath to keep him asleep, then stood at the foot of the bed, hypnotized by his tall body's outline beneath the bed's soft gray sheet. Packages of unopened condoms were scattered on the covers, waiting like opportunities. He had been prepared for me, and I didn't know what to think of that, either. I dug my bare toes into the carpeted floor among our strewn clothes. *Move. Go. Stop trying to understand him or yourself.* I hurried to the suite's large bathroom and stared at myself naked in a huge mirror embellished with a frame of white seashells. What kind of careless mermaid was I? I saw blue eyes fevered with emotion, my face gaunt, my brunette hair in tangles around my shoulders, my body flushed and glistening with sweat, his and mine. Three days ago I'd watched Frog Marvin die. I'd been devastated, numb, suicidal. No one could have made me believe what had happened since then.

Now I knew who I was. I was a survivor at all costs. I had the Hardigree strength, but also the Hardigree weakness for men. I turned and staggered into the shower, slamming my palms into the faucet ontrols until ice-cold water gushed down on my upturned face and gritted teeth. It washed away Solo's sweet taste with the acrid flavor of coastal wells.

I shivered as I toweled myself and belted a thin white robe

around my waist. For all I knew I'd walk out of the bathroom, dress, pack, and tell him good bye. I couldn't begin to share the truth about the peculiar motivations of my dirty soul. When I stepped into the bedroom with my hands knotted by my sides I halted abruptly. He stood with his back to me, looking out toward the ocean on the balcony beyond the bedroom's open glass doors. He had pulled on his rumpled khaki trousers. He smoked another of his small cigars. I inhaled its woodsy aroma in the salt air. As I watched he rolled his broad, bare shoulders, the muscles taut enough to snap. The broad white bandage on his injured forearm was speckled with blood at the center. We'd been too rough at times during the night, but never noticed. One hand pinched the cigar tightly as he pulled it from his lips. He raised the other to his tossled hair and clawed his fingers to the nape of his neck, the gesture seething with frustration.

I froze there, watching him, suddenly realizing he might have something worse to tell me than I could tell him. I didn't want to lose him that way, didn't want to ruin our brief time together. He pivoted as if sensing me. He held my stark gaze, then went down my robed body and back to my face. He tossed the cigar's remnant into the dunes beneath the balcony, then walked inside the room. "We have to talk," he said.

"I agree. Maybe it's a little late to be old-fashioned, but I'd like to know your full name. I'd like to know where you live, and what kind of family you have, and what you really do for a living. And I'd like to know what you've been trying to tell me for the past three days, because I see a lot of regret in your eyes."

"Don't mistake that for a change of heart. Whatever I've done here, I wanted it to happen. And I'll always want you. I don't have the words to tell you how much."

I held out my hands. "Then what you have to say can wait a little while longer." His face convulsed in a smile, a rebuke, surrender. We were lost. He pulled me to him then picked me up off the floor. We kissed like lovers after a long separation. I dug my fingers into his back and arched against him. Instantly we were on the bed again, him twisting sideways and jerking my robe open, his mouth on my breasts and stomach and lower, then holding my face and kissing me on the lips as I cried out along with him.

I loved him, whoever he was. I simply did.

*

The phone rang as we held each other afterwards. I had my back to him, and he'd fitted his body to me, wrapped me in his arms, fully naked, as he was. The breeze was only beginning to cool the sheen of sweat on us, and I hadn't begun to breathe normally. I was frozen inside my dilemmas, but couldn't stop stroking his hands. "Let it go," he asked, as the phone shrilled in the living room. I flinched.

Through the open bedroom door we heard an answering machine click on. An aged, elegant southern voice introduced one of Swan's matronly Asheville friends. "Honey," the woman said, "It's an emergency." That made me lunge up to my elbows, with Solo rising behind me. "Your grandmother and Miss Matilda," she went on, "are in the hospital."

14

Swan had suffered a heart attack during the night. Matilda, after rushing to the hospital to be with her, had collapsed in a waiting room. She'd had a mild stroke. In the rush to pack and leave St. George Island I did little more than nod when Solo said, "You care for your grandma and her friend, I can see that." He withdrew from me, grew very quiet and seemed burdened, then said simply, "Of course I'll take you right to them."

"Thank you."

*Please don't die, Grandmother.*

That was my first thought, an honest bellweather that curdled me inside. I'd fantasized about Swan's death for years, back when I deluded myself into thinking I'd find Eli some day and tell him the truth. I loved Swan Hardigree Samples, my grandmother, my nemesis. It was a helpless devotion, as strong as the hate I also felt, as complex as the bitterness I held toward her. I didn't know what to do with the emotion, anymore than I'd known as a child.

By afternoon we'd left the Gulf behind and followed the continent inward. Solo guided his small plane over the rich cotton and peanut plains of south Georgia, then the forested hills and sprawling suburbs of Atlanta, rising higher as the rounded, blue-green Appalachians climbed to meet us. On the cusp of entering the skies over western North Carolina I broke my moody silence. "Almost there," I said. As the steep wilderness and small towns of my homeland crept under us, I looked at Solo's profile. His mouth was set in a grim line. His hands lightly clenched the controls. He'd dressed in a soft white pullover, gray trousers, and hiking boots, while I'd naturally returned to a blue business suit. We looked so different, now. He was a study in concentration, as reserved as myself. I called out to him over the roar of the plane's engines. "Have you ever been to these mountains, before?"

After a stretch of silence he nodded. "As a kid."

"We have a small hospital in my hometown now, and it's not far from the new airport. A small airport, but still. Once we land I'll call my grandmother's business manager and he'll send a car." Solo nodded but said nothing. I went on carefully. "You'll be welcome to stay at my grandmother's estate."

He glanced at me with poker-faced calm, but I noticed his hands clenching harder, going white-knuckled on the controls. "I'll find myself a place, don't worry."

"I'm not just being polite. I'd like to have you nearby." I hesitated. "I know your job is finished, but—"

"You think you're just a job to me?"

I struggled with my voice, made a pretense of looking out the window, then back at him. "I'm trying to make it easy, if you want to leave."

He put a hand on mine briefly, and stroked my palm with his thumb. "I'm in this for the long haul," he said. "I'm here because I care about you. Remember that."

After a moment he banked the plane and we curved down over the tops of the mountains, gliding lower as the old granite balds and fir-shrouded ridges opened into the small valley that made my heart twist with memories. Below us, the white-pink marble homes and stores of Burnt Stand appeared among the trees, majestic and unchanged.

"Home," I said grimly. I slid one hand into my slender leather purse and cupped the infinity stone Eli had chipped from the bedrock beneath our lives there.

Even the stone knew where it belonged.

*

Cool autumn weather had already descended on the valley, and the dogwoods—almost always the first trees to turn—had taken on the first tinge of red. Solo taxied his plane to a halt at the county airport in a whirl of brisk air and red-green forest. As soon as the plane came to a full stop a tall, rangy black man walked toward us from the airport's one-room office. A dusty SUV waited behind him. He was about 40 years old, with close-cropped hair and a thin white scar across his right jaw. His dark corduroys, pin-striped shirt, leather suspenders and silk tie moderated some of the edge in his eyes. Marble dust clung to his heavy-soled work shoes, and he had the large, sinewed hands of a stonecutter. He was Leon Forrest.

"Leon," I said, and went to him with both hands out. "Talk to me."

He grasped my hands firmly in his. "You know that grandma of yours is not goin' to break. The doctors told us she's doing all right. They call it a mild heart attack. And Miss Matilda's all right. Just got a little slur to her words and can't see quite right."

Relief felt like lemons squeezing behind my eyes. I turned to Solo and made the introductions. "Mr. Forrest is executive manager at the quarry. Leon, Mr. Solo is a friend of mine, and a security consultant at Phoenix." Solo was looking at Leon with a gleam in his eyes—I would have called it surprise and affection, but that made no sense about two strangers. For his part, Leon frowned as he and Solo shook hands. "Man, there's something familiar about you."

Solo said quietly, "It's good to see you. That is, good to meet you." He paused, his jaw working. "Even under the circumstances."

As the three of us walked to the SUV I looked at Leon somberly. "Did my grandmother say anything when she heard I was coming?"

He looked at me apologetically, then sighed. "She told Miss Matilda you were probably surprised to hear she has a heart."

*

The new county hospital, situated on a small knoll north of town, reflected the afternoon sunshine from its pink-marble façade. I left Solo and Leon in a lobby that included Swan and Matilda's elegant portraits as members of the hospital board, and headed for an elevator to the fourth-story cardiac unit. On the way I passed a directory listing the second-floor wing dedicated to Julia Samples Union, my mother. A few years earlier I'd come home briefly for the dedication ceremony, made a small speech in my mother's honor, and asked Swan flatly why she'd pushed for a public memorial to a daughter she'd rejected.

"I never rejected her, only her choices," Swan replied.

"I grew up thinking she deserted me."

"Anyone who told you that was cruel and sadly mistaken."

"You let me believe it."

"I wanted to believe it myself. It was much less painful than admitting I drove her away and caused her death." With that astonishing and brutal honesty she ended the conversation and refused to discuss my mother again. I was still working as a public defender in Atlanta then, and I cried during the entire four-hour drive from North Carolina.

Now I rode the elevator past my mother's crisply clinical memorial floor with my foot making a nervous tap and my hands wound in the strap of my shoulder purse. I had myself under control by the time I exited into a hallway. A sign pointed me to ICU. And there, sitting in a hallway wheelchair, a flowing blue robe covering her hospital gown, was Matilda.

"My god," I said under my breath. I rushed to her. "Darl," she whispered, wrapping my slurred name in the damaged silk of her voice.

"What are you doing out of bed?"

"Waiting for you. And staying near her."

I got down on one knee and hugged her. She felt so frail. She was thin, with stark white hair and skin as easily torn as golden-brown tissue paper. "Where's your room?" I demanded. "I'll take you back right now."

"You will not. I promised her I'd come in with you. She's been napping." Every word was slow and tortured, but she looked determined. "They have her in one of those just-awful cubicles. She hates it. You know how dearly she loves her privacy. Let's go see her. She's been so worried about you."

I said nothing as I wheeled her through the doors of the cardiac intensive-care ward. She guided me to a curtained area, curving a shaky hand at the nurses who looked up from their station. They all straightened as if for inspection and spoke to me politely in their melodic mountain voices, as if I might threaten their jobs or demand special treatment. My stomach twisted. Was that my image now?

We went down a line of cubicles where half-drawn curtains offered wrenching glimpses of cardiac patients dozing among lines and tubes and monitors. Outside the cubicle windows a magenta sunset gathered over the mountains towering around us, and a low, silver mist began to settle like smoke on the hills. Our home, our birthplace, was impossibly beautiful and lonely. "This one," Matilda said. We stopped. I pulled the curtain back slowly.

The lights had been turned down, so that Swan's face was illuminated only by a small lamp above the head of her hospital bed. She was hooked to a half-dozen wires and IV's. A clear, slender oxygen tube curled beneath her aquiline nostrils. Her eyes were closed. I eased Matilda's wheelchair close to the bed then went to the other side and stood, not touching Swan, just looking down at her and steadying myself. Her face was ashen and lined, but still compelling. Her beautiful hair was now silver-gray. She defiantly wore it longer than most ladies of a certain age would dare, the thick silver strands curling around her shoulders. I touched a fingertip to the lace collar of a white silk robe tied at her throat. Matilda whispered, "Of course she wouldn't wear a hospital gown."

"Of course not."

She bent to Swan's ear. "Swan, she's here. Darl's here." My grandmother breathed deeply in sleep and didn't respond. Matilda bent closer. "*Sister*," she whispered as if it were a command, then gave a poignant glance toward the curtain in case someone might overhear—as if most the town didn't already know. That nearly broke me. She and Swan were so much alike, guarding their old ways and secrets, their tangled reputation.

My grandmother opened her eyes abruptly. There had never been any half-measures in her nature. She was either in hibernation or fully alert. Her blue eyes were dulled by medication, but her gaze went straight to me. I saw a flash of pleasure followed by quick self-control. She cleared her throat. "If you've come to see me die, I'll disappoint you."

I leaned over her. My voice barely a whisper, I said, "I've come to take care of you while you recuperate. If that's what you want."

"What have I done to earn such sudden devotion?"

"I have no idea."

"Was this the only way you'd come home for good?"

"I haven't come home for good. I've come to see my sick grandmother. There's a difference."

"Duty, not devotion."

"You expect me to be sentimental? You hate that kind of thing."

"Absolutely. So you'll stay?"

"Until you're well."

"Perhaps I'll become a chronic invalid. Then you'll be forced to smother me with my own pillow."

"I'll give it some thought, in that case."

Matilda gasped. The cruel banter between Swan and I had become a routine over the years, but we'd never indulged in front of anyone else. I looked at Matilda apologetically, then back down at Swan. "I'll be staying at Marble Hall. I'll visit you again early tomorrow morning." I paused. "Did someone upset you yesterday? I heard you had a visitor at the office, and you weren't yourself after that."

Her eyes flared. "Leon is spying on me?"

"Oh, please. He told me a young woman came by and you shut yourself away with her. And that you didn't look well after she left. He was worried. That's his job. Who was she?"

"That's my business, for now. I'll discuss it with you later, when I have a private room. In the meantime, tell Leon I want you to oversee the company business while I'll ill. If anyone's going to spy on me, it might as well be my own granddaughter."

"Leon's doing a perfectly fine job. He doesn't need my interference."

"He's a hired manager, not family. He's not one of us."

I could have laughed, if the sound would have gotten past my locked throat. In Swan's terms, 'one of us' wasn't about race, but about Hardigree status. I bent closer to her and whispered, "Good for him. We tend to kill our own kind—or let others die for the crime. So don't joke about me smothering you. It's a little too close to our family traditions for comfort." Matilda heard every word, and moaned.

Swan stared at me with a kind of fierce pride. "Come back tomorrow. We do have to talk. I have something very important to tell you. We'll see how strong you are, then."

I frowned at her. "No games, Grandmother. I'm not in the mood."

"This is no game, I assure you." With that, she turned her head and ignored me. "Now go and be the lady of Marble Hall. Go on and take Matilda to her own room. I need my rest. I intend to recover in record time." She gazed at Matilda sternly. "You go and rest, too. I'll be checking up on you. Tomorrow I'll insist they move me to your room."

We had been dismissed. Matilda touched her hand in goodbye, and Swan acknowledged her with another quiet look. Matilda nodded. They held silent conversations, like twins sharing an unspoken language. I quickly wheeled Matilda from the ward, moving like a woman on a tightrope. Small, shooting pains began to creep up the back of my neck and into my scalp. My temples ached. As soon as I cleared the ICU doors Matilda looked up at me. Her mouth worked to form the words. Her eyes glittered. "How could you speak to her so cruelly about . . . the past?"

"I'm sorry. It's our way of counting coup on each other."

She clenched a thin fist to her chest. "Why? Why?"

I leaned toward her, quivering. In a hoarse whisper I begged, "Don't the memories stab you a little every day? They haunt me. And lately it's been nearly unbearable."

"It was an accident."

"You know what I mean. Not just Clara."

"An accident, all of it. How can you blame Swan after all these years?"

I sagged with defeat. "Matilda, you've always looked the other way."

"Can't you—just once? You are the only family she has. You cannot treat her badly."

"The only family? Times have changed. The rules have changed. Isn't it time this town learns you're her sister?"

"Half-sister. Her colored half-sister." Matilda was trembling so hard it frightened me, but she drew herself proudly. "And I will never have the world know how I came to be born a colored Hardigree. It would humiliate Karen and cause gossip in her career."

"I'll call her in New York and tell her you need her."

Matilda's lips moved faintly. "I won't ask her to come."

"I came back for Swan. She'll come back for you." I pressed my fingertips to my temples. "Can't there ever be a time when we simply tell the truth and accept what we did and who we are?"

Matilda looked at me with the restraint of an old lioness. "No. Hearts are broken for the sake of the truth. Keep your truth, and I shall keep mine."

*

Burnt Stand. Blood and death and Darl. Eli felt all three fighting for his soul as he waited in the hospital lobby. A few miles from there Pa had died on the ground in front of the Stone Cottage, his eyes searching Ma's face for some kind of forgiveness as she cradled him in her arms. If there was any chance in hell of proving Pa didn't kill Clara Hardigree, it meant someone else had. Probably someone who knew her. Someone from Burnt Stand. That person could be within the sound of Eli's voice right now.

Leon asked Eli a few questions about himself, which Eli circled without really answering. That brought a look of acidic scrutiny into the big man's black eyes, and soured Eli's stomach. He wasn't accustomed to hedging his words, and he wanted Leon's respect. "Well, I better leave you to yourself," Leon said without sparing another slicing look. "I've got a little girl and boy at home, and an old daddy who'll overcook the collard greens and yell at the kids if I don't get there."

"You have kids. That's good."

Leon studied him hard for that curious remark. "Yeah. My wife died a few years ago, so I've got kids to raise alone. Good kids." He tossed him a set of car keys. "Use that Explorer I drove here. It's a company car. I've got a man bringing me another one."

"I appreciate it."

"Hope you'll be around later for more questions. We're pretty nosy about *strangers*."

"You're out of luck. I don't have much to say."

"It's what you don't say that's got my curiosity." Eli chewed his tongue. "Well, Mr. Solo, I'll be talkin' to you again. Good evening, you hear?" Leon nodded to him curtly and turned to walk away.

"Leon, wait." The man halted, frowning at the familiar way a stranger used his name. "Yeah?"

Eli held his gaze evenly. "The name's not Solo. It's Wade. Eli Wade."

For a moment Leon stared at him, scrutinized him, shock and disbelief stamped on his face, then a slow merging of recognition and inevitable resemblance. Eli saw the decision on Leon's face even before the big man raised a finger to his cheek and touched the scar. Slowly he walked back to Eli, then thrust out a massive hand, one stonecutter to another.

They shook on the past.

\*

The two most important women in my life were old and sick and now both lay in hospital beds. When I reached the lobby, Solo met me. My stomach crowded up beneath my breastbone. Suddenly I couldn't breathe. My head throbbed. "I have a good deal of work to do tonight. Phone calls to my grandmother's friends and associates. Business files to read. You don't have to stay with me. There are several inns around town, and two chain motels."

"If you're kickin' me out, Darl, you'll have be blunt. I'm fairly dense. Some people take a hint. Some people take the cake. Me? I need to hear, 'Get outta my sight, you big hick bastard,' before I understand."

I stared at him. "All right. I want you to stay. I'll take you to my family's dark lair."

"Marble Hall?"

"Yes." I must have mentioned the name to him. I couldn't remember. "We'll have more privacy there." I told him the driving directions. Pain shot through my head. I abruptly had to shut my eyes and hold my face, as if it would burst. He put an arm around me. "Talk to me. What's wrong?"

"Headache," I admitted. "I have them. This is a bad one. I've got medicine in my luggage."

"You don't need a pill. You need to cry." He slid an arm around me with ferocious support. "Want me to make you cry?"

"No. You're the only part of my life that doesn't hurt. Let's keep it that way."

Solo chewed his lower lip, looked like a man caught between two trains, and simmered with some misery of his own. "All right," he said finally. "You've got your wish for tonight." He led me outside, where I threw up in the meditation garden my own grandmother had donated to the hospital. He held my hair back and wiped my mouth with the back of his own hand when I tried to turn away. My homecoming complete, I walked to Leon's SUV two paces ahead of him, numb but determined to preserve some dignity. He let me. During the drive I laid my head back on the passenger seat and tried to forget where I was and why. I hoped he could find Marble Hall without my further help.

Surprisingly, he had no trouble at all.

*

The pink mansion existed as it always did in my dreams—looming above me as we drove up the front lane of crushed marble rock, waiting for me to be swallowed inside its cool grandeur. Hooded by firs like enormous Christmas trees and surrounded by manicured shrubs, it made a dark obelisk against the fading light of the sky. Deep woods rose around it on the hills, and mountains behind that. To our left, beyond the back gardens, the pool, the terrace, and the old koi pond, a short walk through those woods, I could always visit Clara's secret grave at the base of the moss-speckled statuary of the Stone Flower Garden. Beyond that garden, the Stone Cottage sat empty in its deep mountain hollow, its boarded-over doors and windows sagging under the weight of the wild muscadine vines that shrouded it. Those vines would be turning bright gold soon, and jewel-toned autumn leaves would sift down gently atop the old yard, the lost garden, Clara's buried bones. I knew exactly what I would see if I had the guts to walk through those woods.

I didn't.

"Home sweet home," I managed through a veil of nausea and pain.

Solo took a key from my hand and strode up the wide steps of the portico as I climbed leadenly behind him. Gloria, Swan's South American housekeeper, had left the portico's chandelier burning and lamps turned on in the mansion's lower windows. We entered the central foyer, our footsteps hidden on Swan's antique Persian rugs. A note from Gloria, written in careful English on a slip of Hardigree Marble Company stationary, said I'd find roast beef, cold salads, and casseroles to microwave in the kitchen.

But I hurried straight to the back of the house like a trapped animal seeks air, staggering in the dark past every fine piece of furniture and object d'art, every portrait of Swan, Esta, and my mother. I flung open the row of tall French doors that led to the back gardens and the pool, then sank down on the front end of a plush wicker lounge. I heard Solo's footsteps behind me. "No lights," I said. "Please. Just give me a moment and I'll take a pill."

He sat down behind me on the lounge. "Let's try this first." Slowly, he rested his broad hands on the tops of my shoulders, then hooked his fingers in the jacket of my suit and pulled it backwards. I stiffened. "I'm not tryin' to undress you for my own interests," he said quietly, his voice laced with dark humor. "I'm tryin' to get you cleaned up. There's one thing you don't do real well. You're not neat when you heave."

I straightened. Prickles of embarrassment crawled over my skin. I let the soiled garment slide down my arms. "Aren't you lucky to be the man who gets to see me—and smell me—this way? You're the only one who's had the privilege."

He tossed the jacket aside. "I bled on you just yesterday, so now we're even." He slid his hands over my shoulders again, puckering the soft material of my white blouse. "I've been inside you. I've tasted you. I've held you around me. There's not a part of you I mind knowin' all about."

I uttered a low sound then reached up, grasping one of his hands. Together we gazed out into the ghostly silhouettes of the forest. His fingers knotted in my blouse. He gave off an energy as bleak as my own. What made him so in tune with my unhappiness? God, I needed him, this intimate stranger. But I had no right to drag him deeper into the pit of complications and old tensions that made up my life. If there was any chance for us, I had to save him from myself. "I want you to leave tomorrow," I announced. "In a week or so, when I have this situation under control, I'll visit you. Somewhere. You pick the place. I'll come there. And we *will* talk about ourselves. I swear to you. But I already care about you too much to let you stay here and get involved."

He said nothing for a moment. Then, "We'll talk this over tomorrow." He sank his fingertips into the bound muscles along the nape of my neck. I moaned with the exquisite pain as he probed and rubbed, forcing the sinews to let go. The massage seemed to go on forever. Tears came to my eyes. I forced them back. It hurt. It helped. Release was never easy. I wouldn't give in. Finally he worked his hands up the back of my skull, cradled my head beneath the jaw, and lifted gently. I felt my spine stretch, and then some of the pain in my head seemed to flow backwards down an open channel, evaporating. I turned, astonished, and stared at him. "What did you do?"

"It's just something I learned along the way in my world travels. I unblocked your chakras or called up your spirit guide or hell—I don't know—changed your brain oil. Whatever. Who knows about the mysteries of universe. However it works, it does." He stood, walked around in front of me, and held down a hand. "That pool out there has a mist over it. It's heated?"

"Yes. My grandmother swims for exercise all year. She loves the water. When she was a child there was a fire in town. Water has made her feel safe, ever since."

"Then let's go. There's no mystery about soakin' in water. That'll feel good, too."

I got to my feet unsteadily. He bent and picked me up. "I don't want to be this dependent on you," I said.

"Let me do what I can. I can't dance, but I tote well."

When we reached the poolside he set me down. We undressed each other as awkwardly as teenagers, then stepped into the warm water, holding hands. We sank down on a low step in the shallow end. I eased between his spread thighs with my back against his chest, then rested my head on his shoulder. I cupped water to my face and rinsed my mouth while he curved his arms around me. He rested one hand atop my left breast, idly stroking a nipple with the rough pad of his thumb.

I sighed as pleasure mingled with pain. The dark, soothing water encased us. His erection prodded the soft spot at the base of my spine. I adjusted the soaked bandage on his arm. "Not hygienic," I said. He brushed his jaw along mine. "Stop thinkin'." He pulled lightly on my nipple in rebuke. I sank closer to him, arching my back against his penis. It was good to be wanted by him, amazing to be this comfortable. I turned my face into the crook of his neck and shut my eyes. He kissed the bridge of my nose.

In the darkness behind my eyes I searched out the tainted place that always kept me by myself. It was in me but out *there*, too, in the earth of the deep mountain woods beyond the terrace. I opened my eyes guiltily and twisted to gaze across at the marble swans that still guarded the terrace walls. They looked back, relentless.

Solo spoke in a gruff whisper. "There could be anything out there. What do you see?"

Whether he was speaking to himself or asking me what I saw in the shadows, it was all the same. I inhaled sharply. "The memory of a boy I loved, named Eli."

Silence. The air became electric. His arms tightened around me. "*Darl.*" There was no censure in his tone.

I shivered. "You remind me of him. Even the way you say my name. I look at you and see the man he might have become. That's why you're special to me. *I'm sorry.* I should have told you in Florida."

"Sssh. Tell me. I want to know about him."

"He was only thirteen the last time I saw him. And I was only ten. I know it sounds impossible." I rushed on, my voice hoarse. "But I can still see him out there in those woods—I can imagine him. He and his family lived not far away. I used to walk over . . . he'd wait. We had a place. It was all innocent." I halted. "This isn't fair to you. You don't deserve to be a stand-in for a memory like that."

"If I'm the kind of man you hoped he'd be, then I've done all right." Solo turned me to face him. Even in the dark I sensed him searching my face. New pain soared through my skull. I winced and jerked back. He released me as if I'd slapped him, then sank his hand into my hair, stroking quickly. We stared at each other. I felt beads of sweat on my forehead, and he breathed roughly. "Jesus," he said.

"You didn't hurt me. It's my headache again." He wound his arms around me fiercely. "Cry," he ordered, his own voice hoarse. "Cry for that boy. It's a blessing to be loved by you. So cry for yourself, because your Eli loved you, and he was *right* to love you. *Cry.*"

He was no more sure of my mysteries than I could be of his, but he broke me. I did something I'd never done before, not with anyone. I sobbed helplessly.

And he held me.

## 15

*Comeon, Eli. Be quiet. Be quiet on your big feet,"* Darl whispered, grinning at him as she led him up the backstairs to her bedroom. It was a summer day, Swan was at a meeting in Asheville, and Mama had brought him and Bell with her to work at the mansion. He and Darl had spent the morning unpacking and arranging boxes of canned goods in the pantry, while Bell watched, reciting solemnly, "String beans. Tomatoes. Potatoes. Squash," because she had finally learned to read. Now Mama had fallen asleep over her mid-day bologna sandwich in one of the library's fat leather easy chairs, and Bell lay napping in the floor by her feet.

"I'll get my behind torn up in Mama catches me upstairs," Eli hissed, but followed Darl anyway. She grabbed his hand and pulled him down a side hallway, then shoved open a pink lacquered door. "*Voila,*" she said, spreading a hand at a pink, fluffy wonderland of girly furniture, a canopied bed, piles of dolls, and books stacked everywhere. "My boudoir."

"Voila," he repeated in awe, drawling the French word like a mule pulling a plow. He stared at the books. "Good godawmighty."

"Here. Sit down." She pushed books and dolls aside on the high pink bed. He shook his head. He was only eleven then, but Pa already had told him the rules about boys, girls, and furniture to lay down on. "I'm not sittin' on your bed."

"Well, suit yourself." She gathered a pile of books into her arms. "Sit over there, then." They huddled side-by-side in a window seat stuffed with pink brocade pillows. "You want Huckleberry Finn?" She held out a book.

"Sure!"

"Okay." She put that in his lap then dug into the novels and held up another one. "I'm reading the Casey Girl mysteries right now. I'm up to book four. 'The Mummy On Oak Street.'"

"Hmmm." He was already deeply intrigued with the first page

of the Twain classic. He pushed his glasses up his nose, settled back on the girly cushions and drew up his legs, skinny and sunburned beneath cut-off jeans. Darl propped herself in the window seat's opposite corner, opening her Casey Girl mystery to a page marked with a string of yarn. She bent her head and began reading as avidly as he, stretching out her long legs in pink shorts with lace edging. Her bare feet collided with his, but both he and she pretended not to notice. They read in perfectly silent friendship, warmed by the sun on that good day, their toes kissing without any embarrassment at all.

*The window seat is gone,* Eli thought when he woke up in that room as a grown man. *The whole damn window's gone.* In the heat and the anguish of the night before, he'd noticed very little about the room. Swan must have remodeled it at some point after Darl left home. Not a sign of that pink girl existed anywhere now. The furniture was dark and elaborately carved, the wall paper a burnished silver pattern, the lamps sleek and contemporary. Swan had done her best to mimic Darl's adult personality.

And had gotten it all wrong.

He rose on one elbow and watched Darl sleep beside him. The tenderness in him fought for release. She looked like hell—her hair tangled and matted, her eyes shadowed—but that only made him love her more. Love her. *I love you with all my heart,* he mouthed. He slid carefully from beneath pale sheets, then smoothed them over her bare shoulders, tucking her in. Grabbing a thick blue towel from the floor, he wrapped it around his waist then walked downstairs.

He padded around a corner into the main foyer. Twin gasps greeted him. Two black-haired women stood there, one in a tailored dress, the other, younger, in a maid's uniform. "Excuse me, ladies," he said. The maid burst out laughing. The older woman did not. "I was not informed there was a guest." She spoke in heavily accented English.

"You Gloria, ma'am?"

"Yes, Miss Swan's housekeeper." She turned and sternly ordered the maid in Spanish. The young woman, giggling, fled toward the kitchen.

This was no time for explanations, Eli thought. He apologized in good Spanish. Continuing in that language, he told Gloria that Miss Swan's granddaughter had been sick the night before, and would sleep late. "When she gets up, tell her I'll be back soon. I'm just going to look around town."

Whether his fluent command of her language impressed her or not, Gloria looked at him grimly but nodded. He flexed his naked shoulders, kept his head up and his back straight, then walked calmly out the elaborate front door of Marble Hall, wearing nothing but a towel. *I'm back, Swan. You don't own me and my family this time. I slept in your house. I slept with your granddaughter. I've staked my place in your territory.* He hated thinking of Darl as a prize even as he indulged the idea. Once in the bright autumn sunshine he exhaled and strode to the big Explorer. He opened the back luggage door, pawed underwear, jeans, and a gray thermal pullover to the surface, got dressed, then shaved as best he could with a dry razor, knicking himself twice. He wiped the tiny smears of blood and thought, *You look rough and no-account.* Next he reached for the carrying case that held his computer and other devices, including a cell phone.

He called William in D.C. Eli had left him a message last night.

"Finally. You call in," William said tensely.

"Any luck? What's wrong?"

"I'm leaving for the airport within the hour. I've located Karen Noland. She's filming a guest part in a music video in Los Angeles. I'll speak to her in person."

"Good." The night before, Darl had left several messages at Karen's New York apartment and at the production offices for *Attractions.* None had yet been returned. Eli found his wristwatch in the luggage. It was nearly ten a.m., eastern time. Los Angeles was four hours earlier. With any luck, William would find Karen and convince her to come home by nightfall. "I owe you, man. Is there anything else?"

"Unfortunately, yes." For once, even William's smooth Jamaican voice sounded tense. "I would have told you yesterday if I'd known. I just learned of it."

"What?"

There was pause. "Your sister. Your mother. They are there."

"What do you mean?"

"Two days ago, they went to Burnt Stand. Your sister met with Swan Samples. Two days ago. They are still there." He paused. "They believe they are taking some of the burden of surprise off you."

Eli's mouth went dry. He listened vaguely as William gave him the name of the inn where Bell and Mama had set up camp. A few seconds later he was in the Explorer, and driving.

*

Solo had deserted me to go exploring. That worried me. After three days of devoted companionship he'd suddenly decided to tour Burnt Stand alone? I showered and dressed in creased slacks, a pullover, and brown-leather mules. I stood in my old bedroom braiding my hair into a rigid twist and wondering grimly what he hoped to learn about my hometown. About me—after my embarassing breakdown the night before.

I pulled the infinity stone from my slacks' pocket and looked at it a long time. I laid it on a dresser as if it belonged there. I gazed around the room. Swan had redone it after I left home, and I knew she'd deliberately removed the window had overlooked the woods leading to the stone flower garden and the stone cottage.

"The truth's still out there, even without a window to see it," I told her once.

She had looked completely unmoved. "I have memories so painful I'll never even whisper them to you. But I've put them away. Closed the window. You will, too."

Now I'd let Solo into this private sanctuary. Maybe I *did* want to forget what had happened to Eli and his family. Maybe I was turning into Swan without realizing it. People changed minute by minute, until they didn't recognize who they once were, and by then the passions that drove them had faded away. One day I'd look up and realize I'd walled off the memories, the truth, and could live with what was left of myself.

I shivered, picked up the infinity stone, and put it back in my pocket.

*

The Rakelow Inn sat on a shady back street in Burnt Stand, surrounded by flower beds and lawn. The style was vaguely colonial, and of course it was built entirely of marble. It was one of the Esta Houses. Eli grimaced.

Mama had cleaned for the Rakelow family before Matilda hired her at Marble Hall. Mama had wiped Rakelow toilets, scrubbed up the shit their poodle dog left on the rugs, smiled and said nothing when the Rakelow kids smeared mud on the doorsills she'd just washed. Eli kept thinking of that as he tried to understand why she and Bell had decided to come back to Burnt Stand without him—ahead of the schedule on which they'd agreed before he left for Florida. Now Mama sat firmly on a fancy divan in the inn's biggest upstairs suite, her hard-working hands knotted in the skirt of a handsome tailored dress of fine blue material. Bell stood by an arched window looking like a silk butterfly with long colorful scarves floating over her blouse and jeans. She was teary but adamant about her decisions. Her baby, Jessie, slept in the center of an antique bed covered in down comforters.

The Wade family had returned, and not as poor white trash.

"I see y'all needed to make a point to the people around here," Eli said wearily. "I've got no problem with that. Just wish you'd warned me." Seated on a couch in the big suite, he levered his elbows on his knees and rubbed his jaw. Mama kept staring at the dingy bandage on his left forearm.

"If we'd wanted to make a grand entrance," Bell said hotly, "We'd have made sure everyone knew our names. But I registered here under Bell Canetree."

"All right then, so why did you have to visit Swan and tell her who you are?"

"I wanted to be honest with her. I wanted her to know who really bought her land. I thought she might appreciate me coming forward and explaining what we intended to do with the property. That we only want to find out the truth. I thought she might be happy to know something that'd give her peace of mind and us, too. Eli, don't you think she's been dogged by terrible wonderings over how her sister died?"

Eli laughed. "I don't think Swan Samples has lost too much sleep over where or how Clara took her last breath."

Her face colored. "Just because you think Swan's mean doesn't *make* it so. Surely she wants to know who really killed Clara. She wants her sister's body found. *Surely.*"

"She thinks Pa did it. She thinks Clara's bones are lost in the bottom of a lake."

Bell thrust out her hands. "Eli, I told her the truth and that ought to make it easier for us, and her, too." She paused, scanning him with a frown. "And easier for you to chase Darl."

Eli straightened angrily. "All you had to do was get in touch with me down in Florida, and I'd have told you to leave it alone for now."

Mama spoke quietly. "Son, what *exactly* were you doing with Darl down there?"

"Taking care of her. She's in a bad way."

"And you thought it wise not to tell her who you are?"

"No, Mama, I didn't think it was wise at all. I just got caught up in the situation."

"I'm ashamed of you."

Her words cut into him, hitting home because he knew she was right. He exhaled wearily and nodded. "None of it worked out the way I expected. Things happened too fast. She needed me to be a stranger, and I played along. But I believe she recognized me. She may not realize it yet, but she did."

"You lied to her," Mama insisted.

He stared grimly at the floor, and hunched his shoulders. "I did."

"Just like Bell lied to get Miss Swan's land."

"*Mama,*" Bell said.

Their mother stood. "We've none of us got a lot to be proud of right this second. When Bell decided to see Miss Swan in person and tell her the truth, I said, 'Yes, we need to do that. This family is not going to sink deeper into shenanigans and ugly ways.' That kind of thing does no honor to your pa's memory. Son, you have to tell Darl who you are. *Today.*"

Eli nodded, but leveled a somber gaze at his sister. "I want you to be prepared for what people'll say when word gets out about us bein' back here. They're goin' to say we caused Swan's heart attack and Matilda's stroke."

Bell gasped. "That's not true! Swan and I had a nice conversation. She wasn't upset at all. She told me she needed to think about what we planned to do with the land—digging around, and all that—and she'd talk to us some more when you got here. I said you were away on business. I didn't say where. Eli—I swear to you—she was cool as a cucumber."

Eli smiled thinly. "You didn't win her over. She just lay there like a snake, waitin' for you to trust her and get close. You're lucky she didn't strike. I expect she's plannin' to eat us alive."

"Miss Swan was always fair to me," Mama said firmly.

Eli sighed. "She thinks Pa killed her sister. That's a closed case to her. I guarantee she's not happy about us stirrin' up the ugliness, again."

Mama looked at him wistfully. "But Darl will talk to her for us. You say Darl wants to believe your pa is innocent. You say Darl is a good person."

Eli looked away. His throat worked. "She's the best."

"Then you tell her who you are, and if you've already proved yourself to be a good man in her eyes, she'll trust you and she'll forgive you—and she'll honor what we came here for."

He stood and touched his mother's shoulder. "There's the test we both have to pass."

Mama nodded.

*

Gloria, the new housekeeper, didn't like me. I sat at the dining room table with a cup of coffee and some toast I'd made in the kitchen while she and the maid watched unhappily. I spread my grandmother's files around me on the gleaming mahogany table. Gloria stood by the door, adjusting the lights on the room's chandelier, and glared at me as if I'd killed Swan then assumed her throne. "I called the hospital," she said in her heavily accented voice. "Miss Swan and Miss Matilda were just moved. They are now sharing a hospital room." Her tone was slightly dismissive, as if she assumed she were more concerned with their well-being than I.

"Yes, I know. I'm leaving in a few minutes to see them, but I need to go over these papers, first."

"I've packed some things for your grandmother and Miss Matilda. Fruit. Muffins. Miss Swan likes blueberry. And I've included some sliced ham and sugarless cookies for Miss Matilda. You know she has the diabetes."

"Thank you. You're very efficient."

"I've put out car keys for you. Miss Swan bought a Lexus this spring."

"That will be fine." I picked up some papers and began to scan them. Gloria cleared her throat. "There is a meeting here in a few days. There will be houseguests. It is a very important meeting."

I frowned. "Is this the guest list?" I held up a sheet. She nodded. I read a dozen names, including the directors of several state social agencies and the outreach chairs of major interfaith church organizations. VIPs. What was this about?

"Should I cancel the arrangements?" Gloria asked.

"No."

"You will be in charge?"

"I think I can manage."

"Where I come from, a granddaughter honors her grandmother. I hope you will find it in your heart to stay here and do this work. I would give you the same respect I give your grandmother."

"Good. Then help me out, here. Did my grandmother have a guest recently—a woman she met two days ago? Did she say anything about that?"

Gloria stared at me. "I know of no one."

*And you wouldn't tell me if you did*, I thought. I eyed her bluntly. "My grandmother is not exactly a warm and lovable person who inspires adoration. Why are you so loyal?"

Disdain gleamed in her eyes. "She pays fairly and she treats people with respect. I have worked for Americans who did neither. In my part of the world, we don't expect an employer to be our friend. We understand that the strong protect the weak, and the weak owe loyalty to the strong."

"That's called a dictatorship, Gloria."

"When the strong are true ladies, as is so with Miss Swan, it is a fine system."

*So Swan's right up there with Eva Peron and Imelda Marcos*, I thought to myself. "Thank you. I was just curious." Gloria clamped her lips tightly and made no move to leave. I'd had enough, and gave her a look that told her so. Her eyes widened. She saw my grandmother in me, cold and dangerous. She nodded and left the room.

I went over the rest of the papers quickly. What I found stopped me with my mouth open in dismay. Swan had committed half-a-million dollars of her own money toward the purchase of land and construction of buildings for something called *Stand Tall*. It was an enormous amount of money, even by Swan's standards. The project would be some kind of group home and educational center for troubled children from all over the state.

I put the papers down and sat there staring into space. Either this was her most cold-blooded effort yet to lure me back to Burnt Stand, or she was trying to buy her way into heaven with good deeds.

*No way, Grandmother. We're both going to hell.*

\*

Swan and Matilda's shared hospital room was large, but flower arrangements filled it like a greenhouse. Their well-wishers included the governor, several state representatives, and every important mining official or quarry owner in the south. I set Gloria's food basket on the stand between the matching beds. My grandmother looked tired but otherwise regal, though she was still attached to oxygen and an IV tube. "I made it out of intensive care in record time," she said. "Are you frightened by my superhuman abilities?"

"It doesn't count if you're a member of the hospital board and threaten to have your cardiologist's license pulled unless he does your bidding."

"If I had such power, I'd use it to make you do what I want."

"I think you are. Tell me about *Stand Tall.*"

"It's a children's home. A guidance center for troubled youth. Run by the Hardigree Foundation, which I have newly created just for the purpose. My lawyer will bring you all the paperwork. I'm sure you'll want to get involved. It's a legacy you can be proud of." She paused, her eyes glittering with cool amusement. "One you can't escape, if I work it just right."

"Please, don't start this again, you two," Matilda said with quiet distress, dragging the words across her slanted lips. She lay curled on her side in her bed, a swath of pale blue silk robe and nightgown enveloping her thin brown body, a light afghan pulled over her legs. Swan was all in white, as usual. They made a grand duo, two white-haired matriarchs, sisters beneath pale skin and brown. My heart twisted. "I apologize, Matilda."

"Have you talked to Karen?"

"Not yet. She must be away from New York. I've left messages. I'll try again this afternoon." Matilda sighed. Swan pointed to a phone on their shared nightstand. "Matilda, you should leave a message for her yourself. Let her hear your voice."

Matilda shook her head. "I won't beg."

Someone knocked on the door. "Come in," I called. Leon eased into the room, frowning, a big man trying to negotiate small spaces. He looked almost dapper in a tweed sports coat and tan trousers. But as before, marble dust coated his shoes. "Good mornin'. Stopped by to see if there's anything you ladies need." He shifted awkwardly.

"To be young again," Swan said.

"Well, now—"

"You've brought me a card?" Matilda asked. Her eyes went to a folded sheet of construction paper in his hand.

"Yes, ma'am. Carla Ann drew it for you." He handed her the crayon drawing and sweet message. His daughter, Carla Ann, was six years old. He had a son, Reggie, who was only three. Leon's wife, who I'd heard described as 'a good Yankee' he'd met at the University of North Carolina, had died of cancer. Matilda doted on Leon's children. She held the homemade card to her chest.

Leon turned to me. "Mornin'."

"Good morning."

"Your friend and I had a nice talk downstairs in the lobby last night. You know, I believe he's a fine man."

I looked at him warily. I'd never gotten the impression Leon gave his instant respect to strangers. "Thank you. I'll tell him you said so."

With a look on his face that said he was protecting my reputation in front of my grandmother, Leon added, "I see you got him a room at the Rakelow last night." My blank stare raised consternation in his eyes. "I, uh, saw my Explorer parked in front on my way here."

"Oh. Yes." I saved poor Leon, while my mind whirled. Why was Solo at the Rakelow Inn? Had he decided to book a room? Why? I chewed the information silently as Leon made small talk. Swan's gaze bored into me. The moment Leon said his goodbyes and left the room, she sat up in bed. "Tell me about this friend." I explained about Solo. Just the facts.

"That's all you know about him?"

"I only met him a few days ago."

"I see."

"No, you don't. He's a remarkable person, and he came here because I asked him to. I can depend on him."

"You should have told me sooner," Swan said curtly.

"I couldn't last night."

Swan looked at me. "Shut the door. We have to talk."

I closed the room's heavy door then moved uneasily to the foot of Swan's bed. Swan lay back on her pillows with lethargic calm, undoubtedly due to medication as well as willpower. But as her gaze swiveled to me I saw worry, and my stomach twisted. "I said yesterday I have something to tell you," she said.

"I don't know what this has to do with my friend."

"Perhaps nothing. Or perhaps you've been the victim of a very disturbing deception."

"Grandmother, what are you hinting at?"

She straightened her bed covers, an almost unselfconscious

act that alarmed me because Swan never fidgeted and never hesitated. Abruptly she spread her pale, fine-boned hands on the blanket. She was settled. Ready for battle. "I've sold the two hundred acres behind Marble Hall."

I stared at her. That land had been in the Hardigree family for over sixty years. Esta had put the estate together. The Stone Cottage was there. And the Stone Flower Garden. *And Clara's grave.* I clutched the steel footboard of her bed and leaned towards her. "Is this a joke?" I managed finally.

"Not at all. I sold the land to a buyer from Memphis. An attorney who said he was acquiring investment properties for his clients." She paused. "The agreement includes certain covenants. Primarily, that the garden be preserved."

"How could you risk that? People break covenants all the time." I looked at Matilda. Her breath rattled in a coarse wheeze. "Did you know about this?" She nodded. "*You agreed?*" She nodded again.

"We did it for your sake," Swan went on. "To show you the place has no power over us, and shouldn't have any over you."

"I don't believe this. I don't believe you turned the garden over to strangers." My voice rose. "*Covenants can be broken.*"

"We're willing to take that chance. I'm committing the money from the sale to Stand Tall."

So that was where the half-million had come from. Sweat broke out on my face. "What are you really trying to prove? That we're invincible? That we can *still* get away with murder—"

"Stop it." Matilda's voice. She was quivering. "We're risking it in order to do something good for our family. To create something that will keep you here and bring Karen back. A legacy you'll both be proud of. *Something that turns a terrible mistake into a blessing.*"

Swan pointed at me. "You think I'm arrogant and reckless?" A brittle smile drew at her mouth. "Perhaps you're right. The attorney was merely a broker—I knew that. But I failed to find out that he had only *one* client, or that his client has some very peculiar ideas about the land."

I straightened. How much worse could this possibly be? "Tell me."

Swan hesitated. "The woman who came to see me two days

ago was Bell Wade. She bought the land."

A clinical wall clock ticked off the seconds. Matilda slowly put her hands to her face, then lay back and shut her eyes. Once the shock wave swept over me I resurfaced and felt everything click into place. Swan was speaking. "And she intends—with her brother's help and approval—to search for clues on the land to prove their father's innocence."

*Eli.*

"You had better go speak with your 'friend,'" Swan said. "I hope for your sake he's not Eli Wade."

*

Eli was on his way to find Darl, and had just stepped off the stair landing at the Rakelow, entering a broad foyer. The inn's double doors stood open, allowing the cool fall air to seep through screen doors from the marble veranda. The manicured front yard was visible. A smooth marble walkway led up the center of the lawn directly to the front steps.

Darl was walking slowly up that path.

Eli halted. *Godawmighty. She knows.* One look at her measured stride, her frozen expression, her rigid posture confirmed it. *She knows.* He shoved the screened doors open and stepped onto the veranda as Darl reached the lowest step. She halted and raised her gaze to him. Her face was chilling in its resistance, but her eyes were full of pain. "Eli?" she asked in a low voice.

He nodded.

She wavered as if he'd hit her, then turned and walked away.

Eli leapt down the steps. When he blocked her she swayed a little. He reached for her. "Don't," she ordered, and the look of her said he'd do more harm than good. He lowered his hands but bent his head close to hers. "I've only said one word to you that isn't true. The name *Solo.* And even it's an honest name. I know I've got a lot to explain—and I will. But right now you need to know I didn't lie to hurt you or to use you."

She said nothing. He wished she'd scream at him or call him names, but she didn't. The emotion, the tension, the bleak vibration in her and in him electrified the air. He could see the finest tremor in her, and his own hands were shaking. He couldn't help himself. He took her by the shoulders. "Please come with me," he ordered in a low voice. "Let me drive us somewhere quiet and we'll talk about everything. I'll tell you whatever you want to know. I've got nothing to hide, and I want to make things right for you and me, too. I know how that sounds right now, but it's true."

Darl gave an almost imperceptible shake of her head. "You lied to get the land."

"That was a mistake."

"Let me go. You have no idea what you're getting into."

"Please, listen." He held onto her harshly, squeezing her shoulders. "Over the past few days you and me—we *found* each other, Darl. Two strangers. We built up more trust and kindness and love than most people get in a whole lifetime. Don't let me ruin it with one mistake, and don't you ruin it with fast judgements."

"It was ruined from the beginning. It was ruined twenty-five years ago. Let me go."

He had to concentrate to unfurl his fingers when every instinct urged him to hold her closer, to break through, to make her listen. *It was ruined twenty-five years ago.* "When you thought I was a stranger, I was special. Now I'm just someone you want to forget." He lowered his hands. She stared up at him. "I want you to forget *me*," she corrected. He could make no sense of that. He started to tell her so.

"Darl!" Bell's voice. Darl slowly swiveled her attention to the veranda behind him. Her face softened in convulsive welcome. Bell and Mama stood there, Bell holding the baby, Mama with her hands pressed to her throat. "*Please* forgive Eli," Mama said. "He only meant to help you. He was sure you wouldn't have a thing to do with him if he told you who he was right off. He was wrong to lie to you, and Bell was wrong was wrong to go behind Miss Swan's back and buy the land. But they did it with a good heart. None of us want to cause more misery. We want peace. We want—" her voice broke—"some kind of saving grace for my Jasper. And for ourselves."

Her eyes hard but shimmering with tears, Darl nodded. When she looked at Eli he thought his heart would break from frustration. What was going through her mind? Why was she rejecting him but also rejecting herself? "You do what you have to do," she said. "But I can't help you."

She walked away, and for the moment, he let her.

# 16

Los Angeles was just a hot, smoggy dream outside the dark confines of the studio where Karen writhed on the hood of a gleaming black Jaguar. Cameras recorded every movement. Behind her and around her, a dozen nearly naked women pumped their pelvises to the hard-driving playback of a rap song.

"Cut," the director yelled. "*Shit.*" The choreographer, a muscular Nigerian-born woman who wore colorful kinte cloth sashes tied around her forehead, began cursing the dancers for a misstep. "Let's take a fuckin' break here," the director bellowed.

Karen slid off the prop car, sweating, then weakly made her way through the dancers. A tide of vomit rose in her throat. Her breasts felt like overfilled balloons bursting from the top of her skintight leather mini-dress. The hem was so short she could feel the breeze from a stage fan on the cheeks of her butt. "Miss Soap Opera's too clean to listen to this shit," one of the girls sneered, loud enough for Karen to hear. Holding her stomach, she kept walking, well aware that the ambitious dancers—black girls, Latino girls, and blonde white girls—watched her like gleeful hawks. *You yellow bitch, Cool T dumped you and we know it.*

All of them sneered at her for what they saw as her desperate attempt to hang onto the attentions of Cool T by appearing in his latest video. In fact she'd dumped *him* a few weeks ago, right after he slapped her for the first and only time. But during the height of their brief romance she'd agreed to wiggle her ass in his video, and he'd held her to the contract. Thank god he hadn't come to the set to watch her humiliation, at least. Let him keep his streetwise pride. She only wanted to get this over with and find some peace in her life.

Karen rushed down a narrow hallway and into a small restroom used by the crew, where she threw up violently in the sink. When her stomach was under control again she rinsed her mouth and glared at herself in a small mirror. Her agent had warned her not to get involved with Cool T. He had an arrest record as long as his arm, and his videos were nasty—just plain nasty. The producers of *Attractions* had threatened to write her out of the show if she appeared in one.

"Why did I do this?" she asked the mirror.

*Because you wanted out. Because you hate your life.*

She walked out of the restroom then leaned against a wall with her eyes shut and one hand splayed over her stomach. A melodic male voice said, "Miss Noland? I'm very sorry to bother you."

She jumped and looked around quickly. A pleasant-faced, dapper black man with the thick build of a weightlifter stood there, dressed in a sports coat and slacks. He wasn't from L.A., she decided — and clearly was not in show business. He looked like an ordinary human being. She stared at him warily. "What do you want?"

"I apologize for my timing. Are you ill? Can I help?" His Carribean voice lulled her, but she noticed instantly he wore no security pass. Karen tensed. "Who are you and how did you get on this soundstage without permission?"

"My name is William Leyland. I'm a security consultant, and I have considerable connections in the security industry. I'm in quite a hurry, so I'm afraid I didn't follow much protocol." He paused. "Also, my wife owns a large publicity firm in Washington D.C. She's an avid fan of yours. She made some calls to Mr. Cool T's record company and that opened doors. Sorry to surprise you."

Karen's skin chilled. Stalkers and crazy fans always concocted the most creative stories. She began to ease down the hallway toward the safety of the cast and crew. "That's allright. Let's walk this way while we talk."

"Miss Noland. Please. I'm here on behalf of Darl Union."

She halted. *Darl.* "Is she all right?"

"Oh, yes. Yes. She hates to alarm you, but both her grandmother and yours are hospitalized in Burnt Stand."

Karen froze, struggling. Years of estrangement—her own doing—could not stop the flood of anxiety and love that rose in her now. *My only family.* "My grandmother is, is she . . . what's wrong?"

He explained her grandmother's mild stroke. Karen sagged against the wall, fighting back tears. How long had Grandmother been in such poor health without telling her? They did talk on the phone regularly, albeit without saying much. Grandmother was just too damned proud. *And so am I*, Karen thought in agony.

"Will you come right away?" Darl's strange emissary asked. "I've arranged a first-class ticket for you on a flight leaving LAX in one hour. And I have a limosine waiting."

"Yo," a thick voice called out. A burly young manager with dread locks, a lot of attitude, and a clipboard, waved at her from the end of the hallway. "You're due," he said, and jerked his thumb toward the stage. Karen looked at him grimly. *I was raised in the South and people down there expect better manners*, she wanted to yell. *My grandmother is a lady, and so am I.* Bile rose in her throat again. Heavy, lurid makeup itched on her face. Her breasts ached and bulged, and her ass was cold. For good or bad, this was a turning point in her life. Darl had sent for her, and Grandmother needed her. She had family.

"Mr. Leyland," she said. "Let's go home."

*

How many clues there were. How blind I'd been. Eli had tried to tell me about himself several times. I gave him credit for that.

There was a great settling inside me, shock and meaning and the numb instinctive confusion anyone would expect. Nothing and everything, a thousand sharp points waiting to tear me apart—so many questions, so much to make me reel back, hold up my hands, sob with disbelief, anger, frustration. He had no idea what I'd hidden from *him.* All of that scalded my mind, and worst of all, in the pit of my stomach, under my ribs, where I lived inside my deepest needs, there existed the pure, resilient, unspeakable joy of reunion. *Eli.*

"So, it is him," Swan said calmly. I nodded. I sat in a low chair beside her bed, my head bent, my shoulders hunched. We were alone. Matilda had been taken out of the room for an EKG. My grandmother smiled thinly. "A *psychic* told his sister they'd find evidence on the property."

I uttered a bleak laugh. "We've been caught by the spirit world."

Swan sank one slender hand onto my shoulder and dug in her fingernails. The line of her IV swung gently with the sudden movement. I lifted my head in warning and held her stern gaze. "What are you thinking?" she demanded.

"I'm thinking I'll tell him the truth. If he's the man I believe he is, he won't hurt you or Matilda."

Her fingernails pinched into my skin through my shirt. "Let's discuss the man you *think* you know. A man who was willing to lie to you about his identity. To win your trust when he knew he'd be coming here to cause trouble. A man who could have contacted you at any time over the years, but didn't. A man who left the country and became a criminal. You don't even know how he managed to return."

I considered every argument, but realized they all came down to one irrational point: *I slept with him. That has to mean something.* The most pathetic excuse a woman could offer. "Whatever he's done or whatever he intended," I said, "he deserves to know the truth."

"Does he? Does he deserve to destroy your life without any consideration? My dear granddaughter, I know what I did to you. I know you have a right to hate me. But I also see that I've created a strong, proud woman who fights for good causes and does good in the world. You did not kill Clara. You did not kill Jasper Wade. If I could have saved you from seeing any of that—from knowing any of that—I would die happy at this moment. But the fact that you *do* know what happened shouldn't condemn you. If you tell Eli Wade the truth, and he is not the merciful man you hope for, he will ruin you. He will ruin your legacy as a Hardigree, and he'll ruin your own name. And your career—your ability to command respect and trust from your clients, from jurors, from judges, from the media. All ruined."

"If I were only worried about myself, I'd have told him already."

"All right, then, let me be more self-serving. *If you tell, it will kill Matilda.* No matter how Eli reacts. Merely knowing that the truth is out will kill her. And if you have any hopes of Karen ever coming back here, it will kill those, too. If she learns her grandmother was involved in Clara's *circumstance,* could she understand? Could she cope with the knowledge? Would she feel nothing but pity and disgust for her grandmother? Does Karen's public career deserve to be hurt? Does this entire town need to learn something that can only harm the decency and charm that makes life here special?"

I felt strangled. Weighed down. Burdened. Hopeless. "Eli deserves to know," I said quietly. "And nothing can change that fact."

*"Then let him find out."* I stared at her. She nodded. "Do you seriously think it matters? Let him search. If he finds Clara's grave, what will it prove?" She leaned closer to me. "Hmmm? Found on land he has bought, land where his family lived at the time she disappeared? People will simply believe that his father buried her there. And so will he."

I stared at her. "You *want* him to find her body."

"Now that the situation has taken this turn, *yes.* The gossip about Clara's disappearance will end, once and for all. Eli and his family will gain a certain peace from simply answering the question they set out to answer, and we'll all bow our heads in a moment of prayer." She settled back, but her hand still clutched me. "Then I'll re-bury Clara with more graciousness than she deserves."

I said very slowly, and very quietly, "You'll ruin him if you can, but I won't let you."

She said nothing for a moment. Then, "You'll have to choose between him and your family. You decide." She would have been a good lawyer, but a hanging judge. I said nothing but she knew she had me. "I have to think," I said.

Silence. Finally, her voice low, she said, "In your eyes, the whole world is innocent except me."

I looked at her quietly. "Once upon a time, you *were* my whole world."

She let go of my shoulder. I would have five tiny, crescent-shaped bruises there.

Small marks. Branded.

*

Tommy Rakelow had been one of the meanest little well-off bastards in school. He was always behind the group taunts, the jabs and jokes that led to fist fights. Eli had never punched the little bastard because he *was* little. Tommy, like Eli, was nearly forty years old now but *still* little—plus half-bald and paunchy, to boot. He and his wife ran the inn. He stopped Eli in the veranda where Eli was pacing with a cigar in his fist.

"I'm afraid those ladies of yours will have to stay somewhere else," Tommy said.

"What's the problem?"

"My wife made a mistake on our calendar. We'd booked their suite upstairs for the rest of the week. The guests get here today."

"Then my mother and sister can move downstairs."

"Those rooms are all booked, too."

Eli saw the deceit in Tommy's eyes. A chill ran through him. "You know who I am," he said.

Tommy took a step back. "Now look, Wade, I don't want trouble."

"Did Swan Samples tell you to kick my family out?"

"I said I don't want any trouble. Let's be honest. You and your family don't look like you have the money to stay here."

Goddamn Swan. Trouble was already starting. "If you say anything to my mother or sister I'll do what I should've done when we were kids. I'll nail your little ass to one of these marble walls."

Tommy blanched.

Eli left him standing there.

It was time to play this game by the numbers.

*

Burnt Stand Realty. Eli walked inside the marble storefront without pausing to slam the wooden door behind him. It swung shut with a clatter. A neatly dressed young man gawked up at him from a front desk. "You the receptionist?" Eli asked.

The man blinked hard. "Uh, no sir. I'm an agent."

Eli studied him. "Did you grow up here?"

"Uh, uh, no. I grew up in Asheville. My wife and I just moved here last year. But I assure you I am very knowledgeable about all the property listings in this wonderful, historic—"

"Good." Eli jerked a chair to the man's desk and sat down. "Are any of the Esta Houses up for sale?"

"Oh! I see you're familiar with our charming traditions and our finest homes. Why, yes, several are on the market—all in splendid condition—and two of them are partially furnished. Antiques, fine rugs—" He paused, eyeing Eli's faded jeans, the arm bandage, the specks of blood where he'd cut himself shaving, and lastly dropping his gaze to Eli's large, callused hands. "Now you understand, these houses are quite expensive. But I have several very nice listings for much smaller homes outside town—"

"I'll take the Esta Houses."

The man blinked at him. "Sir?"

"All the Esta Houses. Furnished, unfurnished, whatever. And once my mother picks out the one she likes best, I want you to get me a decorator, and I want that decorator to finish the decoratin'. And I want it done by tomorrow. I'll put my mother and a sister and a baby niece in a motel for tonight, but by dinnertime tomorrow I want 'em sittin' in their favorite Esta House. And *then* I want you to find me some tenants for the others. Yeah—get me some stonecutters and other folk who wouldn't have the wherewithal ordinarily. I won't charge any rent. Don't you think that'd be nice? Givin' regular folk a chance to raise their kids in an Esta House? I believe I'll like being a landlord in this town." He stared at the agent. "Can do?"

The agent stared at him, open-mouthed. "We're talking about upwards of two million dollars for those houses. This, this, this will take time and paperwork—"

"No, bubba—" Eli jerked a cell phone from his shirt pocket— "all it takes is one call to my bank. I'm payin' cash."

*

I swam laps in the pool at Marble Hall until my chest hurt and I could barely raise my arms, but I couldn't stop the chant of hopeless choices in my brain. When Gloria ushered Leon onto the patio she sniffed at the sight of my slacks and shoes tossed at poolside. *You're not a lady like your grandmother.* I was swimming in my underwear and shirt. But Leon noticed and halted awkwardly, giving my behavior a worried frown. I hung on the pool's marble lip, trying to breathe, and shook my head. *Don't try to understand.* He scowled harder. "I came to tell you I'm not taking sides against Eli Wade." He said that quietly, just as a plain fact.

I nodded, struggling for air, for perspective. "Won't ask you to."

"Your grandma did. I told her no, and she fired me."

My lungs began to recover. "I'll take care of it. You're not fired. Keep doing your job."

"You've got to understand something. I know Swan makes decisions based on what's best for her company and her reputation. I don't fool myself thinkin' she'd have put me in charge if she thought it'd hurt her business to let a black man run Hardigree Marble. Hell, some people told *me* I ought not to work for her. Said I could leave here and run my own business anywhere I wanted."

"Why did you stay?"

"This is my town, too—my roots, my people." He jabbed his hand down at the bedrock. "This is where I can make a difference. This is where people can see how things can change the most." He paused, then smiled grimly. "And Eli's part of that. He's my people, too. A stonecutter. White as flour, but still."

"I don't doubt he's proud to be considered that way."

"Good. Just so you understand. I'll give up my job rather than get in Eli's way. If he thinks his daddy was innocent and maybe there's some way to prove it by digging in the land behind this place, then by god I'll help him look. There's always been talk that Jasper Wade got a raw deal. Talk that your grandma was lookin' for somebody to blame and he was convenient. I'm not sayin' I believe it, but the talk was there, and still is. Eli's got friends he doesn't know about. Men who were stonecutters then. Men who respected his daddy."

"I want you to give Eli all the help you can." Leon stared at me in surprise. I nodded. "I want you to put the word out. Invite him to the quarry. Make sure the men see him with you. I want people to help him." I paused. "Because I can't help him, myself."

"But you'll keep your grandma calmed down?" I nodded. He pondered that a moment, as if stunned. "All right, then. Let me tell you what kind of job you got cut out for you. A little while ago Eli walked into the real estate office and bought five Esta Houses. Nearly two-million-dollars worth of property. His bank is sendin' the money. All of it."

*Why?* I clung to the side of the pool and listened in disbelief as Leon explained. "Tommy Rakelow kicked his mama and sister out of the inn. I feel sure your grandma had something to do with that. So Eli's moving his mama and his sister into one of the fine Esta Houses tomorrow. He says he's goin' to rent the others out cheap, to stonecutters. Word's already all over the quarry. The men are excited. He's staking his claim. Telling us all we better not mess with him—and sure better not mess with his family. The man's here to make a point. Swan's not goin' to stop him."

The slow burn of despair and fury over Swan's tactics kept me quiet. *Grandmother, don't push me.* Leon shook his head in dismay when I said nothing. "Eli told me his real name last night. He asked me to keep it to myself. I said I would. I don't think the man's a cheat or a liar. He hasn't seen me for twenty-five years, but he still trusted me. And so I'm goin' to trust him. I hope you will, too."

"I intend to do all I can to give him the opportunity he deserves."

"You're willin' to hold the door open, but you won't walk through it with him?"

"That's right."

I saw Leon's respect for me erode a little. His face grim, he said, "Well, I guess that's fair enough. You're a Hardigree." I felt scalded. He turned to go. "Eli says he wants to meet you in the stone garden before dark." My heart twisted. So this was the message Leon had been asked to deliver. "If you really want to be fair to him," Leon went on, "you'll go and listen." He nodded to me, then walked out through the front gate.

I levered myself onto the lip of the pool and sat there staring into the back woods. *Eli.* His name, his identity, was the doomed song in me. Stranger, lover, mystery man, rich man, trustee of souls, seeker of truth, victim of Swan's design.

Standing over Clara's bones.

\*

Eli sat on his heels among the briars and weeds that filled the front yard of the  Stone Cottage. The small marble house was hemmed in by tall young maples that had grown up at the foundation's edge over the years. Muscadine and honeysuckle vines covered the marble walls and slate roof. Here and there between the vines he glimpsed pink stone or the weathered boards that had been placed over the windows and doors.

He reached down through the briars, scraped away the leafy loam of twenty-five  seasons, and dug his fingers into the soil. This was where Pa had died. His blood had soaked the dirt. Right here. Eli studied the granules of fine, dark soil, rubbed them between his fingers, brought the earth to his face and smelled it. Then he bent his head and prayed. *Lead us to the truth, even if it hurts like Hell.*

Goosebumps spread over his skin, and he stood quickly. Instinct alone made him swivel his gaze up the hill behind the house. In the steep afternoon shadows only a few rays of sunlight poured through the huge firs and hardwoods. Darl stood at the top of that knoll, watching him through the forest. She had been caught not quite in the light, haloed by shadows. A slip of breeze stirred her hair and moved the material of a white blouse she'd tucked into a long, flowing skirt the color of wood. She might have been there all his life, waiting, timeless and trapped in Swan's hard world. She raised a hand slowly, as if swearing herself to give testimony, then turned and disappeared down the other side of the hill, along the overgrown path to the Stone Flower Garden.

He followed.

*

My nightmares about Clara were never surreal or vaguely symbolic, but instead played out in vivid detail, a small horror film I was forced to watch. Clara always clawed her way out of her grave. She lurched upright like a ghoul, spilling dirt and leaves and writhing worms from her decayed skin. Her sunken eyes gleamed bright, fierce blue. Her Hardigree pendant was twisted in the gore and the dirt of her ruined clothing. She wrapped one arm around the moss-speckled base of the stone flower statue beside her, caressed it, then looked up at the intricately carved flowers cascading from its wide vase. *These stone flowers will talk for me some day.*

My mouth tasted sour and my legs went weak. I stood with my head up and my hands clenched in front of me, well outside the lost garden's bowl-shaped cove and circle of mossy marble benches, keeping myself on the slope above that haunted place. I watched as Eli crested the low ridge facing me, but I never fully ignored the leaf-matted ground beside the statuary's base. No rational part of my brain could make me turn my back on Clara.

Eli Wade walked down the slope as a grown man—broad-shouldered, big, lean, with the large, dark eyes that made my heart race a little whenever I studied his face. At almost forty his face had taken on a seasoned character. His eyes were still compelling, but hard. He didn't need any pretense. He simply took the place of his own ghost, that boy I'd loved so innocently. Solo merged with the image, too. Eli was now whole and real, and he'd come back. The slow twisting of joy, pain and frustration in my chest nearly choked me.

He halted at the opposite side of the garden his own grandfather had built at my great-grandmother's command. "I knew you'd come," he said. "You can't help rememberin' how much we meant to each other, any more than I can." He took a step toward me, then stopped again when I held up a warning hand. He obviously meant to close in on me by slow degrees, as if I were a deer who might turn and run. "I didn't know Bell tricked your grandmother out of this property," he went on. "I wouldn't have let her do it. She's got some crazy ideas about the land.  But once she told me what she'd done I realized how much the past hangs over me, too. And over our mother. And over you. I saw in Florida how much you need to get out from under it."

"What else hangs over you? The gambling? Did you come back here with a price on your head and the Justice Department looking for you?"

"Prosecuting sports bookies—even big-time ones—is low on the government's list of things to do. I made things right. I'm clean, Darl."

"But you've made a lot of money."

"I invested my ill-gotten gains pretty well. High-tech companies, high-tech stocks. I was in on the start of a few prime Silicon Valley outfits."

I balanced on the balls of my feet, dazed. "Where did you meet William?"

"We were partners in the islands. He handled security. He made money, too. He doesn't need to work anymore."

"And he just happens to like the challenge of coordinating security for the Phoenix Group. Where I work."

"He believes in the group's mission. He likes being part of that."

"I'm trying to understand your connections there."

"I'll tell you everything. Just calm down and listen."

"You maneuvered to place your old friend where he could watch me. Is that it?"

His face tightened. "No. Please let me—"

"You could have come to me. You could have told me about yourself. I'd have understood."

"I know that now."

My shoulders sagged. "Please promise me you won't tear up this garden."

"I can't promise you that. I came here thinking that digging up this land is a crazy plan, and maybe it is, but I'll follow it through."

*He'll dig up everything. He'll find Clara, and  believe the wrong answer.* "If you find evidence that someone else killed Clara, what will you do?"

His eyes filled with cold determination. "I'll track the bastard down and put him in prison. Isn't that what you'd want? Wouldn't you help me?"

I swayed. If I'd had any doubts about his goals or his passion, it vanished. He wanted revenge, justice, a pound of flesh. Hardigree flesh, if he knew. "My grandmother is sick, and old. So is Matilda. If you'd just wait—"

"Until they die?" I nodded. He stared at me grimly. "You're saying the gossip I might stir up is more important to them than finding out who really killed Clara? Look, I know there was no love lost between Swan and Clara, but deep down your grandma's *got* to want to know what really happened to her sister."

I felt as if my skin were separating from my bones. "I support what you have to do for your family. But I don't support your plan."

He took another step toward me, the tension hanging thicker in the air, his eyes boring into me. "You think my pa did it. That's it, isn't? You're afraid he did it. And you can't let yourself be with me if this is true."

I stared at him. "I'd never, *never*—"

"You're a bad liar, Darl. I see it in your eyes. You're hiding something. And that's it. That's the only thing that makes sense. You'd have to turn your back on me if I proved my pa really killed Clara. You'd have to uphold the Hardigree reputation. Is that it?"

"Please don't make any assumptions about me. You barely know me."

"What the hell else am I supposed to think? Goddammit, *talk to me.*" He strode down into the garden, across Clara's grave, and up the slope to me with furious speed. Before I could back away he caught me in his arms. I braced my hands against his chest, pushing, pulling, in agony. "Barely know you?" he echoed. "Don't you *ever* say that to me again. You know that's not true."

"I can't help you, I can't give you my blessing, I can't . . . go on with you the way we were in Florida. It's not the same, now."

"Don't let Swan keep hold of you. What has she *done* to you? Has she twisted you so much that you *are* turning into her? The girl I knew—hell, the woman I knew in Florida—would never turn her back on me. Is this about protecting the Hardigree name? You're a Hardigree, so you can't love me unless I've got the right pedigree? I can't believe it."

"I do love you," I said. "I'll love you all my life."

"*Darl.*" He searched my eyes, lifted a hand to my face, stroked his thumb roughly, lovingly across my cheek. Imprinting me, my words, on his skin. We were both on the verge of tears. A bell began to ring in the distance—the old bell that Matilda had used to call Karen and me to the house when we roamed.

"I have to go. Dear God, just let me go."

He slowly released me and stepped back. "This isn't over. I'm not goin' to let you give up on happiness the way your grandmother'd have you do. Whatever else is drivin' you, I'll dig that up, too."

Those words tore at me along with the peeling of the old brass bell. I was being split in two. I backed up the slope. "Don't ever ask me to meet you here, again. It's haunted."

"*I love you.*"

I shook my head. "You can't."

We were haunted, too.

*

William stood at the top of the back terrace, among the marble swans. And standing beside him, posed in the fading light of the day, golden brown and beautiful in simple black slacks and a sweater, Karen saw me come out of the woods. For the first time in twenty-five years, my beloved cousin ran down the terrace steps to hug me.

She had no idea.

*

When I ushered Karen into Swan and Matilda's hospital room I noticed a new IV unit next to Matilda's bed. The device's long, thin tube ran to a needle taped to her right forearm. She napped under the utilitarian bedcovers, and suddenly I saw her as she was:

A thin, sick old woman with fuzzy gray hair. Karen halted in the center of the room with her hands over her mouth and shock in her eyes. Swan lounged like a pale empress in the other bed, a small book of haiku poetry open in her hands. She still wore her own IV line, and an oxygen tube remained attached across her face. Her white hair streamed over the shoulders of a fresh silk gown and robe I'd brought her. She looked tired, but her blue eyes bored into Karen mercilessly. "Karen," she said in a strong voice. "Don't overreact. You'll do her no good."

I stared at Matilda with fear pulsing in my throat. "What's happened since I was here this morning?"

"Some tests showed a little trouble with her heart function. The doctors have put her on some new medications."

Karen walked unsteadily to Matilda's bedside. "Grandmother?" Matilda stirred, opened her eyes, and uttered a low, keening sound. Karen sat down beside her on the bed. *"Grandmother."* Matilda held up trembling arms. Karen swept her up in a convulsive embrace. As the soft, muffled sounds of their crying emerged, I sat down stiffly in a chair near Swan's bed. Our eyes met. I leaned close and whispered bitterly, "I know about the Rakelow Inn. And I know about Leon's job."

Swan's face remained impassive except for a wicked gleam of humor that rose in her eyes. She picked up an extra pillow she'd been using as an arm rest, pushed it toward me, and asked in a soft, mocking tone, "Tempted to put this over my face?"

"Yes." Her amusement faded. Across from us, Karen and Matilda continued to hold each other and sob. Swan and I would never hug, never cry on each other's shoulders. "I'll do whatever you want," I whispered. "But leave everyone else out of it."

She looked at me with dull victory, and nodded.

\*

Outside a motel on the edge of town, a crowd gathered that night. "Stay back," Eli told Mama and Bell. "We don't know these folks. They may be blamin' us for Swan and Matilda's sickness, like I warned you." Eli stepped outside the simple, one-story building, facing a parking lot full of old cars, pick-up trucks, and motorcycles. Several dozen rough-hewn men and stalwart women stood there. Stonecutters and their wives. Leon walked out of the crowd. "We brought you something to take back to your daddy's gravesite in Tennessee," he said. Eli exhaled with relief then called Mama and Bell outside. The three of them watched as the people parted around a small trailer. On it sat a tall marble monument with the most beautiful hand carving Eli had ever seen.

Jasper Wade

Husband

Father

Stonecutter

Rest in peace and justice

"We gave you these words from the heart," Leon said. "You'll have to make 'em come true."

## 17

As Karen and I left the hospital lobby after a visit the next morning the information ladies gaped at us, and two of them hurried over. "Kare Noland," they exclaimed in unison. "*Cassandra*. We love you on the show. Your grandmother is so proud." I stood watching her graciously give the two white-haired white ladies her autograph, and I watched them thank her. "Does Grandmother really talk about me?" she asked, as we walked outside. We sat down in a meditation garden of azaleas and marble benches. A marble plaque proclaimed the garden a donation of Hardigree Marble.

I nodded. "She told me she never misses an episode. I've heard that people stop her on the street to discuss your character's storylines. She loves discussing you." We stepped into the meditation garden and went to the bench there. In that small, private world Karen hunched forward and said quietly. "My contract's up. I've told my agent I'm leaving the show. I've already taped my last scenes." She shrugged. "Cassandra lives on. They've already got a new actress to play her." She raised her hands. "So I'm not going to be a celebrity for much longer."

I absorbed this morbid information with a puzzled frown. "Why are you giving it all up?"

"I'm pregnant."

I waited two beats, then asked calmly, "How far along are you?"

"Just two months."

"You love the baby's father?"

"No, and he's made it clear he doesn't want to *be* a father. Just as well. He's trash."

"Anyone I know?"

"Not unless you keep up with gangster rap."

"What happened?"

She stared at the marble walkway beneath our feet. "Looking for love in all the wrong places. Who knows? I've got money. I look good. I could go white or black, upscale or downtown—you know, I have my choice of men. I just can't seem to find one of any color who's worth it." Her face stilled. She bit her lip and looked away. "Being a mother is the first thing that's made sense."

"You need to tell your grandmother."

"I don't know how. She always wanted me to be above reproach. Pure class. Lena Horne." Karen laughed wearily. "I can't be Lena Horne. *She's* Lena Horne. So I guess I'll just be a glamorous unwed mother." She bent her head in her hands.

Slowly, I eased an arm around her shoulders. "Maybe you should start looking for love where it's simple, and where it will always be. Right here."

She straightened. We shared a fragile, searching pinpoint of emotion, then a tide of relief. "I've missed you, you fool," she whispered.

We tilted our heads together. "I've missed you, too."

Leon emerged from the hospital in the company of several men. We watched as he held a conversation with them. Stonecutters. White and black, a mixed group united in one trait—they listened with obvious deference and respect to whatever he was saying. I expected he was talking to them about Eli, and my heart twisted. "That's Leon Forrest," I whispered. "Do you remember him?"

Karen straightened, gave me a stunned look, then gazed at him. "Leon," she said softly.

Leon turned, scanning the garden casually, and saw us. We stood. His face went blank when he realized who Karen was, as if everything he knew about himself had suddenly deserted him and had to be reinstated one piece at a time. "Karen?" he said in a deep voice simmering with pleasure and disbelief. She walked over to him and held out a perfect hand. I watched Karen look up into Leon's somber, scarred face and I saw how he looked down at her. He clasped her hand like fine china between his big palms. They barely moved, they barely spoke. They traded welcomes, they traded lives.

*Look what's happening to them.* The slow prickle on my spine and the tears burning behind my eyes said my cousin was finding her way home with unerring instinct. I couldn't ruin that for her. Instead I mourned everything that had gone wrong in my own life. I thought of Eli, and ached for what we'd never have.

*

Eli woke, sweating, in an elegant bedroom in a fine new queen-sized bed with designer sheets and feather pillows, courtesy of the decorator who'd filled out an Esta House called the Broadside. The Broadside covered an entire large corner on two handsome, oak-shaded back streets in Burnt Stand. An Asheville executive and his wife—friends of Swan's—had retired there, but both had died in recent years, leaving their scattered children to sell the villa-like house with its marble porticos and piazzas, its chandeliered rooms and European antiques. The children—like the other mostly absentee owners of the other empty, expensive Esta Houses in Burnt Stand—had been very happy to receive a check for the full price, with no questions asked.

Mama and Bell had settled with Bell's baby in pretty bedrooms sporting private balconies and whirlpool tubs in giant bathrooms. Bell spent hours every night on a phone in the house's library, talking to her psychic or her husband, Alton. Every night, crying, she promised Alton they would all come to her senses soon.

"You have to let Mama do this alone. It's about *her* pride, we're *her* children, and we've been *wronged*, so she has to stand up for us." Bell said all that in a hissed whisper as she clutched Eli's arm and held him still. He chewed his tongue and tried not to walk after Mama, who was slowly making her way toward the hospital lobby's elevators. Mama gazed up at the board of directors' portraits, stopping before the elegant, gilt-framed paintings of Swan and Matilda. Modest and deliberately plain in a brown wool suit with soft brown loafers, Mama set her mouth and looked up at them firmly. She made Eli think of a determined gray-haired mouse gazing up at two languid cats.

"Can't do it," he announced to Bell. "Can't let her meet with

Swan alone. Wait here with little Jessie. I'm going with Mama."

"Brother, you stop it, stop, don't you—" An elevator door opened as Bell tugged furiously on Eli's long arm. To his surprise, Darl stepped out. She was dressed in trim gray slacks and a soft white sweater. She'd put her hair up in some kind of clasp, trickling a fine brunette strand or two over her forehead. The lovely shape of her, the sleek look of her, the tormented yet aloof set of her face all filled Eli with helpless wanting, angry and sad. Her stark blue gaze from him and Bell to Mama, where it warmed into a troubled welcome. "I heard you asked to see my grandmother," she said to Mama.

"I've got a bone to pick with her," Mama answered. "I'm sorry, Darl, I know she's sickly, and I won't visit long, but I sure do have to speak my piece."

"About the problem at the Rakelow Inn?"

Mama nodded. "Nobody tells my children they're not good enough to stay somewhere. I'm hopin' your grandma's just sick and not thinkin' right, treatin' my family that way."

"No, she knew exactly what she was doing, and there's no excuse for it. You, Bell and Eli—" her eyes moved to Eli's, then Bell's briefly—"have my heartfelt apology. You all don't have to live in a house in town. I'm inviting you all to please move your things to Marble Hall. As my guests."

Mama gaped at her. So did Bell. When Darl met Eli's eyes, he knew he looked angry but her offer had gotten to him. He shook his head slightly. "Please," Darl repeated.

"I appreciate it," he answered. "But we're set up at a good house in town. We don't need the charity."

"*Eli,*" Bell hissed. And Mama scowled at him.

Darl seemed to flinch, and it tore at him. "I didn't mean it that way."

Mama patted her arm. "We know that. Thank you kindly, but I'd just like to have my say with your grandma."

"All right. I'll go up with you." Darl turned to leave, guiding Mama into the elevator with one hand gently on her shoulder. Once inside the elevator, Darl looked back at Eli. "Take care of her," he commanded in a low voice. She nodded.

*And yourself,* he added silently, as the doors closed.

*

Annie Gwen was the widow of the man we had killed, Jasper Wade, Karen's full blood uncle and the son of Anthony Wade, whom Matilda had dearly loved. That was how I silently presented Annie Gwen Wade to Swan and Matilda—as a kinswoman and a symbol, a woman wronged by her own family. Which included us.

Matilda welcomed her politely but said little, rigid with dignity even while encased in a hospital bed. Swan lay back with the pose of a monarch receiving a courier from a poorer country. Annie Gwen and I stood between the beds. I stayed by her side. She kept her head up. "I didn't come here to do you wrong," she said to Swan. "And I expect fair treatment from you in return. You were always fair to me, before."

"Annie Gwen," I interjected before Swan could speak, "*no* one was fair to you and your family twenty-five years ago. You deserve an apology for the way my Great Aunt Clara misrepresented Anthony Wade's history in this town. And for the way my grandmother turned her back on your family." I paused. "Then, and now."

Swan gazed at me with icy warning over the oxygen tube that still rimmed her lower face. Then she looked at Annie Gwen. "Everything about the situation was chaotic. I do regret how it was all handled. Just as I regret giving the owner of the Rakelow Inn the impression the other day that your family was not welcome in this town. I assure you, he misunderstood my anxiety. I merely asked him about your lodgings."

I waited one second for the drama of that lie to sink in. "That's not true. Many of my grandmother's out-of- town guests stay at the Rakelow. She's responsible for a sizable amount of the Inn's income. She told the owner she didn't want your family there, and he evicted you."

This blunt rebuttal stiffened the room's air and made Swan's face a little paler. Annie Gwen didn't seem to know how to deal with my dark honesty any more than Swan's cool silence. Finally she said, "Mrs. Samples, you owe me and my children an apology."

"I most certainly do apologize," Swan said, giving me a bitter retaliatory glare. Then, to Annie Gwen, "You've gotten on with your life, I understand. From what I hear, Eli has done very well for himself. Your daughter is well-married. You have a lovely grandchild. You've been blessed."

Annie Gwen frowned. "My family's come out of hard times pretty well, due to hard work and good hearts."

"Then why pursue something so sad about the past that it can only hurt us all?"

"We just want the truth about my Jasper. This notion about the land hiding some secret is my daughter's pain talking, and I know it sounds awful silly, but maybe the Lord sent us here for other purposes, and we have just have to figure out what those purposes are."

Matilda, who had become increasingly restless as Annie Gwen spoke, pressed a frail hand to her heart. "I believe I can tell you one good purpose we can all serve. The Stand Tall project." The air froze. Swan's expression said this was a rare time when Matilda had surprised her and defied her. "I speak for Swan," Matilda said, "when I say we'd consider it an honor if you'd participate."

"What is this project?" Annie Gwen asked me. I quickly described the mountain school for troubled and homeless children. As I spoke, her eyes gleamed with sincere interest. "I'll speak to Eli about it. He handles the bookkeeping on my charity work. It's too much money for me to keep up with. He talks to my accountant for me."

"Annie Gwen, you don't have to give money to Stand Tall," I said hurriedly.

"Oh, I'd want a seat on the board if I gave a lot of money." With that cagey indication that she was nobody's fool, she nodded to Swan and Matilda. "Thank you kindly. My son will be speakin' to you about it." She patted my hand. "Thank you. I'll walk myself downstairs."

She left the room, small and modest, about ten feet tall.

Swan rose up in her bed and stared at Matilda. Matilda said quietly, "She's the widow of Anthony's son." Matilda turned her back to us, moving like a slow, tired bird, and pulled the bedcovers over her shoulder.

Swan and I traded a look. Hers was dark. Mine celebrated a small, unexpected victory.

*

Frog's ashes arrived in a plain cardboard package by regular mail. I took the box from Gloria at the door of Marble Hall, carried it into the library, placed it on a parquet table between a marble chessboard and a small marble bust of Esta, then sat down in a chair across from it as if greeting a surprise guest. After my lungs settled back into place, I began to talk to Frog.

*Life is all about control, Froggie, and I lost that. I'm not sure I'll ever be in control of my life again – and I don't want to be responsible for anyone else's.*

Karen was at the hospital. The house was quiet, holding its breath, empty without Swan. Finally I went upstairs, dressed in a pale gray business suit, then came back down with my purse on one shoulder and car keys in my hands. "I'm going to the Asheville airport," I told Gloria. "Call the hospital, please, and tell Karen I'm taking a flight to Washington D.C. I'll be back tonight."

"You're leaving that . . . that box with that man's burned body in it . . . here?"

"He won't hurt you."

"He killed two people. Why does he deserve a welcome place in this house?"

I stopped and looked at her until she backed up. "Why does anyone deserve forgiveness in this house?" I said.

"What kind of talk is that? What do you mean?"

I walked out.

*

The offices of the Phoenix Group overlooked the busy boulevards of Washington from a small brownstone building off Pennsylvania Avenue. Within minutes I could be at the White

House, the Washington Monument, Lincoln Center. My nearby apartment, in a well-kept brick complex with small balconies and a lawn, occupied one of the shady in-town neighborhoods surrounded by small restaurants and good shops, with a subway station only a block away. D.C. had become as much of a home to me as any city ever would.

When I got out of the cab in front of the office building I looked around me dully, as if the familiar sights had faded, or I had faded instead. "Ms. Union, so glad you're back," a guard said at the lobby desk. I walked through the darkly paneled lobby, took an elevator to the fourth floor, and stepped into a simple reception area with comfortable chairs and deep carpet. I laid my finger to my lips as our receptionist, a pretty young college student, gasped and grinned. "Irene's expecting me." I didn't want to talk to the other five lawyers who made up the group. I had a very simple, painful mission.

The girl buzzed her. Irene met me at her office door. She was a short round black woman with grizzled gray hair pulled back in a neat style. She wore tailored gray pantsuits and always a colorful scarf at her throat, held by a gold bar. Everything about her spoke of solid wisdom. "I don't like the expression on your face," she said as she ushered me in. "I was hoping for a rested look, but you look as if you've been at war."

"I have something to tell you." I sat down across from her desk cluttered with files and a computer, and she frowned as she lowered herself in a leather executive chair. She had been one of the first minority women appointed as a federal judge, and within a year of her retirement from the justice system she'd organized the Phoenix Group. As a young woman in Alabama she'd marched with Dr. King. In legal circles, her intelligence and fairness had made her a legend. What I had come to say was the hardest thing I'd ever imagined in my work for her. "I'm resigning from the foundation."

"Why?"

"The short version is that I'm not capable of seeing myself as an advocate for truth, justice, and the American Way, anymore."

"You didn't fail Frog Marvin. I won't accept your resignation.

You'll have to be more specific."

"I have duties at home."

She bowed her head to her fingertips and looked at me sternly, her dark eyes hooded by graying brows. "Something very destructive is happening to you. I'd like to understand."

"I may have to take over my grandmother's business in North Carolina."

"It's not just that. Tell me."

"Everything's changed. My personal life is chaotic."

She hesitated, then said quietly, "I know about your relationship with Eli Wade."

Silence. I stared at her. The slow ticking of an antique clock on the office's dark bookcases echoed loudly in my brain. I felt disoriented. "I can only assume William told you."

"I know everything."

"I don't condone the situation William put me in, but I'd hate to see this damage his status with the foundation. Let me try to explain my relationship with Eli Wade—"

"You don't have to." She stood. "Come with me."

I followed her from the office and down a back hall to a small conference room. She opened the room's door and gestured for me to enter. I stepped inside and halted, my heart in my throat. Eli rose from a chair at the board table. The overhead lights gleamed on his hair. He wore tan trousers with a pin-striped shirt and leather suspenders. I was dimly aware of Irene closing the door behind me, leaving us alone. "I obviously have no clue what's happening here," I finally said.

"That's my fault. Have a seat and let me tell you, please."

I sat down slowly in a chair at my end of the table, then spread my hands on the cool, dark wood. Eli leaned atop a chair, levering one forearm along the high back. He looked more comfortable in a board room than I'd ever imagined. "I thought I'd never come back from the islands," he said. "But my mother and Bell didn't really like livin' down there. Bell had met Alton Canetree by then, and they'd fallen in love. He was a good ol' boy real estate developer from Tennessee, and he was already askin' her to marry him and come home to live." He paused, then blew out a long breath.

"William and me were partners, like I already told you, running an offshore sports bettin' operation that had already made us a fortune. I got into gamblin' when I was a teenager, Darl. I was good at it. It's all mathematics—odds and calculated risks, statistics. We were dirt poor after we left Burnt Stand, and I was willin' to make money any way I could. Word got around about my *talent*, and by the time I was eighteen I was lyin' about my age, workin' casinos and hangin' out with bookies. It just went from there. I'm not sayin' I was right to do it. I'm just tellin' you how it was."

"How did you get involved with this?" I gestured numbly, indicating Phoenix.

"William was tired of being a man without a country, too. He was born in Jamaica, but he has a lot of relatives in the States." Eli paused. "Including Irene. Who's his grandmother."

My hand still hung in the air. I lowered it slowly. "All right."

"I slipped back into the country. Trying to decide what to do. Stay and get a lawyer—confess, pay up, take my chances on going to prison for a year or two? Or bring Mama and Bell back then hit the road? See the world. I'd already done a lot of travelin', playin' high-stakes poker here and there, checking out things that interested me, like computer systems and gadgets. So maybe I'd just make that my life, I said to myself. I came back to the States to decide." He walked down the side of the table, resting a broad hand on each conference chair as he passed it, halting when he was halfway to me. "One thing I knew I had to do. *I had to see you, again.*"

I exhaled slowly. "Why?"

"It'd been nearly twenty years, then. Not a day had gone by when I didn't think about you. I figured you wanted nothing to do with me or my family or the memories. If you thought my father killed Clara, why would you ever want to see me, again? But I had to see *you*, just once. I tracked you down in Atlanta. Found out you were a lawyer—a damned fine lawyer, judging by your credentials. I had to know why were you interested in defending poor folk and lowlifes. I'd always pictured you doing something good, but not that.

"I went downtown to watch you work. I sat in the back of a courtroom, waitin'." He paused. "And then, you walked in. There you were. *There you were.* You had this little black lady for a client. She'd shot her ex-boyfriend. Just winged him, as I recall, but still. He'd been beatin' her for years. Threatened her children, and wouldn't leave her be. She looked like hell warmed over—just nobody and nothin', poor, ugly, scared. But you got up and gave the jury this speech that made me want to cheer. How the dignity of a person in bad circumstances deserves compassion. How judgement can only be served with common sense and mercy. You had that jury lookin' at you as if you were a minister preaching your best sermon. And that lady—your client—she looked up at you with pure awe on her face." He paused, chewing his lower lip. "*And you won.* You won that case for her. And I sat there falling in love with you all over again, and knowing I had to make everything right—I had to live up to your standards."

I bowed my head. His words hurt in ways he couldn't know. He had nothing to be ashamed of. The guilt was all mine. "You were misled," I said.

"I went to Irene. Sort of turned myself in, since she was a judge. I told her to do what she wanted with me. I'd keep William out of it. Get things fixed for him, take the blame for our gambling business. She'd been after William to get out of the gambling business for a long time. She asked me why I'd risked everything to come back to the States—why it was worth it. I told her about you. She just sat there, listening. And then she said, *I'm not going to let you go to jail. Get William back here and we'll straighten this out. And then I want you to introduce me to this incredible young woman. This Darl Union.*

"I said that wasn't possible. I didn't want to mess up your life." He paused, and disgust crossed his face. "All right, I didn't want to look in your eyes and see what I was afraid I'd see when you met me."

"Eli, I would never have looked at you that way—"

"I wanted to help you. I wanted you to do the good work you were doin'. I wanted to be part of that. I thought of an idea, and I pitched it to Irene. She was about to retire as a judge. Would she be interested in using my money to run some kind of free legal aide service?" He hesitated, studying me as if he couldn't be sure

I wouldn't walk out when he finished. "She said she'd do it. We got it set up. She got in touch with you and offered you a job." He raised both hands, palm up, presenting himself to me very quietly. "That's how I came back to the straight and narrow. And why you and me are sittin' here, today."

"Phoenix is entirely funded with your money?"

He nodded. "Yeah." He paused. "I have a lot of money."

I was silent. I found myself studying a detail in the wood grain of the conference table, seeking some small focus. He watched me wearily. "I didn't set this up to spy on you or run your life. I'm apologizing to you. I'm askin' for your forgiveness."

My forgiveness. My throat closed. *Tell him. Tell him everything. Take him home and show him Clara's bones in the garden.*

And lose him forever. I wanted more time.

"Come with me," I said.

*

*Tell him. Tell him about Clara. Trust him to forgive you.* We stood in my apartment in the afternoon. I pulled a drape over the balcony window, walked into the bedroom, opened the curtains, where an old oak tree screened the view. Eli walked in after me. We looked from the bed to each other. "There's so much you don't know about me," I began.

"Shussh." He pulled my suit jacket open a little, unbuttoned the top of my blouse then put his spread hand on the warm skin above my bra, one finger resting in the crook of my throat, the heel of his hand riding gently on the swell of my breasts. "I'm a simple man," he said, though I knew he wasn't. "Let's go to bed right now, and later we'll talk."

*No, we won't.* "Eli—"

He cupped his hand over my mouth. "You're the one person who always understood me. It's just like when we were kids. Only better, now. "Don't think. Don't talk. And I won't either, right now." I gave in helplessly. He picked me up high against his body with his arms wound below my hips. He kissed the tops of my breasts, and I bent my head over his. He carried me to my own bed, and we pretended nothing else mattered.

When we lay naked in each other's arms, satiated and quiet, he said, "Are you still going to quit the Phoenix Group?"

It was a matter of honor, now. When the time came and I showed him the garden, he'd be free of me in every way. "Yes," I said quietly.

"You don't want to be associated with my name."

"That's not it."

"I don't believe you. Nothing else makes sense."

"After what we just shared, you think I feel that way?"

"I don't know what to think, Darl. Why don't you tell me the truth?" My silence came with a slow withdrawing, as we both sat up. "Then I'm going," he said without any joy.

I nodded. "I understand." We said nothing else to each other. He dressed and left as I wrapped myself in a sheet. I felt naked and ugly.

I could not force a confession out of my mouth.

*

Karen and I lingered over the breakfast table in the sunroom. She wore a nightshirt and robe of red silk. I'd unpacked a pale red robe that once belonged to my mother. I'd told her about my trip to Washington, D.C., and what I'd learned about Eli and the Phoenix Group. We'd talked all night, and now looked like tired red roses after a long rain. "After I learned about our family," Karen said quietly, "I couldn't wait to get out of this town. I wanted to go where no one knew me." She hesitated. "But the lonelier I felt, the angrier I got. I didn't want to miss anyone or any place that had been part of the lie. Not Grandmother. Not you. Not the house. But I did." She bowed her head. "Now it all seems like a waste of energy. The past never left us. Just like with you and Eli."

"No. You had to go away in order to come back and make peace with it."

"Is that what you're trying to do?"

"I'm not sure what I'm trying to do, at the moment."

"What do you think Eli will find out there?" She nodded toward the woods behind the pool and gardens. "You know, I'm afraid he'll just find something that proves his father did it."

I looked at my hands, clenching a pale mug filled with black coffee. "His father was innocent. I have no doubt."

"Then who in the world could have done it? Who'd have had any motive to kill Clara?"

"A lot of people. She was evil."

"Evil? That sounds medieval. Biblical. Not like a lawyer. Surely you can't possibly mean—"

"Evil." I raised my eyes to hers. "Maybe everything here is built on the wrong values. And she was just the tip of the Hardigree iceberg."

Karen shook her head at such talk. "Swan and Grandmother don't deserve to have this time of their lives polluted with ugly memories. They've done nothing wrong. I don't want to accuse Eli and his family of provoking their illness, but it's obvious the stress doesn't help."

I gave her a steady gaze. "Does he owe them more consideration than he owes his own family? His own father's reputation? He's a good man. He's not trying to hurt anyone."

"You've already decided you love him again," she announced quietly, squinting at me in the morning sunshine. "I can see that. I can hear it in every word you say about him." She folded her hands around a glass of milk as if it were the purity of passion.

After a moment, I nodded. "I know it sounds reckless and impossible, but it's true."

"No, it sounds like *you*. The old you. The open-hearted girl I grew up with."

"Have I changed that much?"

"Oh, Darl, you changed *completely* after Clara disappeared and Eli's father was killed. You barely seemed to notice me anymore. You withdrew in your own world. I was miserable." She paused. "I was different too. I admit it. I felt totally ashamed to be part of the history here. I felt totally alone in the world. I decided not to need anyone. You. My grandmother. No one. But the thing is—God! I love this place. This house, this town. Isn't that sick?"

"No. I understand. My family built this town. Your family built this town. And Eli's. Hardigrees and Wades." The coffee burned like acid in my throat. I rose and went to one of the French doors, opened it, and took a deep breath. "Why don't we get dressed and stop by the new restaurant on the square on the way to the hospital? They have bagels and cream cheese on the breakfast menu. Can you imagine, in Burnt Stand? We're practically cosmopolitan . . . " My voice trailed off as a low rumbling sound reached my ears. I frowned and walked out onto the pool patio. There. Again. Heavy equipment, deep in the back woods. Bulldozers, scraping the land.

Eli.

*

By the time Karen and I dressed and hurried across the steep hills and deep hollows, Eli had cleared all the old yard around the Stone Cottage. He sat high in one orange bulldozer, operating it with expert skill—another of his talents. Leon maneuvered a second machine. A dozen men I recognized as stonecutters sifted through the dirt and debris with their gloved hands. Searching. Nearby, Bell lingered over a shovel full of dirt, peering down into it like an archaeologist. She was as delicate as ever in jeans and a bright green t-shirt, her soft brown hair pulled up in a girlish braid, her baby nestled in a colorful woven sling against her breasts. Annie Gwen sat in a lawn chair, a broad straw hat shielding her face, a Bible open on the lap of her denim jumper.

"What can they possibly hope to find?" Karen said under her breath. "Darl, this is sad."

The futility of Eli's mission tore at me, holding me in place. When Eli saw us he stopped his bulldozer and climbed down. Leon pulled his machine so close to us the dust rose in a cloud around our feet. The stonecutters who'd come to help stopped working. Bell and Annie Gwen looked up. In that poignant theater, smelling of torn wood and earth, we became the focus of attention. As Eli walked up to me his intense gaze shifted to Karen, then back to me. I nodded. "Thank you for sending William to find her."

"No problem."

"Thank you, Eli," Karen echoed. The awkward moment rose up like a cloud. They shared a grandfather. They were close cousins, this golden, black-haired woman and ruddy backwoodsman.

"Karen?" Bell's voice, quiet and tearful. She was standing beside us. Annie Gwen joined her. Bell lifted a small crocheted cap from the head of her baby. "This is your newest Wade cousin. She's glad to meet you."

"Mighty glad," Annie Gwen added softly.

Karen began to cry, silent tears streaming down her face. Leon climbed out on the huge metal caterpillar tread of the machine he'd driven. He held down his hand to Karen. "Want to take a look at the world from up here with me?" As if hypnotized, she took his hand, climbed up, and left me standing there. I suddenly felt very alone. Eli looked at me. "That invitation goes for you, too." He held out a hand.

*Please, don't do this to me. I'd tell you where to tear apart this land if I could. I'd do anything you wanted, if it were just about me.* I shook my head. "I can't, Eli." He continued to stand there, his face resolute, his hand thrust out. "You mean you *won't*," he said gruffly.

"Eli, don't make it harder for her," Bell said. I turned to her and Annie Gwen. "I know I seem heartless," I said. "I'm not. I'm caught between your wishes and my grandmother's. I'm sorry all of this is happening."

Annie Gwen said quietly, "We know you're not against us. We've heard." She held out a hand, and I did the same. I touched just my fingertips to Bell's shoulder, then to the head of her child, and finally to Annie Gwen's outstretched fingers. Asking for their blessing, wanting their forgiveness for sins they didn't know I'd committed. "I wish it were this simple," I said.

I walked back into the woods without looking at Eli again. That took all my willpower.

*

Neddler's Place was still up on the mountain, though old Bill Neddler had died long ago. The new owner called the bar The

Quarry Pit. The stonecutters who went there just called it The Pit. Eli stood in the center of the main room that evening, surrounded by dusty men with beer mugs and pool cues frozen in their hands. They gaped at the blank check he held up. "Fifty thousand dollars," Eli said loudly, "to every man, woman , or child who tells me something that leads to the truth. That's the standin' offer."

No one said a word.

He walked out.

*

"He's hired a dozen divers to go to up to Briscoe Lake," Leon told me as he walked into Swan's office at the quarry. I was hunched over her magnificent desk, studying computer printouts of accounts and bills. Leon had insisted I look over the company's books.

I sat back slowly. "Oh, Leon."

"Man's got to look everywhere. Scratching for needles in a haystack, but he says it's got to be that way. He's bringing in high-tech equipment, too—sonar, underwater cameras, things like that. He's got a whole team set up. That friend of his—the Jamaican—is up there running the operation."

Leon left the office. I put my head in my hands. Eli was looking for clues that didn't exist. The answers were buried in the earth, not the water. And they were buried in me.

## 18

A week passed in the forest, killing the trees, scalping the hills, pushing up nothing. In his sleep Eli dreamed of finding spheres of light, of unearthing stones that talked. He tossed and turned, his brain trying to calculate the endless tons of empty dirt—weight, volume, the grains of granite and mica, the invisible universe of marble dust, the infinite solar systems whirling around him. The truth was the tiniest speck of gold. Faceless miseries  sent him floating back to Tennessee. *Look in your own pa's grave. There's the murderer.*

During the day Eli ate dust until it choked him atop the bulldozer. He tasted it in his sleep, scrubbed it from his body at night, and lay naked but not clean in the fine bed pride had bought him, alone, unhappy, and thinking of Darl.

Thoughts of Darl wrapped him up every day, hurtful and warm, loving, proud, desperate. She was just on the other side of a forest that seemed to shrink by only inches, becoming piles of stripped logs he sold for timber, because he couldn't bear the waste.

Nothing was just weights and lengths and prices.  Nothing could be reduced to mere numbers, anymore. In a few weeks he'd clear the whole forest. He'd leave just an island of trees around the Stone Flower Garden, and if he'd found nothing by then, the garden would go, too.

Mama fervently read and re-read a file of information Darl had sent her concerning the Stand Tall project. She came to Eli one night as he scrubbed dirt from his hands in the sink of the Broadside's handsome kitchen, and the hopeful look in her eyes filled him with quiet misery. She held the dog-earred Stand Tall file. "No matter what else comes of us being here," she told Eli, pressing the file to her heart, "we were meant to take part in this good work."

He nodded, for her sake. "I'll set up a meeting with Swan," he said.

*

Swan's hospital bed was empty. "Where is she?" I asked, as if she could make herself invisible at will. Afternoon sun poured through the room's window. Karen sat next to Matilda's bed, looking a little dusty and guilty. Matilda, who looked gaunt, raised a hand and pointed to the window, the IV tube moving along with her. "She insisted on being taken outside."

"Outside?"

"To a more private garden on the other side of the building. Ask the ladies at the lobby desk to direct you. It's called the chapel garden."

"I'll still be here when you come back," Karen said. "I told Grandmother we'd stay through dinner. All right?" I nodded, watching Karen and Matilda link hands. Karen was determined to explain her life and her homecoming to Matilda without upsetting her, though she still wasn't ready to announce her pregnancy. She'd already told Matilda about meeting Leon and the Wades. In return, Matilda had filled Karen with glowing accounts of Leon's rise to executive status at Hardigree Marble. She'd also told Karen all about his wife's death, the two fine children Leon was raising alone, and the nice marble house he'd built for his family on the old Forrest farm. She was matchmaking, no doubt.

I went downstairs reluctantly. Talking to Swan always made me aware of my place in her universe, where the weight of loving her and hating her made me too heavy to escape her gravity. The information ladies pointed me to a narrow alcove between the main hospital building and auxiliary offices. Beyond a glass exterior door, the tiny garden mostly hidden by high, see-through walls of marble block draped in confederate jasmine. A placid-looking woman dressed in the blue scrubs and the bright smiley buttons of a nurse's aid stood politely by the door. She recognized me and gave me a hang-dog look. "I'm not supposed to let anybody go in. Your grandma said she wanted to be alone."

"I'll take the rap for invading her privacy. It's all right. Thank you." As I reached for the door the aide said, "She paid for computers at the new elementary school last year. And my boy won a computer contest Hardigree Marble sponsored. He got his own laptop. She's such a good person. She makes this town a paradise on God's green earth."

*Buying off the old sins with good deeds.* "I hope God likes pink marble." The woman laughed. I stepped outside and entered the garden through an opening in the green-and-pink walls. A small fountain bubbled at the center of marble walkways. Unlike the meditation garden, this one had a spartan, Asian feel. Gnarled miniature maples shaded the corners. Feather-thin clumps of ornamental grasses grew from beds of pebbles. My grandmother sat in her wheelchair before the fountain. An oxygen tank was attached to the chair's back, and her IV bag hung from a movable pole beside her. She had bowed her head and steepled her hands to her mouth. Her white hair glowed in the sunlight. The wing-like arms of her white silk robe moved gently in a wisp of autumn air.

I halted. Painful wonder cooled my skin. Swan, praying?

She sensed me and raised her head sharply. As I walked up beside her, her stern expression softened enough to say she was relieved. Then the sardonic gleam returned to her eyes. "We all have our gardens," she said. "We all go where our memories take us."

"Some gardens are kinder than others." I sat down on a marble bench, feeling more depressed than angry. Swan wasn't God here, but only an aging woman losing her closest friends and companions. Carl McCarl had died years ago. The Italian marble baron, as well. "Are you worried about Matilda?"

"Possibly. Does it strike you as unbelievable that I pray when I'm distressed? Is my piety obscene? Hypocritical?" She smiled like a cat.

"When I was a little girl, I always watched you in church. When you prayed you never shut your eyes."

"Indeed. I've never believed God requires blind faith. He expects common sense."

"I used to think you were just determined to look him in the eye if he showed up in your Methodist sanctuary." I mimicked her drily. *"God, I built this church for you. You'd better answer my prayers and destroy my enemies."* I paused, watching her. "And I pictured God shuffling and nodding as if he were a stonecutter standing on your office rug with his hat in his hands. *"Yes, ma'am, Miss Swan. Whatever you want, Miss Swan. I'll get to answerin' prayers and smitin' enemies right away, ma'am."*

"I expect you didn't come here to debate my spiritual virtue." Swan brushed off my sarcasm—and God's too, for all I knew—with a wave of one hand. I said very quietly, "I'm here because your secrets are hurting everyone around you." I told her about finding the bulldozers at the Stone Cottage. Her face remained neutral, but her chest moved in a deep sigh. "Great thoughts and great deeds are torn out of plain dirt," she said. "The most beautiful stone rises from the ugliest muck of the earth. You can hate the process, but you have to love the results."

"The ends justify the means?"

"Exactly."

*"You're wrong."*

"Oh? Look at all the good that's come out of my wicked life." She smiled grimly as she said that. "A lovely town, steady jobs for several hundred citizens, and so many generous, charitable donations that I've made. Because of me—because of the Hardigree success and reputation—life is good here in our small, special part of the world. When the children's home opens it will be a haven and a fresh start for small, troubled souls from all over North Carolina. So let's not whine and gnash our teeth about the sad decisions and occasional regrets that accompanied us to this point."

"Those decisions and regrets ruined Eli's family."

"Ruined? *Ruined?* From what I've been able to gather, his hard experiences here spurred him to seek his own fortune—and he wasn't particularly choosy about how he did that. A practical soul, like me, you see? Now he's wealthy. He indulges his mother and sister and does as he pleases. If tragedy hadn't struck him, would he have simply made do? Been an ordinary man? I think so."

"So you'll take credit for how he's turned out?"

"No, but I won't take the blame for how he didn't."

"I doubt he'd see it that way."

"I doubt you see how well *you've* turned out because of me."

"Stop. I won't even dignify this line of reasoning."

"Do this much for me. Proceed with the board meeting for Stand Tall. Represent me. Represent our family. Create something wonderful."

"I've told you already I'd handle it."

"And I'll do something for you. If you want Eli Wade, I'll give him to you." She lifted a platinum watch from a fine long necklace. It was a gift the Italian had given her years earlier. "He should be here any minute. He wants to meet with me. He was always a punctual little boy. Let's see if that discipline has continued."

I had no time to react, to ask questions, to do more than stare at her in grim suspicion. Eli opened the glass door from the main building and stepped between the garden walls. "Ah," Swan said, and smiled at me. Eli met my eyes with a look of troubled surprise. His jeans and plaid shirt were stained by red clay dust. He'd washed his arms and face, but his dark hair had a dull patina of the dust, too. He crossed the small garden space and turned to face Swan. It was the first time they'd confronted each other since his return. He gazed down at her with a clamped set to his mouth, then gallantly nodded to her. "Miss Swan," he said.

He looked at me and gestured toward a bench, but I shook my head. He took the bench. I remained standing.

Swan cleared her throat. "Now let me confess something. I despise what you came to my town to do. I think it's ridiculous and demeaning to us all. I loathe your sister's tactics in getting the land, but I blame myself for foolishly allowing that to happen."

"You sure know how to sweet-talk a person."

"However, I apologize for any mistake of pride I made years ago. If anything I said or did contributed to the situation that resulted in your father's death, I take full responsibility." At this point I could only stare at her, frozen in disbelief and vividly suspicious. Eli frowned at her but leaned forward, listening intently.

She went on. "I would rather never mention my sister Clara's name again, and I consider her death a tragic event that is no longer of importance. However she died—and by whoever's hands—she is, undoubtedly, *dead*. That can't be changed. But if you need to prove your father did not kill her, you have my blessings."

"I came here for one reason. To tell you I want a place for me and my mother on the board of Stand Tall."

I groaned inside. Swan never blinked. "I intended to issue an invitation to you both."

I nearly choked. What a lie. I looked at Eli quietly. "She's bribing you."

"Oh?" He calmly swiveled his attention to Swan. "What do you want in return?"

"Nothing," Swan countered. "I want the entire town to know that Swan Hardigree Samples welcomes the Wade family. Are you going to turn my offer down? Why would you?"

He stood. "My fight's not with you. It's with whoever killed your sister and let my pa die for it."

"As it should be."

"What's in this for you and your family name?"

"To use a popular term, *Closure*." She glanced at me. "And reconciliation with my granddaughter. If I involve you in Stand Tall, she'll participate wholeheartedly, too."

"Then I accept your offer." It was that simple. He looked at me, his eyes sad but determined. He nodded to Swan and left the garden.

I simply stood there in his wake, and when I was alone with Swan I stared at her furiously. She looked back with the same unyielding blue gaze. "I will always try to give you what will do you the most good."

"You're trying to buy his friendship."

"And succeeding."

"Tell me if you've ever loved a man so much you'd be honest with him. So much you'd sacrifice yourself." She said nothing. I circled her as if she were a criminal client I had to interrogate. "Did you love the Italian?"

"I cared for him deeply. I miss him very much."

"Did you sleep with him?" My tone sliced at her.

"Of course."

"You never considered marrying him?"

"No."

I swept around her and abruptly leaned over her, bracing my

arms on the arms of her chair. "Because you thought all he really wanted was Hardigree Marble?"

"My dear, he wanted *me*. He adored me. He was wonderful to me. When I was still young and beautiful he would have whisked me away to Europe and I'd have lived like a *contesa*."

My voice rose. "He was rich, he was pedigreed, he was perfect for you, he loved you. Marrying him would have been the ultimate step up the social ladder. And you 'cared' for him. So why didn't you marry him? *Tell me why you manipulate everyone who cares about you and reject their love. Tell me why you even rejected a man you admit you needed.*"

She looked up at me quietly. "Because you were the center of my life, and he hated children. He wanted me, but he didn't want *you*."

*

I stood atop the low marble wall of the back terrace that evening with a tall glass of bourbon in one hand, bathed in the sunset, drunk enough to sway, listening to Eli's bulldozers. They were over a half-mile away across the ridges and hollows, but when the wind was right they sounded as if they were just beyond the darkening trees. I looked down thirty feet to the deceptively innocent surface of the koi pond. How easy it had been, in all the confusion, for Clara to fall. How easy for anyone to fall from grace. Karen spotted me from a window and ran to my side. "Have you lost your mind?" She pulled me back to the lawn.

"My soul," I corrected.

"What happened between you and your grandmother today? Will you stop drinking and tell me?"

I looked at her without any hope. "She made me hate her. She made me love her. She bought Eli's loyalty. And she kept mine."

## 19

Webs of stone were closing around us. I could feel them in my sleep. Secrets and lies, old shames, old loves. All there, with faces or without. Karen felt them, too—our mixed heritage, our awkward relationship in a modern world where everything was supposed to be so easy, so fashionably equal. One afternoon Leon drove up to the Hall with his children, a boy and a girl, well-behaved and well-spoken, who melted into pools of awe when Karen shook their hands. "*Cassandra*," the little girl said. "Daddy lets me watch your TV show, except when you kiss Jeremy. You're so pretty. I want to be just like you." She touched Karen's pale brown skin and chocolate hair.

"No, I want to be just like *you*," Karen replied, smiling and gently caressing the girl's stiff black braids and darker skin. "Because you're the most beautiful little girl I've ever seen."

The girl beamed at her. And the boy, a little shy, said, "Ma'am, I'd like to kiss you on the cheek when I'm older."

"Well, for now, may I kiss *you*?"

His dark eyes went wide. He looked at his father, who said, "I wouldn't turn the opportunity down, son." And so he stood stock still while Karen planted a feather-soft kiss on his cheek.

The children dissolved into broad smiles. Karen looked at them as if she could taste their sweet innocence on her tongue, and then her eyes filled with tears. "Excuse me, I'll be right back," she said in a strained voice, and left the living room hurriedly. I gave Leon a worried look, asked the maid to bring the kids some ice cream, then went after her.

I found her in a linen room off the kitchen, sobbing into the folded softness of a monogrammed tablecloth. "Leon asked me to go to dinner with him the other day," she explained. "I put him off. But now he's brought his kids to meet me. You know what this all means."

"He's a gentleman and he's crazy about you."

"But he doesn't know I'm pregnant."

I sighed and sat down on a heavy oak trunk where Swan's monogrammed silver flatware was stored. The heavy flatware bore an H for Hardigree, not an S for Samples. I'd always found that telling. "You're a Noland," I said to Karen. "Your father was a Marine and a war hero. And you're a Wade. Your grandfather was the finest stonecutter in the south. I believe he was a good man caught up in a bad situation. And you're a Dove. Your grandmother has survived unspeakable prejudice and unfairness in her life, but she's kept her dignity." I paused. "And you're a Hardigree. That means—" she looked at me as if expecting the worst—"that means you can't hide this from me, anymore." I reached up and hooked a finger in the collar of her soft blue sweater, then filched the Hardigree chain and pendant from beneath it.

She sighed raggedly. "Grandmother gave it to me when I was a teenager. I refused to wear it. Until now."

"You're a Hardigree," I repeated quietly. "And that means you and I will always be here for each other, because that's the best tradition in this family."

She took my hand. "You're saying I have to tell Leon the truth and live up to what got me here?"

"Live up to it, or live it down," I said with a tired smile. "But just never forget who you are, and that you have a family who is proud of you no matter what."

She blew out a long breath. "I'll tell him in private, when his kids aren't with us, and take my chances."

As we left the room, she stopped me. "Are *you* proud to be a Hardigree?"

No one had ever asked me that question before. It struck at a tangled push-pull of emotions. I couldn't divorce the shame from the success, the love from the regret. "I haven't proved I'm strong enough to survive the name," I said.

\*

"A man shouldn't stand outside when the beer is inside," Leon said as he walked up to Eli outside The Quarry Pit's rust-streaked steel door.

"I've been inside already. I came to see if anybody had anything to tell me, yet. Nobody did. I don't know if I want to drink, here. I have bad memories."

"The men aren't holding back. They just don't know anything to tell."

"I've had divers at the lake for days, now. Findin' nothing." Eli spread his hands. "Nothing in the lake, nothing in the land, nothing in the people. Nothing. My sister's sittin' at the Broadside crying to her husband every night, and my mama's stiff with misery."

"Comeon. Come on in. You can't give a place too much power over you."

Eli chewed his tongue. *Too late*, he thought. But he went inside with Leon and sat at the bar. "My kids met Karen," Leon said. "They think she's a fairy princess. Just goggled at her. She had 'em wrapped around her little finger just like that." He snapped his fingers. "They talked to her for two hours."

"Good for you. Good for her."

"I asked Karen would she come out to my farm and have dinner with me and the kids and my ol' daddy soon. And she said yes. So then I said, 'This is a good place to raise kids. Not like a city somewhere.' I wasn't exactly subtle."

"What'd she say?"

"Said I was right. Said she wanted her children to grow up with woods to roam. So she wants kids. That's what she was tellin' me, you know? So then I said, 'Well, *I've* got woods.' And she looked at me with those cool eyes that can heat a man right to the bottom of his furnace, and she said, 'I'll come to dinner one day soon and have a look at your forest, Mr. Forrest.'" Leon emitted a long, deep laugh.

Eli opened his silver cigar tube, pulled a fine Macanudo from it, and handed the cigar to Leon. "Celebrate."

"What do you think? Old scar-face like me, country-boy-made-good? You think I've got a chance?" Leon shook his head and stuck the cigar between his teeth. "Any of this makin' sense to you?"

Eli nodded. Loneliness clung to his skin like marble dust. "Sometimes you just know she's the right one and she knows you're right for her. That's the easy part." He downed a second beer and ordered another round. "The rest is what tears your heart out."

*

The first official board meeting for Stand Tall convened at Marble Hall with me in charge and people whispering that I would be elected president of the newly formed foundation. I did not want the job but the tangle in my mind had begun to tighten in strange ways. By taking control I might protect Eli and his family from Swan's maneuvers. She was drawing them in, waiting for the moment when she could count coup on them. This was the beginning of her conquest by assimilation.

Karen and I ushered a dozen socially, spiritually, and politically prominent North Carolinians into the library, where caterers had moved the furniture aside and set up a long temporary table covered in white linen. Notepads and folders filled with paperwork waited before each chair. An architect's painting of Stand Tall's large main building, a rambling home of marble and wood, sat on an easel in one corner.

There was an undercurrent of curiosity and excitement—looks were darted at Karen, our celebrity. "The colored babe," as she put it wryly earlier that day, as she lay on a couch suffering morning sickness, with a cold washcloth to her forehead. She hadn't talked to Leon about her pregnancy, yet. Now she looked perfectly in command of her body, slender and stunning in a trim black suit with thin silver jewelry. I was dressed in pale camel-colored silk pants and a flowing white blouse she'd forced on me instead of a business suit. "How beautiful you are when you're not trying to look like Joan Crawford," Karen had joked gently. I caught a glimpse of us in a large mirror on one wall. Sunlight and shadow. Cream and honey.

Leon arrived at the house five minutes before the meeting was to start. When he walked into the library looking tall, dark and not-quite-elegant in a brown suit with a hint of marble dust on one sleeve, the others gave him awkward or dismissive glances, which he caught with a frown. As I started across the large room to welcome him Karen strode past me with her chin up and her brightest Cassandra smile beaming. "Leon," she said, turning his name into a friendly caress, her voice ringing above the conversations. She tucked her arm through his. "You're sitting beside *me*." And he looked down at her with an expression that caught my breath. He would have fought tigers for her at that moment.

I turned to study two table settings with place cards that drew everyone's attention. Eli Wade. Annie Gwen Wade, they announced. With only a minute or two remaining I walked into the hall and waited anxiously. My skin tightened as the front bell chimed. I nodded to the maid and she opened the ornate double doors. Annie Gwen stepped inside, followed by Eli. A soft, chic blue suit gave Annie Gwen a stately air, but she gazed around the foyer with tearful eyes and a wistful smile, remembering Marble Hall. "I used to do this very same job," she said to the maid. Her face said she wished she could return to that time, when Jasper was alive.

Eli, standing behind her, stole my thoughts, my concentration, the pulse in my veins. I had never seen him in a suit before, and that day he wore a fine one, dark and well-tailored for his broad-shouldered body, with a loosely knotted silk tie. He filled even the big foyer with a calm, righteous presence. He held my gaze and went over me the way I looked at him. The intensity burned me.

I took Annie Gwen's hand. "I'm glad you're part of this." She reached up and straightened a lock of my hair from my cheek. The gesture was motherly and kind, though her eyes seemed sad. "There are blessings," she said. My throat ached. I nodded to Eli, then walked Annie Gwen into the library with him behind us, so close I could smell the good scent of his fine linen and subtle cologne. The other board members stared at them. I could imagine the gossip. Swan had generously made peace with the family of her sister's murderer—even invited them into her home. How big-hearted, how noble. If Eli found Clara's bones, people would feel so sorry for Swan.

"First I'd like for each of you to introduce yourself," I said as I started the meeting. Heads of large ministries, presidents of prestigious charities, a former congressman, and the directors of several vital service agencies each stood and listed his or her credentials. The resumes included doctorates, awards, and exclusive executive positions. But Leon stood and said simply, "I grew up cuttin' stone for Hardigree Marble, went to business school at the university on a Hardigree scholarship, and now I run the whole shebang for Mrs. Samples. I'm a widower, a part-time farmer, a daddy, and a son. I want to help other kids have the good life I'm tryin' to give mine. That's why I accept Mrs. Samples' invitation to serve on this board." He sat down. Karen watched him the entire time with sheer respect in her eyes.

Finally, it came to Eli. He stood, and everyone in the room grew very still. His presence had a remarkable effect. He was solid, he was comfortable, he needed elaborate credentials even less than Leon did. "I grew up alongside Leon," he said, "and my cousin Karen." *That* stilled the air in the room.

He paused, his eyes meeting mine, dissolving me. "And I grew up with Darl. I'm not a hometown boy here, but I had a home, here, for awhile." He touched Annie Gwen's shoulder. "My mother and sister ask me to speak for them, too, and so I am. We lost somebody we love here, and we've come to find him, if we can. But we've come to find ourselves, too. I've been a gambler, an investor, and an inventor. I was a criminal for awhile, but I'm right with God and the government now." People gasped. "I've made a lot of money." He met my eyes again. "When I was a boy Darl Union believed in me. Her family gave mine a chance, and even though things went wrong that chance has taken us a long way. So on behalf of my family, I'm giving five million dollars to Stand Tall. In the name of my father, Jasper Wade."

He sat down.

The rest of the twelve-hour meeting was just talk, after that.

*

The world wasn't doomed by flood and fire, as the Bible said.

*Mountain rain and red mud would do the trick just as good*, Eli thought. The day after the board meeting the autumn weather turned nasty. Cold water slithered down the back of his neck and followed his spine beneath a wet pullover sweater. Rusty droplets dripped from the brim of a Braves baseball cap just beyond the tip of his nose, carrying off residues of clay dust the cap had collected at the clearing site in the past week. He shrugged off the five million dollars he'd promised to Stand Tall. It was only money. He had more to prove.

He went on working with dogged determination, a battery-powered mason's drill whining in one big hand as he bored a second neat screw hole in the hard marble of a flat-faced Esta House he now owned. The place was beautiful, grand. It towered over a backstreet on a knoll hooded by huge oaks. People called it Olson Manor, after the heir to a railroad fortune who had moved his family to Burnt Stand in the 1940's. Olson Manor had elaborate marble eaves and cornices, doorsills carved with fleur de lis patterns—all handiwork of Eli's own grandfather's, the finest craftsmanship Eli had ever seen.

It made his chest swell with painful confusion. *What my family might have been, except for bad odds and Hardigrees. Or would we still be poor nobodies without them?* Fine stone came out of the ground dirty and dull. It had to be recognized—cut, carved, polished. Maybe all this misery had a sheen of purpose. Maybe Wades were the rough material and Hardigrees the craftsman. One couldn't exist without the other. That was why he'd donated the money. Trying to heal the wound where his family ended and Darl's began.

Philosophy on a gray day. He turned to blunt logic. "This house needed a porch, Grandpa," he said aloud as the rain increased. Eli picked up the last of five identical marble plaques. He'd made them with Leon's expert help at the quarry factory, carved the words into them himself, beveled the edges, polished the stone. He fitted one on the walls beside the main entrances to all the Esta Houses he'd bought. Now he set the last one about head high beside the grand front door of the Olson House, and riveted it there with long brass screws. Eli stepped back on the marble floor of a wide stoop, removed his cap, and read the inscription aloud, a small ritual christened in the rain.

*Built By Anthony E. Wade, Master Stonecutter.*

The initial in his grandfather's name stood for Elijah. Eli bowed his head for a moment, honoring the imperfect namesake who had left behind an imperfect legacy. Maybe his grandfather had been no better than a gigolo, letting women use him and using them back. Or maybe just a buck-wild fool with a talent for stonework. Either way, this wasn't going to be an Esta House anymore. It was a Wade House. Eli wanted people to know.

The soft sound of footsteps on the sidewalk made him pivot quickly. This was a quiet neighborhood of old homes, and the street had been deserted. Even the soft shush of a distant car could have been heard. Darl stood there at the edge of the front lawn, her long hair matted to her head and shoulders, a blue dress suit soaked where a gray raincoat hung open. An enormous oak draped over a glistening golden bower over her. She was beautiful and unreal and so lost looking it broke his heart. She looked from the plaque to him, and the despair in her face was edged with pride for him.

"You're a hard man to find," she said in a hollow voice. "I've been to all the other houses."

He threw his cap aside and went to her without a word, taking her by the arm and leading her up a front walkway hedged by low boxwoods in marble urns. "You're no smarter than me, gettin' all wet, " he said, as water ran down his face. He shoved open a heavily carved front door and they stepped inside a broad, empty foyer hung with a chandelier. This house was unfurnished, and every footstep echoed on the marble floor. "Comeon, there's a back porch, at least." He pulled her along a central hallway and out a door onto a small veranda. They looked out on a fading autumn lawn and more oaks. The yard was hemmed by sculpted shrubs nearly twenty feet tall. "Eli," she said urgently. "Let me talk. I won't let you donate money to—"

"It's done. I wanted to. I'll buy a place by your side, if I have to."

"No, no, Eli—"

"Sssh. Let's not make the mistake of talking." He wiped her

face with his bare hands. She uttered a soft, poignant sound of rebuke under her breath, but by then he had sunk his hands into her hair, and without any word at all they came together. As they kissed wildly he picked her up then sat down on the edge of the veranda's stone steps. She settled on the floor between his splayed thighs, both of her legs draped over one of his, and he bent her backward. As easily as rain on dust he gathered her in his hands, touching, stroking, as she kissed him and moaned. She knotted her hands in his sweater, slid them underneath and explored him, then stroked down, along his legs and groin through his soft khakis, touching him. He was nearly gone by the time she moved her hands to his hips, then around his waist and up his back, beneath the sweater. She spread her fingers on the bare skin between his shoulder blades and burrowed her face in the curve of his neck, kissing the wet skin, licking, tasting.

A patch of acorns showered the veranda roof with the rattle of firecrackers. Both he and she flinched as if guilty. His grandpa had let himself be owned by Hardigree women. *What am I doing?* Eli thought. If Darl wouldn't be with him because he was a Wade, then he shouldn't encourage her. *But she is with me.* Just as suddenly as they tore into each other he and she bent their heads to each other's necks and sat there motionless, quivering, holding tightly. It was three weeks to the day since they'd met in Florida as strangers.

She raised her head and pulled back from him. "This is the house in the picture," she admitted. His skin chilled. So she meant that decades ago his grandpa had stood in the unfinished upper wall here, looking as if nothing could bring him down. But his smile, angled in secret at Matilda behind old Esta's back, was already giving him away. The Hardigree women would destroy him, and he would let them.

"If you want me to give up on you because you're a goddamned Hardigree," Eli said quietly, "I won't do it. I'm making the rules, this time. I won't end up like my grandpa. And you won't end up mournin' for me."

She rose, touched his face, ruined him with a look. "It's too late to stop me from that," she whispered, and left him there.

\*

I sat down at Swan's library desk in the darkest part of the night, when the Hall was as quiet as a marble tomb. I took a stack of fine linen sheets of Hardigree Marble Company stationary from a drawer, and picked up the old-fashioned ink pen the Italian marble baron had given Swan when I was a child. And I began to write. *Twenty-five years ago, I witnessed the murder of my great aunt, Clara Hardigree, by her sister, my grandmother, Swan Hardigree Samples. And I have hidden that crime ever since.*

I wrote until dawn, relating every detail before and after Clara's death, but leaving out any mention of Matilda. This confession would damn Swan and me, but no one else. When I finished I slid the thick stack of paper into a large manila envelope, sealed it, wrote the name of our local District Attorney on the front, then carried the envelope to the library shelves and hid it high up, between two aging texts on geology. The science of bedrock and hard forces.

When the time came, I wouldn't ask for Eli's silence and mercy. Because now I was certain he'd give both.

\*

"You're abusing his kindness," Matilda hurled at Swan in slow but fervent words. She stood beside her hospital bed, holding the pole of her IV unit for support, ignoring my efforts to make her lay down, and glaring at Swan, who sat demurely on her own bed, her legs curled beneath her in an almost girlish pose. I felt like a boxer who'd taken one punch too many. "You cannot accept millions of dollars from Eli Wade," Matilda went on. "People believe he's admitting his father's guilt. I won't have it. It's not fair."

"I'm making a very public show of accepting the Wades' into society. For your sake." She glanced at me. "And for Darl's sake."

"Eli's donating money as a public apology *to you*," I said evenly. "For a crime his father didn't commit. I'm not going to let you do it."

"What would you have me do instead?" Swan asked. "Reject

him and his family? Or feed his revenge by telling him the truth? Matilda, do you want Karen to know the truth about what we did?" An icy tinge colored Matilda's face. "Look at my Darl. Look at her—so agonized, so bitter toward me. I wish I could erase the memory from *her* mind. You don't want to infect Karen, as well. Not now that she's come home."

Matilda moaned and shut her eyes. "But what am I doing to *Anthony's grandson?* What kind of heartless monster have I become? I loved him, and he loved me. I'm betraying him." She put a hand to her forehead and swayed against the side of her bed. I went to her quickly as she began to collapse. Swan sat forward with sudden urgency. "*Matilda.*"

"Call for a nurse," I said. I lowered Matilda to the bed.

# 20

A pall of fear hung in the air. Swan spent most of her waking hours in a chair close beside Matilda's bed, watching her with cat-like concentration, her hands folded in her lap, her shoulders straight. *She's afraid of losing the one person who understands her better than I do,* I realized. Karen, her face often streaked with tears, gave up decorum entirely and laid down next to her grandmother, holding her left hand tightly. Matilda was awake and alert, but her right eyelid and the right corner of her mouth drooped noticeably, and she was very weak.

"I'm dying," she said softly, just managing to form the words.

Karen flinched. "Please don't say that. It's not true." Swan stiffened in the chair. She and Matilda held each other's gaze as if transmitting lifetimes of shared experiences—this just another one—with a kind of tragic grace.

"I want to go home," Matilda said slowly, working at every word. "To Marble Hall."

Swan nodded.

*

Eli sat with Mama and Bell in the handsome kitchen of the Broadside House, where Bell jostled Jessie beneath a thin towel as the baby nursed. Leon had just sent word that Matilda was failing. Eli turned his gaze from his sister when she put the baby to her breast, though she was smooth as butter when it came to hiding the process behind a baby blanket or burping towel.

"Family recognizes family," he said quietly, realizing that was an old saw and often not true, but it should be. Bell slipped Jessie from beneath the towel and wiped the baby's pink mouth. Eli watched her care for her child, his niece, with a growing sense of finality, then met his mother's somber eyes.

Mama knew what he was thinking. "Whose family are we goin' to hurt most with all this searchin' for answers?" she asked. "The

Hardigrees, Matilda, ourselves? Or is it all one in the same, if we're all related one way or another. These people are Karen's kin. And we're Karen's kin, too. I've prayed on this, and I keep asking the Lord, 'Where does justice stop and mercy begin?' When do we have to stop lookin' for answers that only hurt the livin'?"

"Here. Now," Eli said. "We're killin' Matilda. We're hurtin' Karen. And Darl. And even Swan, damn her." He paused. "We're hurtin' ourselves." He looked at Bell gently. "I'm sorry, Sister. If there's any truth buried in the earth or the water or the memories of people in this town, we have to just trust it'll come out on its own."

Bell nodded but bowed her head to one hand, and cried.

*

"Thank you for coming. Matilda asked for you." I led Eli through Marble Hall, the cool rooms bright with warm light and fires in the hearths, to chase away the spectres that evening. "Leon and Karen are out on the back patio. Come and speak to them first."

Eli put a hand on my arm. "Do I make you so uncomfortable you can't talk to me alone?" We stopped in a shadowed hallway near a small portrait of Swan and my mother that Swan had displayed in recent years. Eli brought the chilly night air with him, washing over me along with the good scent of his hair and clothes, his warmth.

"Yes," I admitted. "I tend to throw myself at you. That's not good for either of us."

"Maybe if you trusted me more you wouldn't worry."

I glanced at my mother's naïve eyes. She'd loved my father regardless of Swan's opposition. She and he had died defying Swan. *Have courage*, she whispered to me.

*Trust him.* Every instinct told me my only redemption was complete trust of Eli. A rush of dark fear filled me, fear of losing him, fear of hurting others, but also the fear of giving into an urge to take the easy way out and never tell him what was buried in the garden. I latched my hands in the front of the soft canvas jacket he wore. He reached for me. I let go and took a step back, trembling. "We'll talk later," I said. I turned numbly and continued outside.

Leon and Karen stood in the edge of light from a lamppost near the pool. The pool's heated water gave off a white fog in the cool autumn air, damp with mist. Karen hugged herself in a soft wool sweater, her face turned up to Leon's above a cowl collar. Leon took off a quilted jacket he wore and offered it to her. She shook her head but he put the jacket around her shoulders, anyway. When they saw us approach Karen strode to me. "This is ridiculous." She looked up to the second story window and its balcony. We glimpsed a pair of private nurses moving about. Matilda and Swan were there. "My grandmother needs to be in the hospital. I can't accept this. In the morning she's going back."

I put an arm around her. "Where did you get the notion that you can tell your grandmother what to do, anymore than I can tell mine?"

"She's sick, she's not thinking right. Someone has to make decisions for her." Karen sagged a little, her voice breaking. "I'm so worried."

Leon put a hand on her shoulder. "Your grandma has always said to me that a life without dignity isn't worth living. She wants to be home. Leave her be."

Karen jabbed a finger at herself. "*I'm* her closest family, and I should be the one she—"

"A life without dignity isn't worth living," Leon repeated firmly. "She raised you to respect her. Now do it."

Karen whirled toward him. "I need her. You don't understand."

"I understand you're mighty selfish."

"*I'm pregnant.*"

Stunned silence. She went on in a tearful, angry rush, telling him she was going to have another man's child, a man who didn't want the baby, and good riddance. It was brutal news, striking right at the heart. I watched them worriedly. Leon's face tightened, and he got tears in his eyes. She saw them and said hoarsely, "*Leon.* I'm sorry. I'm not that sweet little girl you tried to protect. I am trying to make my life right, but not at your expense."

He exploded. "You do right by your grandma. That's how you

start fixing your life so you can raise a baby with the dignity your grandma taught you."

His tone stiffened her, humiliated her. She left us standing there and walked inside. Leon's big shoulders slumped.

There was enough misery to go around.

*

Eli and I walked into Swan's big bedroom, a room of soaring windows, heavy antiques, and delicate linens. I had rarely been allowed to enter it as a child, and never as an adult. Matilda lay in the middle of Swan's own bedstead, a queenly thing with a headboard of mahogany and marble. The strange sight of someone else in grandmother's private sanctuary completed the sensation that the world as I knew it was crumbling, that the bedrock falling away beneath my feet. Swan sat up in a luxurious day bed nearby, her white gown and robe spread around her on a down comforter encased in soft pearl-gray silk. She watched Matilda.

Karen stood near a window. She hugged herself and stared into the night. Swan shooed a nurse out of the shadowy room with a flick of one hand. I met my grandmother's troubled eyes, which instantly hardened at the sight of Eli. He nodded to her but went to Matilda. Matilda struggled, then slowly raised her left hand. "The other one shakes," she said slowly, her mouth a little twisted.

He pulled a chair close to her side and sat down, holding her proffered hand in both of his. "My mother and sister send you their prayers."

"I want you to know something." It made me ache to watch her laboriously form her lips around words. "Karen, come here. I want you to listen, too."

Karen moved slowly to her side. "Grandmother, you're not going to die, so there's no need for you to gather people around you—"

"Be quiet," Swan interjected. Her voice vibrated. "Listen to her."

Matilda looked at Eli. "Your grandfather was a good person. Not a lady's man, not the way it sounded." Eli stiffened with surprise. So did I. The last thing I'd expected was this. "He didn't have many choices in his life. Not many choices for me, either. A colored girl." She took several short breaths, running out of strength. Her eyes went back to Eli. "But I loved him, your grandfather. I loved Anthony Wade. And he loved me."

Karen picked up her right hand. "That's the shaking hand," Matilda said, frowning.

"I don't mind. It's still strong." Karen tucked Matilda's hand in both of hers, and brought it to her stomach. Her throat worked. "*Grandmother*," she said in a low voice. "Don't talk yourself into deathbed confessions. You're not going to die. You can't. You're going to be a great-grandmother. I'm going to have a baby."

Matilda's face stilled. As Karen explained the circumstances, every word seemed to sink into Matilda's heart then rise through her eyes, which filled with tears. "I was happy enough just to be a mother," she whispered when Karen finished. "Are you?"

Karen put a hand to her throat. Her face convulsed, and she nodded.

"Then I'm proud of you," Matilda said. In the sweet, tragic silence that followed, Karen bent her head to her grandmother's hand, and all the years of estrangement faded away.

"Miss Matilda, I'm going to ask her to marry me," Leon announced from the doorway. We all turned, stunned. Karen gasped. "I've loved her since I was a boy," Leon went on firmly, his fists clenched by his side. "I still love everything about her. I'll take care of her and her baby. I swear to you, Miss Matilda. I swear to everybody here." He looked at Karen. "I'll be your husband. I'll be your baby's daddy. If you'll have me. Just think about it and don't say anything yet. We'll talk later." Karen stared at him in tearful shock until he turned on one heel and left the room.

Matilda turned her head slowly toward Swan. The look they traded chilled me,  awed me, made me want to cry. Silent communication, choices, battles, tragedy, strength the click of time changing hands. "I want a future here for our granddaughters and their children," Matilda whispered.

Swan looked away.

\*

The house was quiet, late at night. Eli leaned by a fireplace in a small parlor off the main rooms, a half-smoked cigar in his hand. It was a place filled with books and thick reading chairs. Karen went upstairs to a guest bedroom and stretched out to sleep. Leon dozed in a kitchen chair. A nurse slept on a settee outside Swan's room. Eli and I spoke very few words. Finally he tossed the cigar in the fire and sat down. We shared a couch at opposite ends. Sometime after midnight he said, "I want you to tell Matilda I won't do any more digging."

I turned toward him. "What do you mean?"

"I'm leavin', Darl. Taking Mama and Bell back to Tennessee." He paused. "I won't hurt my family and yours. You're part of me. You always have been. I'm only hurtin' your people. Hurtin' you. This was a sad plan from the start. There's nothing I can do to save my father's soul."

*She's won. Swan has won. If you let her.* I got up, moved over, sat down. I was suddenly the calmest I'd ever been. Close beside him, I put my hands to his face, stroked my fingers over his skin, touched my fingertips to his mouth. He inhaled sharply. "You haven't hurt anyone," I said. "Everything that's happening here started a long time ago."

He pulled me to him, stroked my hair roughly, held me. "Walk away from this place. Come with me. I'll wait for you. I'll make it all up to you."

"No, you come with me," I said, quiet despair merging with victory. I would show him the truth. I would lose him. I would set him free. "We're going to the Stone Flower Garden."

\*

The rain had stopped. A cold high white moon cleared the mountains among scudding gray clouds, luminescent and ethereal. The forest's heavy firs brushed us with their rough fronds and dripped their dew on our faces and hair like cold tears as we climbed the hills and followed the hollows. I still wore the day's silk trousers and a soft gray sweater. Briars tore at the silk and clawed my walking shoes. I shivered. Long streamers of my hair clung to my cheeks and throat.

Eli carried a shovel, and I carried a small pickax. He didn't ask why and I didn't say. His hair was damp with the forest, his face was strained. I beamed a flashlight across the ground. He held up a camp lantern, its hissing glow wrapping me in quiet horror. He didn't know what we were about to dig up. I did.

When we crested the ridge of the small cove that held the garden, I halted. Eli raised the lantern. Below us, the massive stone vase and its perpetual bouquet gleamed in the lights and cast long shadows. The old marble benches seemed to be sinking into the ground. Mired in loam and vine, their tops might have been the covers of small tombs. Children's souls, trapped inside.

I walked down the slope, every step sinking me into that place, dragging me closer to Clara's bones. I reached the bottom and staggered to the vase, shoving matted leaves aside with my feet, shaking. Eli stepped down behind me. "Where?" he asked grimly. I pointed to the space only inches from the vase's bottom. He set the lantern on the ground and lifted the shovel from his shoulder.

I shook my head. "Let me start." I tossed the flashlight aside, took the pickax in both hands, and sunk its narrow blade into earth as wet and soft as flesh. Every muscle in my body pulled back from the task. I chopped at the ground, scraping, clawing, dragging clumps of rotted soil toward me. The soggy pile grew around my feet. The past was surrounding me. Keening sounds grew helplessly in my exploding breath. Every nightmare, every moment of guilt and despair for twenty-five years, was boiling up under me, exposed to Eli's judgement.

He clamped a hand on my shoulder. I was so dazed it took a moment to respond to the sensation. "Don't," I begged. But he pulled me upright and wiped my face, studying my eyes, his own face carved with bleak determination. "You're not in this alone. That's the big mistake in your thinkin'. Whatever's in this ground, it's my misery, too."

"*You can't imagine.*"

"Maybe not, but don't tell me we're not in this together." He angled in front of me, levered the shovel into the earth, and began to dig. I scrubbed an arm over my sweating face and fell to my knees beside the small but deepening hole. I racked my brain for details I'd tried so hard to forget. The open grave had seemed like a bottomless cavern to me as a child, but I knew Swan and Matilda hadn't buried Clara more than a few feet deep. I shivered with every movement of Eli's shovel, every sharp scrape that might mean the tip had struck a rock—or a bone.

I gagged on that thought, lurched forward, and grabbed the shovel's shank. "No more. I have to do the rest with my fingers." I hunched over the hole and reached down with both bare hands, shaking, sinking my fingers into the dirt. The nerves seemed to retract with revulsion as black topsoil gave way to clammy red clay. I clawed slowly. Eli dropped to his heels beside me. I looked up once, wild and disheveled, and he was looking at me as if I were ripping his heart out. His face flooded with pain. "Stop. Stop right now. I don't know what you're doing to yourself, but I'm stoppin' it. You saw my pa bury something of Clara's here, didn't you? You saw something happen. That's what you know. That's what torments you." He reached down and clamped both hands to my wrists.

I jerked them away. "Oh, God. No. No, Eli." I stabbed my hands into the dirt again. Eli grabbed for them again. "Darl, I won't let—"

I cut him off with a ragged groan. My fingers curled around something small and oval, maybe a rock, maybe not. I pulled upward. The small object fit neatly in the palm of my hand, encased in wet clay. I lifted it into the lantern light between Eli and I, scrubbing it with my thumbs, the damp red dirt falling away. A texture as fine as hair emerged. I speared my fingers through that, and stretched it out. A thin necklace. Before I brushed the last crust of dirt from the object attached to that necklace, I knew what it was. A moment later—the marble crusted and dirty but the tiny diamond catching the lantern light—Clara's family pendant lay in the light for the first time in a quarter-century. In the bottom of the hole the puddled clay showed just the edges of what must be vertabra. I had pulled the necklace from the bones of Clara's throat.

I looked at Eli's stunned expression. Comprehension, agony, pity, and fury filled his eyes, until I couldn't bear his sight or mine. I closed the pendant in my fist and bowed my head.

"Tell me what you've always known," he said.

*"I was here when Swan killed her."*

He sagged back on his heels, free of the past, but ruined. Both of us. We sat across from each other, and cried.

*

Restless, Swan had been standing at her bedroom window when she saw Darl and Eli left the mansion, crossed the back lawn and went down the terrace steps. The light from the terrace lamppost showed the tools they carried. Swan pressed a hand to her heart, measured the painful, racing beat, turned slowly, and sat down on the day bed. *I've lost. I'm losing Matilda and I've lost Darl, and this is how it ends.* She was suddenly very tired.

Across the room, Matilda stirred. A nightlight cast soft shadows on her. From that darkness, her slurred voice rose urgently. "Swan. Swan."

Swan held the daybed's white-iron footboard, rose weakly to her feet, and crossed the room with the thudding in her chest making it hard to breathe. When she reached Matilda she knew instantly it was very bad. Matilda gasped a strange sound. Swan sank down beside her, slid one arm beneath her neck, took her trembling hand, and bent over her. "Something's wrong," Matilda whispered. "With me. With us." Shards of fear joined, hardened, began to shine. Intuition or coincidence, fate, timing, the arrival of last chances and lost hopes. "I'll call the nurse," Swan said.

"No. Please. I don't want to be an invalid. I see that coming."

Small agonies rose in Swan's chest. She bowed her head to Matilda's. "Don't go."

"Set them free. Save them. Our granddaughters. Save them from our mistakes."

*"Stay and help me."*

"Let me go. Let yourself go. That's the love we have to give them."

Matilda did not quite shut her eyes. She sighed. Swan gathered her closer, rocked her, and cried very quietly, the only safe way. "*Sister*," she whispered.

\*

Eli looked at Darl across Clara's grave, listening as she told him everything, how it all happened, and why. He watched the pain pour through her, like a ripple in her skin, and it twisted him inside. She looked at him as if there was no doubt he hated her, and he didn't know how, yet, to admit he could forgive her. A part of him said he shouldn't. A part of him said nothing should have mattered to her but the truth, and goddamn her family. Rage boiled up in him.

She finished speaking—ragged, exhausted, covered in tears and the dirt of Clara's grave, on her knees—like him. He stood, took the shovel that lay beside them, turned, and slammed it against the stone flower vase. Sparks flew from the steel on marble. The sound rang through the forest. The shovel's handle split in two, and chips of marble cascaded around them. A shard of it flicked across Eli's face beneath one eye, leaving a bloody welt. Darl didn't move. A trickle of blood slid from a scratch on her chin. She never took her eyes off him.

"I've written it all down," she said. "Everything about my grandmother and me. What happened, and how. Everything except Matilda. I left her out. My confession is in an envelope in the library. Tomorrow I'll take that envelope to the courthouse and hand it to the district attorney. All I ask you—all I beg you—is that you never tell anyone about Matilda's involvement."

Her sacrificing words make Eli's knees weak. "I want to know why you couldn't tell me before."

She sagged a little. "God help me," she whispered. "I love you, but I love my grandmother, too."

Eli stepped around the open grave and dropped to his knees in front of her. "Give me the necklace," he ordered hoarsely, and held out his hand. *She has to choose, and she'll choose me.* Darl placed

Clara's pendant on his palm. "Choose," he ordered. "Choose between me and what this stands for. Choose between me and Swan. *Choose*, and walk away with me, and never look back."

"I can't," she whispered. "Swan's in me, she's part of me—everything we are, everything she suffered through to make a life for herself, for Matilda, for Karen. For me. I won't leave her."

Eli took Darl by the shoulders. "You just gave me my pa back. Free and clear, innocent. *But I want my girl, too.*" Tears slid down her face. She shook her head. "You have to let go of me. I'll punish Swan my own way."

The bell at Marble Hall began to ring.

*

I was numb. Eli wanted to forgive me, but I wouldn't let him. Leon, who had sequestered himself in a downstairs room that night, stood by the big iron bell on its marble post, shadowed by the landscape lights and the weird cast of the swimming pool's submerged lamps. When Eli and I climbed the terrace steps I saw the tears on Leon's face and the water running from his soggy clothes. He jerked his head toward the pool.

Swan lay on wide marble steps that descended into the shallow end, her head pillowed on one arm along the marble lip, her hair streaming in the water around her shoulders. A fine mist rose from the pool. Her white gown and robe floated around her. The sight she made was haunting and unreal. Angel and spirit, free of gravity, unbound by anyone's rules but her own.

"I found her and pulled her to the edge," Leon said. "She'd come down from her room. Nobody saw her." He paused. His throat worked. "I've called for an ambulance." Another pause. "Karen's upstairs with her grandma." Leon looked over at the mansion with grief in his face. "Miss Matilda's dead."

I lunged past him, running towards the pool, and heard Eli's strides behind me. Plowing into the water around the steps, I sank down beside my grandmother, pushed her hair back, and took her face between my hands. Her eyes were shut; even in the dim light I saw the terrible, pinched color of her skin. "Swan," I called quietly.

"Grandmother." She opened her eyes, those stark blue orbs going lifeless even then, and looked up at me. "I know where you took Eli," she said.

I nodded. "I'm in charge, now. I've told him everything."

Her gaze flickered beyond me as Eli stepped down into the water on her other side. His face grim, he leaned over her, simply holding her gaze. I realized dimly that Leon had followed and now stood over us all, on the pool's edge. "I have to go see about Karen," he said grimly, then left us for the house. Alone with Swan and Eli, I repeated what I'd said. "I'm in charge, now, Grandmother. I make the decisions. I've told Eli what we did. I'll deal with the consequences."

"You always amaze me." Her gaze remained on Eli. His eyes bored into her mercilessly. He slowly raised his hand before her face, then let Clara's pendant descend from the dirt-encrusted necklace clenched in his fingers. It shimmered in the misty light. "You killed your sister," he said. "And you let my pa die for it."

She acknowledged the truth with a dip of her eyelids, then wet her lips with her tongue. "Push me under the water. Do it. My family carved yours from the finest stone. I made you what you are. I made you worthy of my Darl. You're strong enough to kill me."

My skin crawled. I hunched over her and watched Eli with open agony. His face tightened. Tears glimmered in his eyes, but the goodness in him surfaced like a hard polish. "I can't hate you more than I love Darl." He flung the pendant aside.

I was crying now, silently but with blessings. Swan's eyes went to me. "Then *you* do it." Her voice was a bare breath, wheezing and pained. "Prove you can do what you have to do. I taught you how."

I shook my head. She had brought us there for a perverse baptism—returning her soul to her, but also giving ours back. I slid one arm under her shoulders and stroked her cheek with my fingertips covered in the soil of the stone flower garden. "I love you. You never understood that."

"Yes, I did. But I couldn't let you. For your sake. And for mine. Love is so hard."

"No, it's not. Let me just hold you, now. Whatever happens, I'll be here."

I broke her. I saw the love in her face, the apology, the lonely peace. Eli had asked me to choose, but I couldn't, so Swan was choosing for me. Setting me free but settling the truth on me like a stone weight, my choice being how to carry it. *"Granddaughter,"* she whispered. "My heart is gone. You have it."

I kissed her forehead, her eyes, her cheeks. It was the first time in my life I had ever touched my lips to her skin. She died in my arms, floating.

*

Darl refused to leave her grandmother's body, or Matilda's. She and Karen, who was fractured with grief, followed their grandmothers' corpses to the hospital morgue, and then the Burnt Stand Funeral Home. Holding hands, they sat all night with the sheeted bodies in a cool, shadowed room with marble floors. People from all over the county heard of the two deaths and came in silent respect, sitting on blankets in the darkness, under the cloudy moon and the shadows of the autumn mountains, until by dawn the rain-dampened lawn of the funeral home was filled with a waiting crowd.

Eli walked the blocks through town to the Broadside house, turned on the lights downstairs, woke Mama and Bell, and told them simply that Swan and Matilda had died in the night. Mama bent her head in prayer. Bell cried. Eli tried to decide what truth he needed to tell them, but couldn't. Pa was innocent. They had to hear that, and soon. He groaned inside himself and heard Darl's words, over and over. *I was there when Swan killed Clara.*

"What's troublin' your heart?" Mama asked Eli. He shook his head. She let him alone, for the moment. Bell stayed with little Jessie but Mama dressed and walked back through town with him. The crowd on the lawn—stonecutters and merchants, townsfolk and farmers—parted for her to pass. She settled on the funeral home's veranda and began to read out loud from her Bible. People nodded along with her. Eli seated himself in a straight chair next to Leon, in a dark corner. "What were you and Darl doing in the woods?" Leon ventured wearily.

"I'll tell you when I know how to say the words," Eli said. *Or what words to say*, he added silently. Leon nodded. They smoked cigars and said little else. It was easy to imagine Swan and Matilda gliding past the veranda with youthful hope, easy to curl smoke into the air and picture the tragic half-sisters stepping through its veil toward their lost loved ones—their beloved daughters, their innocence. Eli looked into the cold autumn morning, hidden in smoke and silver mountain mist. He thought his grandpa must be watching from the vapors, reunited at last with Matilda. And Pa was watching from that other world, too. Eli hunched over, his head down as he pretended to nurture the cigar, hiding his emotions. *Pa, I know you're with me right now. Forgive me for ever doubtin' you. Forgive me. I love you. Talk to me. Tell me what to do.*

The answer rose silently in Eli, echoing his father's heart, letting him know how to offer and receive forgiveness.

*Leave no stone unturned, no love forgotten.*

Carve the rest away.

*

Dawn cast shards of light through pale curtains, dappling our grandmothers' shrouded forms. Karen and I sat on a couch across from the draped gurneys that held their bodies, in a small room at the funeral home, not meant for the public. A single wall sconce lit our faces. Karen rested her head on my shoulder. I put my arms around her and closed my eyes against her thick chocolate hair. We had cried all we could.

*You have my heart.*

Swan's words hurt and hurt again, painful with their irony, their joy, their confession. I missed her, I mourned her, I hated her, I loved her. Most of all, I knew what she'd left me to do. I'd tell everyone the truth about Swan and me. About Clara. My heart was gone, too. Only the truth and Eli could give it back.

"I don't know what else to say to my grandmother or yours," Karen whispered in a tear-soaked voice. "What will we do without them?"

I kissed her hair.

"We'll love as best we can and never give up," I said.

Just as we'd been taught.

*

Eli rose to his feet as Darl stepped out onto the veranda of the funeral home as the sun rose higher over the mountains. Leon stood at the sight of Karen, who followed Darl. The crowd got to its feet respectfully. Mama closed her Bible and folded her hands over the fine, parched white leather, burnished by her fingertips. Her eyes, beneath tossled gray hair, shimmered with sorrow. Darl's haunted blue gaze went to her, then to Eli, asking for no mercy. Everything inside him twisted at the sight of her, unfurled, coiled, demanded release, and found calm. She gripped Karen's hand, then released it. Karen stared at the respectful crowd in dull amazement, then found herself in Leon's capable bear hug, and wound her arms around his waist.

Darl stepped to the edge of the veranda. "I have something to tell all of you," she began, and understanding knifed through Eli. She turned to him and Mama. "To you, most of all," she said. And then, to Karen. "And to my cousin, Karen. I'm sorry to do it this way, but if I learned anything from our grandmothers, it's the strength to do what has to be done."

Her head up, Darl riveted her eyes to Eli's. The love in her gaze tore him apart. She was about to ruin herself for his sake, and he couldn't let her. He leapt forward, startling her. "Let me," he said. She opened her mouth in protest, but he slid a hand along her jaw and pressed his little finger over her lips. Before she could speak again he looked at Mama. "Swan told us the truth before she died. She's the one who killed her sister twenty-five years ago. Her by herself. She confessed to Darl and me before she died."

The crowd gasped. Karen made a garbled sound and said, "Oh, Darl," in incredulous sympathy, and when Eli looked at her and Leon, even Leon couldn't help a stare of horrified surprise. Mama's face stilled, and a look of beseeching hope mingled with sorrow in her eyes. That hope burst into full understanding. She clasped her hands to her heart. Pa was innocent. It had been proved. It had been proclaimed.

Eli turned his gaze back to Darl's stunned, upturned face. She searched his eyes. He kept his finger over her lips and said to the crowd again, "She killed her sister and let my Pa get the blame. It was all her doing. Just her."

Darl's lips moved slightly. *Why?*

"I love you," Eli said, and slowly enclosed her in his arms.

She slid trembling hands up his back and held onto him for dear life.

*

It all happened so fast after that, as if Swan's death had been the key to a door that now swung open easily. That afternoon Eli and I led Leon and Karen to the Stone Flower Garden along with the county sheriff, the coroner, the funeral home director, and several other local officials. There, with due process, we dug up Clara's bones. I forced myself to look at them, and felt Eli's strong grip on my hand as I did. The funeral director carried the remains away in a rubber bag, followed by the others. Eli, Leon, Karen and I stood by the empty grave alone as autumn leaves sifted down on us, already filling the hole.

"I'm so sorry for you," Karen said to me, hugging me, then stepping back, her face anguished. "For what your grandmother did. And that you have to live with it."

"I'll be all right. I can manage better than I realized." I looked up at Eli. His dark eyes were quiet and sad, supportive and victorious. There was too much emotion for either of us to sort through, at the moment. Karen touched his arm. "I'm sorry for you, too. For what our family did to yours." Her voice broke. "I'm sure if my grandmother were here she'd apologize for Swan and beg us to understand how Swan could do something so horrible—"

"We're all family," Eli said quietly. "And we'll still be family. It all comes down to that."

Leon cleared his throat. "It's the end of Hardigree Marble. The company'll never be the same without Swan and Matilda. Neither will the town."

"I disagree," I said. I turned to Karen. "My grandmother's will divides the company between you and me." I paused. "And the mansion, too. We both own Marble Hall, now."

"Oh, Darl."

"It's only fair. She and Matilda were both Hardigrees. Everything belonged to the two of them, whether people knew it, or not." We all stood there for a minute, absorbing the news. Swan's attorney had brought me a copy of her will only hours earlier. I put a hand over hers. "Are you sure you're going to stay here?"

She looked at Leon. "Yes."

"Then I'm giving my half to you. The company, and the estate." I nodded to Leon. "To both of you."

"Darl, you can't," Karen began, and Leon was already shaking his head.

"Someone needs to be the lady of the manor, and you'll be perfect. And Leon was meant to own the quarry."

"I'm not a Hardigree," he put in.

"Marry Karen, and you will be."

The thought settled on him, and on my cousin. I watched the decision sink in, and I felt Eli's gaze on me. I met his troubled but proud eyes. "We'll come back to visit," I said. "We'll be involved in Stand Tall."

"What if it was built on these grounds?" he asked. "Something good, set on this property. Put the buildings on the land I cleared. Make the Stone Cottage the center of it. What do you think?"

I stepped away from Clara's empty grave, then touched my fingertips to the towering stone vase with its hopeful marble flowers, always imitating life, waiting for the magic Eli and I had always tried to make there. "I think that would be perfect," I said.

\*

Matilda and Swan lay in state in the main living room at Marble Hall. I had sat with their bodies all morning, alone, talking to them.

Now I kept myself in the library, smoothing my pale gray suit, fingering the Hardigree pendant that still bound my neck. In an hour, I would open the house to all the people who would come to pay their respects. Flowers and cards filled the mansion. Karen had escaped to Leon's farm, crying. I ached with fatigue, with grief, with the hard tug of unfinished debts. Eli and I had barely been alone together, and had not talked much in the two days since the deaths. There was too much to say. We didn't know how to start over, or when the words would suddenly be free in us, again. I knew why we were held back, even if he didn't.

Gloria, who had transferred her affections to Karen but not to me, glumly opened the library door. Eli walked in with Annie Gwen and Bell. Bell's husband had rushed to North Carolina and reunited tearfully with her. He was caring for their baby at the Broadside house.

I looked at Eli with quiet reserve, him as foreign to me in a handsome suit as a suit of armor. Everything about his grim face said my request to talk to his mother and sister in private worried him. He didn't know what I intended, and he was right to worry. I was frightened, myself.

"Poor child," Annie Gwen said, and hugged me. So did Bell.

I hugged them back. "It's a miracle you don't hate me for what I represent," I said wearily.

"How could we blame *you* for what your grandma did?" Bell cried.

*You'll see*, I thought. I went behind Swan's desk, to the bookcases, reached up between the two heavy textbooks where I'd hidden my confession, and pulled it out. Eli realized then what I meant to do. He stepped close to me and clamped a hand on the large brown envelope. I shook my head and spoke around a knot in my throat. "I have to do what's right. The secret will always be between us, if I don't. No more secrets."

"Goddammit," he said very softly, in pain. "Some things don't have to be told, if they only hurt people."

"I love you too much—and your family too much—to let this stay hidden." I turned to Annie Gwen and Bell, held out the envelope, and said in a low, strained voice, "I knew about Clara's murder when I was a child. I wrote down all the details here. I knew what my grandmother did. I've always known, but I was too afraid to tell anyone." My hand shaking, I laid the envelope on Swan's desk. "I have to share the blame for what she did."

Slowly, Annie Gwen and Bell's faces compressed in sorrow. I watched a dozen emotions wash across their eyes, until finally, to my amazement, only sorrow remained. "I figured you knew," Annie Gwen whispered. "I could see the guilt in your face at the funeral home." She looked at Eli. "I could see it in yours, too."

I put a hand to my throat and shut my eyes. Beside me, Eli said gruffly, "I won't have Darl blamed for any of this. I didn't want you and Bell to know something that ought not make a difference. Something that only hurts."

Bell surged forward, her eyes fervent and gleaming with tears. "Are you saying your grandma told you about the murder when you were a girl? Why did she *do* that to you?"

"She didn't have to tell me. I saw it happen. I saw her shove Clara over the terrace wall. I watched Clara die. And that night I watched Swan bury her." Breaking down, I leaned on the desk for support. Eli grasped me around the waist, but I was frozen in place. "I don't expect your forgiveness."

Annie Gwen's mouth flattened. She came around the massive desk like a small, determined hen in a blue suit, followed by Bell, and in the next moment she took my face between her hands. "Poor child," she whispered again. "Justice has been done, here, already. Me and my family, we . . . *we killed your grandma*. We killed her by comin' back."

"Annie Gwen, that's not so—"

"Oh, yes, it is. In her heart she knew she had a debt to pay, and her heart paid it. But we killed poor innocent Matilda, too, god help us." Annie Gwen pressed her hands tighter around my face, as if impressing her faith on me. "What's done is done, child. On both sides."

"Let it go," Eli said softly, and curved a hand down my hair. And I did. I had been forgiven, and could start forgiving myself. The next thing I knew, I was encased in Annie Gwen's arms, and Bell's, and Eli's.

*

"I want to see Swan," Annie Gwen said, her voice firm.

I ushered her into the tall-windowed living room, then stood back. Even the sight of the twin coffins set among towering flower arrangements across the large room broke my heart. I had looked at my grandmother's face for the last time, and Matilda's, and would not look again.

Annie Gwen made her way to Swan's coffin and stood quietly beside it, gazing down at her. Annie Gwen spoke softly but firmly. "I'll take your granddaughter into my heart," she told Swan, "and make her part of my family. I'll be a good grandmother to her children with my son—and they'll honor me. You'll just be a bad memory—somebody we don't talk about much, for Darl's sake. You took my husband. But I'll take your whole family. I'll take the future. And that's my revenge, Swan Samples. That's the hell you made for yourself."

Annie Gwen Wade turned her back to my grandmother's memory, and faced me.

"You love my son, and I love you," she said.

"I'll never make you regret that," I answered.

She, Bell, Eli and I carried the envelope with my confession in it outside to the pale pink marble patio, and Eli held his lighter beneath one corner, and we burned all those words.

The first Burnt Stand fire gave my family a name and a clean past. The second one, there on the marble patio that day, gave my family a soul and a clean future.

*

They were buried in the Hardigree mausoleum in the Methodist cemetery—Swan, Matilda, and Clara—all with their separate names carved on the faces of their crypts. And where there had been a blank space on the secret crypt beside my mother's, we carved the name of Karen's mother. Katherine Wade.

It was all set in stone, now.

*

"Come with me," Eli said after the funerals. It wasn't so much an order as a plea.

We drove to the Stone Cottage, sitting forlornly in a scalped hollow that would soon revive with the buildings and lawns of Stand Tall. Eli and I walked inside the cottage's cool, haunted beauty, silent acknowledging the love that had been nurtured there by Anthony and Matilda, the close family that had blossomed there when Jasper and Annie Gwen moved in, and now, the redemption and devotion Eli and I brought to the rooms his own grandfather had built.

I followed Eli to a back bedroom, where we faced each other beside a simple bedstead and mattress we'd covered with white sheets, broad pillows, and deep comforters. There was just that bed in that marble cottage, and us. He held out his hands and I went to him. He took a small set of pliers from his suit pocket, slid his fingers beneath the collar of my blouse, lifted the chain of my pendant, and cut it.

I laid the necklace on a marble sill, and never touched it, again.

We undressed each other, becoming pure and naked, and got into bed. We stayed there for the afternoon and the night, taking each other as full and trusting lovers, never letting go, making the sorrow all right, turning back time.

The next morning we threw our belongings together, said goodbye to Karen and Leon, to Annie Gwen and Bell, then went to the airstrip outside town. I wore jeans and a t-shirt, a leather jacket of Eli's, and old shoes. He was just as comfortable. We flew out over the town, circling for a moment, looking down at the pale blush majesty of Burnt Stand among the golden mountains. "Time to go," Eli said, and I nodded. We moved away on high currents of autumn air. In a few hours we were free of the land and the past, soaring over the southern ocean toward some exotic and warm adventure, skimming over the unpolished face of the world, weightless.

Loving each other, and forgetting the coldness of stone.

# Also From Deborah Smith

# A Gentle Rain

## Available from BelleBooks

## Excerpt

Kara
My birth, 1974

In my mother's innocent world of Saturday morning cartoons, babies wearing name sashes fluttered about a cartoon garden after being delivered by a heavenly stork. Lily Akens had no reason to doubt the obstetrics of a TV show.

My teenaged father, Mac Tolbert, knew better, since he often helped birth calves and foals at River Bluff, his family's elegant, northern Florida farm, but he didn't know how to warn my mother about the process. Besides, he wasn't certain human babies were born the same way as livestock.

He could only assume a baby came out from the same spot where the boy put it in.

"Lily, L-lily, don't c-cry," Mac stuttered, kneeling over her helplessly in the sweaty, sub-tropical darkness, swatting at mosquitoes that flitted in the beam of his shaking flashlight. Tall pines shifted above them in a swampy breeze. Bullfrogs chortled in the creek bottoms. Somewhere in a sumpy ditch, an alligator grunted. The dark forests of inland Florida breathe and talk at night, drawing mysterious memories from the porous limestone bedrock. Though far from either ocean, the air carries a faint hint of saltwater.

"But it hurts!" Lily sobbed, pounding her palms on her distended stomach. Her cheap, flowery mumu was soaked with fluid and clotted around her thighs.

"I t-think it's s-*supposed* to hurt," Mac told her. "Maybe you should stand u-up. Like a m-mare."

"I don't think I can! Oh, Mac! It hurts so bad! Mac! Something's trying to come out of me down there!"

Trembling, Mac pointed the flashlight between her legs. Horses and cattle were born front feet first, as if diving into the world. Mac looked closely but saw no baby hands, just the bloody pate of a tiny head. It terrified him, but he hid the emotion. He had to be strong for Lily. They were different from other teenagers; they had taken care of each other since childhood. "It's just the b-baby." He sounded more confident than he felt. He knew how to turn a breeched calf or foal but could not imagine sticking his big hand inside Lily.

"Mac! It's moving!"

He grabbed her hands as she sat up. She rocked and he held her. The heels of her tennis shoes plowed furrows in the soft, damp loam. Lily began to yell. After what seemed like forever she went quiet and collapsed against him. "The baby fell out," she moaned. "Why doesn't it flap its wings? Something must be wrong with it. Oh, *Mac*."

My father turned the flashlight between her thighs, again. He and my mother stared in horror. Neither had seen a newborn child, before. I was not a cute little doll or a smiling cherub. I was nearly purple. My head was misshapen. Bloody mucous plastered a feathery dab of red hair to my skull. I opened my shriveled mouth and took a big yawn of air. To them, the effort looked like a dying gasp.

They bent their heads over me and cried.

Searchlights pierced the woods. Mac's older brother, Glen, found them first. "What the hell have you done?" he said.

Mac and Lily sobbed. Before they could hold me even once, before they could realize I was alive and normal, I was taken from them.

I would be grown before I knew Mac and Lily existed. Grown before I knew they had birthed me in the wilds of Florida. Grown, before I knew they had wanted me.

Grown and orphaned before I was born into my parents' lives, again.

## About Deborah Smith

Deborah Smith is the award-winning, New York Times bestselling author of A PLACE TO CALL HOME, A GENTLE RAIN, and many others. She has written over forty novels including series romance, women's fiction, mainstream fiction and fantasy. As editorial director and partner in BelleBooks, a small publishing company she co-owns with three other veteran authors, Deborah edits and writes for a variety of books including the Mossy Creek Hometown Series and the Sweet Tea story collections. She also manages BelleBooks Audio. You can now purchase audio downloads of Deb's newest novels, read by the author. Visit Deb at www.deborah-smith.com or www.bellebooks.com. Send comments to her at BelleBooks@bellebooks.com.

CPSIA information can be obtained at www.ICGtesting.com

231646LV00002B/51/P